TANGLED IN LIES

Also by Jasmin Miller

Kings Of The Water Series

Secret Plunge - An Accidental Pregnancy Sports Romance

Fresh Meet - A Single Dad Sports Romance

Second Dive - A Second Chance Sports Romance

Fake Start - A Fake Relationship Sports Romance

Standalones

Forbidden Freedom - A Forbidden Romance

The Husband Checklist - A Brother's Best Friend Romance

Mitchell Brothers Series

Baking With A Rockstar - A Single Parent Romance

Tempted By My Roommate - A Friends to Lovers Romance

Mitchell Brothers Box Set

TANGLED IN LIES

USA TODAY BESTSELLING AUTHOR
JASMIN MILLER

WUNDERLAND
PRESS

Published: Wunderland Press, Jasmin Miller 2024
jasmin@jasminmiller.com
www.jasminmiller.com
Editing: Rebecca, Fairest Reviews Editing Services;
Emmy Ellis, Studioenp
Proofreading: Karen Hrdlicka, Barren Acres Editing
Cover Art: Najla Qamber, Qamber Designs & Media

BLURB AND CONTENT WARNINGS

Phoenix Montgomery is my sister's ex-fiancé.
Billionaire heir and freshly released from prison.
One glance is all it takes to rekindle our old hatred.

Now, I'm forced to marry him.
To live with him.
To pretend I'm in love with him.

But he doesn't know our lives are tangled in lies.
He doesn't know I have a stalker.
And now, he's a target too.

My goal is to survive.
His is to make my life hell.

However, the past doesn't stay in the past.
And soon, old emotions re-appear.
It's messy. Forbidden. Addictive.

He can't ever find out I was the one who put him in prison.
Or all the other terrible things I'm responsible for.
Neither one of us would survive that.

Tangled in Lies is a steamy enemies-to-lovers arranged marriage standalone romance with a HEA, no third-act breakup, and no cliffhanger. It features mature themes and content that may not be suitable for all audiences. Reader discretion is advised.

Content warnings: This story contains explicit sexual content, profanity, suspense with mild violence (not between the MCs), and topics that may be sensitive to some readers.

PLAYLIST

"Who" — Lauv, BTS
"Hate You" — Jung Kook
"It'll Be Okay" — Shawn Mendes
"Alone" — Jimin
"Don't Blame Me" — Taylor Swift
"In My Blood" — Shawn Mendes
"Leaving My Love Behind" — Lewis Capaldi
"Work Song" — Hozier
"Mercy" — Shawn Mendes
"Would've, Could've, Should've" — Taylor Swift
"Everything I Did To Get To You" — Ben Platt
"If The World Was Ending" — JP Saxe, Julia Michaels
"There's Nothing Holdin' Me Back" — Shawn Mendes
"When The Party's Over" — Billie Eilish
"Tides" — Ed Sheeran
"Dynasty" — MIIA

To everyone who has ever spiraled because their life was completely out of control.

Let karma be your next book boyfriend, giving you much-needed relief and calling you a good girl.

You deserve it.

CHAPTER 1

EVANGELINE

My phone chimes a few feet away on my bed, and I freeze.

There's only one contact I assigned the creepy sound to, and it immediately gives me the proper reaction the person behind the number deserves: a pounding heart, trouble breathing, and a lot of gut-wrenching nausea.

The phone is buried under several financial management textbooks, and I reach for it with a shaky hand. But before I can read the message, there's a knock on the door.

"Ready or not, here I come."

I grab the phone and push it into the side pocket of my leggings just as the door swings open, and my best friend, Ruby, waltzes in with her fluffy pink bathrobe floating behind her and her hair twisted in a towel atop her head. Even in this getup, she's dazzling.

She stops in her tracks when her gaze settles on me, her eyes wide. "Evangeline Caldwell, what the hell do you think you're doing?"

I take a steadying breath and shrug, not trusting my voice.

Ruby tilts her head toward the open door and yells, "Mason."

Great, now I really need to make sure my poker face is in position.

One best friend is hard enough to fool, but both of them together? It will take a little miracle.

Mason, our third roommate, joins us. One glance at me, and his eyebrows dip. "Did someone die?"

The second I turned eighteen, I bought a house and asked my two best friends if they wanted to move in with me for college. It's nothing like the million-dollar mansions we grew up in, but big enough to accommodate a large family. Thank goodness my parents have given me a significant allowance ever since I was a teen, and I actually listened to my sister and saved as much of it as possible so I could buy a house when I was old enough and could get out from under my parents' thumb.

Ruby smacks him on the arm. "No one died, you sourpuss." She leans my way and whispers, "Right?"

I shake my head. "No one died, no."

At least, I hope not.

Mason gestures from me to my bed and back to me again. "Why on earth are you sitting here, looking like *that*, and doing *this* then?"

I assume by *that* he means my slightly unkempt appearance, or at least I'm sure I don't look my finest. I haven't taken a shower yet or touched a hairbrush to appear more human.

And *this* is the scattered schoolwork around me on my crumpled duvet.

I glance at the clock on my bookshelf. "I still have time. We don't have to leave for another two and a half hours."

Ruby sighs like I just confessed I prefer to hang the toilet paper roll under. "The makeup and hair stylists will be here in about half an hour."

My brows draw together. "Huh?"

"Didn't your mom tell you she booked a team for us? There will be photographers at the party."

I shake my head to indicate I didn't have a clue and because I can't—and don't—want to deal with this right now. None of it.

I'm not a masochist, so being stuffed in a room with a bunch of people I mostly don't care about sounds like torture. It's almost impossible to feel anything but dread over it, especially after receiving a text message from *Freddy*. I'm sure he'll try to ruin my life even more than he already has.

You're almost there, Eve. Next year, you're done with school, and you can finally leave this place to work overseas.

Mason's voice pulls me out of my thoughts, and I catch the end of whatever he's saying. "Well, you only turn twenty-one once, and we all know that public image is at the top of the priority list for our parents."

"Right alongside making more money than we'll ever know what to do with," Ruby chimes in.

He raises his brows. "That goes without saying."

I only half listen to their conversation because my brain is still stuck on something Mason said.

"You only turn twenty-one once."

If you make it to that point.

I'm now officially older than my sister was. She only had a few more days until her twenty-first birthday.

My gaze automatically moves to my shelf and the picture of my sister and me. People always thought we were twins, although she was three years older. I never saw it. Her hair was golden brown, whereas mine is almost black, and she had our dad's dark-blue eyes, whereas I inherited my mom's brown ones.

Our smiles were similar, though, and we looked so happy in the picture. It was taken just months before everything went to shit. We had our differences, especially toward the end, but she was my sister, and I still miss her like crazy.

You can't change what happened.

"Evie."

I start and gape at Mason with wide eyes.

"You okay?" His voice is soft and gentle.

The lump in my throat is almost impossible to swallow, but I manage after several tries. "Yeah, sorry. Long day of studying."

Because we've been best friends for ten years, I don't need to look at them to know they don't believe a single word I'm saying, just like they know I won't tell them anything if I'm not ready.

It's become an unspoken rule among us over the last few years.

Even if I wanted to tell them what was happening, I couldn't. Not without someone paying the price for it.

Oblivious to my inner turmoil, Ruby grabs my hand and pulls me off the bed while Mason attacks the mess on my duvet, gathering all of my schoolwork and putting it in a neat pile on my desk. Then he disappears in my closet for a moment and returns with my glittering designer dress in one hand and matching shoes in the other.

He smiles at me. "You'll be stunning in this."

Somehow, I muster a smile back. "Thank you."

Like me, Mason is the victim of ultra-wealthy parents with no time for him but all the expectations. Sometimes, it makes him a brat but with a heart of gold.

Ruby taps a finger on her wrist. "You have twenty minutes to shower, birthday girl. Hurry."

They escort me to my en suite bathroom like I'm a kindergartener.

My phone replays the awful notification sound for the unread message in my pocket as Ruby shuts the door. Not quick enough though. I still see the worried glance they exchange.

As usual, I'm alone with my thoughts and a sense of dread that always goes hand in hand whenever I receive messages from *him*. My stalker, my tormenter, the man who's single-handedly brought so much destruction to my life and others that I can barely hold myself upright some days.

When he started messaging me, he told me to call him Devil, but I saved his number under Freddy. Like Freddy Krueger, my personal nightmare come to life.

FREDDY

Happy birthday, pet. Enjoy your party tonight. There will be a surprise waiting for you.

The message vanishes shortly after, like it does every

time, and the phone clangs to the floor. I didn't even know there was such a thing as disappearing messages until I got my first one from Freddy, and it was gone after a few minutes. My stomach lurches at the memory, and I barely reach the toilet in time to empty my stomach contents. I allow myself two minutes to freak out on the bathroom floor. After that, I pick myself back up and take a shower.

I'll get through this day like any other day.

Three hours later, we're at my parents' estate. I'm primped and preened, ready to face the elite of Ansonville, New York, who my parents value above all else. Or at least, they like to pretend they do. Behind the curtain, there's nothing but gossiping, backstabbing, and swindling people out of their money to enrich us further.

My stomach roils, and every cell in my body is telling me to turn around and escape. To hide somewhere, to pretend Freddy didn't message me about a surprise. Coming from him, it can't be good.

Sadly, my brother is by my side the second we walk into the ballroom of my parents' estate. "Happy birthday, Evangeline."

That's all he says and all I'm going to get. We're basically strangers, always have been.

Everything around me immediately adds to my discomfort: the noise of the crowd, the change from cool evening air to humid, this packed room, the overwhelming smell of food.

I inhale deeply and dip my chin. "Thank you."

A photographer from the society pages stops us, and we pose for a photo together. My parents' friends smile at us from all sides, wishing me a happy birthday. Not that any of them are actually here for me. A waiter walks by us with a tray of champagne, but I shake my head when Alex tries to hand me one.

"I'll get one later."

He only shrugs and takes a sip of his.

Much to our father's delight, Alex is also the spitting image of him: tall, lean, with brown hair that's almost black, and dark-blue eyes. On the other hand, I lean more toward my mom with her average height, brown eyes, olive skin, and curves—that she pretends to love for the public but secretly hates.

While it's easy to spot the family resemblance between Alex and me, we might as well have grown up in two families on opposite sides of the world instead of the same house for how estranged we are. Alex is living proof of how astute my father and his grooming skills are, at least as long as he's dealt with a child who worships him and is easy to influence.

Which is not me.

Consequently, Alex has pretty much ignored me ever since my parents discovered I'm not like my older siblings. I have zero interest in the family business or playing an overzealous socialite.

There is no room in the Caldwell family for a child who would much rather "make noise"—as my parents used to call my music behind closed doors—than shove my nose in a book and talk about economic statistics or the future of the global financial market.

I disappointed the family, and they do their best to ignore me as much as possible.

And after what happened to my sister, they've barely been able to look at me for more than a few seconds.

Not that I blame them. They all heard our fight that dreadful night three years ago.

"I hope one day you can forgive me, Angie."

The parting words my sister whispered to me before she sped off in her car will forever haunt me.

Her *last* words.

It's a miracle I have people in my life who talk to me, let alone care about me, like Mason and Ruby.

That's because they don't know what you did.

As if summoned, my friends walk up next to me, giving me reassuring squeezes on my hand and shoulder. It's enough to drag me out of my destructive thoughts.

Alex steers me past tables with elaborate floral decorations and toward our parents, who are already waiting for us on the other side of the room with fake smiles. As always, they are ideally situated in front of the thick velvet drapes over large gold-rimmed French windows. My mom once told me it's the perfect backdrop for pictures because it makes her skin glow.

I've never seen her as disappointed as when I didn't share her enthusiasm at that moment.

By now, my parents know I hate gatherings like this and I most likely won't last more than an hour. The only saving grace is no one will miss me when I disappear.

My mom's gaze travels over my meticulous makeup and lavish curls, down to my perfectly fitted floor-length designer dress and the thin heels that show with every step I take on the polished hardwood floors, due to the generous slit in the skirt.

Her smile doesn't falter as I approach, which is as much

of a sign that nothing is amiss with my appearance as any word could be.

She wraps her arms around me when I'm within reach and squeezes. "Happy birthday, Evangeline."

For those fleeting few seconds, I close my eyes and take in as much of her warmth and familiar scent of roses as possible. My dad clears his throat loudly, and the rare moment is over.

All noise in the room immediately ceases, everyone's focus shifting to him.

"We've gathered today to celebrate the birthday of our beautiful daughter, Evangeline. May this evening be a celebration of joy, love, and family."

The crowd erupts into applause. My dad's gaze lands on me for half a breath, and he's back to his speech.

"Furthermore, I'd also like tonight to stand for forgiveness and community as we welcome home one of our own."

Murmurs erupt around us at his declaration.

I search for Ruby and Mason, who only shrug when I find them standing to the side a few feet away.

My dad raises his champagne glass. "We're glad you're back, Son. Welcome home."

Someone in the back raises their glass as well, and I get my first glimpse of the man. My stomach roils so violently I grab on to my brother's arm to keep myself upright.

Phoenix Montgomery.

My dad continues to talk, but everything sounds like I'm underwater.

The crowd parts for Phoenix. He casually makes his way over to us with a smile plastered on his stupidly handsome face—the same sharp jawline, straight nose, and well-defined outline of his mouth with the small scar on his upper lip that always added to his male beauty.

Meanwhile, my heart is trying to pull the plug on itself.

This is impossible.

This can't be happening.

Yet, he's almost reached us like this is just another ordinary day.

And he definitely fits right in too, clad in a pristine black suit.

Have his shoulders always been this wide though?

I don't notice much else about his body, or our surroundings. I'm transfixed. Unable to avert my gaze from his face.

The dark depths of his eyes are holding me hostage, and he stares at me with nothing but warmth in them.

There will be a surprise waiting for you.

The words from Freddy's text message filter back into my head.

I knew it couldn't be anything good, but I didn't expect it to be this fucked up.

Phoenix Montgomery is my surprise.

My dead sister's fiancé.

The man who was in prison for the last three years.

And he has no idea I'm the one who put him there.

CHAPTER 2

PHOENIX

I've waited for this moment for so long, and now that it's finally happening, I can't take my eyes off Evangeline.

The blood roaring in my ears is so loud, everything around me changes to background noise. The whispers and subtle stares of judgment when I walk past the people I once wanted to impress so badly don't bother me anymore.

Some of them only see the criminal in me. Someone who was put in prison for doing something illegal.

Others see past that—mostly for their own agenda, or pockets—and focus on the billionaire heir of Montgomery Enterprises, the largest merger and acquisitions firm in the world. The same person they shun one second and try to kiss his ass the next.

Senator Walsh is in the crowd, his hand a bit too firm on his young assistant's lower back, something I file away for later.

Right now, they don't matter.

No one does, except for one person.

My body hums at seeing the panicked expression on her face, and I don't dare glance away. Since she set eyes on me, her gaze hasn't wavered once. It's like she knows I'm the predator and she's the prey, and if she looks away from me for only one second, I'll pounce and kill her.

Little does she know what I have in mind for her is far worse.

If everything goes according to plan, she'll be begging for death. But she doesn't deserve the luxury of a quick death. What she deserves is drawn-out torture.

And that's what I'm here for.

She was my downfall, and I'm here to return the favor.

But first, she needs to know I'm back.

This is the first public outing since I was released almost two weeks ago, and being here, surrounded by so many people, makes my skin itch. The fact something so simple is such a shock to my system only fuels the hate and the need for revenge further.

Even though Evangeline's father told the crowd to enjoy the party, most attendees are still staring. I practically feel their gazes searing into my back like pins and needles.

Her dad takes a step toward me and to the side, severing my view from Evangeline.

My muscles tense.

"Good to see you, Phoenix. Welcome home."

I shake his outstretched hand and smile. Time to play my part in this game. "Thanks, Mr. Caldwell."

He chuckles, his large midsection shaking from the action. "Oh, stop with the formalities and call me Byron."

I nod. "Byron."

He motions toward his wife. "And my beautiful wife, Audrey, of course."

I take her hand and lift it to my lips. "Lovely to see you again, Audrey."

The smile she gives me is warm and welcoming. Entirely pleasant to the naked eye. If I hadn't grown up in this environment, surrounded by phony people my entire life, she could have fooled me too. But I know better.

And as much as prison was an . . . inconvenience, to say the least, it allowed me to hone my people-reading skills further. There's only so much you can do and focus on when you're locked away. Unless you want to waste your time staring at a blank concrete wall or wallowing in self-pity.

It also gave me ample time to prepare for the moment I'd come face-to-face with Evangeline again.

Ignoring her, I focus on her brother first, studying his face.

He doesn't hold my gaze for long, his posture slightly sagging when he says, "Hey, man."

Alex and I weren't close friends, but we spent enough time together that it stung when he, just like everyone else in our circle, cut all ties with me when the news broke of my arrest.

Bunch of spineless bastards.

When I can't prolong it any longer, I turn toward Evangeline and drink her in.

Eve, the sweet girl I was obsessed with years ago but couldn't have.

But she's not my Eve, my Angel, anymore. She hasn't been in a very long time.

She's Evangeline now.

The photos I've seen of her while I was locked up haven't done her justice. She's matured, and even I can admit she's done so beautifully. What makes her appear even more devastating now are her trembling chin and her wide eyes. I hope it's out of fear. I hope she imagines me slitting her throat or something equally terrible to pay her back for what she did to me.

But that would be too easy.

Too quick and too final.

She deserves something a lot more painful and torturous.

Revenge won't bring back what I lost, but it will make me feel better.

Just like she's been occupying my thoughts for the bigger part of the last three years, I want her to experience the same inconvenience now that I'm back. The same compulsion. To have her constantly glancing over her shoulder and incapable of sleeping at night.

But she doesn't know any of that yet. That's a surprise for later.

With a smile that should pass as genuine, I close the distance between us and wrap her in my arms. "Happy birthday, *Angie.*"

She stiffens under my touch. Without having to see her, I know I hit my mark with the nickname, as intended, since her sister was the only one who called her that.

Her familiar floral scent floods my nose, still the same lavender fragrance. It's still as delicate and sweet as before, hitting my depraved nervous system with a ferocity I didn't anticipate. Unexpectedly, it's not unpleasant, a good thing if I go through with my plan.

I pull back enough to graze her cheek with a kiss, the

perfect gentleman. Her skin is soft under my lips, and I have to use every ounce of control in my body to refrain from biting her. The urge to inflict even the smallest fraction of pain is almost impossible to resist.

Reluctantly, I let go of her and push my hands into my pockets, pretending nothing's amiss.

She's still holding on to her brother's arm as though it's the only thing keeping her upright. I hope like hell it is.

Directing my attention to her dad, I dip my head. "Thanks for the invitation, Byron. I appreciate it."

Evangeline's head snaps in her father's direction. It seems she didn't know about her father's involvement in my appearance today.

Byron chuckles. "You're always welcome here."

He doesn't specify what *here* means, but if I'm correct and he refers to his family, he might truly not know what his daughter did. How else could he possibly think I'd forget his own daughter was the one who put me behind bars? Let alone forgive such a betrayal. Impossible.

Since he seems very secure in his hospitality, I put it on extra thick and place a hand on my chest. Right over my heart and the tattoo that'll forever be my reminder of a hard-learned lesson. Trusting people will leave you with two outcomes: either you gain a person for life, or you learn a lesson for life. "That means a lot."

"Let me know if you need anything."

I only smile and nod, unsure if I can keep up the act if I speak right now.

Unable to stay in their, in *her,* presence for any longer tonight, I clap him on the upper arm and lean in so only he can hear me. "I have some people who're waiting for me to mingle, but we're still on for our meeting tomorrow, correct?"

Another overeager smile for me. "Absolutely. Your parents will be there as well?"

"Yes, they're scheduled to return in the morning from their trip and will meet with us right away."

"Perfect."

I lower my voice. "I want Evangeline to be there too."

Byron stares at me with a small frown marring his forehead but quickly schools his expression.

Before he can ask any questions, I add, "But let's keep it between us. It's supposed to be a surprise, one I'm sure you'll like a lot."

He nods curtly, the excited gleam reentering his dark eyes. "Yes, of course."

"Enjoy your evening." I glance at each of them, ready to get the hell away from them before my control slips, but then I catch *her* gaze, and the blood rushes too loudly through my body again. My mask disappears, and for a moment, I let her see a sliver of the darkness and pain to come.

With my hands in tight fists in my pockets, I somehow manage a wink. "Bye, Angie."

This time, she doesn't flinch. This time, she expected it because she got a glimpse of the monster I've turned into. The monster *she* created.

Unable to look at her for another second, I spin around and quickly disappear into the crowd. Everything's too loud, too crowded. A bead of sweat rolls down my back, and I despise every second of it.

I don't make it far when a hand grabs my bicep and I freeze.

Bad move.

People should know better than to just touch others, especially a man like me.

I spin around—too quickly—and smack Alex's hand away.

He raises it in front of him. "Sorry, man. I wasn't thinking."

"No worries." I stare at him, waiting for him to make the first move and say what he came here to say.

"Listen. My father thought it would be best if I didn't visit. I'm sure you understand. You know how our parents are about appearances and all." He rubs a hand over his jaw. "So are we . . . are we good?"

Alex could have found other ways to get in contact with me, but he didn't. And I got over it. Eventually. The question is, does he know about his sister's involvement in my downfall? Like he said, public image is a top priority for most people in our circle, and most would go to great lengths to keep their family's reputation in a positive light, no matter the cost.

My old friend is still waiting for an answer, and I appreciate he hasn't run off with his tail tucked between his legs.

I hold out my fist to him. "Yeah, we're good."

With a sigh of what is undoubtedly relief, he bumps his curled-up hand against mine. "Thanks, bro. Glad you're back."

None of this means shit to me, but even if he truly has no clue about the little snitch in his family, I doubt he'll want to be friends once he realizes what I have in mind for his sister.

You gain some, you lose some.

Holden—my partner in crime, so to speak, and best

friend—steps up beside Alex and claps him on the back. "What a *nice* welcome." He stresses *nice* like the troublemaker he is. "Great party, man. Your family knows how to be hospitable."

Alex sways forward from the impact of Holden's paw and stares at the newcomer.

I wave my hand between the two. "Alex, meet Holden Donahue. Holden, this is Alex Caldwell."

The two size each other up for a moment, with Holden not once dropping his shit-eating grin. I'm not sure if it's because he knows he could easily take Alex if it came to that, seeing as he's built like a tank, or if he just wants to get a rise out of him. Nothing is ever certain with Holden. But he's one of the best guys I've ever met and has been my steady companion in the last few years until he was released two months ago. He's proven his loyalty over and over when people wanted to take a chunk out of the billionaire inmate and earned his spot by my side.

I might not have survived my time in prison unscathed if it wasn't for him. Well, mostly unscathed. There were times when I wanted to shed blood, both mine and others. Mostly at the beginning of my sentence when I was still grappling with what had transpired outside my new home.

Not just Evangeline's utter betrayal, but also her sister's death.

My fiancée's death.

Alex takes a step back from Holden and dips his head in my direction. "Let's catch up soon, yeah?"

I nod. "Sure thing."

We watch Alex's retreating figure until he disappears from sight.

Holden chuckles. "Look at him scuttle with his tail between his legs. I thought the Caldwells were all such badasses."

I raise a brow. "Have you seen yourself in the mirror lately? It's called self-preservation."

He puts a hand on his chest. "Aww, thank you."

I shake my head at his antics.

Holden rubs his hands together. "So, what's the deal? Are we leaving, or are we mingling? I saw some ladies checking me out." He flexes his biceps as if there's a single person in this room who hasn't witnessed the way his suit jacket strains at the seams.

I roll my lips. "Not sure."

Michael Simmons, a former investor of my father's company, walks by, and our gazes collide. His eyes narrow at me, but to my surprise, he stops.

After scanning the crowd around us, he takes a step closer to me. "I'm only doing this because your grandfather was a dear friend of mine. Your father is a cunning man and ruining the company your grandfather had spent most of his life creating. He's made a lot of enemies, and if you stand by his side, he'll drag you right to Hell with him."

I stare at him. "I'm afraid I'm already there, actually have been for the last few years."

He nods. "Very well. Watch your back then. A lot of people are out for blood."

Holden and I both watch the old man making his way toward the exit.

He asks, "What was that about?"

I shrug. "No clue. I'm sure he lost a lot of money, like so

many others did when the stock prices dropped after my arrest. It created a lot of disgruntled investors."

Holden hums, knowing my father's business isn't my priority at the moment.

My gaze wanders across the room to take in the pretentious crowd as they chitchat their night away. Observing. Searching.

It doesn't take long for me to find *her*.

Evangeline's walking away from her parents, her gaze glued to the phone in her hand. Her friends join her, both talking to her, as she points to the hallway on the opposite side of the room. Mason rubs her lower back in small circles, and she leans into him. Next to her, Ruby takes Evangeline's hand, and the three of them make their way through the throng of people.

Something hard presses against my chest.

I stare down at Holden's arm keeping me in place.

He *tsks* in my ear. "Easy there, tiger. It won't help you if you make a scene right now. You'll get your hands on her soon enough. Stick to the plan."

An edgy, twitchy feeling overtakes my body, but I force myself not to react.

Holden moves his arm up to my shoulder, still keeping a tight grip on me. "Let's get out of here before we need a body bag."

His previous words are in my head on repeat and the only reason why I let him drag me out of here.

You'll get your hands on her soon enough.

CHAPTER 3

EVANGELINE

The door slams into the wall, but I don't slow down. I push my way into the restroom and into the large enclosed stall at the end. My breaths are coming in fast and shallow as I pace back and forth in the space.

"Shit." Ruby's voice filters through the thin wall.

"What the hell is going on?" Mason hisses. "I thought this was supposed to be Evie's birthday party and not some fucked-up reunion with the ex-con."

"Mason, will you shut up?"

He makes a frustrated sound. "What? I'm just saying it like it is. I'm not even sure who the biggest asshole is tonight after that little stunt her dad pulled with Phoenix. Even though, did you see the guy Phoenix stood with when we left? He looks like that thing?"

Ruby sighs. "What thing?"

"You know, The Fantastic Four Thing."

"Oh my God. Do you mean Ben Grimm? His name is *The Thing*, not that thing."

"Whatever."

Their ridiculous argument is enough to distract me for a moment, but then my thoughts grow louder. Seeing Phoenix was bad enough, but what made it a million times worse was Freddy's text message I received minutes ago.

Did you like my surprise?

I need to get out of here. I need to get away from this place and all of these people.

I fumble my phone out of my purse and stare at it like it personally offended me. What I wouldn't give to throw it away and flee the country right now, or at the very least block Freddy's number. But I can't do that, or bad things will happen to my friends. Freddy made that more than clear.

After a deep inhale, I pull up my messages and text my driver, Darryl, to get the car. He tells me to meet him out back in ten minutes.

Ten minutes. I can keep it together for that long. Hide in here until I can go straight to the back exit, hopefully without running into anyone.

The door creaks outside, and a new voice filters in.

"Is she okay?"

No, damn it. What is Tyler doing here? I don't need more people witnessing my meltdown.

I sigh and get out of the stall. "I'm fine, Ty."

"Are you sure? You look a bit green." Our friend studies me and hands me a bottle of water.

"Thank you." A quick glance in the mirror confirms his statement. My skin does have a sick gleam to it. "My stomach is just a little upset."

"I'm sorry. Did you eat or drink something bad?" He

pushes his hands into his pockets, relaxing now that he can see I'm okay. His right cheek lifts in the devilish smirk I know so well. "Any punch at this party I should know about?"

Mason groans. "Oh my God. We said we'd never talk about that punch again. I still believe the assholes who added that entire vodka bottle were trying to murder all of us. Our parents were so mad we got that hammered at Evie's sweet sixteen." He laughs. "It's a miracle any of us remember that night at all."

Tyler laughs. "Only bits and pieces."

"Fuck, you feel so good, Evie."

Flashes of him with his head between my legs before he crawled up my body and thrust into me race through my mind. The memories are a bit blurry, but most of them are there.

I shake off the memory. We hooked up once, and that was many years ago. Well, at least this brief walk down memory lane distracted me for another two to three minutes.

Almost time to escape this shit show.

It's okay. Everything's okay. I'm going to be fine.

Yes, Phoenix is back, but maybe I won't see him again.

I mean, there's no reason for us to cross paths. And if we happen to attend the same parties, I can easily avoid him, right?

Plus, I'll be gone next year once I'm done with school anyway, and all of this will be behind me.

I focus back on Tyler and the fact he's wearing his pristine vest, crisp white shirt, and black slacks. Damn it. I forgot he's working tonight.

"Ty, get back out there. I don't want you to get in trouble."

"Stop worrying about me. I just wanted to make sure you're okay." He brushes a hand through his messy dark-blond hair. He must have done that a lot tonight. Waiting on the rich can do that to you. He walks to the door and eyes me over his shoulder. "See you Monday?"

I give him a small smile. "Bright and early, as usual."

He nods and leaves, and I catch Ruby's gaze in the mirror.

She shakes her head at me. "Don't give me that look. You know I couldn't stop him. He came barging in here like a white knight in shining armor. Nothing and no one can stop him once he's set his eyes on something."

"I just don't want to get him in trouble."

The corner of her mouth quirks up. "I know, babe. But he's a big boy who can take care of himself." She winks at me. "A really *nice* big boy."

"You're so bad." I grab my phone and check the time. "Darryl will be out back in two minutes. Are you guys staying or coming with me?"

Mason snorts. "As if you even have to ask. Of course we're coming with you."

"Evie." Ruby's sudden soft voice draws my attention from the screen.

She stares at me with her eyebrows pulled together. "You good?"

We both know I'm not, but I nod anyway.

"Sure. I mean, it'll be fine, right? I just didn't expect to see Phoenix tonight, and it's brought up a crap ton of memories, that's all."

The look she gives me says it all. She doesn't believe a

single piece of the crap that just came out of my mouth, but thankfully, she doesn't press any further.

THE NEXT MORNING, I wake up to a text message from my father.

DAD

Be at the office at 10 a.m.

Yeah, sure. I don't think so. Whatever he wants can wait.

ME

Sorry, I'm busy today.

DAD

I wasn't asking, Evangeline. Be there at 10, or I'll cut off your money.

I'm still staring at the screen when another message comes through.

DAD

All of the money.

I want to strangle him.

ME

I'll be there.

I'm sure he figured out I don't use all of my allowance with how comparatively modest we live here, so now he goes straight for the jugular by threatening to take away *all of my money*, which includes a nice sum I donate in his name every month to the local women's shelter I volunteer at. It's a nice tax write-off for him but has also become his new favorite tool to force my hand at the first sign of noncompliance.

And he knows I'd never let him cut off their money. They've been working so hard on expanding their housing to offer more women and their children a safe place. They need every cent they can get, and I will not be the reason they lose it.

So until I graduate and get the heck out of here, I have to keep up the false friendliness and obey my parents.

Two hours later, I walk down the hallway that leads to my father's home office, and it feels like I'm on the way to my own execution. Like my life will end here today. For good.

Don't be so dramatic. That's the lack of sleep talking.

Yes, I barely got any sleep. And the little I got was total crap, considering recent events. Add a healthy dose of anxiety over what my dad wants from me, and voilà, here I am, ready to jump out of my skin.

My stomach churns more with each step I take across the polished marble floor, reminding me I have more than just sleep deprivation to deal with. The overwhelming nausea that started yesterday still hasn't fully subsided, and the lack of food in my system has only added to the misery, making me slightly lightheaded too.

The electrolyte drink Ruby pressed into my hand when she and Mason dropped me off at the waiting car by the curb has been fighting to come back up ever since I gulped it down on the way to my parents' estate.

I can't wait to go home after this meeting and hide under the covers for the rest of the day. To be back in my own four walls that feel safer and more me than any other place has ever felt in my life. Sure, the comparably modest house I acquired near campus is almost a disgrace in my parents' eyes, and nothing they'd ever set foot in willingly, but it's all mine. That fact, plus sharing it with my best friends, is what makes it a home.

Our home. My home. Something this place with the shiny floors, crystal chandeliers, and more rooms than anyone could ever use was never able to accomplish. Though I do miss the library a lot, especially my personal one. Since I wasn't able to fit all of my books in my room at our house, they're stored away for now, alongside all of my sheet music I can't bear to look at anymore.

The door at the far end is open, and loud male voices drift out into the hallway. Each step is harder to take than the previous one, and I fight the liquid in my stomach every inch of the way.

Stupid nervous stomach.

All eyes are on me when I enter the large space, and my heartbeat picks up immediately at the sight in front of me. Not only are both of my parents here and my brother, but also Phoenix and his parents.

This can't be good.

The dark leather and wood decor blends into the background. All I can focus on are the people in the room.

Phoenix lounges in the brown leather love seat that's perpendicular to the one his parents occupy. My father sits in his massive wing chair opposite them, like the king he deems himself to be, with my mother dutifully standing by his side, though slightly behind, and my brother in a chair beside them. As always. Them versus me.

"There you are, Evangeline. We've been waiting for you." My father's slightly narrowed eyes don't hide the annoyance his voice manages to. He points at the spot on the couch next to Phoenix. "Sit."

I walk to the couch but stay standing beside it. No way in hell am I willingly going to sit next to Phoenix. "I'll stand for now, thank you."

Knowing it's expected of me, I shift my attention to Phoenix's parents and dip my head. "It's lovely to see you, Mr. and Mrs. Montgomery."

A small smile is all I can muster, but it has to be enough. They both give me their own practiced smiles, the one you learn early on in these circles. It passes as socially acceptable and friendly enough without being over the top.

However, Mr. Montgomery might have to practice some more. His was gone before it ever fully formed on his face, transforming it into a grimace. He openly studies me, taking me in from top to bottom, like he's trying to figure out if I'll pass the test. A test I'm unaware of.

The scrutiny continues as I stay frozen in place, the brown rug at my feet suddenly the most interesting thing in this room.

"You're in your last year at AV University?"

Mr. Montgomery's question catches me off guard. I can't remember if he's ever directly talked to me before, and I'm also fairly certain he already knows the answer to that question.

I clear my throat. "Yes, sir. I'll graduate next spring."

He nods, immediately reminding me of those strange bobblehead figures Mason finds hilarious.

"And you're planning on heading to the UK office right after graduation?"

Where is he going with this?

Let's just get through this and go back home, and then we can forget about this strange interaction.

"Mmm, yes. That's still the plan. To learn the ropes while I get my MBA."

I don't glance at my father for confirmation. I might break down right this very second if I saw a single speck of doubt in his gaze. Getting out of here and as far away from my family and all the other crap in my life is the only good thing about having to work in a job, in an industry, I've never wanted anything to do with.

Whereas I was always just interested in my piano and escaping into the made-up world of my favorite books, my sister inherited our dad's brain for business and finances. She was basically a numbers wizard, which made her the perfect candidate to take over the UK office of Caldwell & Company, our global management consulting firm, while my brother will take over the U.S. main office. But if dealing with numbers and business procedures for the foreseeable future will allow me to get out of here, I'll pay that price.

Phoenix's father hums under his breath but stops questioning me.

My dad takes that as his cue and clasps his hands together. He's suddenly sporting a huge grin, his joyful attitude immediately putting me on edge. My insides feel like they're quivering, and I hold on to the back of the couch for support.

My death grip on the cool material gets even worse when my father focuses his smile on me.

"Evangeline, we had a lovely conversation with the Montgomerys, and we all agreed it's best to leave the past in the past and focus on the future instead. We once had great plans for our families and empires, and we'd like to circle back to that great partnership with you."

My breathing has sped up with every word from his mouth.

We once had great plans.

My sister marrying Phoenix.

We'd like to circle back to that great partnership with you.

With you.

With. Me.

"Evangeline, you're going to take over Constance's spot and marry Phoenix."

That's the last thing I hear before my body decides it's had enough and everything goes black.

CHAPTER 4

PHOENIX

It would be so easy to kill her.

So easy to walk up to the bed, slit her throat, and let her bleed out.

Yet, after everything that happened, there's still no satisfaction at the thought. No punishment will ever be enough. Nothing will give me back the last three years of my life or the hit my reputation, as well as my family's, took.

Nothing will ever make up for it.

But making her life a living hell will help some.

She'll be mine to ruin, and having her become my wife is only the first step, one I know she'll resent me for with all her being. All while I have a front-row seat to her misery.

I can't wait.

And maybe this was a long time coming. Who knows? Perhaps we were always inevitable, our life paths chosen long before we ever stepped foot on them.

Everything started falling apart when I got engaged to Connie. Though, to be fair, I knew this might be an issue for Eve. I didn't anticipate such a strong reaction from her, though, to the point where she put a wedge between her and her sister. I don't know everything that went on between them, but as far as I'm aware, their relationship went from good to rocky when Eve—no more nicknames, it's Evangeline now—found out about us.

Then Connie died, and everything went to shit from there. I didn't even have the chance to pay my respects to her before the police arrested me.

Granted, the charges were warranted, but they should have never happened in the first place. I just wanted to dish out some much-deserved punishment because Chris Wellinger deserved it. Of course, the police didn't agree with me. My father had groomed me for years, having me do a ton of shady shit for him, but I was never caught. Until that dreadful night.

Unfortunately, this time, the judge couldn't be bought. To say my father was livid is the understatement of the year. No one ever says no to Spencer Montgomery; it was the reality check he didn't want or need. I certainly didn't either.

Evangeline groans on the bed. "What . . ."

Her parents asked me to carry her into the closest guest bedroom after she fainted. Yes, *carry*, because my dumb-ass reflexes kicked in and overrode everything else when I saw her collapse. I jumped up and caught her before she hit her head on the floor. I should have been so lucky. Instead, I was the white knight everyone was grateful for.

I had to hold her in my arms like she was precious, with her lush curves pressed against me. My traitorous former self came to the surface and wanted to touch her some more, to trace her high cheekbones and grab her hips. Why does she have to be so damn beautiful? I thought all of these old feelings and the desire would be gone forever with how much hatred I have for her in my heart.

She shifts again, lifting her hand to her head and resting it on her dark hair. Her eyes flutter as she slowly blinks them open and stares at the ceiling. I know the second her memories come back to her. She gasps and sits upright, her gaze immediately zooming around the room until it lands on me with wide eyes.

"Welcome back, *fiancée*." I push my hands in my pockets and don't move from where I stand, with several feet between us.

Be nice. You want to keep the upper hand and not let her immediately see all of your cards.

Her head goes left and right several times. "That can't be . . . No . . . We can't."

"Well, it seems like the decision was already made for us, but feel free to try and get us out of it. You can go find Daddy and tell him the business deal of his dreams will go up in flames after all."

I try to be nonchalant without sounding too desperate. I didn't expect her to go along with our engagement, but I'm also banking on her dad holding up his end of the bargain. There's a reason I made sure my father dangled the biggest carrot under his nose we could offer. Dropping our current consulting firm and using Byron's instead. My future father-in-law doesn't need to know my father was planning on switching companies anyway.

Evangeline could still say screw it and leave her princess life behind in favor of not getting married to me, but I don't think she'll do that.

At least, that's what I'm banking on. If she proves me

wrong and her father can't convince her, I still have an ace up my sleeve.

Because if she doesn't play along, I'll ruin her and her whole family.

No matter how much she doesn't agree with them, her reputation means something to her. It'll be tainted enough now that she's marrying an ex-con.

Her gaze fixates on the wall, her lip tucked between her teeth to the point where it has lost almost all its color. Maybe I will get lucky and see some spilled blood today after all.

"How are you feeling? Are you okay?" Every passing second in her company makes it harder to keep my tone in check.

But she doesn't need to know any of that yet, or she'll run for sure.

Agreeing to a marriage with a white knight is very different from agreeing to a marriage with the big bad wolf.

So, for now, I have to hide in my sheep's clothing.

She finally glances my way at my question, and something that resembles guilt a whole lot flashes in her dark eyes. But she averts her gaze almost immediately to stare at her hands in her lap, so I can't be sure.

Can't stand to look at me, my fallen angel? Well, too fucking bad. You made your bed, and now you have to lie in it, sharp thorns and all.

She gives a little nod. "Yes, I'm okay. Thank you for asking."

Always so polite.

"I'm glad you didn't get hurt. That could have been a hard fall." At this rate, I might need to visit my dentist soon for the tooth damage I'll cause from all the clenching and grinding when I'm in Evangeline's presence.

Her hand goes to the back of her head like it just now occurred to her she didn't get injured. "What happened?"

"I caught you and carried you to this room."

Her breath hisses between her lips at the sharp inhale. "Thank you."

She pulls the blanket off her body and slowly swings her legs over the side of the bed. "I . . . I need to find my parents." She clears her throat and straightens her spine. "They can't make us get married. No way in hell are you and I . . ."

She glances my way and licks her lips.

Finish your sentence, Princess, and tell me how you really feel.

But she doesn't. Instead, she pushes off the bed and lands on her feet.

She wobbles immediately, and I rush forward and grab her by the arm.

What a fucking white knight you are.

It only takes her a second to steady herself, but I continue to hold her anyway.

"You can let go of me. I'm good." Her voice shakes the tiniest amount. "Just didn't think about the heels."

I nod as if I care.

"Phoenix, I said I'm good. Please let go." This time, her voice has that signature Caldwell steel back.

"Phoenix, please don't marry Connie. I don't know what's happening, but please don't ruin her life."

Three years, and her sharp words still hit home. It's crystal clear her low opinion of me hasn't changed a single bit. With my stint in prison, it's probably only gotten worse.

I draw on every ounce of control I possess and let go of her. One finger at a time.

"I just wanted to make sure you're stable enough." I shove my hands into my pockets to keep myself from grabbing her again, but this time to shake her.

She huffs out a breath. "Sorry, I'm not trying to be a bitch, but I didn't expect this mess to happen today. We both know this would never work between us. I mean, neither of us wants this, and we live in the twenty-first century, for crying out loud. They can't make us."

"I'd be willing to try if you are." The second the words leave my mouth, I have to bite the inside of my cheek to keep from doing something stupid like laughing at the pure insanity of my statement. My control has already been stretched to its maximum capacity today, and I need to get away from her as soon as possible before it snaps.

Evangeline regards me as if I slapped her. "You can't mean that. An arranged marriage? Us? Never."

My dick twitches behind my zipper.

Fuck.

Of course, I'd get off on seeing that fire, that hatred for me and the accompanying misery in her eyes. After all, that's exactly what I want to see.

However, I won't deny she's a total beauty either. She's always been beautiful, but the last three years have matured and sharpened her features, turning her into a total showstopper.

She shakes her head. "After everything that happened, you can't possibly want to be near me any more than I want to be near you."

Her voice is the slap back to reality I needed.

"Going for the throat today, Angie?" My smile slips as I take a step toward her.

She takes a step back.

Good. Maybe it's time to remind her who I am without spilling my secret. "Maybe the time I spent in *prison* has helped put some things in perspective for me. I know I can't change past events, regardless of how much I want to. The only thing that's left is to move on. Maybe you should try the same."

Her mouth opens and closes several times, and she doesn't look away this time.

Our stare down is interrupted when a knock sounds at the door.

"Come in." The words come out clipped, but I'm beyond caring.

I need to get out of here. Away from her until I can learn how to handle her presence better. This is only a short preview of what I'll have to withstand when we're in the same room.

A woman with salt-and-pepper hair opens the door and pokes her head in. One of the housekeepers, if I remember correctly.

She scans over us and swallows, her gaze settling on Evangeline. "I wanted to see if you're awake and need anything."

Evangeline smiles at the woman. "You're the best, Patricia, thank you. I'm much better now. Do you know where my parents are? I need to talk to them."

Patricia frowns. "I'm so sorry, miss, but your parents have left for lunch."

I take Evangeline's frustrated expression as my cue to leave, desperate to escape from her for a while.

With a casual "Goodbye," I head toward the door, adding, "I expect you at my place tonight for dinner, Angie," over my shoulder.

I can't help myself. I don't want to miss a single opportunity to dig that knife in deeper.

That's as much of a promise to myself as it is to my future wife.

CHAPTER 5

EVANGELINE

"If they think I'm going to just lie down and marry Phoenix like a good little girl, they're officially delusional." I pace the length of our living room over and over. Back and forth. Back and forth.

"Babe, please, you're making me dizzy. Sit down," Ruby whines from the couch she and Mason are sitting on.

They've been there for the last ten or so minutes while I told them what happened. While I told them I was supposed to marry Phoenix. That I had to track down my parents to confront them, and that my dad expected me to marry him out of *family duty*. Those were his exact words. That it's my job, part of the business. They've all lost their fucking minds.

Of course, he brought up the donations again, but there's only so far I'll take that. I'll just have to find another way to help Doreen at the shelter. And the fact that Phoenix is going along with it like it's totally normal to have an arranged marriage like this in the twenty-first century is insane, and to the sister of his dead fiancée, no less. What is he thinking?

I plop down onto the empty couch and stare at the coffee

table, unable to look at my friends. I don't want to see the pity in their eyes.

"You know, I'm not even too surprised about my dad pushing this. He's greedy and has been very vocal about wanting to work with Montgomery Enterprises. This is his chance to get the piece of the pie he's been wanting so badly. But to sell off his daughter for it? After everything that happened with Connie?"

I heave a sigh and drop back into the cushions.

The desire to throw a blanket over my head and pretend life isn't happening is overwhelmingly high.

"Evie." Mason's gentle tone is accompanied by the couch dipping next to me, right before he wraps his arms around my shoulders and pulls me closer. "We'll figure this out, okay? I mean, they can't *make* you, right?"

No, they can't.

That's my only silver lining.

Am I going to lose my family and possibly more if I refuse?

It's not like they hold you in high regard anyway.

No . . . no, they don't.

Because they blame you for your sister's death.

Because it was my fault.

It's my fucking fault she died.

"Shh." Mason rubs my back. "You're starting to hyper-ventilate. You need to breathe."

I gasp for air and close my eyes. I was so lost in my head, the past dragging me into its dark depths like so often, I didn't even realize what I was doing.

Inhaling deeply, I try to calm my erratic breathing. Cold sweat runs down my back, and my eyes burn.

Sometimes, I really wish it had been me in that car accident and not my sister.

I bet she would have had a better shot at life and happiness. She always saw the cup half full instead of half empty, even when she was ruining her life.

"I don't know exactly how, Angie, but it'll all work out. You just need to trust me to do the right thing, even if you think I'm making a mistake right now. Phoenix is my saving grace, and I need him more than you'll ever understand."

I was shaking uncontrollably when she said those words to me, every word piercing my whole being once again. Like I was the problem in that situation and couldn't see the beauty before me. Like she wasn't the one cutting out my heart by marrying Phoenix.

I will not make the same mistake she did. No way in hell am I going to marry that man.

I can't.

I wouldn't survive it.

"Babe, look at me." Ruby crouches before me on the floor and takes my hands into hers.

After a moment, I manage to lift my gaze.

"Breathe with me, okay?"

Shit. Did I lose it again? I pause and peer down at my heaving chest. Yup, way too fast.

"Evie, focus." Ruby gets in my face again, her eyes narrowed. "I need you with me."

It's hard to read her face. She might be close to either slapping me or starting to cry. Fifty-fifty. Since I don't want her to do either, I drive through the thick fog in my mind and focus on her as best as possible.

She nods. "Good. Deep breath in . . . and then out."

I stare at her mouth and follow her instructions.

When she seems satisfied, she sits back on her heels. "Shit, man. This is all really bad, isn't it?"

I'm about to reply just as the doorbell rings.

We all stare toward the entryway like the Devil himself is waiting on the other side of the door, ready to collect our souls.

Mason gets up. "Stay here, I'll get it."

Since we're seated around the corner, I don't have an actual view of the front door or the visitor. The swoosh of the door is the only indication Mason actually opened it. Other than that, there are several beats of silence.

I'm about to jump off the couch to see what's going on when Mason sighs.

"What do *you* want?"

"I'm here to get Evangeline." The deep voice is laced with both amusement and authority. What a strange combination.

"She's not going anywhere with you. Tell Phoenix the deal is off." Mason's voice is low and surprisingly hard.

My mouth drops open.

He's usually so calm-mannered and gentle.

The other guy chuckles. "Good to know. Tell her she's got five minutes."

I'm out of my seat this time, ready to tell whoever's at the door to screw themselves.

But by the time I reach the door, it's already closed, with Mason sagging against it.

He presses a hand to his chest. "Shit. That guy is a scary motherfucker."

"Who?" I halt in front of him, rising onto my toes to see through the peephole.

Of course, I can't make out anything but a black SUV parked by the curb.

Mason gives a shaky laugh. "That huge guy Phoenix was with at the party. He gives the impression he could snap anyone in half in less than a second."

I think for a moment but shake my head when I come up empty. "I remember you talking about him, but I can't remember what he looks like."

"Probably for the best." Mason checks all the locks and takes my hand to drag me after him through the open living room and into the kitchen. "I need a drink."

"Already on it." Ruby is in front of us.

She climbs on the counter with one knee to reach the shot glasses before lining them neatly on the island between us. Mason fills them with clear liquor. I have no idea what it is or where it came from. One of them shoves a glass into my hand, and I take it, working on autopilot. We clink glasses, and I down the shot. The liquid burns in my throat and all the way down to my stomach, slowly settling into a comforting warmth.

"Another one." My voice sounds weird, even to my ears, but I ignore it. I need this.

After my third shot, the burning travels through my entire body. It feels incredible.

I hold out my glass for another refill at the same time as an ear-splitting noise fills the room.

"Fuck. Get down and behind the island," Mason yells.

I'm frozen, unable to take my eyes off the massive man striding toward me.

His stride is casual like he doesn't have a care in the world.

If he were walking past me on the street, I'd probably stop and stare too. It's impossible not to. He's dressed entirely in black, with his dark hair pulled away from his face in what seems to be a man bun. I can't be sure from this angle. A thick, well-groomed beard covers the bottom half of his face, somehow accentuating his smile.

Why is he smiling at me?

"Your time is up, Princess."

Without any preamble, he squats in front of me. With his body bent in my direction, I'm heaved into the air, my midsection hitting his hard shoulder.

My world turns upside down.

"Ooof." I'm still trying to figure out what just happened when I sway around like I'm on a boat.

My stomach is unsure how to feel about that, but thankfully, it decides it's okay for now.

Mostly.

Did this guy . . . did he seriously just throw me over his shoulder?

What the fuck?

"Let her go," Mason yells from somewhere behind me.

Or in front of me? I'm not even sure anymore.

I stare at the floor as we move away from my friends.

No, no, no.

I finally find my brain again and pound on him with my fists. "Let me down."

His shoulders shake underneath my stomach. Is he laughing at me?

Hurried footsteps come closer, and I try to hit him harder.

"You can't just take her." Ruby's voice is loud with the slightest slur to it.

The guy holding me stops and spins around. "Try and stop me."

Another spin, and we're on the move again. The guy steps over strewn pieces of splintered wood and walks outside.

What the hell?

Was that our front door?

Or rather, what's left of it?

Who does something like this?

The Thing.

That's what Mason called him yesterday. This first impression might have been spot on.

I stare at the damage in disbelief, and then Ruby's collection of garden gnomes which has, thankfully, come away unharmed. She'd be livid otherwise.

"Watch your head."

That's all the warning I get. One of the man's hands leaves my thighs and goes to my back, and two seconds later, I'm in the back of a car. I'm unsure how he managed to get me in here like this, but I'm too stunned to react. Then the door closes, and I'm locked in.

I blink.

He steps away from the door and intercepts Ruby and Mason, who are frantically trying to get to me, while I yank on the door handle, push every available button, and hammer on the darkened windows.

The stranger ignores me and talks to my friends for a

moment. After that, he goes to the front of the car and gets into the driver's seat.

I gasp, all I'm capable of, while my brain tries to force its way through the fogginess in my head. But to no avail. The alcohol has fully hit my system—hard and fast—just like the brute leisurely driving away from my house.

No screeching tires or speeding, like I'd normally associate with a kidnapping. This man is way too chill for my taste, which might be even worse.

There's a partition between the front and the back, but it's down enough for me to glare at the burly man behind the wheel. "Where are you taking me?"

He glances at me in the rearview mirror. At least, I think he is since his eyes hide behind his aviators.

"To Phoenix."

Although I'm not surprised about the answer, adrenaline still shoots through my system. "I need you to let me go, please."

He shifts his focus back to the road. "Can't do that, Princess."

I try again, pleading and begging, but he ignores me.

With every passing second, the overwhelming sense of dread grows.

I need to get out of here.

I'm not having Phoenix steamroller all over me like this.

He can't do that. I won't let him.

With each turn, hole, or bump we hit, my stomach complains, and my nausea grows to terrifying heights.

I don't drink often, not liking the lack of control, but I usually handle my alcohol better than this.

A normal person would also make sure to eat something before you take shots like someone whose life isn't blowing to shit.

Ugh.

How could I forget I'd barely eaten anything substantial in the last twenty-four hours?

My phone vibrates in my pocket, and I stiffen.

Of course, I forgot I had it on me.

I pull it out quickly, excited to be able to call someone for help.

But the moment I see the name on the screen, a new wave of nausea hits me.

I click on the notification to open the message.

FREDDY

I heard congratulations are in order. You'll be a good fiancée and wife, won't you, pet?

I stare and stare, and stare some more until the phone becomes blurry in my hands.

FREDDY

We don't want your friend's career to end before it ever begins, do we?

A photo comes through. Ruby on stage during one of her rehearsals from last week.

My stomach gives a warning, wordlessly telling me that no one should drink several shots on a stomach that's not just empty but also upset.

I have to agree. That was a really bad idea.

"Stop the car."

The man ignores me.

"I'm going to be sick."

This time, he inspects me in the rearview mirror just as I slap a hand over my mouth.

The tires screech. He pulls the car sharply to the right, and we bump for several feet until we come to a complete stop.

He's out of the car and in the back to open my door.

Just in time, too, because everything comes out in a big gush of liquids.

CHAPTER 6

PHOENIX

"She just fell asleep?" I take in Evangeline's comatose form on the bed.

Holden nods. "Yeah. They were drinking when I got there. Not that I blame her. I'd get hammered too in her situation."

I ignore his comment.

Much like earlier, her first sign of life is a groan.

This one isn't a soft one, though, like this morning, but rather one of someone who's on the brink of dying. Or, at the very least, feels like it.

"Imma adhdilsgfergbwlkiefsfbdhgwek."

Holden and I stare at each other at the gibberish that just came out of her mouth. He only raises his brows.

I sigh, something it seems I'll be doing a lot around this woman. I have no patience for her and her antics.

Don't want them.

Don't need them.

Won't tolerate them.

She's quiet after that, and soft snores fill the room instead.

Shifting my gaze away from her, I focus on my friend. "Did you really have to break down her door? I thought we said we're keeping a low profile?"

Holden just smiles—his way of dealing with pretty much anything. "I got a little carried away. I already have some guys working on it."

I nod. "Good."

One thing I like about Holden is I don't need to babysit him. He knows his role and can deal with shit by himself without having to be told. We didn't have much contact in the last few months between his release and mine, and I quickly realized it wasn't necessary. He had everything ready for my arrival, had assembled a crew he instinctively trusted, and started delving into our new business venture.

We both know the police will most likely scrutinize every move I make, happy to bust me again at the slightest infraction, so all illegal activity is on pause until we can be sure they're off my case. And what better way to show you're an invaluable part of society than giving away some of your money for a good cause? Or several good causes as we grow our charitable foundation legally, with the possibility of using it to wash money down the road. That's at least what I told my dad to keep him from constantly looking over my shoulder.

And while putting money in other people's pockets instead of our own isn't how he raised me, I'm excited for this opportunity. I've met a lot of guys in prison who didn't grow up as fortunate as I did but were better people than most in our rich circle, which says more about them than us.

Holden hasn't told me everything about his past and demons, but I know enough about him to understand he didn't have the best upbringing. He was actually the one who suggested starting a charity for teenagers, and I can't fault him for wanting to offer others a better chance at life. So the Foxhole Foundation was born: a charity to support teenagers who need a helping hand in life.

Holden's phone chimes, and he reads something on his screen. "Thomas wants to know if his team is supposed to handle Evangeline's clothes as well."

I think about it for a moment. Without a doubt, Evangeline has an impeccable wardrobe, but I know she'll hate everything she gets from me, even if my personal shopper picks it. "Tell Thomas to buy everything Evangeline could possibly need and to have her formal wardrobe for the upcoming events complement my own."

Holden chuckles. "You're evil; I like it."

Evil, I'm not sure. But definitely petty and hateful enough to turn over as many rocks in Evangeline's life as possible. That's the whole reason for this charade.

Holden puts his phone back into his pocket. "And you really think she'll play along and attend the events with you?"

I tilt my head to the side. "If she refuses, I'll just have to play my ace earlier than I want to."

He slaps his large hand on my back. "It'll be fun to watch either way. So far, she's been wearing her emotions on her face, so I'm not sure she possesses the acting skills she needs to pull this off."

"Only one way to find out." I glance at the clock on the wall and sigh. "I have to meet with my father."

"Go. I'll keep an eye on her."

AFTER THIS MORNING'S meeting with the Caldwells, my father went straight to his office in the city. Although he has a big office at his estate, he still prefers the city one where he can revel in everyone's admiration and fear. I hate having to make the drive, but when my dad calls, I come. Since I want to take over Montgomery Enterprises one day, just like I promised my grandfather I would, I need to play along with my dad's dominion for as long as necessary.

Since it's Sunday, the building is mostly empty as I go up to the thirty-second floor. The secretary's desk was left in pristine condition, like everything else under my father's control, and I'm tempted to move some things around, but no one deserves my father's wrath.

As if he heard me, his door opens, and his large body fills the frame. "Get your ass in here."

He sighs and disappears, leaving the door open for me.

The moment I close it behind me, his voice echoes around me.

"I wanted to see how things are going with your little project."

Damn, has his office always been this big?

This is my first time back here since my release, and everywhere I go, I can't help but notice how massive everything is. The change from a small cell to the expansive nature of our homes and businesses isn't as terrible as it was to get used to the cramped space when I first entered my prison cell, but it's still an adjustment.

Everything is almost too big.

Is there such a thing as reverse claustrophobia?

"Phoenix."

My father's sharp voice snaps me out of my thoughts and the perusal of his executive office with a view of Central Park. "Sorry. What?"

He regards me with narrowed eyes. "I said I want a report on the charity."

"I'm meeting with the lawyers this week to ensure we have everything we need to get going as soon as possible." I push both hands in my pockets and stare out the window.

Since we're heading into fall, the leaves have been creating stunning foliage amidst the skyscrapers. Reds, oranges, and yellows interspersed with greens and browns.

Of all the things I thought I'd miss the most in prison, nature wasn't one of them. Yet, I've been staring at flowers and trees way more in the past couple of weeks since Holden picked me up than ever before.

My father steps in front of me, successfully cutting off my view. We're around the same height, so the two inches I have on him with my six-foot-four frame unfortunately aren't enough to secure my vantage point.

His eyes narrow. "You know, this entire time, I thought you'd return to your old position."

Of course he thought that. He's groomed me to be what he calls an enforcer, which was never a surprise, considering he loves to use any and all measures to get what he wants. And what's some blackmail, or violence, when it secures you the companies you lust after?

You're better than this, Phoenix. Listen to your gut; it will show you the right path.

My grandfather's words of wisdom could be categorized as famous last words, considering that listening to him ultimately ended with me in prison.

Nevertheless, it felt right to do this from the moment Holden first brought it up.

I push back my shoulders and stare straight into my father's dark-brown eyes, which is always a bit like staring into a mirror. But I always try not to react to our clone-like appearances since, like the true narcissist he is, he takes pride in the fact that I resemble him so much.

"It's too soon for that. I've thought about this long and hard, and at this point, the foundation is the best thing for me to do to clear my name. Unless you want the company stocks to dip again."

That shuts him up fast because there isn't much that my father cares about more than his money.

After my arrest, many investors jumped ship, and it took my father a while to get the enterprise value back to where it used to be. He wouldn't risk that again. I'm surprised he didn't think about that himself.

I shrug. "Plus, this will be a nice opportunity to launder money in the future."

"Fine, have it your way." He stays quiet and studies me until his facial muscles relax slightly. "Evangeline will certainly be your golden ticket with this. Someone with her social standing might be the only one who can convince people to do business with you. Smart move."

I want to tell him to screw himself, that I don't need Evangeline's help for anything, but that would blow up my whole cover. He doesn't know Evangeline put me in prison, or he would have never agreed to do business with Byron.

And that would have prevented me from getting my hands on my little traitor, at least in the way I have now.

"I'm sure she'll be a great asset." I push the words through gritted teeth.

"Good." He claps me on the shoulder once before he makes his way back to his oversized mahogany desk. "I don't have to remind you not to screw this up. I don't care if you fuck her, but don't let your emotions get involved. I've raised you better than that."

I want to laugh at the ridiculousness of ever having feelings for Evangeline, but the admonishment he just delivered has me biting the inside of my cheek hard enough to taste the coppery tinge of blood. God, how badly I want to give him a piece of my mind, but I can't do that if I ever want to take over the company. I wouldn't put it past my father to keep it from me as punishment for getting in his way, or even for standing up to him.

Just like my parents never visited me while I was in prison. I saw them once before my trial, and my dad used that opportunity to tell me if I was stupid enough to get caught, I'd have to deal with the consequences by myself too. He sent someone to check on me in prison periodically to make sure I wasn't stepping out of line.

So, I nod. "Of course, Father."

"Visit your mother sometime soon so she stops whining." He waves a hand toward the door, his attention already back on the papers in front of him.

My dismissal.

What a waste of time to come here for this instead of having the conversation on the phone. Just another one of his many tactics to show his power over me.

I march toward the bank of elevators. One opens, and the two men who were animatedly chatting scurry toward the corner when they see me.

Scary ex-con, yes.

I lean back against the wall and close my eyes. My father has a gift to rile me up like no one else.

Except for Evangeline. She's on a whole different level.

My phone buzzes, and I take it out to check the screen.

CANARY

Have you told the bitch yet? Maybe it's time to reveal your secret.

CHAPTER 7

EVANGELINE

S top pacing and just open the damn door. What could possibly go wrong?

I want to snort at the ridiculous voice in my head because what *hasn't* gone wrong in the last few days?

No, make that years.

Not a lot of things, that is.

The pain in my head rises to near-impossible levels, and I stop in the middle of the room.

In a bedroom.

At Phoenix's house.

Where I was taken without my consent.

After I got the text message on the drive here.

I heard congratulations are in order. You'll be a good fiancée and wife, won't you, pet?

The *or else* is implied.

But why? A few years ago, I went on one date, and the

guy never talked to me again because Freddy vandalized his car and told him to stay away from me. But now he wants me to marry Phoenix? The more I think about it, the less it makes sense.

Being forced into an engagement, into an impending marriage, takes my life to a whole new level of ruin, especially when it's with the man who will surely kill me if he ever finds out what I did.

And I couldn't even explain to him why I did it, not without putting Ruby or anyone else in my life in danger.

Angry and frustrated tears well in my eyes, but I will the emotions away. I have to, or they'll eat me alive.

At least then, you wouldn't have to deal with all of this shit anymore. Then you'd finally be at peace.

Shut up, shut up, shut up.

I grasp my head, willing that malicious voice to go away. I can't deal with it right now, not when I'm already so close to crumbling, so close to giving in and ignoring the warning my devil once gave me all those years ago.

If you ever think about taking yourself out of the equation, think again, because everyone will suffer for that. Every last person in your life.

A knock at the door saves me from spiraling further. The door opens after a few seconds without anyone waiting for a response.

I guess any form of decency is gone when you're a prisoner in your own life.

"Miss Evangeline, are you all right?"

The gentle voice pulls me out of my head long enough to look up.

A tall, thin man with a full head of gray hair stands in the doorway, staring at me with a worried frown.

I let go of my hair and wipe at my face, painfully aware I probably resemble a complete nutcase and nothing like the put-together heiress I am supposed to be.

My spine straightens as I plaster on a smile and nod. "Of course, yes. Sorry about that."

Old habits die hard—good manners that have been drilled into you your entire life even more so.

I'm unsure if he buys my terrible act, but he nods and pushes a cart I didn't notice into the room.

"Mister Phoenix said you'd probably be hungry by now, so I brought you breakfast. Our chef said the food shouldn't upset your stomach." He wheels the cart to the table in the corner and glances at me with a more relaxed, pleasant expression. "Would you like me to set it up for you, or do you want to freshen up first?"

I blink at him, taken back by his friendly demeanor and the fact that someone must have told the chef I had an upset stomach.

"Miss?"

"Sorry. Freshening up sounds perfect."

With a gentle smile, he takes a few steps back and gestures to the hallway opposite the giant four-poster bed I slept in. "In case you haven't wandered, this hallway leads to the bathroom and the walk-in closet. Mister Holden will have your school items ready at your departure, and the remainder of your belongings should arrive later today. But I took the liberty to stock everything for you, so please alert me if anything is amiss or not to your liking, and I'll attend to it immediately."

With my head pounding now, and dumbfounded by this whole interaction, I manage another smile and a "Thank you."

The man drops his hands to his sides and bows a little. "My pleasure, miss."

When he reaches the open door, he grabs the doorknob and regards me. "Before I forget, my name is Huxley. If there's anything I can do for you, please don't hesitate to find me. I'll see to it immediately if it's within my power."

The wooden door closes before I get my brain to form a reply and I stare at it. It takes me several beats to get back to my senses.

Putting aside my current situation, Huxley was right. I'm hungry and need a shower to feel more human again.

I examine the cart and lift the lids one by one, groaning at the sight and smell. Poached eggs, crispy bacon, avocado toast, and a bowl of yogurt with fresh fruit and drizzled honey on top. My gaze snatches on the small package of painkillers, and I instantly grab it, silently sending a thank you to whoever took pity on me. I rip it open, toss the two pills into my mouth, and gulp them down with some orange juice. After taking a bite out of the avocado toast, I cover the food again.

Shower first, then more food.

I stride down the hallway into the bathroom, taking in the modern aesthetic with its warm, neutral colors that give it an almost cozy feel. Wood, brass, and glass are all well-balanced with sharp, clean lines, uncluttered counter spaces, and geometric shapes.

The large walk-in shower greets me with the perfectly tuned water temperature, the six jet sprays and wide rainfall showerhead effectively lifting my mood while I try to scrub away the events from the past few days. Unfortunately, without much success. But at least I've gotten rid of the yucky layer of repulsion that only a hangover can cause.

The closet brings me to an immediate halt since it's entirely filled. Clothes, shoes, stacks of unopened boxes. Brand names. Famous designers. A mix of business and casual attire. Whose closet is this because these are definitely not my clothes. Nothing in this room belongs to me. I inspect the racks and pause. Everything is in my size, even the underwear in the drawers. When Huxley said he took the liberty to stock everything for me, was he talking about my entire wardrobe as well?

Deep breath. That's the least of your problems right now.

I mumble some choice words for Phoenix and pick some simple cotton panties alongside a pair of jeans and a sweater I find toward the back.

Returning to the bathroom, I give myself a once-over in the mirror.

Ouch.

There's a reason I usually don't drink a lot.

I look like I've been doing drugs for a week straight.

Thankfully, Huxley was right, and a quick glance into the drawers reveals everything I need.

I apply some lotion and light makeup, but not until I smother my dark circles with several levels of concealer. After a round with the hair dryer, I stop. This will have to be enough to blend in with the college crowd. At school, I'm only Evie, nothing more and nothing less, at least not to most of the students. So hopefully, it'll do.

Feeling marginally better than when I first woke up, I'm

ready to devour as much delicious-smelling food as possible before heading out.

I make my way back into the bedroom, my footsteps quiet on the plush carpet.

The moment the table comes into view, I stop and stare at it with wide eyes. It's no longer unoccupied.

Phoenix is lounging in one of the chairs like the king personified.

Well, I guess he *is* the king of this castle.

Does that make me his queen now?

A groan works up my throat at my random thoughts, but Phoenix only raises a brow.

He leans forward and pulls out the chair next to him. "Sit."

I ignore him and sit in the chair next to the one he offered me, successfully putting as much distance between us as possible.

Feeling his gaze on me, I stare at him and sigh. "What do you want, Phoenix? I'd like to enjoy the food, so say what you came here to say and leave."

"Why so prickly this morning, Angie?"

No one has called me that in three years, and the nickname sends an ice-cold chill down my spine. "Stop calling me that."

"Why? I think I rather like it." He leans back and puts his right arm on the back of the one I ignored.

Even though my head feels a lot better, I still have no energy to deal with this crap. I refuse to. I need at least three days of good sleep and my life to give me a momentary break from all this bullshit to digest this new episode of *My Fucked-Up Life* I suddenly stumbled into. Or rather, was forced into.

My stomach rumbles loudly, so I turn my eyes to the food now laid out on the table and begin adding things to my plate.

Just when I think the universe might give me two minutes of quiet to eat, Phoenix clears his throat.

"I thought it would be best to talk about the rules and what's expected of you so we don't run into any trouble."

I wave my hand in a go-on gesture and take a bite of the eggs and avocado toast. Damn, that's good. I hope the chef gets compensated well. I chew but try to focus on Phoenix. The faster he spits out what he came here for, the sooner I can eat this delicious food in peace.

"You're allowed to wander around the house at your discretion and use all available facilities. Just stay away from my wing, and don't leave the premises by yourself."

My utensils clank to the plate, and I snort. "So you're keeping me here as a prisoner?"

His friendly demeanor is instantly gone, replaced by something much harder.

With his eyes narrowed on me, he leans forward. "Trust me, this couldn't be further from a prison, and you'd do well to remember where I've been for the last three years. I wouldn't wish the humiliating treatment, inhumane conditions, or abusive interactions on anyone. Not even you."

Well, shit.

Now, my appetite is definitely gone.

Ignoring the immense guilt bubbling inside me, I find an ounce of my backbone, even when I know deep down it's pointless. Under normal circumstances, I'd hightail it out of here, but sadly, nothing about my life is normal anymore. It hasn't been since that very first text message Freddy sent me.

"Just so we're clear, I won't be your sex slave."

CHAPTER 8

PHOENIX

I stare at her for a beat, then laugh.

Her back straightens at the noise. "I am not kidding, Phoenix. I am not going to have sex with you. Ever."

I shake my head and *tsk*. "Careful with those absolutes."

She huffs but stays quiet.

I use that moment and lean forward to minimize the space between us she very clearly wanted. "But trust me, no matter how hot you are, unwilling women aren't my thing. Neither are backstabbing and vindictive ones, in case you were wondering."

She flinches and averts her gaze. Good.

Picking up a piece of bacon from the plate, I pop it into my mouth and chew, watching her every move.

My gaze focuses on how she gnaws on her plump bottom lip and how her right hand taps on her leg. It's rhythmic and oddly fascinating. A little birdie told me she hasn't played piano since her sister died, which makes me wonder if her fingers have a mind of their own, and she's not even aware of it. Although, it's a shame she doesn't play anymore. She's an amazing musician and absolutely mesmerizing to watch.

Stop.

Fuck. It's only day one, and I already can't keep my eyes off her or have my thoughts veer in directions they have no business going.

Just because I haven't had pussy in years doesn't mean I should look at her as anything other than a means to an end.

That's all she is.

A means to get my revenge and cause her demise.

"Phoenix." She lets out a long, tired sigh. "We both know you don't really want to marry me, so can we stop with this charade?"

When I stay quiet, she sighs again. "Why are you doing this?"

I shrug. "I have my reasons."

"What reasons could you possibly have? Don't you see how insane this is?" She gets out of her chair and walks across the room, just to pace back again.

I watch her like a predator, not wanting to miss a single move she makes.

She stops several feet away and puts her hands on her hips. "Do you really want to be stuck in an arranged marriage for the rest of your life? I know you hate how your parents treat their marriage like a business transaction."

"You want me to call off the engagement?"

She throws her hands up. "Oh my God, yes. Of course I do."

"Beg me."

Her eyebrows pinch together. "What?"

"I said, beg me." I pronounce each word slowly. "Get on

your knees right now and beg me to call off the engagement."

She snorts. "Don't be an ass. That's ridiculous."

I push out of the chair and stalk toward her with unhurried steps. At some point, she takes a step back for each one I advance.

Am I getting too close, my little traitor?

"I said, get on your knees."

She lifts her chin. "No."

An image of her on her knees doing other things fills my head, and I grind my teeth. This old attraction to her only fuels the anger inside me. It bubbles hotter and hotter until my vision turns red. "It's the least you could do after what you did. You should *want* to get on your knees and beg me for forgiveness."

The words are out of my mouth before I can stop them. Damn it. So much for keeping my secret for a while longer.

Don't let her get under your skin.

Easier said than done.

Her gaze darts around, glancing everywhere but at me. "What?"

"Come on. Stupid doesn't suit you." I stop a few feet in front of her when she bumps into the wall. I bend down, trying to catch her gaze, but she's staring at her feet. "I know what you did."

She swallows loudly. "I don't know what you're talking about."

The blood in my veins boils, and I close the distance between us, grab her chin, and tilt it up. Forcing her to look at me.

My body hums in triumph when her gaze is back on me.

All the fight has left her eyes, the flash of fear not leaving room for anything else.

For over three years, the question of why she stabbed me in the back has been plaguing my every thought. Day in and day out. Distracting me during the day. Keeping me up at night. I want to know how she could betray me like this. I *deserve* to know. She's going to tell me why, and then she's going to beg me for forgiveness.

Yet, she remains quiet, simply staring at me, and part of my control slips.

I slam my other hand on the wall next to her and half-growl. "Tell me why you did it."

Our fronts touch, and that dark hole inside me takes sick pleasure in feeling her rapid chest movements against mine.

Still, nothing. I want to shake the words out of her. I want to turn her inside out and let every last depraved thought of hers leak out.

I need *something* from her.

Something that will make me feel less out of control.

I need to know why she did it.

Make her.

My hands move on their own accord, fueled by my vicious thoughts. One moment, my hand is on her chin, and the next, I'm pressing her against the wall with my hand around her throat. "Tell me why you called the cops on me."

Realization kicks in, and she stares at me with wide eyes.

To anyone else, it might seem like she isn't affected by my revelation, considering she's still frozen in place, not even trying to fight back.

But I know better.

Her pulse just turned even more erratic under my fingertips, which tells me exactly how rattled she is. And I'm so close I see every popped blood vessel that frames her dilated pupils. Would her eyes bulge even more if I squeezed just a little tighter? Would her face morph into an even darker shade of red?

It would be so easy too. Just a bit more pressure.

I thought I wanted her to suffer for a long time, just like I did during my prison sentence, but I also didn't expect her presence to screw with me so much. Every time I see her, the imaginary knife digs deeper in my flesh.

Maybe it would make it better if I knew why. If I could understand.

I tighten my hand a fraction around the soft skin of her throat. "Tell me, and I'll let you go."

Again, no reply.

To make matters worse, she closes her eyes. Shutting me out.

It's almost like the hope from earlier, to still get out of this arrangement and away from me, has vanished, and now there's nothing left for her.

A loud bang pulls me out of my murderous haze as the door swings open, and Holden waltzes inside the room.

He winks at me. "Hey, boss."

I let go of Evangeline, who folds over with her hands on her knees and gulps in big lungfuls of air.

"Spencer, please." My mother's words are barely audible, but I hear them just fine through the small gap in the closet door.

"Do not ever disobey me again." My father lets go of her throat, and she crumples to the floor.

He walks out without another look back at her, and I stumble out of my hiding spot to make sure she's okay. The moment she notices me, she curls even more into herself, leaving me to stare at her back. She doesn't want me right now; she never does.

I stare at my hands. What the fuck did I just do?

You're becoming the person you never wanted to be.

Holden claps me on the shoulder and pushes me toward the open door. He keeps his hand on me as he utters something to Evangeline that I can't make out.

The urge to hit something, someone, is even worse than before. The red cloud in my vision is too much to break through, and I need an outlet.

Once we're in the hallway, Holden grabs me by the neck. Hard.

"Bro, eyes on me."

I comply and tilt my head back.

"Do you want me to send someone else to campus with her so we can spar?"

Sparring is what kept both of us sane in prison. It was also a great way to stay in shape and to let the other inmates know not to fuck with us.

I shake my head at his question, at least as much as possible, with how he still holds my neck tightly. "Only you."

That's all I get out, but he nods.

"Are you gonna be okay until I'm back later?" The corner of his mouth tilts up. "I don't want to miss out on a surprise killing spree if I can avoid it."

I huff out a half-grunt and push him away. "Dickhead."

"Just saying." He shrugs and steps back. "You know I'd hate to miss a good bloodbath."

I rub a hand over my face. "I'm fine."

"Okay."

I drop my hand and stare at him. "Thank you."

"No worries." His big shoulders rise. "That's what I'm here for."

"And because I pay you a shit ton of money."

He chuckles. "Of course you do. You'd be fucked without me."

This time, a chuckle escapes my mouth because he isn't wrong. While there's a large staff working on the estate, I'm not close with any of them. Huxley is probably the one I'm friendliest with, but I've also known him my entire life. He used to work for my grandparents and was in charge of the estate after my grandfather passed away and while I was gone. There are a few other employees left from before, but most of the staff are new and vetted by Holden and his security team. Other than that, I don't have anyone in my life. Not anymore.

Holden nods in the direction of the hallway behind me. "It's probably better for you to be gone when she comes out. We don't want to have another incident."

I stare daggers at the wall, but I know he's right. I hate that I snapped, and keeping some distance between us is better for now. At least until I can control my anger better around her.

Lifting my hand to my forehead, I give him a small salute and walk away.

Away from the person who ruined my life.

With every step I take, the urge to spin around and go back to her grows.

I should be running away, but instead, I wish I could undo what I did to study her more.

She's like a puzzle I need to solve, but the pieces don't fit together, no matter which way I try.

An enigma that still keeps me occupied during the day and up at night.

When it comes to Evangeline, nothing makes sense.

Of course, there's a chance I'm wrong, and she really is a conniving bitch who deserves everything coming her way, but I feel this inexplicable need to find out everything there is to know about what happened.

For the next few hours, I lose myself in work. Reading the reports my dad sent me about new and upcoming acquisitions and mergers. Even though he doesn't want me officially back at work until my public image is better, he still wants me to know everything about what's going on.

After an hour, I'm bored to death and switch over to my Foxhole Foundation files. There are several documents from our accountant for the IRS and the state that need signing. I also want to delve into other charities to analyze their business models in more depth.

Holden asked me a few days ago if I wanted my focus to be supporting other charities and institutions that are already helping teens, or if I wanted to take it a step farther and also create my own safe place for teenagers to fall back on when they don't have anywhere else to go. It would transform the project into something much bigger than I had initially intended for it to be, but there was something in Holden's gaze when he suggested it that I haven't been able to shake.

It would require more planning, more staff, and a lot more money, but that's where the sponsors will come in. A task Evangeline will help me with, even though she doesn't know it yet. It would certainly boost my public image even more.

We even thought of a name already: The Fox Hideout.

Kids deserve to have a safe place. A refuge. Although my dad is an asshole, and my family has never been warm and fuzzy, I at least never had to worry about going hungry or having a secure place to sleep.

My phone buzzes on the table, and I lean over the screen to read it.

There are two text messages from Holden. One from a few hours ago, and then the one that just came in.

HOLDEN

Shit. School is boring. I don't know how the princess does it. She's like a damn robot.

HOLDEN

Did you know she does volunteer work a few times a week after school? That wasn't on the schedule. How did that slip through?

ME

Seriously? I think the private investigator we fired gave us that schedule.

The three dots at the bottom appear and disappear.

HOLDEN

I still think he faked his license. No one can be that stupid.

I think back to the day we found the PI sleeping in his car while he was on the job for us, and Holden hammered on the guy's car window. He got so scared he stumbled out of the driver's door with a wet stain on his pants.

Such a dumbass.

My phone pings with an incoming picture message.

HOLDEN

I'm not sure I get paid handsomely enough
for this, boss.

I laugh the second the image of Holden loads. His hair is
tucked underneath a hair net, and he frowns at the camera.

ME

Where the fuck are you?

HOLDEN

Women's shelter.

I lower the phone to the desk.

A women's shelter?

That's where Evangeline volunteers?

I can't remember seeing any mention of that online when
I did an in-depth internet search of her either. And I mean in-
depth, with a fine-tooth comb. How is that possible?

Opening my browser on the phone, I type in *Evangeline
Caldwell women's shelter*. A few entries appear regarding
donations from her family, but nothing beyond that.

Another thing that doesn't add up.

ME

See if you can get any info out of her about
it. I'll talk to her about her schedule when
you get back.

HOLDEN

Sounds good. We'll be back in a couple of
hours.

ME

You can come home now. This wasn't part
of the plan.

I stretch my head left and right until my neck makes a satisfying *crack*, trying to push the growing irritation away.

Unexpected events always get my blood boiling.

The only reason I could stay sane in prison and actually manage to get my university degree was because of the strict routine they implemented. My mind thrives on that. Give me a spontaneous and impulsive schedule, and my mind switches to a bloodthirsty hound in point-five seconds.

I flex my right hand, waiting for Holden to finish typing.

HOLDEN

Nah. We may as well stay, seeing as we're already here.

Another message pops up before I have time to respond.

HOLDEN

I'll find you when we're home. If you haven't yet, get your workout in before you lose the last bit of your muscle mass.

ME

middle finger emoji

We both know my muscles aren't small by any means, and he's the biggest reason for it. I'm not nearly as bulky as his fridge-sized frame, but I'm undoubtedly in the best shape ever.

But he isn't wrong. A workout is exactly what I need to mellow out before they get back. I have a feeling I need to be as calm as possible around Evangeline so I don't accidentally kill her.

She still has to pay her dues before then.

And there's a whole list of them.

CHAPTER 9

EVANGELINE

I jolt awake with my heart hammering wildly behind my rib cage, the seat belt the only thing keeping me from leaping forward.

Crap, I must have fallen asleep after we left the shelter. I blink at the window and the winding road toward my new home.

My new home.

My stomach churns at what's waiting for me behind the gorgeous façade.

Groaning, I rub at my right temple.

My life has turned into a joke.

A fucking joke.

Or maybe a horror show.

Possibly both.

"Something wrong?" Holden slows down as we near the gate and the security post, glancing in the rearview mirror. "You don't need to puke again, do you?"

I shake my head. "I'm good."

That's all I say because Holden doesn't actually care about anything other than me not making a mess of the car.

He's barely spoken to me all day, just a quiet shadow in the background. A constant reminder of my new situation.

The only saving grace I was granted was that Monday is the only day I don't have any classes with my friends, so I could go as unnoticed as possible in the back of my lectures and feign a migraine when someone approached me.

Tomorrow will look very different. Tyler shouldn't be a problem once he can see for himself I'm okay. Hopefully. But there will be no escaping Ruby or Mason. I'm sure by now there will be dozens of missed phone calls and messages waiting for me from the two of them. I haven't been able to check because, of course, in my hurry to get out of the house this morning, and as far away as possible from Phoenix, I forgot my phone. They're probably out of their mind with worry. I just hope they didn't do anything hasty, like show up on Phoenix's doorstep or something like that.

That also meant I couldn't call the shelter and get out of volunteering without leaving them one person short. Not that I wanted to, but I expected Holden to throw a fit. Weirdly enough, he didn't.

Due to his size, they didn't want him out in the front where the women would see him, so he helped in the kitchen with me since I like to stay out of sight in the back too. I'm just glad I had enough brain cells left this morning to grab a scarf on the way out, or today might have gone very differently. I only got a quick peek at my throat in the bathroom earlier, but there's no denying someone had their hands around my neck and squeezed.

Just as I'd expected.

I should feel disgusted and angry about what happened, but there's this little voice in the very back of my head that has been yelling the most random things at me all day long, probably playing a huge role in the massive headache I have.

You deserve whatever Phoenix throws your way.

Why didn't he squeeze harder and finally put you out of your misery?

Don't pretend you didn't like it. It's been years since you felt this alive.

The first two don't surprise me; they are pretty much regular thoughts at this point. But the third one did throw me for a bit. I might not like this situation with Phoenix, but I can't deny I felt something when he had his hand around my neck. Not in a sexual way like I've read about in books, but more so in a way that had all my worries go away.

In those minutes where he slowly increased the pressure on my windpipe, this strange sense of peace and freedom spread through me. The spot in my heart that has been filled with nothing but dread, fear, death, and constant anxiety for so many years now was suddenly quiet. So quiet that for a blissful moment, there was enough room for me to feel the energy, vibrancy, and excitement of being alive. But just as fast as it appeared, it was gone again.

The more I think about it, the less it makes sense, and I'm glad I don't have to share these thoughts with anyone. Someone would probably admit me to a mental hospital.

Nevertheless, it has made me very tired of feeling the way I've been feeling the last few years, more so than before. And since I had all day long to think about all of my depraved thoughts, I've also come to the conclusion that just because I'm stuck in this unfortunate situation at the moment, it doesn't mean I have to for the rest of my life. I just need to figure out what this new life of mine entails and then play my cards right when the time comes.

I sense Holden's gaze on me and clear my throat.

"Thanks for helping out at the shelter. That was very nice of you." And I mean it too. He didn't have to, and extra hands are always appreciated.

The rows of trees on either side of the road gently sway in the breeze as we drive by. It's easier to focus on them than on Holden. I'm sure his name is right below Phoenix's on the list of people who'd like to kill me, seeing as he's Phoenix's right-hand man. Although, he did save me this morning.

"How did you end up volunteering there?"

With my gaze on the greenery outside, I think back to that day I met Doreen, the woman running the shelter. "I wasn't . . . you know, I wasn't in a good place after my sister died and everything happened with Phoenix. I felt like I was suffocating at home, so I wandered around the city for hours. I didn't have a clear goal in mind. I just knew I was looking for something.

"One day, a storm blew in when I was miles away from home. I walked past the shelter and recognized the name from one of the charity galas I'd been to. I stopped and stood there, completely drenched, until an older woman ran out to drag me inside. She took care of me. Gave me some dry clothes and a hot meal. She didn't know me or know if I was rich or homeless, yet she cared more for me than most people ever had. I wanted to help her help others, and with more than just a check."

Holden parks in the garage, the gray Mercedes fitting right in with the other expensive cars.

He opens my door and studies me. "Let me guess, Doreen?"

I nod.

After closing the door behind me, he strides toward the entrance that leads into the mudroom. "Boss wants to see you."

I follow him without replying because, of course, Phoenix wants to see me. I didn't think we were done after what happened this morning.

I'm still wondering if he would have finished the job if Holden hadn't intervened. His dark gaze and the pure hatred in it has me leaning toward yes. At the very least, he wanted to.

"Princess."

Holden's voice brings me back to reality.

I'd tailed him like a lost puppy through the maze of hallways and stairs without paying attention to where we were going.

To my surprise, the door he holds open takes us outside.

He must see the confusion on my face because he says, "Gym."

"The gym is outside?" I step onto the pebble pathway leading away from the house.

"Different building." He points toward a black rectangular structure on one side of the vast grounds.

Loud music greets us when we enter. This place must be soundproof because I didn't hear a thing from outside.

I pause and take in the ample space that resembles a state-of-the-art gym. One side has more workout gear and machines than I even knew existed, and the other one houses a boxing ring and mats.

The music abruptly stops, snapping my attention to the man approaching us—the half-naked man.

Phoenix strolls over with a water bottle in his hand and his black shorts sitting so low on his hips the waistband of his underwear peeks out. Right below the narrow line of dark hair that disappears behind said waistband.

My gaze travels up his muscular abs and chest, momentarily stopping when something shiny glints in the light—a nipple piercing on his right pec.

I falter for a moment when I see a compass tattoo right above his heart, but that can't be right. No way. I must be seeing things. Why would he ever mark his skin with that permanently?

Fully aware I'm staring, I swallow and drag my gaze up to meet his.

He stops a few feet before us, grabs his shirt from the bench next to us, and puts it on. I continue to stare at him like he's some mystical creature while also trying to ignore any reaction my body might have to him.

Because no, I'm most definitely not blind, and beauty doesn't seem to have an asshole meter. Even psychos and assholes can look like they were carved from marble.

The one standing in front of me gives me a cocky smirk, probably knowing what he's doing to me. But I'm not the only one checking the other one out. Phoenix's gaze flicks down my body so lazily, and with such open appreciation, it almost feels like a phantom touch. A low buzz fills my veins with every inch his gaze travels. The same weightless euphoria as this morning sings in my body, sending me a little dizzy. It's so compelling, I can't resist it. Nor do I want to.

Holden clears his throat. "You okay, man?"

Crap. I totally forgot he was still here.

I don't look at him, but Phoenix turns his way and nods.

Holden sighs. "Good, because I need a shower and to get rid of this food smell."

I wrinkle my nose because what is he talking about? I don't smell anything. Maybe it's because I'm used to the smell of food from the shelter? I've been helping there for so long, I barely even register anything when I enter the building.

Something touches my arm, and I jerk, blinking several times.

I seriously have to stop zoning out so much.

Phoenix is much closer than before, and Holden is nowhere to be seen.

Great.

Yet again, alone with the devil.

Not the same kind of devil like Freddy, but one nonetheless. They're both trying to ruin my life, just in different ways. One has already done a decent job, destroying several lives along the way, while the other one is just getting started.

"About this morning." Phoenix brushes his fingers through his damp hair, his gaze moving down my throat. "I went too far, and it won't happen again."

Not exactly an apology, but close enough, I suppose.

I can still feel his hand around my throat, each finger biting into my skin as my air supply slowly dwindled.

He narrows his eyes at me. "Did you hear what I said?"

I just stand there like a total moron and nod.

Because how am I supposed to reply to that? I won't

thank him for attempting to act like a civilized human and not kill me.

Bummer he didn't finish the job, isn't it?

There's that crazy thought again.

Would he feel bad, or guilty, if he'd actually killed me this morning? Without regard to if it was done by accident or on purpose?

I can't figure out what that would have made him in my life. Would he have been the villain of my story, or would he have been my salvation after all, just not in the way either one of us could have ever predicted?

The backs of my eyes burn, but I'm not sure anymore if it's because he almost ended my life or because he didn't.

This whole time, Phoenix stares at me, the frown on his face etching deeper into his skin.

Maybe he's starting to see what a nutcase you are.

Maybe.

Maybe not.

I'm not sure anymore what's better.

He probably thought he'd get a "well-trained" socialite princess as a future wife, someone like my sister. Instead, he ended up with me.

Too bad I didn't come with a warranty.

Phoenix grabs my arm and pulls me with him. "Come on, we need to finish our conversation from this morning."

We head out of the building and back into the main house. Up a flight of stairs and a few turns toward his wing, and we enter a large office that screams masculinity with its dark wooden furniture and leather scent in the air.

Phoenix deposits me in front of an oversized armchair and says, "Sit."

I humor him and listen.

He moves around the spacious desk and sits behind it.

He's a living visual contradiction in his gym clothes with sweat glistening on his skin, sitting behind the executive desk in this grand office. It's almost like a child playing dress-up.

The computer screen illuminates his elegant features as he ignores me and stares at whatever is in front of him.

A mechanical crackling sounds from all around me.

"Nine-one-one. What's your emergency?" The female voice echoes around the room.

All life drains out of me.

Despite knowing exactly what's coming next, my heart still goes into overdrive, and I can't stop it.

"A man is being held hostage in the 2338 West Forrest Avenue warehouse. Come quickly." My voice sounds shaky but is easily identifiable.

I've often wondered why I didn't think to muffle it somehow.

Probably because you were scared shitless and your brain didn't work right.

I made the call mere minutes after I'd heard the news from my father.

"Evangeline, your sister was in a car accident. She didn't make it."

Just like that. He'd patted my shoulder once, then left my room.

A text message came moments after.

FREDDY

> See what you did, pet? Maybe you should have done what I asked you to do the first time. Now, make the call. A man is being held hostage in the 2338 West Forrest Avenue warehouse.

A single tear runs down my face.

I killed my sister. I'm the reason her car crashed that night. Someone tampered with it because I thought the person sending me text messages was just some idiot playing games. Never in a million years did I think he'd go through with it and hurt someone I loved. Not just hurt, but kill.

The tear slips off my chin and onto my lap. I watch the moisture seep into my pants, disappearing into the material like it's not a part of me anymore. I wish the pain and sorrow would disappear alongside it, instead of always staying behind.

"How did you know about the guy and where he was?" Phoenix's voice is calm enough that I look up.

I can't tell him what happened; Freddy made sure of that almost immediately after he'd killed my sister. The text message he sent all those years ago still haunts me.

FREDDY

> If you ever tell anyone about my messages, Ruby will be next. Then Mason, Tyler, and the rest of your family.

I've already lost one person I love to Freddy. I can't lose another one.

Not to mention, I have no proof. Every single message

he's sent vanished. And for good reason. A few weeks after my sister died, I had a terrible nightmare and wandered around the house to calm down. I ran into my dad in the kitchen and broke down, telling him about what had happened.

When he'd asked me if I had proof, and I told him about the vanishing messages, he'd finished the rest of his whiskey, stared me straight in the eye, and said, *"Stop trying to gain attention by spreading ridiculous lies like this. It only makes you look pathetic."* And then he'd just left.

Phoenix clenches his jaw at my silence and slams his hand on the desk. "Damn it, Evangeline."

I jump.

Phoenix shakes his head at me and paces behind the desk. The vein on his temple pulses furiously. "Why would you make a call to incriminate me, have me locked up for three years, and then refuse to tell me why? It makes no sense. None of this does."

I don't reply because what can I possibly say to that? Of course, he's right. It *can't* make sense to him.

Just like it still makes no sense to me why some random psychopath chose me as their human torture device, forcing me to do things I never thought in a million years I'd do.

Because life can be cruel sometimes, and all we can do is try our best to make it through.

One day at a time.

One moment at a time.

And I'll get through this mess, too, because people depend on me.

An epiphany hits me then, and my entire being sags in relief. I can handle whatever Phoenix has in store for me because *nothing* he'll do to me could possibly be worse than what Freddy would do or has already done.

While I completely understand Phoenix's confusion and anger toward me, and don't fault him at all for wanting to understand the situation, it still doesn't erase the fact that before he ever went to prison, he ripped my heart into so many pieces, it never quite fit back together right.

And I'm tired of being everyone's punching bag. So damn tired.

With my hands interlaced in my lap, I meet Phoenix's steely gaze and school my expression into a neutral one. "You said something about rules?"

CHAPTER 10

PHOENIX

I stare at Evangeline, and then I laugh.

And then I laugh some more.

It's way louder and longer than would be considered socially acceptable.

This woman.

This damn woman.

What the fuck is wrong with her?

Once I'm calm enough to continue this ridiculous conversation, I lower myself back in my office chair, the leather squeaking when I put my whole weight into it.

Are you just going to let her get away without getting any more information?

She's playing you for a fool.

Don't be weak, Son.

I inhale deeply and push the suffocating thoughts aside, especially when they come in the form of my dad's voice.

Sure, I could use my dad's techniques and torture the answers out of her. Eventually, she would give them to me because everyone has a breaking point. Even my fallen angel does. But to what avail? That she'd be broken and bloodied and never able to act the part I need her to play?

Not worth it.

I want answers, yes. But I also want to get my new business endeavor off the ground, and I need her for that. In one piece.

So, I nod and say, "Yes, there are rules, and I expect you to follow them."

She stares at me, clearly waiting for me to lay them out so she can leave. To get away from me as fast as possible, just like she continues to do.

"When we're both home, I expect you to eat with me in the dining room. For all intents and purposes, we will present this as a real marriage, and I will not tolerate anyone questioning the integrity of it, inside my home or otherwise."

"Just remember, I told you I won't sleep with you."

Her voice is almost friendly, and I'm taken aback by it. What game is she playing now?

I focus back on the conversation and her ludicrous sex statement. "Yes, you're unwilling to have sex with me. Got that loud and clear. I also remember telling you I don't take women without their consent. It's truly not my thing."

"No sharing a bedroom either."

I thought about that one for a long time. I know it would drive her crazy if I made her share a bed with me, but then I came to one conclusion: I don't think I could handle it either. I'd probably end up killing her in my sleep one night, which would be incredibly inconvenient.

I nod but stay quiet as she continues.

"I'd also appreciate it if you could keep your affairs low-key and out of the press."

So matter of fact, as if we're discussing the weather.

I know some of this is how we grew up and how particular manners and expectations were drilled into us. It's like this neutral to slightly friendly state is her norm, and real emotions are slipups, like when she was lost to something in her mind earlier.

The more time I spend with her, the less anything about her or what happened makes sense.

It's also crystal clear she's not the same girl I used to know.

If I didn't see her sitting in front of me with my own two eyes, I'd swear she's an imposter.

I got a few real glimpses of her old self in the past few days when that fire I was so used to sparked in her eyes. That version seems years away from who's sitting in front of me now. This person is a cheap copy of her. A robot. The urge to ask her, "Who are you?" is strong, but what's the point?

I clear my throat. "We will start attending events together this weekend, and I expect you to act appropriately. Pretending is your specialty, so you shouldn't have any problem with that."

"I need to know what events and when they occur to prepare accordingly and see if it works for me."

Leaning back, I steeple my fingers in front of me. "Evangeline, let me make one thing very clear. I don't give a fuck about your social calendar. You're mine now, and you will do as I say. If I tell you to be somewhere, you better be there."

Her jaw flexing is the only outward sign she isn't happy about this. "I'm going to marry you because I have to, but I'm not your property. I have my own life and engagements I will continue."

The control she has over most of her emotions is strangely fascinating. If I had to guess, she's ready to scratch out my eyes with her fingernails. She must be.

She shifts in her seat, uncrossing and crossing her legs. "I also need keys and access codes to the house."

I smile at her. "You don't need them. Someone will drive you and be with you at all times."

This time, her eyes flash. "That's ridiculous. I'm a big girl, and I can drive myself."

I shrug. "You're my responsibility now, and I'll provide you with everything you need, but my rules are nonnegotiable."

She throws her arms in the air. "Fine, if you want to punish me, I'll let someone chauffeur me around."

Punish her?

Punish her?

Punish. Her.

Images of me balls-deep inside her and spanking her pink pussy while she moans my name race through my mind.

Fuck.

No.

Where did that come from?

I barely manage to refrain from adjusting my already hard cock.

I wasn't lying when I said I don't do non-consent, and I won't break my rules, especially for her.

Her glare pulls me out of my head, and I want to wrap my hand around her neck once more and squeeze.

Watch that fear slither into her irises and darken them.

She deserves everything coming her way, and she'll take it, no matter what.

She'll take everything I will give her and say thank you.

The chair scrapes across the floor as she abruptly stands and walks toward the door.

Jumping out of my chair, I shove my hands into my shorts and ball them into fists. "Don't test me, Evangeline. You might be used to wrapping everyone around your little finger and getting whatever you want, but I advise you not to try the same with me. It won't end well."

At that, she stops. She still doesn't face me, and I watch every single one of her movements to see what she'll do next. I thought she'd be easy to bend to my will, easy to break. Instead, she's a total loose cannon. Utterly unpredictable, and if I'm not mistaken, also slightly broken.

I guess that will make her utter destruction that much sweeter.

Her head is tilted toward the floor, her shoulders shaking.

She's crying.

There, finally, a more fitting response.

A sound escapes her, and I freeze.

No.

Is she fucking laughing?

My feet advance before I make the conscious decision. I stop in front of her, grab her chin between my fingers, and press her against the wall.

She gasps at the contact and blinks, a few more silent tears running down her face.

"Why are you laughing?" The words come out in a low, threatening tone.

I have no control around this woman. She pushes my buttons without even trying, and I hate it.

I hate it.

I hate *her*.

And I hate that this stupid act of craziness mixed with all her defiance has my cock harder than it's been in years.

She ignores the firm grip I have on her and wrinkles her nose to sniffle.

After a deep inhale, she fixes her tear-streaked gaze on mine. "You just said something funny, that's all."

Her cheeks are lined with dark mascara, and I can only stare at her.

One corner of her mouth twitches, and she directs her gaze downward. "You might want to take care of that, it feels painful."

She'd be a vision on her knees choking on my dick.

I let go of her as if she burned me and stalk over to the window, giving her my back.

Her reflection in the glass is almost as clear as looking in a mirror. She takes my reaction for what it is and leaves, light filtering in from the bright hallway.

Closing my eyes, I get myself under control until heavy footsteps enter and the door clicks shut.

Holden snorts. "You made the princess cry again, huh?"

I continue to stare outside at the darkening sky.

The gray clouds are almost black now, slowly gearing up for the rain promised in the next few days.

How fitting.

Holden comes up next to me, and I face him.

He hisses. "That bad, huh?"

I let out a heavy sigh. "You have no idea."

Going back to the desk, I plop into my chair while he takes the one Evangeline just vacated.

My fiancée.

My soon-to-be wife.

Fuck.

I thought this was going to be an easy transition.

I expected her to balk at marrying me, and to try and convince her father that merging families with an ex-convict was a terrible idea.

I even wondered if she'd run away.

What I didn't expect was for her to accept this. I know she's not happy about it, but part of the time, she doesn't act like it's the life-destroying event I wanted it to be for her either.

Holden gets something black out of his pocket and extends it my way. "Conveniently, she forgot her phone today, and I took advantage of that while you guys were having your little tête-à-tête."

I grab the sleek phone from him and unlock the screen, staring at a picture of Evangeline with her friends Ruby and Mason. The three of them all smile at the camera.

A genuine smile that's reflected in Evangeline's eyes.

I can't remember the last time I've seen one of those on her face. Not in a long time.

"Phoenix, could you hand me some water, please?"

I glance up from the outdoor fridge to stare at a smiling Evangeline in the pool and nod.

She's turning sixteen in a week, and her parents left Alex in charge of watching his sister. Alongside the staff, of course. To Alex, that means cockblocking since he has extreme feelings about either of his sisters becoming teen moms. That would be an utter disgrace to the family. Any scandal would be. Alex has done the same with Constance for years, and since she's starting her first year of college with us in a few weeks, I guess he has been successful with her so far. And there is no doubt the guys in Evangeline's friend group want to fuck her. But none of them are good enough for her.

"... you wanted."

I blink at Holden, who tilts his head to the side to study me.

Clearing my throat, I focus back on him. "Sorry, what?"

He stays silent for another beat before answering. "I said everything is done the way you wanted."

"Good, thank you."

"I added the camera feed from her room to the others so you can access it from your phone and computer."

Turning toward my computer, I log in and pull up the security cameras. Holden stands beside me to point out the added screen in the large quadrant of video feeds.

Evangeline is lying on her bed, phone in her hand.

And just like magic, the phone in my hand vibrates, mirroring what she's doing on hers.

TYLER

You didn't stop by this morning. Everything okay?

EVIE

Yeah, all good. I thought it might be better to avoid coffee with my upset stomach, you know? But I'll pop in tomorrow.

A grunt erupts from my throat just as another message pops up.

TYLER

Deal :)

She exits the conversation and opens the group chat with Ruby and Mason. Several dots in different colors dance across the bottom of the screen.

RUBY

Evangeline Caldwell. You're in so much trouble ghosting us all day. How dare you? Next time, at least let us know you're not lying in a ditch somewhere.

EVIE

Sorry, I got sick last night and passed out. And then I forgot my phone today and just got back.

MASON

Are you okay?

EVIE

Yeah, I'm good.

RUBY

I swear to you, if Phoenix or The Thing lays a hand on you, I'll murder them. I know people who can make bodies disappear.

Holden snorts behind me, reading over my shoulder. "The Thing? I like it."

MASON

I'll help.

EVIE

No, everything's fine, guys.

RUBY

I don't care if Phoenix looks like a Greek god with tattoos, or if he has this whole bad-boy vibe down to a T, he will not get to keep you there against your will and force you to throw away your future to marry him.

EVIE

He's not that bad, I promise. This is new, so it'll take some getting used to, but I'm sure it'll all turn out okay.

"What the fuck?" Holden says.

My sentiment exactly.

I read Evangeline's message repeatedly until my stomach churns, then stare over my shoulder at Holden. "They don't know what she did."

He scrubs a hand over his face and blows out a breath. "You think she didn't tell them?"

Another message pops up.

MASON

Ruby, weren't you the one who tried to get Evie to make a move on Phoenix when we were younger?

RUBY

Well, yeah. And I still stand by the fact they'd make the prettiest babies, but a lot of shit happened. We liked him back then, and now we don't. Right?

When Evangeline doesn't answer right away, I check the computer. She's still lying on her bed, but now she's pressing her face into the pillow. After a few seconds, she picks up her phone again.

MASON

Fine.

RUBY

You got it.

EVIE

Maybe he's not the bad guy after all, so let's give him a chance. And please, guys, let's keep everything that's going on between Phoenix and me between the three of us. No one else.

EVIE

Thank you! Okay, guys, I'll see you tomorrow. I'm exhausted and off to bed now. Love you.

Holden huffs. "Fuck. That was a plot twist I didn't see coming. If she didn't even tell her best friends, does that mean she kept this a secret from everyone?"

I stare at the computer monitor and follow Evangeline's every move as she puts her phone away and gets off the bed to walk to the bathroom.

What other secrets are you keeping, my fallen angel?

CHAPTER II

EVANGELINE

The bell above the door chimes as I walk into my favorite coffee shop the following day. It's a small corner shop just a few blocks away from campus, and they have the most delicious drinks and treats.

Tyler looks up from behind the counter and smiles at me. "There you are."

His smile falters the second he glances over my shoulder.

I don't need to turn around to know what he sees.

My mountain of a silent shadow.

At least he didn't complain when I asked if we could stop here since that's my usual morning go-to before school.

The place is quiet, with a few patrons sitting in the black booths off to one side.

I approach the counter, where Tyler has already started making my coffee.

He keeps sending me glances, scanning me from head to toe as if to make sure I'm still in one piece.

Once he's done with my large caramel macchiato, he brings it over and leans closer. "Are you feeling better?"

I nod. "Much better, thank you."

He studies me as if he's trying to figure out if I'm telling the truth. "Everything else okay too? You seemed upset at the party."

My lips tip up at the corners. "Oh yeah. It was just such a big shock. You know I don't like surprises."

He chuckles. "Sometimes they can be good, like when I add extra caramel or whipped cream to your drink."

"That's true." I huff a laugh and reach for my drink.

Instead of giving it to me, Tyler grabs my hand.

My instinct is to pull back, aware of Holden behind me, who probably reports everything I do back to Phoenix. Tyler is my friend, and he doesn't deserve to be dragged into this mess.

He stares at me with big eyes. "You know I'm here if you need me, right? If you need help, I'm your guy."

My heart races with worry for him, and I take the cup he pushes my way. "Thank you. I'm just trying to lie low right now, but I really appreciate it."

He gets the point and turns toward the glass case to his left. "What do you feel like today? Sweet or savory?"

Grateful for the distraction, I let my gaze roam over the food behind the glass case—muffins, cupcakes, croissants, sandwiches—and stop when I see the wraps.

"A spinach, feta, and egg white wrap, please."

He chuckles. "See, that was a good surprise, right?"

I've been whining for weeks about them not having my favorite wrap since they had supplier issues.

"Definitely." I watch him with a smile as he rings me up.

He's matured in the last few years since I've known him. Still as good-looking as before, but now he's also grown into his broad shoulders. He's a nice guy and a good friend, even after our drunken one-night stand. It's too bad I never had any romantic feelings for him.

I pay, grab my coffee and paper bag, and give him a wave. "Thanks, Ty."

He gives me another meaningful glance. "I meant what I said."

I nod. "I know, thank you."

Holden is waiting by the door, opening it for me and doing the same when we reach the car.

I thank him and slide into the back seat, releasing a breath and closing my eyes while Holden gets behind the wheel and heads for campus.

Thankfully, the mix of caffeine, sugar, and carbs does wonders for my system, and by the time we walk into my first class, I feel marginally better.

TODAY, I share a few classes with Ruby and Mason, but I manage to avoid them as much as possible. They seem to have calmed down some after last night's chat, but I know they must still have questions and things they want to say. My luck runs out at the end of a long day when they wait for me in the bathroom, of all places. No wonder they ran out of our math class like their butts were on fire. They know I usually go to the bathroom before I head home and probably thought it would be their best chance to corner me.

I snort. "Mason, you know this is the girls' bathroom, right?"

His only response is a shrug.

Ruby has her Sherlock Holmes face on, staring at me with narrowed eyes like she can see straight into my brain.

Sometimes, I wish she actually had that ability so there wouldn't be any lies or secrets between us.

But then you wouldn't have any friends anymore either.

These two are the only good things in my life, and I can't give them up. I won't survive without them.

"Soooooo?" Ruby waves a hand through the air. "Is this how things are going to go now? You avoid us and sneak around with The Thing?"

I cradle my binder against my chest like a security blanket and sigh. "Honestly, I don't know. I'm still processing what the hell is happening."

Mason steps up and wraps an arm around my shoulder to pull me into his body. "You know we're just worried, right?"

He smells like our laundry detergent, like home.

But their home isn't my home anymore.

Not any longer.

That thought rips another small tear into my already tattered heart.

How can I navigate this mess without them by my side?

My eyes tear up as I lean closer.

"Oh shit, don't cry. I'm sorry, Evie." Ruby steps closer and wraps her arms around me and Mason. "You know I'm shit at handling tough situations sometimes."

I sniffle and sag into the security blanket they've formed around me.

Ruby is definitely a shoot first and ask questions later kind of girl, the first of us to raise her fist in the air and make demands.

Unfortunately, this isn't a situation where I can do either.

I wipe my cheeks. "Things are going to be different—they already are—but I'm going to figure out how to keep as much of my life as normal as possible."

Phoenix will probably cherish the thought of me suffering, but he also told me he needs my help to get donations for his foundation. It's a small bargaining chip, but I'm willing to see how far I can push him and how much of my freedom I can keep while giving him what he wants.

Maybe he'll shut me down at every corner he can, but I have to try.

Almost in unison, we step back, but they both keep their arms around me.

Mason gives me a sad smile. "You're really going to stay with him and marry him?"

The air is tight in my throat, only barely allowing me to suck in a breath. "I have to, for now. Phoenix needs me, so I'm going to be okay."

Ruby sighs, clearly unhappy with this. "He better treat you right, or I'll kick him in the balls."

The door behind us squeaks, and we all turn our heads to look at the intruder.

Holden.

He takes in our small gathering. Nodding toward the hallway, he says, "Come on, Princess. The boss is waiting."

Of course he is.

Ruby mumbles something that's too quiet to hear, but I'm sure it's all sorts of colorful words for my new bodyguard. Security detail. Prisoner guard. All the same at this point. Even though I'm not one-hundred-percent sure if his main job is to keep me from running or if he's supposed to protect me too. Maybe Phoenix gave him the green light to happily stand by and watch me get run over by a bus or something. As long as he records it on video for Phoenix to play on a loop. We couldn't deny the man to bask in the glory of me getting what I deserve.

Thank you, brain. A pleasure, as always.

Pushing up on my toes, I kiss Mason on the cheek before doing the same to Ruby. "Love you, guys."

They both say, "Love you too," as I give them a small smile.

I silently follow Holden out of the building and to the parking lot.

The second I'm in my seat with my seat belt in place, I settle against the door and close my eyes.

Thankfully, Holden takes the hint and stays quiet the whole drive, allowing me to put all my emotions back into their tight spaces where they escaped after seeing Ruby and Mason. Hiding my genuine emotions from them is much more complicated than hiding them from anyone else, except anything related to Freddy. Whenever he's involved, they usually know something is up, but I can't tell them what it is.

At the house, I follow Holden out of the garage and through the kitchen, unbothered when he brings me to my room like a small child. The cracks in my armor are fragile today, and I need all my energy to keep them under wraps when I'm around Phoenix.

Holden doesn't follow me into the room, waiting in front of the open door. "Dinner is in half an hour. Do you know where the dining room is?"

"Yes." I don't look at him as I put my bag on the bed and unpack my things.

I managed to do some of my homework during my free periods, but I still have more to do.

Accounting. My favorite.

Even in my head, it sounds ridiculous. I'm the last person to understand most number-related things. Math just isn't mathing for me. That was Connie's domain. When she died, my dad said it was now my job.

In one day, I lost my sister and the entire future I had dreamed up. Traveling the world, playing music, performing. Now I'll spend my life with my nose in books and behind computers and my butt in a chair.

I can't imagine anything more boring.

At least my dad got his wish for me to end up with a "real job" since I completely stopped with my music after Connie's death, unable to play a single note or even go near a piano.

A noise startles me, and I stare toward the door. But it's closed. Holden must have shut it when he left.

At least he's been decent enough, a far cry from Phoenix's open hatred.

That's because you didn't put Holden in prison.

With a sigh, I drop onto the bed and start my homework.

Sometime later, the door swings open with a loud swoosh, jolting me so much my pencil flies out of my hand and over the side of the bed.

With a hand on my chest, I try to calm my frantic heart and glance toward the door. Phoenix leans against the door-frame like he doesn't have a care in the world. I see it for what it is: yet another reminder of how utterly out of depth I am when it comes to him.

"You're late."

Per usual, he glares at me, and I can see his nostrils flaring from where I'm sitting. I bet he'd spit fire right now if he could.

His words register, and I glance at the clock. Shit. How did time pass so quickly? I barely got anything done. And I was supposed to be at dinner ten minutes ago.

"Sorry." I close the notebook I was working in and slide off the bed without disturbing my things. "Give me five minutes to get changed and freshen up."

I head toward the bathroom and the walk-in closet.

"Evangeline."

Phoenix's voice stops me dead in my tracks, and I glare at him over my shoulder.

"You have two minutes. There's no need to get changed." He drags his gaze over my leggings and oversized sweatshirt. "You look fine."

Before I can reply, he's gone, leaving me to stare at the spot he just vacated.

"One and a half minutes." His voice flows inside the room from the hallway.

I hurry to the bathroom to pee and at least take care of the flyaway hairs that have escaped my messy bun throughout the day.

The dining room is in the opposite wing on the first level, and I'm sure not even running would get me there before Phoenix's time runs out.

I try to rush anyway, slamming into a solid brick wall when I turn the corner to the dining room.

No, not a wall. A chest. Phoenix's rock-hard chest.

He steadies me with his hands on my arms before he grabs my chin and tilts my head back until I gaze at him. My nerve endings stir and tingle from his touch, and my lips part in response.

"The next time you're late, I'll put you over my knee and spank your ass like a petulant child who can't follow simple orders."

CHAPTER 12

EVANGELINE

I swallow and blink up at him.

Did he just say what I think he said, or is my mind playing tricks on me?

I'm surrounded by the dark aroma of his woodsy scent, wrapped in the familiarity of him. Of the old him. The old us. There are two versions of us: one that belongs in a book's "then" section, the other in the "now." One would be pleasant and the other would be cruel.

Tyler is talking to me, but I don't hear a single word. I'm too aware of the way Phoenix's gaze is on me. At least, I think he's looking at me. Since he arrived with my brother at my pool party to babysit, it feels like someone is staring a hole into the side of my head. And it's doing funny things to my body. Despite the warm temperatures in the pool, my nipples are hard, and I have no doubt poor Tyler is getting a front-row seat to that show.

Something like nostalgic longing stabs me in the chest, but I ignore it.

Although, after yesterday when his thick, hard cock pressed against my stomach, I'm wondering if he's struggling with similar issues. Maybe not necessarily any form of emotional longing, but his body is still clearly reacting to mine, just as mine is to his. And I hate it. It's inconvenient and a little concerning, but I'm not sure there's anything I can do about it.

The pressure at my chin increases, homing my focus back in on the man in front of me.

Or rather, the man now looming over me like a fire-breathing dragon, ready to eat me alive. But not in a good way.

His eyes are so dark they are black pools, filled with nothing but pure loathing. "I said, do you understand?"

He's waiting for a reply, and I scramble to remember what he's referring to. His words repeat in my head, and I press my lips together to prevent myself from reacting and nod.

I've never been spanked before, and now is certainly not the time to start.

Especially not with Phoenix.

Why are you clenching your thighs then?

There is that traitorous voice in my head again, loud and impossible to ignore. Something coils tightly in my belly.

Phoenix sighs. "So help me God, Evangeline. Use your damn words."

"Yes, I understand."

The words come out breathless. Too breathless.

Phoenix's gaze roams over my face, scrutinizing me, trying to find a crack in my armor, and I pray he doesn't find one.

After an agonizing moment, and a lingering gaze on my

lips, he finally lets go of my face and steps back, pointing at the empty seat on the left side of the large table. "Sit."

My stomach growls at the sight of the food, distracting me enough from the fact the table is set for only two.

I slide onto the chair, and Phoenix does the same opposite me. I stare at the vast array of options, my mouth watering at the rich scents drifting up my nose. Each dish is more compelling than the next, making it impossible to decide what to eat first.

"I hope you still like Greek food." Phoenix reaches across the table for my plate, putting some of everything on it for me.

"I do." The words come out in a whisper.

I watch him, unsure how to react to this version of Phoenix.

The hard boundaries he drew for us at the beginning of this engagement have quickly turned blurry, transforming him into an enigma. It's not every day my teenage crush, who almost became my brother-in-law, forces me into an arranged marriage, all while knowing I was the one who put him in jail, and now he gets me my favorite dishes for dinner. The chances of something crazy like this happening seem as impossible as catching sight of a unicorn, yet here we are. Is it too late to choose the unicorn?

When Phoenix holds out my plate, I take it with both hands and say, "Thank you."

The only reply I get is a nod, which is ironic, considering he all but growled at me to use my words less than five minutes ago. But since I don't want to talk to him anyway, I focus on the plate in front of me, trying to decide what to eat first.

I might as well enjoy this meal as much as I can, considering every meal has the potential to be my last. I mean, how is it possible he knows about my nine-one-one call, and I'm still alive?

Phoenix finishes serving himself and picks up his utensils, which I take as my green light. The first bite of souvlaki and tzatziki hits my tongue. Fresh and tangy flavors burst in my mouth, and I close my eyes, barely containing the moan that wants to escape. I'm a sucker for good food, not caring if it costs a few bucks and comes from the food stand at the corner.

Phoenix is staring at me. I can feel it, just like I could all those years ago. But now, I ignore it. I focus on eating and nothing else, trying a little bit of everything until I'm full. I leave my silverware on the plate at a perfect four o'clock position and only barely refrain from rubbing my satisfied stomach.

After several breaths, I finally meet Phoenix's gaze head-on.

The next time you're late, I'll put you over my knee and spank your ass.

Of course, my brain uses this moment to replay his earlier words on a loop in my head.

Heat blooms between my legs, and I'm slowly catching on to how seriously screwed I am.

Without thinking, I squirm in my seat, and Phoenix's gaze flares when he catches the movement. Why does he have to have eagle eyes? Nothing ever goes unnoticed.

One side of his mouth lifts in a satisfied smirk, and I fully intend to keep my gaze everywhere but on him. Manners be damned.

For the rest of the week, both at mealtimes and otherwise, our interactions stay as minimal as possible and, thankfully, without any more comments my brain could construe as sexual innuendos. In a way, we've found somewhat of a neutral area for us. A way to co-exist.

During the day, I'm back to my regular schedule of school and volunteering, with Holden as my ever-present shadow. He's been such a good sport about the volunteer work, and I swear, he's got everyone at the shelter wrapped around his little finger. I should have known he'd be a total charmer.

Ruby and Mason haven't cornered me again either, satisfied now that they have seen with their own eyes that I'm okay. At least for now. On the rare occasion that they send me a worried glance, I shut them down quickly, reassuring them I'm truly fine. The last thing I need is for Freddy to get involved because my friends are causing trouble with Phoenix.

Once I'm home and dismissed after dinner, I spend my evenings in my room, catching up on homework and studying.

Just like Huxley promised, my personal items were delivered this week, changing my room into a homier space with photos and my other items. I sorted through all the boxes, and Huxley helped me store the ones I don't need at the moment in the closet. Somehow, I'm not ready to fully unpack my life here.

Although, it's not that different from my previous life, other than having Ruby or Mason occasionally drag me out of my room to watch a movie, telling me I study too hard and need a break. This weekend will be my first real test when I don't have school or work to keep me busy around the clock, at least not the entire day.

But first, I need to survive our first charity event tonight, with another one tomorrow.

I walk out of the bathroom and snatch my phone, groaning at the "check-in" text message from my dad.

DAD

Remember your manners tonight. Everything you do reflects back on us and the company. If the deal with Montgomery Enterprises falls through because of bad press, there will be consequences.

Thanks for the concern and the love, Dad. Much appreciated.

I send him a thumbs-up emoji and open the group chat next. A smile spreads across my face when I see the picture of Ruby, Mason, and Tyler squished together to fit in the frame.

RUBY

Wish you were here. Even you, homebody, would enjoy this party. We miss you!

ME

Miss you too. Looks like fun!

There's a knock on the door, and I put my phone on the table.

"Come in," I call out and cross the room for a drink.

The door swings open, and a tall woman walks in. She glances around until her gaze zooms in on me, openly assessing me.

Once she's done with her perusal, she locks eyes with me. "Evangeline, right?"

I nod, still taking all of her in because there's a lot. The colorful hair, the tattoos peeking out from under her T-shirt, the piercings. It's a whole vibe, and I love it.

"I'm Jo." She strides over to me with a large aluminum trolley behind her.

My brain finally catches up with my vision, and I plaster on a smile. "You're my hair and makeup artist?"

She returns my smile and gives me a salute. "In the flesh."

"Nice to meet you."

"Likewise."

I grab my diet soda and go to the table, where she's opening up her cases, and sit in the chair she points at.

The moment my butt hits the cushion, she pulls out one for herself in front of me, sits, and stares at my face.

A few beats later, she nods and jumps up to dig in her bags.

She spreads out a large microfiber towel on the table and places several makeup items on it. She picks an eyeliner and pauses halfway in the air to examine me. "What color is your dress?"

I pause for a moment and cringe, quickly trying to cover it up with a laugh.

It's time to play your role, dummy.

"I haven't even checked yet." My laugh turns awkward. Damn it. *Keep it together.* "Sorry, Phoenix took care of my wardrobe for me. Let me get it."

The memory of him telling me at dinner last night that my dresses for our events are in my closet swirls around in my head. And the smirk he wore when he informed me that the dates and event names are written on the garment bags.

Control freak.

Jo doesn't say anything. I take the opportunity and rush into the walk-in closet.

The rack on the right side is filled with large garment bags, and I grab the one with today's date. I probably should have checked out the wardrobe when I got home, but Phoenix mentioned a personal shopper, and if there's one thing I'm sure of, it's that Phoenix would never let me accompany him to events in anything less than beautiful haute couture. This is important to him, and he wouldn't risk his image by having me look anything but well put-together.

I tug down the zipper and push the garment bag out of the way.

A low whistle comes from behind me.

"Well, hot damn. Does your fiancé know how to pick a dress, or what?"

Jo steps up beside me, and I don't correct her about the fact a personal shopper is to thank for this and not Phoenix. *Not my fiancé.*

There's no denying the gown is beautiful—with golden beads, a high choker, and elegant off-shoulder pearl sleeves. The dress itself is see-through with a nude underlining attached. Simply breathtaking.

Jo claps her hands and rubs them like an excited child. "Let's get you ready. Phoenix won't know what hit him when I'm done with you."

I settle in the chair and close my eyes.

Jo works in silence, but after a while, I almost sense her curious energy around me.

"So . . ." She studies me. "Holden said you and Phoenix

have known each other since you were younger. Are you childhood sweethearts?"

I stare at her, probably too long, but digesting this takes longer. The urge to snort or laugh at her comment is followed closely by bursting into tears and spilling my guts to this random stranger.

Typically, I excel at putting on a fake mask and charming everyone around me, but those battery levels are almost empty. Occasionally, there are moments when they work perfectly, but then they drain again. Having to be *on* everyday all day this week has been too much.

Her blue eyes bore into mine when I finally manage to look at her again, and she flinches at whatever she sees on my face.

Yup, those fake mask batteries are utterly depleted.

And at what better time than when I have not only one charity event to get through by Phoenix's side this weekend but two?

She shakes her head. "I'm sorry if I overstepped. We don't need to talk about it. I promise."

I sigh and exhale loudly. "No, sorry. It's just complicated."

Her mouth forms an 'O' shape. "I understand complicated."

"Phoenix was engaged to my sister. She died a few days before he went to prison."

Jo stops what she was doing mid-air and stares at me. "Well, maybe I don't understand complicated, after all. Wow. Mmm, okay. I understand why you might feel weird talking about your relationship."

"I guess I'll have to get used to it."

She hisses through her teeth. "I bet the press will have a field day with this, I'm so sorry. Especially since they're still all over Phoenix being a free man again."

"I can imagine." I squeeze my intertwined fingers in my lap, counting to five, then easing the pressure.

She adjusts a clip on top of my head and weaves a strand of hair through her hands. "You haven't seen all the headlines about the prodigal son's return?"

I shake my head as much as I can in this position. "I stopped reading tabloids and online gossip a long time ago. I learned it's better that way."

She briefly considers that, twirling the curling iron in her hand. "I guess I can see why. I probably wouldn't want to read all the gossip about myself either."

"It gets old fast, especially when they flip on you and turn into vultures at the drop of a hat. I've had enough of that with my sister and Phoenix for a lifetime."

Her high ponytail bobs. "I feel bad for even bringing it up. Sometimes, I have a talent for putting my foot in my mouth."

I lift my hand and wave her off. "It's okay. Like I said, I probably have to get used to it anyway. I'm sure the press will go nuts over this new development."

She steps away and admires her handiwork with an excited glimmer in her eyes. "Well, at least you will knock the air out of every single person there tonight. Let's get you in that dress, shall we? I cannot wait to see Phoenix's face when he sets eyes on you. Fiancé or not, he will have to beat the guys away from you with a stick all night long."

Her chuckle is adorable, so at odds with her more tough-looking exterior, and I can't help but smile at her.

A real smile.

After a quick bathroom stop, Jo helps me into the dress.

We walk out of my room together, heading down the long corridor until we reach the large landing leading to the massive staircase.

Phoenix and Holden stand at the bottom of it, deep in conversation, until Jo calls Holden's name, and he glances up at her. His eyes widen when he sees me, but then they volley back to Jo, who's bounding toward him.

With a hand on the rail, I slowly descend the stairs. Each step is measured and careful, giving me the time to school my expression as much as possible.

Like before, I sense Phoenix's gaze on me.

I hate the turmoil it causes inside me. The soft tug at my middle, how my heart switches to an excited gallop, the fire that ignites in my lower belly. A fire I'm sure can burn us both to the ground if we're not careful.

When I can't stand it anymore, I lift my gaze and let it collide with his.

We have barely talked all week, but what started as cold hatred in his gaze has slowly turned into a somewhat neutral, almost civilized gaze over the week.

Now, only undisguised desire and appreciation pool in his dark depths, and that realization stuns me so much I stop paying attention to the stairs and stumble in my heels.

CHAPTER 13

PHOENIX

I jump up the few steps separating us and catch Evangeline before she falls.

Fucking reflexes.

Again.

Her hands circle my neck, digging into my nape.

I grasp her tightly around her waist, pushing her back up to fully standing.

With me still one step below her, and her added inches from the heels, we're at the same height for once.

Which means I'm staring straight at her face. Only a breath away.

Thankfully, her eyes are closed, but as so often when it comes to this woman, luck isn't on my side for long, and she opens them just when I'm about to let go.

Her gaze is unwavering, her brown irises dark and tenacious like she just survived a visit from the devil and somehow succeeded in keeping her soul intact.

I drift toward her, wanting a better glimpse, ready to beg her to spill all her secrets.

For a moment, I'm caught in some alternate reality where Evangeline and I are the same people we were at her birthday party all those years ago, where lines were beginning to blur despite how hard I tried to stay away.

What are you doing, man? She is not your friend. Not anymore.

The invisible bubble around us bursts, returning me to the here and now. In this reality, I was engaged to her sister, who died in a tragic accident a day before Evangeline picked up a knife and shoved it into the already bleeding wound her sister's death had left and ratted me out to the police.

The reminder finally gives me the proverbial cold shower I need, and I step back. Since I require her help tonight, I ensure she's steady on her feet, then turn around and storm out the front door to put as much distance between us as possible.

I slide into the back seat of the blacked-out SUV, staring out the front window as if that'll magically take care of my problems.

You did this to yourself.

You brought her into your life and forced her into this.

And now the past mixes with the present, smudging what was once a strictly black-and-white situation into different shades of gray.

When I was locked up, gone from my everyday life, it was easy to let my anger take over and devise this plan. I thought it would be the easiest thing on earth to come back here, get engaged, then marry Evangeline and make her life hell.

What was I thinking?

When were things ever easy when it came to her?

Shit.

I didn't expect the past to take over my thoughts so much. Yet, whenever I see her, or spend time with her, I'm reminded of what she did to me. But at the same time, I'm also reminded we used to be friends. And we would have been more if I hadn't gone away to college and things hadn't gone down the way they had with Connie.

Now, I have to live daily with the constant reminder that once upon a time, I wanted her with a desperation that nearly brought me to my knees.

Now she's my enemy.

But it doesn't compute in my brain.

I let my head fall against the headrest.

Memories are so fucked up.

Beyond that, the more time I'm around her, the less things add up with her actions. And since Holden agrees with that assessment, I'm not imagining it either. He spends a lot more time with her than I do, and he said while she's often quiet and withdrawn, she's always lovely and friendly to everyone. There isn't a single mean streak in sight. And every single night this week she spent on her homework and doing little else.

Nothing suspicious has popped up from going through her phone either, and I searched in every single corner. It all aligns with the version of Evangeline that Holden has seen. It is undoubtedly a more watered-down and subdued version of the Eve I used to know, but it's still her.

I can still see *my* Eve. My *Angel*.

Fuuuuuuuuuck.

I close my eyes and rub a hand over my face. My skin is too tight, my head spinning in circles.

The door opens on the other side, and I stiffen.

Her sweet floral scent reaches me first, scrambling my already confused thoughts even more.

I study her.

Who are you?

Of course, my silent question goes unanswered, but I continue to stare at her while she buckles her seat belt.

I cannot look away from how breathtaking she is, how heart-stoppingly beautiful. Her dark eyes are framed by long lashes and accentuated with eye makeup, while her hair cascades down her back in soft waves that are held back in the front with golden clips that match her dress. She's an absolute vision, and I want to drag her back into the house so she can change into something that'll draw less attention.

When she glances my way, that nagging feeling that something isn't right intensifies inside my chest.

I will find out what it is, and I think then I'll have to cut her loose, after all.

This arranged marriage isn't worth driving myself crazy over; *she* isn't.

And what secret could she possibly have that would justify what she did to me?

Nothing could.

Holden clears his throat and watches me in the rearview mirror. "Good to go?"

I nod and stare out the window.

He steers the car around the circular driveway, and I absentmindedly realize I was so enthralled by Evangeline I didn't even notice Jo leaving. But her car is gone, leaving the driveway empty.

We stay silent on our drive to the city, and I try to shove

this whole mess inside a box in the farthest corner of my head where it belongs. I can't let Evangeline distract me.

Good luck trying to pretend to be a newly engaged couple in love tonight while also trying to convince people you're a reformed man.

I'm so screwed.

But speaking of engagement . . . I pull the velvety box out of my pocket and all but shove it in Evangeline's face. "Here."

"What is it?" She regards the box like it's personally offending her and doesn't make a move to take it.

"What do you think it is?" I sigh. "We're almost there. Will you take the damn box already?"

"Only because you asked so nicely." She gives me a bright smile that doesn't reach her eyes and snatches the box out of my hand.

After an excruciating moment, she slowly opens it. I don't miss the way her eyes widen, or the way her breath hitches, when she catches the first glimpse of what's inside.

Her engagement ring.

"Phoenix." Evangeline's hand flies to her mouth before she lowers it to the ring, gingerly brushing the gem. "Is that a moonstone?"

I clear my throat. "It is."

"Did you pick it?"

"Yeah."

Her gaze flicks to mine, and I shrug.

"Connie once mentioned it's your sisterhood gemstone or something like that. I thought you might like it." My impatience takes over, and I grab the box from her. "We don't have a lot of time left. Let me help."

Carefully, I take the custom-made piece and gesture for

her hand. I keep my gaze downward as I slide it on her left ring finger. It fits perfectly, and I stare at the glowing oval-shaped moonstone that's nestled within twinkling diamonds.

Then I finally glance up and immediately regret it. There's an undeniable shimmer in her eyes, and I put that there.

"Phoenix, I don't know what to say. It's . . . it's absolutely beautiful. Thank you."

I nod and say, "No problem."

After another long perusal, she gazes at me. Her entire face has transformed. It's softer around the edges, and the tightness around her eyes that's usually there when she looks at me has disappeared too.

"We haven't really talked much about tonight. The gala is for a nonprofit that helps children who are transitioning into foster care, right?"

Grateful for the topic change, I dip my head. "Yes. They also offer support via emergency shelters, or if someone was affected by other traumatic situations."

She stays silent for a moment as if she's processing the information. "Do you sometimes feel guilty that you grew up with so much when others don't even have the necessities?"

I don't want to indulge the many things I thought about during my time in prison. The way it's changed me at my core. When everything you're used to is stripped away without warning, especially if you're used to having whatever you wanted at the snap of a finger, you eat a huge piece of humble pie very quickly. I feel like I ate my body weight of it and then some.

I swallow but hold her gaze. "I don't feel guilty per se,

since I didn't do anything wrong by being born into a rich family, but I definitely have changed the ways I think about money and privileges over the last few years."

"Is that why you're starting your own nonprofit? To help less privileged people?"

I avert my gaze to the front, where it collides with Holden's in the mirror. "Not really. I can make a huge change by just donating money to other charities and organizations. Starting my own nonprofit was a means to an end at first, more busy work than anything else, a tool. But now, I don't know."

I shrug and avert my gaze to the window and the passing city life.

"Now what?"

Of course, she can't just leave it alone.

I sigh. "I don't know. I guess I like it more than I thought. It feels satisfying to build a company by myself, and one that will actually do good too."

"We're almost there," Holden calls from the front at the same time Evangeline mumbles something that sounds like, "The exact opposite of what your dad does."

And she's not wrong. The same thoughts have been occupying my mind. He likes to destroy things. Demolish companies and the people who built them if it's necessary, or just because he feels like it. Devastation is all he does and he enjoys it, revels in it even. And I was going to step right into his shoes, walking down the same path. I would have ended up exactly like him . . . if I hadn't gone to prison.

I don't have time to think more about that little realization. The car stops in front of the carpeted entrance and a valet rushes over to open my door.

Showtime.

After a quick glance at Holden and a deep breath, I get out.

I step to the side to make enough room for Evangeline and hold out my hand toward the still-open car door. Warm fingers grasp mine, sending a spark of electricity through my entire body.

A small gasp comes from the car seconds before Evangeline steps out. With our hands still intertwined, she's only a hair's breadth away, allowing me to spot the golden rays around her irises, which turn her eyes into the most fascinating golden-brown kaleidoscope I've ever seen.

The valet clears his throat behind me. "Welcome, Mr. Montgomery. Miss Caldwell."

I snap out of my trance for the second time in the last hour.

This is going to be a long night.

Evangeline squeezes my hand and gives the man behind me a dazzling smile. "Hi, Paul. It's good to see you."

"The pleasure is all mine, miss."

My head snaps up at something in the man's voice, and I glare at him. He's ogling Evangeline with undisguised interest and appreciation in his eyes. Not that I blame him, she looks mesmerizing, always has been pretty with her curvy figure and dark features, but tonight, her beauty is on a different level.

I step forward, cutting off Paul's view of my *fiancée*.

His eyes widen, and he scrambles a few steps to the side, tipping his head a fraction. "Good to have you back, sir. Enjoy your evening."

With his eyes downcast, he hurries around us and closes the car door.

Evangeline untangles her hand from mine and curls her slender fingers around the crook of my elbow instead, her ring now on full display.

Tonight's event isn't as big as most of the other ones we'll attend, so I thought this would be good practice—a trial run. We don't need every New York paparazzi after us on our first night out together in public. Although, seeing the way Evangeline nails the role of the charming and doting fiancée, all smiles and open adoration, I shouldn't have worried. We've both grown up in the same tank of sharks, but I needed to be sure she'd be able to manage our situation.

Her acting skills around me have been subpar as best, but it seems like she's got it under control when there are cameras around.

We make the rounds, talking to so many people that names and faces blur. It doesn't help either that I'm too busy watching Evangeline while she charms the socks off everyone we come across. Even the ones who approach us with a hint of caution leave with a smile and a promise to connect soon.

Once we're alone, I lean closer and whisper into her ear, "I'm impressed. Honestly, I wasn't sure you could pull it off."

Her shoulder moves against my chest. Did she just shiver?

Just when I think she won't answer, she mimics my position, her warm breath hitting the shell of my ear.

"I've had lots of practice, especially in the last few years. You know that social events were Connie's domain and not mine, but I had to attend them all after . . ." She inhales sharply. "You know, after she was gone."

Her voice trails off at the end like she didn't mean to add on that last part.

I inhale her intoxicating scent and place my hand on her lower back, in what I'm sure comes off as a loving gesture between two people having an intimate conversation. "I'm sorry you lost your sister."

The words are out, and I can't take them back.

For some inexplicable reason, I don't want to either.

Since I was arrested a day after Connie's accident, I couldn't attend her funeral and had to mourn her in my concrete cell. Over the years, my only outside contact was with the people my father periodically sent to ensure I remembered, even though I was in prison, I was still expected to keep our family name in a good light.

And yes, I lost my fiancée—my future family—but Evangeline lost her sister, one she loved dearly. It couldn't have been easy for her.

She studies me, her gaze flitting back and forth between my eyes. "Why did you do it, Phoenix?"

"Why did I do what?" I narrow my eyes at her, suspicion and defensiveness immediately filling my veins. People have often asked me why I did what I did, but I didn't want to rehash any of it, especially not with Evangeline.

"Why did you kidnap Chris Wellinger?"

"Kidnap? I'd hardly call it that. He and I were just having a little . . . chat."

"Was it because you were jealous of him?"

I scoff. "Jealous?"

Evangeline nods. "Yeah. He was very obvious in his

interest in Connie. At least to me. But she kept laughing it off and said I was being silly, that he was just one of Dad's business partners."

It's so easy to forget Evangeline doesn't know what happened back then, and I promised Connie I wouldn't tell anyone. If things were different between Evangeline and me, I might have told her anyway. But since they're not, we both continue with our secrets and lies.

I glance around to make sure no one's within earshot before I hiss at her, "You probably shouldn't be talking about things you know nothing about."

Her eyes light up and she laughs as if I just said the funniest thing ever. When she glances back at me with an enormous smile aimed at me, my mouth opens of its own volition at her radiating beauty.

A flash lights up somewhere close by, and I snap my head toward it, staring at the grinning face of one of the photographers for the evening. He gives me a thumbs-up and moves on to someone else.

She grips my bicep and squeezes. "That should be a good shot for the press. You might look a little dumbfounded, but that's okay. We can say you were utterly spellbound by me."

Damn, this woman and her acting skills. Maybe they work a little too well in public.

I drop my hands from her frame and stare at her. "I need a drink."

"Will you get me another glass of champagne too, please? I need to use the restroom." With that, she spins around and walks across the room, turning heads left and right.

My gaze doesn't leave her swaying hips until she's out of sight and Holden is with her.

It is beyond me how she could ever think she was born for anything less than the spotlight.

Shit, she *is* the spotlight.

And I hate it with every fiber in my body.

As if sensing where my thoughts are going, my phone vibrates with a message, successfully interrupting the train wreck that is my mind.

CANARY

Seems like she's already got you caught in her web.

Under the message, a photo loads.

It's one of Evangeline and me from when the photographer stopped by. But this photo is taken from the other side with the photographer behind us. My "informant" took this photo.

I scan the crowd. What for, I'm not sure, since I still have no clue who's behind these messages. Holden and I have tried everything, but this guy is like a ghost.

Or it could be a woman, as Holden has pointed out several times.

When no one stands out in the crowd, I reread the message.

ME

Where are you?

CANARY

Already left. I just wanted to see the lovely
couple. You looked awfully cozy together,
not like you're with the woman who put you
in prison. I hope you sleep with one eye
open, ready to be stabbed again in the
back. Maybe this time, for real.

CHAPTER 14

EVANGELINE

I should have stopped one champagne ago. Okay, two. But I needed the boost after I got back from the restroom. I don't know what happened, but Phoenix suddenly started acting weird. Well, more bizarre than usual. He was distracted during conversations, kept frowning at me half the time, and I constantly felt his gaze on me, as if he was afraid I'd suddenly pull a gun out of my purse and shoot him.

The champagne helped calm my nerves, maybe too much. My laugh is louder, my grin wider, but at least that bubble of anxiety and dread in my chest has slowly disappeared.

So when the photographer from earlier comes around again sometime later, I'm ready to prove to myself and the entire world Phoenix and I are a couple in love.

The older man smiles at me. "I forgot to congratulate you earlier. I couldn't believe my eyes when I saw the announcement yesterday."

Ah yes, *the announcement* our parents couldn't wait to

make on our behalf. I had to hear about it from my friends. Thanks, Mom and Dad.

The photographer doesn't seem to feel my mood shift, still wearing the same cheerful expression. "When's the big day?"

Phoenix grumbles next to me, "We haven't set a date yet."

The photographer's smile falls at Phoenix's tone, so I playfully shake my head.

"The engagement was such a surprise; we just want to enjoy our time together for now."

The man nods as if my statement makes total sense. "You must be busy with school. It's your last year before you graduate, right?"

I take the breadcrumb eagerly. "Exactly. I want to be able to give my full attention to our wedding, which will be hard to do during the school year."

He smiles as if I've given him an invitation to our wedding. His gaze lowers for just a second to roam over my body. At this point, I don't even care. I'm too relieved he isn't bringing up Phoenix's prison sentence or my sister's death.

But Phoenix stiffens beside me and turns to face me. I automatically gaze up at him, stunned because he's much closer than I thought.

He frowns at me, but I'm not sure if that's in reaction to the photographer or me. Next thing I know, he cups my face and brushes his thumb over my cheek.

My breath hitches.

Oh my God, why is he touching me like this?

My mind is in overdrive, quickly distracted again when his warm breath fans over my face.

Something flutters in my chest.

His hand stills as he stares deep into my eyes. "Or maybe I should drag you to the courthouse right now to make sure everyone knows you're mine."

"Phoenix." His name sounds like a plea on my lips, and I don't know why.

His gaze shifts to my lips, and he says, "Fuck it."

Then he closes the distance between us and kisses me.

At first, it's only a press against my lips.

Firm, almost angry.

A low and pleasant hum warms my blood, quickly heating up my entire body.

I gasp, and several things happen at the same time.

Phoenix's other hand joins my face, now both cupping my cheeks, with his fingertips digging into the sides of my skull. He draws me closer, and I blindly reach out to steady myself. My hands land on his warm chest, where his heart beats wildly under my palm, almost a replica of my own.

The sensation becomes a distant memory when his tongue delves into my mouth and claims mine in a way I've never experienced before. The fact that he isn't exactly gentle in his approach only sends an extra spark of heat between my legs.

Without thought, I let out a quiet whimper, and Phoenix pulls back with wide eyes.

The noise around us slowly breaks through my daze.

We stare at each other, my panicked gaze resembling his.

Someone clears his throat close by. I move my head toward the sound, heat rising to my cheeks when I stare at the photographer.

I swallow my groan. Why is he still here? Did he watch us this whole time like a creep?

Before I can offer an apology, Phoenix grabs my hand and tugs me away.

I give the photographer a half-assed chuckle and wave, barely able to keep up with Phoenix as he marches across the room and toward the exit.

With my hand still firmly clasped in his, we reach the coat check. Phoenix wordlessly hands my ticket to the employee and then types furiously on his phone. I'm still too stunned to speak, my brain busy replaying what happened in my head. Over and over and over.

That did happen, right?

Phoenix just kissed the ever-loving shit out of me . . . at our first outing as an engaged couple.

In a room full of people. With a photographer watching —and probably recording—the entire moment.

And worst of all . . . did I actually kiss him back?

Phoenix holds out my coat for me, and I slip my arms into it on autopilot, utterly lost in my head. Without a word, he drags me out into the cool night air to the already waiting car at the curb.

When on earth did Holden manage to get that?

Phoenix opens the back door for me and motions for me to get in, but I pause and look at him for the first time since our kiss and immediately wish I hadn't. His eyes are cold, his jaw locked tight, and he stares at me with such disgust my stomach plunges.

With a hard swallow, I manage to avert my gaze and climb into the vehicle. Phoenix follows, and Holden pulls into traffic. I keep my gaze solely trained on the busy New

York streets that fade away once we leave the city. Freeways and dark scenery replace skyscrapers and packed streets.

Eventually, we reach the long driveway I've already become so used to.

Holden parks in the garage, the car barely coming to a halt when Phoenix yanks the door open and slams it behind him. Holden stares through the windshield as his friend storms through the vast space and disappears inside the house with another door slam.

He shifts my way with his eyebrows drawn together. "What did I miss?"

"He didn't tell you?"

He shakes his head. "He only messaged me to get the car, and that was it."

I roll my lips together. "Well, you need to ask him then because I have no clue either."

It's not a lie. Well, not really. My brain is still trying to figure out what happened or how what transpired was possible in the first place. Because while I agreed to be his fiancée, or rather was forced to agree, I never said I'd be okay with any kind of public intimacy. Holding hands is one thing, kissing on the cheek bearable, but a kiss like *that*? That's an entirely different thing.

That wasn't just a kiss. He devoured you. He made a statement.

Shit.

I shake my head and open my door. "I can't deal with this right now."

Holden jumps out of the car too, his gaze scrutinizing. "So something did happen."

I shrug. "Yes, but I won't tell you what. Ask Phoenix."

He grumbles under his breath, "Fine."

Once inside, he activates the security system and follows me.

"Miss Caldwell. Ah, there you are. I'm so glad I could catch you." Huxley appears out of nowhere, carrying a rectangular black box. "This was left for you while you were out."

I don't move a muscle. I can't.

After an awkward moment of silence, Holden says, "Thanks, Huxley. I'll take it for her."

"Of course, sir." Huxley hands Holden the box, and disappears with a little head bow.

Poor man did nothing wrong. I'll need to make sure to apologize to him tomorrow.

Holden holds out the box for me, and I lift the lid. I already know what's inside, but I check anyway. A bouquet of withered red roses. Just like the ones *he* sent after Connie died.

Fully aware of Holden's gaze on me, I grab the small card tucked inside and close the lid.

Congratulations on the engagement. You'll make a beautiful bride.

My head spins.

I need to get away.

I school my features the best I can and look at Holden. "Someone must have sent these as a prank. Would you mind tossing them in the trash for me, please?"

He narrows his eyes at me, probably not buying my bullshit, but nods. "Okay. Just wait here for a second. I'll be right back."

I shake my head. "Holden, I don't need a babysitter. I'm a big girl and can walk upstairs by myself."

He raises an eyebrow. "I just wanted to make sure you're okay. But have it your way, Princess."

With that, he spins around and stalks off in the opposite direction.

Way to go, Eve. He was just trying to be nice.

Maybe that's the problem. When this arrangement started, I thought I knew what I was getting into. Not just with Phoenix but also with Holden. Now, all lines are blurred, and I'm constantly confused, especially with Holden. Besides kicking down our door at my old house—which Ruby and Mason assured me was fixed before the end of the day—Holden hasn't been mean to me or mistreated me in any way.

Is this a twisted form of deferred Stockholm syndrome?

With a sigh, I take off my heels. My feet are killing me. I trudge up the stairs, the smooth feel of the rail under my fingers calming me. I tap it the entire way up. At the top, I turn toward the left where my room is, but something stops me.

Maybe the flowers—an absolutely unnecessary reminder from Freddy that my life isn't really my own—finally pushed me over the edge toward insanity.

My chest heaves, and my heartbeat quickens in tune with my shallow breaths. Without overthinking it, I follow the invisible pull and stride in the opposite direction.

Once I reach my destination, I stare at the open door. The soft carpet soothes my aching feet the moment I take a cautious step into the room for the first time. My gaze dashes past the seating arrangement to the grand piano in front of the windows. Last I knew, Phoenix didn't have a musical bone in his body, so I wonder if his grandfather added this music room.

The piano's polished surface shines in the moonlight, the night sky bright enough to illuminate the stark contrast of the white and black keys from the rest of the body. I walk over to it in a daze and circle the black beauty once, twice, sliding my fingers along the glossy sides, a weird mix of panic and anticipation filling my chest at touching the instrument. Familiar, yet foreign. It's been so many years since I last played, and now that I'm this close, I can't resist the draw of it.

I place my purse on the extensive body and sit on the bench.

The magic that used to encompass my entire being whenever I was near a piano slowly weaves its way back into my essence.

Play for me, Angie.

My sister's voice drifts into my mind like she's with me in the room. Although Connie wasn't musical, she shared my love of classical music. She loved to listen to me play, either live or via a recording, which helped her focus better on her school assignments and work. She was such a workaholic, just like my father and brother. There were days when I wondered if I was adopted, but the family resemblances were too uncanny to deny.

I felt about music the way Connie felt about work. It was my favorite escape from life, my way of dreaming about the future, my only way to create that unique spark that lights up my soul like nothing else does.

I move my fingers over the keys.

Connie would have loved tonight.

She wouldn't have had too much champagne and inappropriately kissed her fiancé, not only because of the large crowd but also because she'd have known the media would have a field day with it.

But it's Phoenix's fault, he kissed me first.

My sister's fiancé, who is now *my* fiancé.

I kissed what was hers.

My lower lip trembles, and I bite it.

The room is dim but fully disappears behind my closed eyelids.

My fingers fly over the keys, acting solely on muscle memory. I try to keep it together. Try to hang on to that thin thread of sanity that has been unraveling for so long now, it's a miracle it still exists at all.

Kissing Phoenix tonight opened up a can of worms I thought I'd had a tight lid on.

Pictures of my sister fly through my head, the last glance she sent me over her shoulder before she left the house. If I'd only known it would be the last time I'd ever see her. The things I said to her, and she wasn't even angry at me, only disappointed and sad, which was even worse. I just wanted to understand why she was throwing away her life the way she did. I needed to understand what I ever did to her that she'd hurt me that much on purpose.

"Angie, I know it's a surprise, but please trust me. Phoenix is the best thing that's ever happened to me."

She gives me a pleading look, silently begging me to understand, but I don't. I can't. I yank my hand out of her grasp and watch in horror as she places her fingers on her stomach. She rubs it almost absentmindedly, and we both freeze. Her gaze finds mine again, but I'm already shaking my head and backing away.

"Are you—" I draw in a sharp breath. "Are you pregnant?"

She presses her lips together and nods.

My hands go into my hair, and I pull at my strands. "No, that can't be. How . . . how long have you been seeing him behind my back?"

My voice rises with every word that comes out of my mouth until I'm yelling.

Her hand reaches for me, but I step out of her reach with an ugly snort. "I bet you had a good laugh together about your stupid little sister being in love with your fiancé. With the father of your child."

She stares at me with tears brimming her eyes and shakes her head. "No, Angie. It's not like that at all."

I hold up a hand and turn away from her. "I can't . . . please don't. I can't even look at you right now."

The words 'I hate you' are on the tip of my tongue, but I bite them back for some reason.

She sniffles. "We'll talk tomorrow. Let's cool down, and I'll explain everything tomorrow. Please."

I stay quiet, staring at a hole in the floor while I listen to her retreating footsteps. When they stop and she calls my name, I'm compelled to glance at her, forced to see her beautiful face wholly shadowed in sorrow.

"I love you. I hope one day you can forgive me, Angie."

She waits for another moment, but when I don't say anything, she steps out of the door, closing it quietly.

I snap back to reality with a gasp. The pressure on my chest is so heavy, it feels like my rib cage is going to collapse at any moment. Every inch of skin tingles. All of these emotions rushing through my body. It's too much.

They don't have anywhere to go, so they continue to grow until it feels like I'm going to implode. I want to scratch at my skin, this need to find an outlet impossible to ignore.

I grind my teeth and breathe loudly through my nose.

What am I supposed to do?

I clench my hands into fists so hard, my fingernails dig into my palms. But it's not enough. I stare straight ahead at the piano keys, and without taking a second to think things over, I grip the lid and slam it closed.

The *bang* echoes around the room. It feels good but doesn't keep my body from getting hotter by the second. A bead of sweat runs down my nape.

I stand so abruptly, the bench topples over behind me.

But I don't care.

I'm tired of these stupid recurring thoughts circling almost nonstop in my head.

I'm tired of people using me as a puppet.

Of all the lies and secrets.

Of the people and things I've lost and can never regain.

Of Freddy.

My sister's death.

Phoenix's prison sentence.

The threats to my friends.

The text messages.

The wilted roses.

The kiss.

The touches.

The longing.

The attraction.

The engagement.

Our future marriage.

Losing the possibility to escape this life, the only thing that kept me going.

In one big swoop, I push the sheet music off the top of the piano and watch them scatter across the floor.

My entire body is shaking, my heart dancing at an irregular beat. It's too fast and out of control.

I walk to the seating arrangement, grab the vase from the coffee table, and throw it against the wall. It doesn't smash into a million pieces like I'd hoped, so I pick up the larger piece and fling it at the wall once more, this time with even more force. It does the trick, and glass shards fly everywhere, enabling a whoosh of pent-up air to hiss out of my lungs.

Finally, a small relief.

Fast footsteps come toward me from behind, and I spin, just as strong arms band around me.

Phoenix.

My body tenses, and I try to wiggle out of his hold. "No, let me go. Please. Let me go."

He only holds me tighter, pulling me against his warm chest.

Tremors shake my body almost uncontrollably. "Phoenix, I need to . . . I . . . I can't keep this in. It's too much."

His hold loosens enough for me to hammer on his chest with my fists.

He doesn't stop me or complain. "It's okay, Angel. Let it all out."

His old nickname is like the final stab to my heart, the pain too much, ripping me wide open.

So I do what he says and let it out. All of it.

I don't stop pounding on his chest until this angry energy finally dissipates and my hair sticks to my neck and forehead. I feel like I just ran a marathon and sag against his body, utterly exhausted.

Phoenix holds me for a moment, before he picks me up and cradles me tightly. "Are you okay?"

I try to shake my head, but it's too heavy to move. "I don't know if I'm strong enough to survive all of this. It's so much. Too much. Too damn much. Sometimes, I wish I could just disappear. I bet you'd like that."

CHAPTER 15

PHOENIX

Evangeline rests her head on my chest and stays quiet. I take in the room, careful to avoid the broken glass on the floor on my way to the door.

Fuck.

I've never seen her like this before.

I adjust my grip, and she winces.

"Are you hurt?" I peer down at her, noticing for the first time that she's cradling her hand to her chest.

She opens it, and I stare at her red palm that's dripping blood.

"I think I cut my hand." The words are barely a whisper, her voice devoid of emotion.

Holden sprints up the stairs when I step into the hallway.

"Is she okay?"

Although I know what he's asking, I want to snort at how complex of a question those three words are at this point.

"She cut her hand." My mouth is dry, and the pitch of my voice is all wrong.

"I was worried she got hurt." His gaze goes back and

forth between Evangeline's slouched form in my arms and my face. "I already called the doc."

"Thanks."

He dips his head. "You bet. Anything else?"

I'm back to walking, and he falls in step beside me. "My door, please. And could you get a washcloth or towel from the bathroom for her hand?"

"Of course." He swings the door open and steps aside so I can walk in sideways, careful not to bang Evangeline against the doorframe. He mumbles, "Be right back," before he runs off and meets me at the bed with a washcloth.

He puts it on the nightstand and says, "I'll wait outside."

"Thank you."

The door shuts with a quiet click, and I place Evangeline on my bed as gently as I can while she stares at me through half-lidded eyes.

Her hair has fallen into her face, and I brush the strands off her forehead. She doesn't say a word the entire time, just silently tracks my movements.

She shivers, and I realize her dress is pooling around her hips, exposing her nude underwear. It must have slipped up while I was carrying her.

My cock twitches.

What's wrong with you? This is not the right time to think about her pussy.

I clench my hands into fists and take a step back.

It's never the right time because I'm not interested in her pussy.

Sure, keep telling yourself that, man. You wanted it back then, and you still want it now despite what happened.

Shit.

I can't deal with this right now.

After a few tugs and pulls, I free the blanket from under her body and drape it over her legs. With her underwear successfully hidden, I take a step toward the head of the bed and carefully take her hand to examine her palm. The bleeding seems to have slowed down already, and since I can't see any glass shards in the wound, I gently wrap the washcloth around it.

She smacks her lips. The motion is slow, like the movement takes up all the energy in her body.

"Do you want something to drink?"

She gives me a little nod. "Please."

"One sec." I walk to the fridge I keep in the corner to grab a bottle of water.

Back by her side, I unscrew it and place a hand by her nape to help her up enough to drink.

"Small sips." I watch her like a hawk, satisfied she listens. "Good girl."

At the words, her eyes flicker to mine lazily before dropping to the bed.

She makes a humming sound to indicate she's done, and I put the bottle on the bedside table. She looks exhausted, like whatever just happened in the music room zapped all the energy right out of her. "Rest. The doctor will be here soon."

To my surprise, she listens again and closes her eyes. Her breaths even out, nothing like the erratic breaths when I first found her.

I don't know how long I just stand here, staring at this woman in *my* bed, who is as much of a stranger as she's familiar. However, I can't shake the feeling the needle has unwittingly swung to familiarity after tonight. Our lives are so tangled, I was conceited to think I could bind her to me without our past interfering.

In this relaxed state, she seems so much like her younger self.

What a fool I am, indeed.

After a while, a knock sounds on the door, and I quickly cross the room, slipping outside quietly to not disturb Evangeline.

My best friend peeks past me through the gap in the doorway I left open. "Doc should be here soon. Is she okay? I saw her on the camera feed, man. One second she was fine, and the next she just lost it."

I blow out a breath and shrug. "She didn't really say anything."

"Nothing?"

"No."

We stare at each other for a long beat until Holden shakes his head.

"I don't like this. There's so much not adding up, and things just . . . I don't know." He rubs a hand over his beard. "They just don't feel right."

I sigh and push a hand through my hair for the hundredth time tonight. "I hear ya."

"You know, I'm all about revenge and people getting what they deserve, but is there any chance it wasn't her on the recording?"

My breath stalls for a moment before I shake my head. "No, it's her one-hundred-percent. She didn't deny it either."

Holden crosses his massive arms in front of his chest, his biceps bulging. "Then something else is going on that we aren't aware of. She's hiding something. I can feel it in my gut. I've met many despicable people and have seen them do all sorts of nasty things to others. But they all have that dark spark in their eyes because they enjoy it to their very core. It makes them happy, smug even."

His gaze flickers through the open door to a sleeping Evangeline. "She's as far away from being happy as she could be. And I'm not just saying that about the whole engagement thing. She's sad, Phoenix. Like deeply to the bone. My guess is she has been for years."

"She lost her sister."

He nods. "I know, but I don't think that's all there is. I think there's something else that's dragging her down. Something bigger than that."

"Like what?"

"Fuck. I don't know, okay? That's the whole problem." He almost growls the words.

I lean against the wall and drop my head against it.

Holden blows out a breath, clearly frustrated by this mystery surrounding Evangeline. "Wouldn't you be elated if she were innocent somehow?"

I pin him with a narrowed gaze but stay quiet.

He points at me. "I didn't say anything earlier to the princess, but I saw you with her tonight. You might have entered that event with fake smiles, each of you playing your part, but don't pretend that kiss was an act. I wouldn't buy it for even a second."

"Fuck." I squeeze my hands so tightly my joints scream in protest. "I didn't think it would be like this. You know how much I wanted to make her pay for what she did to me. That was the whole reason for this arrangement. And it was so simple: hating her, making her pay, and finally feeling better after getting my revenge. I didn't expect to have these moments where I don't really hate her at all. She's fucking with my head in a way I wasn't prepared for."

When I became friends with Holden in prison, he told me outright there's only one rule I need to follow with him: no lying. I lie to him, and we're done. I've stood by that rule in all the years I've known him, and it's given me a friendship like I've never had before. Growing up in this world, in a society that thrives on pretense, gossiping, and lies, it's hard to shift gears to pure honesty. But it was worth it. Holden is the only reason I didn't turn into a mess in prison. It truly felt like my life was over, and he's the reason I'm alive.

He tips his chin toward the room. "You two have history. More than maybe even you realized."

"I thought the hate was stronger than the stupid crush I had on her when we were younger. There was a reason why I didn't act on it back then. Everything should have been easy, Hold. Especially after what happened with Connie."

Holden opens his mouth to say something just as his phone rings in his pocket. He pulls it out and holds it up to his ear, nodding and listening. "Thanks, Mike."

"Doc is here."

I push off the wall and roll my shoulders. "Good."

He claps me on the upper arm. "We'll continue this conversation later, okay? Go back to your girl. I'll let the doc in and bring him upstairs."

I stare after him. Two words repeat in my head over and over.

Your girl.

Your girl.

My girl.

But she isn't my girl. How could she be?

Instead of returning to the bedroom, I listen to the quiet voices drifting up from the foyer and meet the two men at the top of the stairs, relaying to Dr. Harvey what happened with Evangeline.

He has a friendly smile and a full head of gray hair. He used to be my grandpa's on-call doctor, only a few years younger than my grandpa would have been now. I thought about my grandpa a lot during my prison sentence, wondering if I would have ended up there if he was still alive. After a while and lots of thinking, as one does in prison, I concluded my life would have turned out very differently if he hadn't died when I was a young teen. He would have prevented my father from digging his rotten claws into me. But I was young and impressionable, without any well-meant guidance besides the big bad wolf himself.

Doc pushes his glasses up his nose and squeezes my arm. "Let's check her out, shall we?"

I nod and lead him into the bedroom where Evangeline has rolled to her side, thankfully still under the blanket and with the washcloth around her hand.

The doctor moves to the foot of the bed and places his black leather bag on it.

Evangeline stirs, and I walk to her side, watching her eyes flutter open.

The corner of her mouth draws up a little the moment she sees me, and a croaky "Hey" escapes her lips.

Fuck me.

I feel like I've entered a time machine.

"Hey." I clear my throat. "The doctor is here to check on you."

Her gaze shifts around the room when she realizes other people are present.

I point at the older man putting a stethoscope around his neck. "That's Dr. Harvey."

The man in question steps closer and smiles at Evangeline. "How are you feeling? I heard you had a small mishap."

As if she only now remembers what happened, Evangeline's eyes widen. "I . . . I guess I did."

The doctor chuckles behind me. "Phoenix, I need to actually get to Miss Caldwell if you want me to examine her."

I stiffen. "Of course, sorry."

Holden laugh-coughs, unable to hide his shit-eating grin when I join him a few feet away.

Evangeline pushes herself up to a sitting position and winces.

Crap. "She said she cut her hand."

"Let's take a look at it, shall we?" He inspects one hand, turning it over to study it from all angles, before he does the same to the other one. "Thankfully you didn't break your skin with all of these marks, although I'm sure you might feel them for a few days. Good news is that the cut is shallow and doesn't need stitches."

Evangeline nods. "Okay."

"Let's clean the wounds and make sure there aren't any glass pieces in there, and then we can put on some ointment and a bandage." The doc walks to his bag to get the supplies he needs before getting started. His gaze remains on Evangeline's hand. "Do you want to tell me what happened?"

Her throat bobs, her gaze flickering in my direction. The doc eyes us too.

Holden is the first to take the hint. "I'll wait outside."

My feet are reluctant, but after a few moments, I follow him to the door.

"Phoenix." My name is quiet on Evangeline's lips.

I turn around and glance at her. Her lips are pressed tightly together, and her eyes shimmer as if she's holding back tears.

When she doesn't say anything, I focus on her pleading eyes. "You want me to stay?"

Her nod is almost indiscernible, but it's there.

Why the fuck would she want me to stay? Me, of all people? At this point, I'd have expected her to pick Holden over me.

Pushing my thoughts aside, I swallow and point toward the couch. "I'll be right there."

"Thank you." She exhales and shifts her focus away from me and back to the man by her bedside.

I instantly miss her eyes on me.

Calm the fuck down.

I'm too wired to sit, so I pace back and forth in front of the couch.

"What happened, Evangeline?" The doc's voice is gentle, as if he's talking to a wounded animal.

Her shoulders lift and drop like she's carrying the world's weight on them. "It's really not a big deal. I just got a little frustrated and threw some things. At first, I thought I was going to have a panic attack, but I haven't had one in a while, so maybe that's why it hit me harder than usual? I don't know."

He nods and grabs the ointment from the small tray he put on the bedside table with his supplies. "Have you been treated for them before?"

She casts a quick look my way before she shakes her head. "No, I . . . mmh, I didn't have the support, so I kind of just dealt with them until life calmed down."

Until life calmed down. Is she talking about her sister's death? My imprisonment?

He lifts his head to study her. "It might be good for you to see someone, especially if the panic attacks return, or more of these rage attacks happen. I believe a great deal in therapy. Frankly, if it were up to me, everyone would go."

Evangeline just nods but stays quiet while the doc finishes up wrapping her hand and checking her vitals.

He jots down a few lines in his notebook and puts everything back into his bag. "I don't want to prescribe you any medicine right now, but please let me know if you're having more attacks or any other symptoms arise. And please think about seeing a therapist. Mental health is just as important as physical health, if not more important sometimes. I'd be happy to give you some recommendations."

Her mouth forms a gentle smile. "I will, thank you."

One second, the words form in my head; the next, they are out of my mouth. "She also fainted last week."

Evangeline and the doc both turn to stare at me before the doc focuses his attention back on his patient.

"Is that true? You fainted?"

She wrings the blanket in her lap and winces. "I did, but it was for a different reason. I had an upset stomach and couldn't keep anything down for a while but then had to attend a meeting the next day when I should have stayed in bed. I was extremely dizzy, probably a little dehydrated, and then fainted."

No wonder she promptly fell asleep when Holden got her later that day. She probably drank on that still-empty and upset stomach. Stubborn woman.

The concern is written all over the doc's face. "And you're sure you're feeling okay?"

She nods. "I think so. My life has been a bit crazy, and a lot has happened in a really short time. Maybe a bit too much."

"Miss Caldwell, that sounds to me like you are in dire need of a vacation."

She chuckles like he just said something funny.

I frown.

"Think about it. I'd also feel more comfortable to get you on the schedule for a more thorough exam and some blood work as well." He closes his bag and gestures toward me. "And please don't hesitate to call if something changes or you need me for anything else. Phoenix has my number."

She nods. "Thank you."

He gives her a small head bow. "It was my pleasure, miss. Feel better soon."

I walk him toward the door and shake hands with him. "Thanks for coming out. I appreciate it."

"Of course." He pats my arm and leans in. "Keep a close eye on her and make sure she gets lots of rest."

"I will try my best."

Holden is waiting on the other side of the door to escort the doctor to his car, so my focus zeroes back in on Evangeline.

My eyes widen when I see she's trying to get out of bed. "What do you think you're doing?"

I rush to her side and reach for her arm, barely in time for her to stand.

She's wobbly on her feet, but at least she's not pushing me away. "Can you help me to my room, please?"

Before she can protest, I lift her into my arms for the second time tonight.

"Phoenix, let me down. I can walk."

The shove at my chest is weak, and I settle her more comfortably in my arms, careful her injured hand is safe.

"Stop fighting me. I'm just going to take you to your room."

I almost tell her to stay here in my bed, but that would be ridiculous.

It's already bad enough that I enjoy the feel of her in my arms way more than I should.

After a moment of silence, she shifts. "Why help me? Why do any of this? You hate me."

"I don't hate you." Clearly, my mouth has no filter tonight. If there was any doubt about my confession to Holden earlier, here's the confirmation I didn't ask for.

I'm a mess over this woman.

Her earlier words rush back into my head. *Sometimes, I wish I could just disappear. I bet you'd like that.*

My throat tightens painfully.

Nothing is black and white anymore; it hasn't been in a while.

Her sharp inhale is loud in the otherwise quiet house. "You should hate me. I deserve it."

I go rigid at her words, her statement catching me off guard.

Why would she say something like this?

Not wanting to disturb this weird calm between us, I keep my voice low and say, "Well, if it's that important to you, I can go back to hating you tomorrow."

CHAPTER 16

EVANGELINE

Sunlight shines through my closed eyelids, and I don't need a mirror to know my eyes are swollen.

Thank you, utter breakdown last night.

Maybe it made Phoenix realize what a basket case he's got on his hands, and he'll let me out of this arrangement.

Yeah, right.

I roll onto my back and stare at the ceiling, unable to keep yesterday's memories at bay.

The gala. The kiss. Playing the piano. The reminder of what a mess my life has turned into. My outburst. Phoenix.

I don't hate you.

His words still float around in my head. He really said that, didn't he? And then he carried me into my room like some dark knight in shining armor, where he waited until I managed to change out of my dress and climb into bed. I'm totally ignoring the memories of how gentle he was with me and that I wanted to stay cocooned in his warm arms.

Although I got a full night's sleep, I feel like I barely slept. My panic attacks always suck the energy right out of me, and this seems to be no different. More than once, I had to spend several days in bed afterward because my body and mind were so sluggish and fatigued, making me utterly useless.

I didn't miss feeling like this, and I'm not sure how I'm supposed to go to another event in mere hours.

With my fiancé.

I look around the room, almost expecting to find him somewhere, which is ridiculous.

That man has zero reasons to care about me. Absolutely zero.

Not hating someone is a far cry from liking or caring about someone.

Regardless of how he feels about me, I need to find him and apologize for last night. My stomach churns uncomfortably at the memory of destroying the music room and facing Phoenix again, but it wasn't okay what I did. Hopefully, it won't ever happen again because this side of myself scares me.

It's okay.

I fill my lungs with air and exhale slowly.

Yes, it's okay. I can't change what happened. All I can do is apologize and move forward.

You won't get to your future if you're stuck in the past.

I've got this. The good thing is when you're at the bottom, there's only one way to go. And up, up, up we go.

My gaze snatches on the couch and the rumpled blankets. Didn't I fold them up yesterday before the gala?

I stretch, checking that heavy feeling in my bones like they're filled with lead. It takes me a good minute to get my phone from the nightstand, and I groan at the multitude of messages and notifications. At least my hand feels mostly okay, just a small pinch under the bandage when I use it.

I click on my group chat with Ruby and Mason first, but there's a knock on the door before I can read them.

Not having the energy to move a muscle right now, I shout, "Yes?"

"Are you decent?"

Holden.

I glance down to double-check and yell, "Yes," again.

The door opens, and Holden walks in. His gaze roams over me. "Hey. How are you feeling?"

What a loaded question. "Okay, I guess."

He walks in and leans against the wall. "Okay?"

I shrug. "A mixture of what I imagine it feels like when you get drunk right after you get hit by a truck."

The corners of his mouth twitch. "Sounds like you've given this some serious thought."

I can't help but smirk. "Maybe?"

Why is this guy so likable? I can't forget he's Phoenix's friend and right-hand man who might chuck me out of a speeding car if given the order.

He nods toward the phone in my hand. "Has Phoenix gotten a hold of you yet?"

I frown. "Phoenix?"

Holden nods. "Yeah. He said he was going to call you, but he might not have had a chance to do so yet. He left for the city this morning to take care of some business and will likely stay there for a few days."

"Oh." I drop my gaze to my hands, certain I imagine the tightness in my chest at the news.

I am not sad Phoenix isn't here.

Nope.

Not happening.

Remembering Holden is still here, I glance back up. Of course, he's already studying me. I wouldn't be in the least bit surprised if this man told me he could read my thoughts. "Well, thanks for letting me know."

"You bet."

I might imagine it, but he looks too smug for my taste.

"The doc said you need lots of rest, so I thought we could camp out in the movie room and watch something."

I blink at him, completely dumbfounded.

After several beats of silence, I finally manage to say, "You want to watch a movie with me?"

He shrugs. "Sure. Why not?"

He says it like it's the most normal thing in the world, like we do this all the time.

My stomach chooses that moment to growl.

Holden chuckles. "Huxley will be so happy to hear you're hungry. He's been driving me nuts all morning asking for you."

"He has?"

"That old man loves to take care of people, so I'll let him know you're up. And you can come to the movie room when you're ready."

The desire to pinch my arm to check if I'm dreaming is strong, but I decide against it. It takes too much energy.

Wasn't there something I needed all of my energy for?

I gasp. "The gala tonight."

Holden shakes his head. "Phoenix canceled your attendance. The media has been going wild, and the phone hasn't stopped ringing. It'll be good to give everyone a break over the next week to calm down before you guys go out again."

Phoenix canceled today. Was it really because of the media? The little voice in the back of my head thinks differently.

He did this for *you.*

No, no, no.

Retreat right now. This path is full of land mines, and we will never reach the other side in one piece. It's impossible.

Holden rubs his hands together. "Okay, Princess. I'll tell Huxley to make you breakfast. Ten minutes? Twenty? How long do you need?"

Knowing that overthinking in my state would only lead to a headache, I decide to just roll with this new development. "Twenty?"

That should give me enough time to use the bathroom, brush my teeth, get changed, and message Ruby and Mason before they call in the cavalry.

"Twenty it is." He salutes me, and then he's gone.

I take care of business and make sure I look decent enough to be around anyone before I finally get to my friends' messages.

RUBY

I admit, I expected to see the first one at some point. The second one, I didn't see coming.

MASON

Is there something you aren't telling us? We need to see you.

Underneath are two screenshots from some gossip pages.

The first is a photo of Phoenix and me posing for the photographer. The second one is a candid of us kissing.

I can't stop staring.

Experiencing it was one thing, but seeing it captured for eternity like this is something else.

No one is going to think our engagement is fake. Or not so much fake, but rather, arranged. If I didn't know better, I wouldn't believe it myself.

Three little dots dance across the bottom of the page.

RUBY

Don't you dare leave us on read. Meet us at the café in two hours?

My fingers move over the keyboard at a sluggish pace.

ME

Hey. Sorry, guys, but I'm afraid I might be out for the next few days.

MASON

What happened? Do we need to call in a SWAT team?

RUBY

Are you okay?

ME

I'm okay, just down with something. I'll explain everything when I'm better. Promise.

RUBY

Fine. It's probably for the best anyway. The press has been absolutely feral, and you don't need to see half of the shit they're saying.

MASON

What Ruby meant to say is get some rest
and feel better soon. And don't worry about
the press or anything else. Just don't go
online.

RUBY

Yes, that. Sorry.

RUBY

Do you need anything?

I swallow past the tightness in my throat.

ME

I'm all good, thank you.

MASON

Let us know if there is anything we can do
for you or if you're up for some company.

ME

I'll do that, thanks. Love you, guys.

RUBY

Love you more.

MASON

Miss and love you.

I'm about to put my phone down when it vibrates with
another incoming message.

Phoenix.

He made me add his and Holden's numbers to my phone
last week, but this is the first time he's contacted me.

PHOENIX

Hold said you're awake. How are you feeling?

Maybe a pinch isn't so bad after all. Phoenix is texting me, asking me how I'm feeling. Did anything life-altering happen that I forgot about? Or some kind of a body swap?

My fingers hover over the screen longer than ever before.

ME

I'm okay.

ME

We could have gone to the gala tonight. I said I'd go.

PHOENIX

Not until you feel better.

Something warm and forbidden blooms in my chest.

PHOENIX

We can't have the press catch on to anything.

And the feeling disappears into thin air again.

I laugh to myself.

I wasn't really thinking he actually cared about my well-being, was I? Not even for a moment?

Because that would be utterly foolish of me.

I have no clue how to respond, so I type out what I wanted to tell him instead.

ME

I'm sorry about last night. Of course, I'll pay for whatever damage I caused and clean it up.

He replies almost immediately.

PHOENIX

Don't worry about it. It's already been taken care of.

ME

Thank you.

I feel like I should say more, but I don't know what, so I sigh and tuck my phone in my pocket.

Unable to help myself, I take a quick glimpse into the piano room, and it's back to its meticulous order, just like Phoenix said. After another long glance at the piano, I drag myself downstairs to the media room just as Huxley wheels a cart into it.

He looks up at me. "Oh, good morning, Miss Caldwell. I'm so happy to see you awake."

"Thank you, Huxley. How are you?"

He smiles at me, his eyes crinkling at the corners. "I'm doing very well, miss. Thank you for asking. I hear you're hungry?"

I nod at him, one of my hands settling on my stomach. "Famished."

Between my upset stomach and all the stress and nerves, I feel like I've only eaten two meals all week.

Huxley inclines his head, still smiling as if I just told him he won the lottery. "Well, enjoy your food. Mr. Montgomery asked us to prepare something special for you this morning to help you feel better."

Too stunned to speak, I simply nod and watch him push the cart to the front of the room where he parks it next to the oversized leather recliner.

A special meal Phoenix arranged for me? He didn't mention anything.

"Don't hesitate to call me over the house line if you need anything, miss. Bon appétit."

"Thank you, Huxley. I appreciate it."

He gives a little bow. "Anytime." He straightens up again and starts when Holden walks into the room. "Oh, Mr. Donahue. Did you change your mind and want something to eat?"

Holden claps him on the arm, much gentler than he does with Phoenix, and shakes his head. "Nah, I'm good for now, but thanks. Her Majesty and I are going to have a movie marathon, and I might give that popcorn machine in the corner a whirl."

He gestures past the other rows of seats toward the back of the room, which houses several snack machines straight out of a movie theater as well as a fridge with cold drinks and a coffee machine, if I'm not mistaken.

Huxley nods at him. "Very well, sir. You know where to find me."

We walk to the front and sink into the plush seats.

Holden grabs the remote and points it at the oversized screen. "What do you want to watch?"

I shrug. "I don't know. I haven't really watched anything in forever."

His stare burns into the side of my head. "What were you doing all week if you weren't watching TV?"

I turn his way. "Studying and reading?"

He makes a noncommittal sound. "Oh my God, you're almost as boring as Phoenix. He reads business reports and looks at houses in his free time."

"Houses?"

"Yeah. He's trying to find something for the foundation. It would be easier to build something from scratch to get exactly what we want, but that would also take a lot longer."

I'm still mulling over that info when Holden directs his attention toward the food cart with undisguised curiosity in his eyes.

"What did he bring you?"

Nerves flutter in my midsection. I sit up taller and lift the lids to store them on the lower part of the cart.

My heart plummets straight into my stomach at the sight in front of me—animal face pancakes.

Connie and I used to make them together every weekend growing up, trying out a different animal every week. I haven't had them in years. Not since before Connie died.

I close my eyes, willing the heat in them to subside. I will not cry over some dang pancakes.

But it's no use. A single tear escapes my eye, and I swipe it off my cheek.

Holden clears his throat. "You okay, Princess?"

"Mmm-hmmm." I hum, not trusting myself enough to speak.

I grab one of the plates and stare down at the lion—a round pancake with a strawberry mane and nose, blueberry eyes, and a chocolate chip mouth.

It's utterly perfect.

This man. I pull out my phone.

ME

> Thank you for the pancakes. That was oddly sweet of you.

PHOENIX

> Maybe they're poisoned.

Given my mental state, I don't react like other sane people would by putting the plate down due to the very high possibility of Phoenix telling the truth. Instead, I laugh, not hesitating for even a second before I get a bite on my fork and put it into my mouth, pushing it past the lump in my throat.

They're sweet and fluffy and utterly delicious.

Eating this transports me back to a time when life was still good.

Where I had dreams and hopes and where my life was my own.

"What do you want to be when you grow up, Angie?" Connie steals one of the chocolate chips from my plate and pops it into her mouth.

"A world-famous piano player who travels around the globe." Pointing my fork at her, I wink. "What do you want to be when you grow up, Connie?"

"I want to be the CFO in Dad's company. You know, because I love numbers."

We giggle, like every time we play this game. I think it's silly that my ten-year-old sister wants to sit in a stuffy office all day long like our dad, but she says that's what she wants to do. Better her than me. I'd suffocate in days.

"You'll be magnificent on stage, Angie. Simply magnificent.

And I'll sit in the front row at every concert, telling everyone you're my sister."

My dream died alongside her, and my parents couldn't have been happier about that.

And I thought I was done for good, that I was too broken to play ever again.

But despite everything that happened last night, I can't regret placing my fingers on those keys and letting go.

One problem (possibly) solved, two more to go.

Phoenix and Freddy.

One first, then the other.

CHAPTER 17

EVANGELINE

The next day goes by similarly. A text message from Phoenix asking me how I'm doing, another special animal face pancake—an owl this time—and more relaxing in front of the TV.

Holden and I thought it would be a fun idea to try and binge-watch all seasons of *Lucifer* this week, so we'll see if we succeed. It's definitely fun to just relax and not stress about school or anything else for a little while.

Although I'm constantly distracted by Phoenix's text messages. After our morning exchange, I asked him how house hunting is going, so most of the messages are now business related. There are a lot of real estate listings, but it's a side of him I haven't been privy to, and I strangely enjoy these back-and-forths.

PHOENIX

> What do you think about this building? It's bigger than the last one, and I think we could push the emergency shelter to 30 beds instead of just 20.

One thing became clear really soon. Phoenix thinks big. He's been telling me about all of these ideas he has for the teens, not just until they age out of the system at eighteen, but also beyond that. He doesn't just want to provide them with a safe place to stay and a warm meal in their stomach, he wants to make a lasting difference in their lives. He wants to teach them things that'll allow them to alter their futures in ways they might never be able to otherwise. It's admirable, and witnessing this side of him makes me want to talk to him a whole lot more. To learn more about him and this project, about his visions. I want to learn everything there is about him.

Which is why I don't hold back, asking questions and offering solutions and ideas. Weirdly enough, I'm not mad about it. It makes me feel useful to help with something that matters and to share my experience from the women's shelter and what I've learned from Doreen over the years.

ME

I like this a lot better, but while it would provide more beds, it has less room for the rest. I don't think you could fit more than the office, a common room, and one, maybe two more "conference" rooms in there. Would you be okay cutting some of the programs you wanted to offer?

On Tuesday, I called Doreen at the shelter to tell her I couldn't stop by this week, and she informed me not to worry, that "Mr. Montgomery" had already taken care of it and hired some people to help. Apparently, Phoenix had also told her he'd be in touch soon to discuss the shelter and how he could help more. I could practically hear the hearts in her eyes over the phone.

Not that I blame her. To say I was immune to hearing what Phoenix did would be a lie.

I also get more messages from my parents, this time my mom, who gives me the same "warning message," just a tad less obnoxious than my dad.

Ruby and Mason also check in almost every day, entertaining me with their antics, sending pictures and videos of what I'm missing, asking if I'm okay and what I'm doing. They've calmed down a bit after I sent them pictures of my animal pancakes and my cozy setup in the movie room.

The two of them, along with Tyler, also keep me up to date on the classes I'm missing, emailing me their notes and assignments. They're the best.

By midweek, Holden grumbles that I spend more time on the phone than I spend watching, and that I haven't even noticed what's going on with Lucifer and Chloe. I just wave him off and get him some popcorn.

By Thursday, after yet another excited text message from Phoenix with a possible building prospect, the inexplicable desire to want to have these conversations with him face-to-face ignites inside me. I want to *see* the excitement on his face and hear the passion in his voice.

I'm so screwed.

Holden and I have also started going on walks in the last few days, once my fatigue finally started to fade, and he showed me around the parts of the property I hadn't seen yet and introduced me to every staff member we crossed paths with, from Mike at the gate to Jean in the kitchen. We don't always talk a lot, and I appreciate him letting me be. There's no need to fulfill any expectations like I so often have to.

For the first time in forever, I feel somewhat relaxed.

Phoenix stays away longer than planned, and by the time the weekend rolls in, I'm almost back to normal.

I'm also ready to see Phoenix again.

Am I the only one who feels like things have changed between us?

What if we're back to weird or hostile again?

Holden said Phoenix finally returned last night, but I haven't caught a glimpse of him yet.

Maybe he came in late, and that's why he didn't stop by my room.

But he'll have to show his face soon since we have our next event tonight, and tonight is a big one for World Vision, an organization that focuses on helping kids in the U.S. and all around the world. I know Phoenix is looking forward to soaking up all the information and to making as many connections as possible, as am I.

Since I gave myself a clean bill of health and have the whole day to pass, I'm finally meeting up with Ruby and Mason, who've been more patient with me this week than they probably wanted to be.

When Holden and I arrive at the coffee shop, Ruby and Mason immediately wave me to the corner booth they snatched. They both send a wary glance at my shadow as he settles into a chair close by that'll allow him to keep an eye on both the door and me.

My friends shower me with hugs and kisses before Mason ushers me into his side of the booth.

He gives me a once-over. "You look healthy. I approve."

I smile at him. "Thank you. I desperately needed this week to feel better."

Mason squeezes my side. "I'm glad you're okay. We weren't sure if you were lying and wanted to see it for ourselves."

Ruby nods. "Yup. Looking good. Now spill the beans, babe. We've been on the edge of our seats all week long. And if I haven't said it yet, I'm glad you weren't on campus this week. People even came up to me to ask about you and Phoenix. Does no one remember what boundaries and privacy are?"

Mason snorts. "It seems to be trendy to be rude and entitled these days. Some people act like it's a new hobby."

"So true." Ruby nods. "You told us you were chilling with your shadow most of this week, but we still have no clue what happened last weekend with Phoenix."

"Well . . . so." I rub my hand over my neck and collarbone. "Remember, I'm okay now, so no freaking out. After we got home from the gala, I found the piano and started playing. And then I kinda lost it and had a bit of a meltdown and threw some stuff."

I say it all quickly, not wanting to draw this out any longer than necessary. I'm met with silence for a beat. Two, three, four.

Ruby's eyes widen, and she takes my hands over the table. "Oh my God, babe."

Then they talk at the same time.

"You didn't think to tell us?"

"Are you okay?"

"Fucking hell."

"You played piano?"

"How was it?"

"I'm so sorry."

The words all blend, but I still hear them so clearly, it should be impossible.

I grab both of their hands and make a *shushing* sound. "I'm sorry I kept it from you, but I had to shake it off first and didn't want to have that conversation over the phone either."

Mason tugs me against his body while Ruby still holds my hand across the table.

His lips touch my hair gently. "I hate we couldn't be there for you, but I'm so glad you're okay."

Reveling in the warmth that is my friends, I lean closer to Mason.

It's so different from when I was cuddled against Phoenix's hard chest last week when my heart skipped beats to keep up with his.

My pulse picks up at the memory alone, and the desire to see him flares brightly in my chest.

Shit. It's really stupid to miss him, isn't it?

My heart needs to stay out of this, or things will get ugly fast.

Not to mention, he might be back to his former asshole self again when I see him next.

"Hey, babe."

At the familiar voice, I untangle myself from Mason's embrace, and Ruby lets go of my hand after squeezing it once more.

It's Tyler.

Wait. Did he just call me babe?

I peer up at him, but he isn't looking at me. His gaze is

fixed on Ruby as he slides onto the bench beside her and presses his lips to hers.

She giggles under her breath and pushes against his chest. "Tyyyyyyyy, stop it."

I stare at the two of them with wide eyes.

Tyler leans back and shifts his attention to me. "Hey, Evie. I'm so glad you're better."

Did I somehow land in an alternate universe?

I blink and nod. "Uh, yes, thank you."

He laughs at my response and gets up after kissing Ruby again. His smile is infectious. "You want your regular, Evie?"

I squeak out a "Yes, please," and he leaves with a small salute.

Ruby throws her hands over her eyes first, then up in the air. "Damn him."

Her glance flickers to Mason, but he holds up his hands and shakes his head.

"Nope, this is all you."

Ruby groans and stares at me with a pleading look in her eyes. "Ty wasn't supposed to give anything away until I gave him the green light."

"Are you guys together? Is this what you wanted to talk about?" My brain is still spinning at this unexpected turn.

Ruby grimaces. "Yes?"

Mason scoffs and leans his head down. "Evie, they've been making out like they're the last two people on earth. You're lucky you haven't been around to witness it. My eyeballs are ready to explode."

Ruby smacks him on the arm again but chuckles. "Stoooop it."

"It's true. Half the guys were adjusting themselves at the party last night because of the show you two put on."

Ruby hides her face behind her hands. "Oh my God."

I tilt my head to the side. "You like him."

She immediately nods. "I think I do."

"She definitely does," Mason pipes up again.

So much for him staying out of this.

Ruby gives me her puppy eyes. "Is this okay with you? Crap, I totally should have talked to you first."

I place my hand on my chest. "With me?"

She waves her hand around in front of me. "Yeah, you know, you and him and your history together."

"Pfft, oh yeah, don't even worry about me." I shake my head and laugh. "You know Ty and I agreed what happened was a huge mistake. If I could go back in time, I'd erase that entire night with him."

Ruby sighs, letting her shoulders slump in relief. She was seriously worried about my reaction.

Tyler steps up with my drink and winks at me. "I put some extra whipped cream on top."

I smile at him. "Thank you, you're the best."

He chuckles. "Whatever I can do to help my favorite ladies."

Mason huffs beside me, but Tyler ignores him, his gaze flicking to my hand around the cup. To my bare fingers.

Crap. I forgot to put on my engagement ring.

"How are you holding up?"

For a moment, I'm so stunned, I don't know what to say. But then I remember this is Tyler, the same one who saw me freak out in the bathroom at my birthday party after I saw Phoenix for the first time again. I didn't tell him what exactly went down, but he probably put two and two together and knows this isn't an engagement based on love.

So I shrug and say, "Hanging in there."

Tyler opens his mouth to say something, but the doorbell chimes, and a group of older ladies walk in the door.

He sighs. "Duty calls."

Ruby watches him with obvious longing in her eyes. Before I get to dig deeper into this surprising turn of events, Mason bumps his elbow into my side.

"You okay?"

"I swear I'm okay with it. There has never been anything between Ty and me." I grab my straw and take a big gulp, sighing happily when the liquid slithers down my throat.

"Evie," Mason's voice is quiet. Gentle. "I'm talking about what happened last week. Not just the piano and meltdown situation, but also everything going on with Phoenix." He shoots a glance in Holden's direction and leans in closer. "He isn't forcing you to do things, is he?"

My eyes widen to unnatural saucers as I simultaneously choke on my drink. My panicked gaze skips to Holden, who's about to get up, probably to check on me, but I wave him off, and he sits back down.

Mason rubs my back until the worst of the coughs have finally subsided. "Sorry about that."

We've been inseparable since the three of us met in middle school, and they've been my rock every moment of these last few fucked-up years, at least for the parts I was able to share with them. I've leaned on them, and they pulled me out of my darkness more times than I could count, especially when no one and nothing else could get through to me during my panic attacks.

Just like Phoenix did last week.

Phoenix cared for me, and if I didn't know better, I'd say he was worried. My mind must have played tricks on me, though, because could Phoenix really ever be concerned about me?

"Evie?" Ruby's voice cuts through my thoughts.

Mason's question pops back to the forefront.

I shake my head so violently, little pins of pain prickle at my temples. "No, never."

Mason levels me with a serious look. "If he lays a finger on you against your will, we'll find a way to off him, and all go into witness protection together."

I huff a quiet laugh and throw my hands around Mason. "Thank you for caring. It means more than I could ever tell you."

He squeezes tight. "Always, Evie. Always."

"Hey, don't forget about me." Ruby leans across the table.

We make room for her in our group hug.

My eyes burn. "Love you guys."

"Love you too." Ruby touches her forehead against my temple.

"Me three." Mason gives both of us another squeeze.

Eventually, we disentangle and sip our drinks as if we need a moment to collect ourselves. I know I do.

Ruby stirs the liquid in her cup. "Soooo, let's talk about that totally willing and unforced kiss."

Ah, yes, *that kiss.*

Heat warms my cheeks before I can rein in my reaction. And it's impossible to think about that kiss without remembering how amazing it felt.

It was exactly how I always thought kissing Phoenix Montgomery would feel.

Utterly addictive and spellbinding.

I lower my head and sigh. "You know it wasn't a real kiss."

Mason drapes his arm over the bench behind me. "Are you sure about that? Because I've watched the video of it several times, and it looked pretty real to me." He snorts. "I bet it was perfect. Because that man doesn't already have everything a guy could ever dream of, he must also have a wicked tongue."

Ruby bursts out laughing. "Careful, Romeo, your green witch is showing."

Mason points at her. "It's true, and you know it."

Ruby's still wearing a stupid grin. "I'm pretty sure having committed a felony and going to prison put a dent in his perfect Prince Charming façade."

Mason gapes at her with raised brows. "You can't be serious right now. The whole bad-boy image only makes it worse."

I shake my head at their antics until the bell at the entrance rings, drawing my attention to the front of the café.

My mouth goes dry when I see who just walked in.

Phoenix.

Phoenix in workout clothes.

His intense gaze immediately zeroes in on me.

What's that saying? Distance makes the heart grow fonder?

I'm sure that's not it, but not seeing him for a week after what transpired between us did something.

My heart does a little flip.

No, no. Bad heart.

He takes in our group, and I see his jaw flexing even from across the room.

Mason retracts his arm from behind me as if our contact burnt him. "Fuck."

"What is it?" I say absentmindedly, unable to tear my gaze away from Phoenix.

But Mason doesn't explain.

Phoenix ignores the female barista talking to him and walks across the room.

His presence is all-consuming, and I know I'm not the only one who feels it.

Ruby squeaks from across the table. "He has a nipple piercing? Someone hand me a fan."

My gaze lowers at her comment, and yup, the silver stud is easy to see under the thin shirt material.

Holden meets Phoenix halfway, breaking our connection. They talk for a moment before Holden heads toward the door.

I want to yell, "Hey, please don't leave me alone with the big bad wolf, he might eat me after all," after his retreating form, but my brain-to-vocal-cords connection doesn't seem to work correctly.

When Phoenix is only a few steps away, Mason scrambles out of the seat, rounds the table, and plops down next to Ruby.

Phoenix gives him a nod and says, "Douglas."

I'll never understand why guys call each other by their last names.

Ruby lifts her chin and says, "Hey, Phoenix. Long time no see." Her eyes go wide the second the words leave her lips.

"Well, I mean, I know I couldn't see you because you were gone. Prison and all. Oh shit . . . sorry." She buries her face in Mason's side.

Phoenix chuckles. "Good to see you, Ruby. Seems like you still like to put your foot in your mouth."

She tilts her head until we can see one of her eyes. Somehow, she manages to glare at him like that.

One corner of Phoenix's mouth twitches, and then he turns to me, finally giving me his attention.

Finally?

No, we don't want his attention. Maybe.

His gaze on me is like a soft caress on my skin.

It makes no sense, but I can't deny that's what it feels like.

He doesn't sit but leans closer, with one hand on the table and the other on the back of the booth. "Hey, fiancée."

Mason's words pop back into my head.

I bet the kiss was perfect.

My gaze drops to Phoenix's lips.

Because, yes, it was a perfect kiss. It was like that first breath you take after a summer rain, when the sun warms your face, and you close your eyes, or when you slip into your bed after you wash your sheets: utter bliss and pure perfection.

For years, I was lying awake in bed, wondering what it would be like to kiss him.

Now I know.

And part of me wishes I could forget about it again.

Because how am I ever going to handle that information?

Especially knowing my sister tasted those lips too, that she had all of him.

It's a tidbit my brain forgets about on the regular.

That realization is like a cold shower to my mind, allowing me to break this weird connection between us. I pick up my drink and finish the rest of it.

"I'm taking you home." Phoenix's tone is clipped. "Let's go."

Home.

During my childhood, Connie was the only reason our mansion ever felt like a home to me. That was until she distanced herself from me in the months before her death. I knew something was up, but no matter what I tried, she wouldn't confide in me.

Until that one day.

"Angie, Phoenix and I are going to get married."

My hand goes to my chest, the phantom pain almost as potent as the day she told me the news. At first, I'd thought she was joking, but when she gave me that small, sad smile so similar to mine, I knew she was telling the truth.

They officially announced their engagement a week later, and my world was never the same. But she wasn't the only one I felt betrayed by. Phoenix never promised me anything, he was never officially mine, but that made no difference to my shattered heart.

With that old hurt and betrayal still thrumming in my veins, I grab my purse and spit out a "Fine."

I was hoping things would be different after this last week, but maybe the pain from the past is too strong that not even the happy nostalgia that continues to drag me into that old, warm cocoon is enough. Maybe that time of my life where my whole world was centered around Phoenix, my personal fantasy, where I would have given everything to be by his side for the rest of my life, will forever be just that: a fantasy.

Because he didn't want me.

He made his choice, and I'm making mine.

I agreed to marry him for practical purposes. Maybe this week was to show us we can work side by side and be civil, but nothing beyond that.

I say my goodbyes to Mason and Ruby, who are eyeing me warily.

I can't blame them. I'm giving myself whiplash.

Phoenix takes my hand, and after a quick glance at the healed skin on my palm, pulls me after him.

His skin is warm, his fingers firm against mine.

I stare at our intertwined hands, trying to keep from tripping over my feet.

It's just for show. You're engaged, remember?

"Evie."

Phoenix stops at the voice, and I almost bump into him.

Tyler runs around the glass case, holding a small brown paper bag with the café logo. "Your favorite cookie for the road?"

I try to disentangle my fingers from Phoenix's, but he's keeping a death grip on my hand.

Not knowing what else to do, I awkwardly attempt to face Tyler.

"You didn't have to, Ty."

He winks at me and hands me the bag. "It's nothing. I know how you can get without your sugar high."

A smile spreads across my face, genuine this time. "Thank you."

He returns my smile, then shifts his attention to Phoenix. "Hey, man, I heard you're back."

Phoenix lifts his chin, his eyes narrowing as he takes in Tyler. "Do I know you?"

I stare at Phoenix. "Seriously?"

He regards me and shrugs, oozing nonchalance.

I sigh. "Tyler went to school with me. You've seen him a gazillion times at the house and the pool parties."

Phoenix stiffens when I mention pool parties, but Tyler only chuckles.

He touches my arm. "Don't worry about it, Evie. It's all good. He was gone for a while, and we have no connection except you."

I huff, unable to hold back my irritation. I don't even know why I'm reacting like this. If Tyler says it's not a big deal, it shouldn't be to me either, but somehow it is.

Because if he doesn't remember Tyler, does that mean he doesn't remember other things either? Like the kiss we almost shared in the pool house? When he fractured my heart for the first time of many.

"Turn around, birthday girl, so I can give you your present."

He's so close, his breath ghosts over my neck.

"Lift your hair."

I barely manage to gather it because my hands are shaking so badly.

Something cool touches my collarbone, and I grasp it with my hand. "A compass?"

He walks around me and nods. "It's supposed to be a reminder to keep moving forward, to follow your dreams."

My breath leaves me in a whoosh.

I stare at him. "I love it, thank you."

He pulls me in for a hug, leaning down enough for his mouth to graze my ear and cheek.

"Happy birthday, Angel."

His lips move toward my cheek at the same time that I shiver, and his lips hit the corner of my mouth instead.

My gasp is loud, and Phoenix draws back.

"Fuck." He leans his forehead against mine and exhales harshly. "I'm sorry, but I can't. There's no place for someone like you in my life."

I ended up getting drunk and losing my virginity to Tyler that night.

Happy birthday to me.

CHAPTER 18

PHOENIX

My foot is heavy on the gas pedal on our way home.

The silence in the car is deafening, and with each passing moment, my grip on the steering wheel tightens.

Evangeline shifts around, one hand still holding that damn paper bag like her life depends on it, and I've never been so offended by a paper bag before. I'm two seconds away from tossing it out the window and reversing over it for good measure.

I glare at her when we stop at a light. "When you agreed to marry me, you agreed not to see other guys. I will not allow you to make a fool of me in public. Was that not clear?"

She doesn't say anything.

"Eve, I'm talking to you. If I ask you a question, I expect a response."

My tone is as cold as ice, but I can't help myself. When it comes to this woman, I feel like someone grabbed me by the arms, pushed me into the vortex of a tornado, and yelled after me, "Good luck finding your way around in there, buddy." An absolute clusterfuck. And while I usually pride myself on my control, I must admit it's mostly absent where Evangeline is concerned.

A week ago, I kissed her like she truly belonged to me and held her in my arms a few hours later, worried sick after I found her in the music room amid a sea of broken glass. I watched over her all night, unable to close my eyes because I had to make sure she was okay.

I thought spending time away from her would clear my head and put things back into perspective. Despite the minor setback of obsessively watching her on the camera feeds, it did help some. Then we started texting more, and I got to know another facet of her. The urge to race back to the house grew, so I stayed away longer than planned. Now, we're at a point where one minute in her presence, one guy looking at her, touching her, tips me over the edge and all bets are off.

No one touches what's mine.

I want to strangle every guy who even glances in her direction. When Holden sent me pictures of her cozying up with Mason, I cut my workout session short and drove here like the Devil was after me.

And, of course, she acts like it's not a big deal. That only makes me want to punish her.

Maybe it's time to teach her a lesson and make use of my threat.

"Evangeline." My voice comes out low, my anger barely disguised.

She sighs like I'm the one who did something wrong.

No matter how much she fights me, she's mine, and the sooner she understands that, the better.

"Yes, Phoenix, I got it." She couldn't have put more attitude into that sentence had she tried.

"Were you trying to get my attention then today, is that it?" I keep my gaze on the road, but I can still see her in my periphery.

Her head snaps my way, her body turning. "What the hell are you talking about?"

The roads start to wind along the tree lines, and I ease my foot off the gas.

I exhale through my nose, probably sounding like an angry bull. "I can't tell if you're playing stupid right now or if you're just completely oblivious."

She holds up her index finger. "Number one, don't talk to me like that." She adds another finger. "And number two, I genuinely have no clue what the hell you're talking about."

I glance at her with narrowed eyes but can't detect a lie on her face. "I'm talking about how you allow guys to fawn over you in public. I was in the café less than five minutes, and you let two men touch you. Anyone could have walked in there and taken a photo or video of you to post it online. And you're not even wearing your ring."

"It's still new, so I forgot it when I got ready, okay? And no one was fawning over me."

"Eve, you were snuggled against Mason's chest. Any closer, and you would have sat on his lap." The words taste like acid on my tongue, and I take a deep breath. "And don't get me started on how that barista was drooling after you. He still has the same stars in his eyes when he sees you as he did back then."

This time, she points her fingers at me. "So you *do* remember him."

I shrug.

"You're such an asshole. Who pretends not to know someone just to fuck with their head? Unbelievable." She shakes her head and turns away from me.

"Careful, Angel. I've given you a warning before. That mouth will get you in trouble. Keep talking to me like that if you want that ass spanking."

She gasps. "You wouldn't."

I slow down as we near the security gate and glance at her. "Do you know me at all?"

She stares at me for a moment before focusing on her lap. "I once thought I did."

The words are so quiet I almost think I imagined them, but she did say them, hitting me right behind my rib cage.

I stop at the security gate and roll down my window while we wait for the metal gates to swing open.

"Sir." Mike nods at me and peeks into the car, a huge smile spreading when he sees who's in the passenger seat. "Miss Caldwell. How are you today? Are you feeling better?"

Evangeline leans across the middle console and lifts a hand in a wave. "Hey, Mike. A lot better, yes, thank you. How are the kids? Better too?"

I press my lips together, trying to understand what's happening. Mike's kids? I think he has a son and a daughter, but why is Evangeline asking about their well-being?

Like a smitten puppy, Mike nods at her. "They finally seem over the worst, thank God."

She gives him a wide smile. A genuine smile. The same smile she used to give me.

"I'm so glad to hear that."

"Me too," Mike says. "Does your offer still stand?"

She nods. "Absolutely. You have my number. Just give me a call."

He touches the brim of his hat and pulls on it. "Will do, thanks."

"Of course."

His gaze moves to me as if he remembered I'm still here too.

Me.

His fucking boss.

He swallows and dips his head. "Sir. You have a lovely fiancée."

I stare at him before I narrow my gaze at said fiancée. She's still draped over the middle console. So close. Close enough for me to see the golden flecks in her eyes. Close enough for me to get a whiff of her floral perfume.

"I do, don't I?"

My cock gives a little twitch, even more so when my gaze goes lower and lands on those lush lips of hers.

Was it only last week when I devoured them?

When I wanted to devour so much more than just her soft mouth?

My gaze roams upward, catching Evangeline glancing at my mouth the same way I imagine I just stared at hers.

Then our gazes meet, and whatever spell we were just under is broken.

She clears her throat and says, "Have a lovely day, Mike," before returning to her seat.

"You too." Mike steps back.

I let the car roar, and we drive through the gate, up the driveway to the house.

My house.

It's pretentious and way too big for me, but my grandfather wanted me to have it. And somehow, it feels a lot more like a home now with Holden and Evangeline in it.

"You have my number. Just give me a call."

My mind circles back over our conversation with my security guard until we drive into the garage. My skin feels too tight.

I kill the engine but keep my focus on the front of the car, not trusting myself to look at Evangeline yet. No one else winds me up the way she does.

My breath escapes out of my nose in an angry swoosh. "Why the fuck does my security guard have your phone number?"

Evangeline lifts her hand toward the door.

Of course, she'd rather run from me than answer a damn question.

I click the lock button on my door console.

"Phoenix." There's that bite again in her voice. "Open the door."

"Not until you answer my question."

She sighs and settles back in her seat. "I don't have to answer all of your questions, okay? Yes, I agreed to marry you, but I'm not your property to do whatever you want with."

But that's where she's wrong.

She might not be my property, but she owes me.

Owes me.

I don't reply; I react.

I push the unlock button, the click loud in the otherwise quiet car, and she immediately grabs the door handle to yank it open.

Then she runs.

A laugh escapes me. "You can run all you want, Angel, but I'll always find you."

She races through the mudroom, across the foyer, and up the stairs.

Once she reaches the top landing, I catch up with her, grab her hand, and drag her in the opposite direction of her room.

"What are you doing?" She tries to yank her hand out of mine. "Phoenix. Let me go."

I ignore her and drag her straight to my office.

Holden sits behind the desk when I burst in and regards us with a confused expression. Once he sees me with my cargo in tow, it quickly turns into amusement.

"Out." I keep my voice restrained with him, barely.

He walks toward the door with a slight shake to his head.

"Hold, help me." Evangeline yanks and wiggles behind me, using her other hand to aid her attempted escape.

Holden lifts his hands and inches toward the door. "Sorry, Princess, but this is between you two."

She huffs at the obvious laughter in his tone before turning her attention back to me once the door clicks shut.

"Phoenix, I swear. If you don't let me go, I will knee you in the balls."

I spin her around so her back is to my front.

Which I realize too late is a big mistake because now my cock is pressed against her backside.

"There's that smart mouth again, Angel. I've warned you."

"Wh-what?" She stiffens in my hold.

I brush all of her hair to one side and run my nose up the delicate curve of her shoulder.

The slight noise she lets out at the contact makes me rock-hard.

"I told you there'd be consequences."

"What kind of consequences?" All the defiance has left her voice.

I trail my lips up her throat to her ear. "The good kind."

All week long she's infiltrated my brain to the point that it was an image of her that appeared in my head when I was stroking my cock in the shower a few days ago. I came harder than I have in years, and I hate it. Now I can't get myself off without thinking about her and what it would feel like to sink deep into her pussy, to make her take my cock to the hilt and moan my name.

And she has to pay for driving me crazy. For making me think of her. For making me want things from her that aren't part of my plan.

I take her earlobe between my teeth, and she shivers in my arms. When she moves this time, it's not to struggle but to get closer.

She whimpers, and the last of my self-control evaporates.

Before she can react, I walk us back to the big armchair by the window. I sink onto the cool leather and pull her with me, flipping her onto her stomach so she lands on my lap.

Her surprised gasp echoes around the room, and she immediately goes back to struggling. I put one arm on her back to keep her in place.

"Let me go."

But my hold is solid. I brush my other hand down her spine and toward that delectable ass of hers. Kneading one cheek several times over her leggings. Repeating the motion on the other side.

Evangeline is still wiggling underneath my touch, trying to get closer.

"Phoenix?"

My name leaves her mouth as a question. I turn my attention away from her lower half and find her facing me. She's staring at me with her plush lips slightly parted and a rosy flush in her cheeks.

"Shh. I'll be gentle this time." I give her no time to react, grabbing the hem of her leggings and yanking them down. I catch a glimpse of her black thong, but not wanting to waste any time, I bring my hand down on her bare skin with a resounding *smack*.

My gaze is fixated on her, unwilling to miss a second of her reaction. The breathy gasp, the widening of her eyes before she squeezes them closed, the moment she pulls her lower lip into her mouth.

I smooth my hand over her soft skin. For an instant, I savor the contact, then I lift my hand again and let it connect with the other side.

Smack.

Evangeline moans, shifting on my hard cock to the point of discomfort.

Wasn't this supposed to be a consequence for *her*? Right now, it feels like I drew the shorter straw.

Once more, I rub over the red spot, my heart speeding up because I left a mark on her.

"Three more." My voice is low and gravelly, and I clear my throat.

Smack.

Smack.

Every gasp turns into a moan.

I caress her cheeks in circles that become bigger and bigger until my fingers graze the edge of her thong, and her reaction is immediate. Evangeline practically bows under my hold in a desperate attempt for more.

"Last one."

CHAPTER 19

EVANGELINE

This must be some alternate reality because there's no way I'm half-naked on Phoenix's lap and getting spanked by him.

His fingers run over my thong again, and I squirm, trying to . . . I don't even know, do something. But every little contact, every brush of his fingers on my skin is like . . .

Smack.

His hand lands on my ass cheek, the same one he started with, and holy shit.

Like every other blow, this one zaps through my body. It's an electric current with one destination in mind. My clit. And boy, does it deliver.

A moan slips through my lips, regardless of how hard I try to keep it in.

Apparently, my self-control and dignity flew out the window the second this man laid a finger on me, especially once I felt him hard behind me. And I'm not going to lie, it feels good to know how affected he is by this too.

"Look at those perfect pink ass cheeks. You did so well." Phoenix's voice sounds strained.

I revel in the sound of it.

His praise is like an aphrodisiac that instantly adds to the desire low in my stomach.

He goes back to massaging my sensitive skin, and I let him.

But that's not all, nope.

I also arch my back and shift around, my body spurring me on to chase this addictive feeling of having his large hands on me.

You've been craving his touch for so long, always wondering what it feels like, and now you know. Is it everything you thought it would be?

Phoenix skims over the fabric again, and all of my thoughts fly out the window.

His cock pulses, and a whimper escapes me.

"Those little noises you make will be the end of me." His ministrations continue.

He shifts around in the chair, pushing his cock harder against my stomach.

I'm worried this overwhelming desire will burn me alive. "Phoenix, please."

The word comes out so quietly, I question for a moment if I said it out loud.

Phoenix's hand stills. "Please, what?"

Reality hauls me back for a second, but it's gone again with his continued movements. Why does his touch feel so good? His fingers brush along the seam of my panties, and I press my eyelids together.

No matter how displaced or wrong this moment of intimacy is, I can't remember the last time I was this turned on.

His fingers are so close to where I need him, and I hum my displeasure at being teased.

He chuckles. "What do you want, Angel?"

"Touch me." With that admission out in the open, the ball is in his court, and my gut twists with a bout of nerves.

What if I read this entire situation wrong? But no, he's clearly turned on. Just like he was last week when he dragged me in here.

His finger brushes the seam of my panties again, and I jolt. This time, his fingers glide over the fabric. I forget how to breathe, my entire body tense when he reaches the spot right over my center.

His groan sounds tortured. "Fuck. You're soaked."

For a moment, I'm so worried he will stop I don't dare move, biting the inside of my cheek to stay quiet.

That lasts for about two seconds. Then his fingers slide the fabric aside, and all that remains is the pulsing need in my core.

"Look at that pretty pink pussy and how it's dripping for me."

He drags his entire hand over my exposed skin, and my nerve endings explode everywhere. My skin tingles, my clit throbs, and I'm pushing my butt up as much as I can in my position, chasing his touch.

Without warning or preamble, he plunges two fingers inside me. "Fuck, you're tight."

I moan. It's so loud, I should probably be embarrassed, but I don't have the brain power to focus on anything other than Phoenix's fingers slowly pumping in and out of me.

I'm sure I'll have plenty of time to overanalyze and regret every part of this later, but right now, all that matters is the euphoric sensation that buzzes low in my stomach.

After working me up, he removes his fingers and spreads the wetness all the way up to my clit.

The first touch on it has me bucking, needing more.

More pressure, more speed, more fingers filling me up. *Him* filling me up.

He rubs my clit so hard, I know I'll feel it tomorrow, but it's perfect. And Phoenix knows that too since there isn't a second where I don't make some kind of desperate sound.

"Come for me, Angel. Soak my fingers."

He switches back and forth between plunging his fingers deep inside me and circling them around my clit, until the familiar warm buzz spreads in my lower body, and I fall over the edge.

"Oh my God." My muscles clench around his fingers, my thighs squeezing together. Wave after wave consumes me. I gasp for air and ride out one of the best orgasms of my life.

Another thing to psychoanalyze later on.

All I can do for now is lie limply on his lap while his rock-hard dick is still digging into my stomach.

Phoenix withdraws his fingers, and I hiss at the slight burning sensation.

I glance at him, finding his gaze already on me. My heart skips a beat when I see the lust and fire in his dark eyes. That look alone would do the trick if I wasn't already drenched.

He lifts his hand to his mouth and puts his index and middle finger between his parted lips, licking off every single drop he wrung from my body. Unable to tear my gaze away from him, I watch in absolute fascination.

My mouth mimics his before I swallow.

He closes his eyes and groans as if he's savoring my taste. "Even better than I thought you'd taste."

He thought about how I tasted?

My core comes back to life. Apparently, this man has a direct line to it, and I'm not sure how to feel about that. All I know is this stolen moment with him was miles better than anything my wildest imagination has ever conjured during the countless times I've pictured us together.

The fact that Phoenix and I seem so compatible goes straight on the list of cruel jokes life has played on me.

My sister.

Prison.

Their unborn baby.

The lust fog in my mind clears, and reality hits me like a hot knife straight to my heart. My eyes burn, the intensity almost unbearable.

Now that Phoenix isn't holding me down anymore, I push myself off the chair to stand there awkwardly while I try to tug up my underwear and leggings without falling over.

Phoenix studies me openly, something he does often and never hides. He's probably always waiting for me to stab him in the back again.

The words "I'm sorry" want to rise to the top of my throat, but I swallow them. The same way I do every single time. Because what am I going to say to him? Sorry I didn't tell you some psychopath forced me to put you in prison? Or sorry, I got my sister killed and didn't want anyone else to die, so you had to go away instead?

It might be the truth, but it sounds far from it.

And he lost so much because of me. Not just three years of his life while he was behind bars, but he also lost part of his reputation and good standing in the community, and his family and their company also suffered.

I swallow back the rising bile in my throat. No punishment will ever be big enough to compensate for the destruction I've brought to so many lives, despite how much I wish there was.

His silent perusal of me makes everything ten times worse because I know he wants me to trip up and spill my deepest, darkest secrets to him. And I don't blame him. Of course he'd like to know why I put him in prison. We were friends, and I was almost his sister-in-law. I once thought we could have something good together. A future even. We never crossed that line, but we got along. We liked each other —a lot.

His phone beeps, and he takes it out of his pocket. "Jo will be here in an hour. Go get cleaned up."

While his voice is gentle, it's still a dismissal, and I take it, rushing out of the room without another glance or word.

Jo CHUCKLES and puts her bags on the table. "It seems like our work last week did the trick. I blushed a little when I saw the video of you guys. That was one hell of a kiss."

I clear my throat, trying not to choke on my spit. "Uh, yeah. That might have been a bit too much for the public."

She pauses with the curling iron halfway out of her bag to look at me. "If anyone ever ravished me the way Phoenix ravished you, someone would probably have to pry my hands off him. That was the kind of kiss you only read about in romance novels. So hot."

I avert my gaze, hoping she takes it as a form of being flustered and not for what it really is: a silent admission to being a screwed-up masochist because, damn it, I liked how he ravished me too.

And the way he made you come just an hour ago when he bent you over his knee and spanked you.

I should hate every single one of his touches, absolutely loathe them.

But I can't.

Instead, my thoughts have been jumping back and forth between memories of how good he made me feel, self-loathing over what we did, guilt because he was my sister's fiancé, and how there's no way to reconcile all of those things. No matter how hard I try, it's impossible to fit all of them into one box.

Is there something like a multiple feelings disorder? I should really talk to a professional about this.

While Jo is still busy setting up her things, I distract myself by eating some of the cheese and grapes Huxley brought up. The food practically melts on my tongue, and I let out a little sigh. There's nothing food can't make better. At least, that's what I like to tell myself.

Jo straightens up once she's done and points at the open garment bag I draped over the edge of the bed. "Are we going all dark era tonight with your dress? It's magnificent. All eyes will be on you in that sexy number, that's for sure."

The black dress is beautiful with its gathered fabric at the bodice and neckline, the floor-sweeping hem, small train, and the leg slit almost up to the hip.

With the media frenzy still at an all-time high, I wish I wouldn't draw much attention tonight.

I'd much rather curl up in a corner somewhere and hide from my life. Hide from Phoenix, my societal responsibilities, my lies and betrayal, and my past. From everything really at this point. What I wouldn't give to dive into a fantasy world with a good book where I live someone else's life for a while and forget my own.

Yet, here I am.

"Ready?" Jo points at the seat.

I shuffle toward it and sit. "Let's do this."

She starts with my hair, turning it into soft waves pinned into a half updo. My makeup is next, with dramatic eyes and red lips. It's a classic style that never gets old.

Either Jo isn't in the mood to chitchat tonight, or she's reading my vibes spot-on.

I let her work in silence, and she helps me into my dress once she's finished.

Her smile is genuine. "Absolutely stunning."

"Thank you, Jo."

She grabs her bag and watches me put on my earrings. "Have fun tonight, okay? I'll see you next week."

I chuckle. "I'll try my best. Thanks."

She winks at me and wheels her trolley out the door.

I take a moment and glance at the engagement ring on my finger, at its absolute beauty, trying hard to forget this ring is undoubtedly the most beautiful and thoughtful gift anyone's ever given me. Of course, it had to come from Phoenix.

With a sigh, I gather my clutch and phone and leave.

The hallway is empty when I walk toward the staircase and slowly down in my heels.

The front door opens, and Holden slips inside. He immediately spots me and whistles like the charmer he is. The noise echoes around the high ceilings of the foyer, and I shake my head at his behavior.

"You look beautiful, Princess."

I smile back at him. "Thank you."

He points a thumb behind him toward the front door. "Phoenix is already outside. He was helping me find something, but we didn't have any luck. I'll go check in my office quickly. Be right back."

I watch him head toward the hallway to the right. The instant I step off the bottom step, my phone vibrates in my hand. I continue and unlock my screen to check the message.

My gaze immediately zeroes in on the name.

Freddy.

The phone shakes in my hand as my brain is trying to make sense of the words on the screen.

FREDDY

What a shame to have that beautiful black car blown to pieces in a minute. Your fiancé could be gone alongside it, solving all of your problems at once. Decisions, decisions. Tick-tock, pet.

Blown to pieces.

Blown to pieces.

Fiancé gone.

Oh my God.

"Phoenix. No, no, no." My voice reaches ear-piercing levels, and I sprint to the door as fast as possible.

"Phoenix."

I yank the door open, half aware of Holden shouting something behind me. I don't want him anywhere near this right now, but I don't have the time to explain things or to tell him to stay away.

"Phoenix. Bomb," I yell through the gap in the door, the hardwood of it pressing against my shoulder as I push through the narrow space before it's fully open.

Stupid heavy door.

"Phoenix." My voice is so shrill it's almost unrecognizable.

But it has the desired effect, and Phoenix glances up at me with a frown from where he stands right next to his black car.

No, no, please don't.

"Car bomb. Ruuuuuuuuuun."

His eyes go wide, and then he's finally moving.

But instead of running away, he's running toward me.

No, what is he doing?

"Fucking run, Angel."

We collide, and Phoenix grabs me by the waist, hurrying away from the car.

Mere seconds later, an ear-deafening noise sounds behind us, and a blast of heat and pressure hits us.

CHAPTER 20

PHOENIX

The pressure hitting my back is too forceful to withstand, and I fly forward with only one goal: to cover Evangeline from the blast.

I have to keep her safe. I have to keep her safe.

Nothing can happen to her.

She's mine.

I can't lose her too.

Heat sears my back, and for a brief moment, everything goes completely silent in my ears before the muffled sound of a blaring car alarm slowly filters in again and absolute chaos breaks out around me.

With some effort, I push myself up enough that I don't crush Evangeline.

Holden drops to the ground next to us. "Are you guys okay?"

But I can't look at him. I can only look at *her*. At her life-less body pinned to the ground underneath me. At the slick blood on my hands when I touch the back of her head.

"Hold." I say his name, my voice breaking. "Why isn't she

moving?"

I stare at him through blurry eyes, a fresh round of panic and devastation gripping my throat so tightly it feels like someone's choking me. The amount of oxygen squeezing past the restriction is so minuscule that small spots form in my vision.

Eve groans, and Holden all but pushes me off her.

"Phoenix, move. Let me check on her. The ambulance will be here soon." He sends me a concerned glance. "She's going to be okay. The team is securing the premises as we speak, so stay right here."

I nod and grab her hand, not letting go as I watch Holden check her breathing and pulse.

"Her pulse is strong." He points at her chest. "Her breathing too. You probably just knocked the wind out of her for a second."

Eve's hand twitches in my own. She gives it a little squeeze, and I hold on to it like it's my lifeline.

Footsteps rush toward us, and Holden aims his gun at the approaching person.

Niko, one of our security guards, holds up his hands, his face remaining calm. "The ambulance is only a mile away. The fire truck has an ETA of six minutes."

"Thanks." Holden lowers his gun and nods at him. "I want you to call Detective O'Neal. Tell him what happened and to meet me at the hospital."

"Yes, sir." He nods at both of us and runs off.

"Phoenix?"

My name on Eve's lips is almost drowned out by the noise around us and the approaching sirens in the distance, but I hear it nonetheless.

I touch the side of her face, accidentally smearing some of the blood from my hand to her cheek. "Please don't move."

"Phoenix?" She repeats my name and slowly blinks her eyes open. "My head."

"I know, Angel." I press a kiss to the back of her hand. "You hit your head, but you're okay. We'll get you to the hospital."

As if on cue, the ambulance races up the driveway, several EMTs jumping out when it comes to a stop. They hurry over to us with a gurney, and I reluctantly let go of Eve's hand to give them the room they need. Once she's safely in the back of the vehicle, I'm back by her side, and I don't let go of her once while we rush to the hospital.

"Why the fuck is it taking them so long?" I pace back and forth in front of the door.

They took Evangeline and told me I had to wait here.

If it wasn't for Holden restraining me, I might have punched someone. I definitely wanted to.

Holden is a few feet away with his phone to his ear, talking to our guys and whoever else is helping us figure out this mess.

The door opens, and an older nurse strides toward me. "Sir, you're injured. We need to get you to an exam room to check you out."

I narrow my eyes at her. "I'm not going anywhere until I've seen my wife."

She doesn't flinch at my tone or react to my lie. She just sighs as if I'm nothing more than an inconvenience, which I probably am to her. "Let me get you something for your wound, at least. You're bleeding all over my floor."

"Fine," I growl at her.

A moment later, she's back and presses a thick gauze pad in my hand before guiding it to my forehead. "Keep pressure on it."

I huff, and she must take that as confirmation enough to walk away, muttering something that sounds like "stubborn men."

Holden lowers his phone and joins me. "She's going to be okay."

I close my eyes and take a deep breath. "Fuuuuuu-uuuuuck."

The nurse shoots me a dirty look from her station, but I ignore her and focus on Holden. "Any news?"

He shakes his head. "I called in the additional team like you wanted. They're going to help ensure the property is safe and go over the security tapes again." He pauses for a moment. "One of the guys saw a drone hovering nearby when the explosion happened, but that's it so far."

I clench my free hand into a fist at my side. "Someone was watching us get blown up?"

"Yup."

A bomb.

A motherfucking bomb.

On my car.

And they watched it all go down.

I take my hand off my face, and Holden presses it back on.

He makes his "don't be stupid" expression. "There's a big

chance it wasn't done at the house. I'm pretty sure it wasn't. Way too risky to get caught."

That was the same thought I had earlier, and I hate it. That makes finding the person who did this much harder, if not impossible. I'm unsure why anyone would want to blow me up anyway. Sure, I've made enemies over the years, probably more in prison, but to the level of murder? Via bomb, nonetheless? Plus, Eve was there too. She . . . she . . .

I stare at Holden and swallow. "She saved me."

"I know."

"She put me in prison, and then she saved me." A laugh bubbles out of my chest.

The corners of Holden's mouth lift. "I know."

I didn't know a smile could be that sad, that pitiful.

"How did she know?" A question that's been plaguing me over and over.

He lifts a shoulder and drops it again. "She was staring at her phone one second and yelled your name the next, then took off running. Her phone broke during the explosion, but I will try to access it when I get home and also check the mirrored phone. There's gotta be something."

Why does it feel like we're so close to figuring things out, yet so far away?

Before I can voice my thoughts, the door behind Holden opens, and the doctor steps out.

My feet move before I fully grasp his presence, and I stop right in front of him. It's probably too close, but it's better than grabbing him by his white doctor coat and shaking the info out of him, which is what I really want to do. I call that compromise.

He inclines his head. "Mr. Montgomery."

I swallow. Hard. "Is she okay?"

He nods. "Miss Caldwell hit her head pretty hard, but she was alert during the exam. She has a mild concussion, and the scans all looked good. No bleeding or anything else unusual, which is what we want. Most cuts and wounds are superficial, but I'm sure she'll feel them for a while. She was lucky."

The breath that leaves my body nearly brings me to my knees. A strong hand wraps around my elbow, and I glance at Holden's equally relieved face.

I focus back on the doctor. "Can I see her?"

"We gave her some medication to rest, so she'll be out for a while." He points at my face. "You need to get checked."

"I won't leave this spot until I've seen her."

I'm ready to get in his face, doing whatever it takes, when he averts his gaze to Holden then back to me.

He lets out a defeated sigh, probably realizing it's not worth the fight, and lifts his index finger in the air. "You have one minute, and then you'll get checked out." He glances around me toward the nurses' desk and murmurs, "And don't touch anything."

I narrow my eyes at him but nod reluctantly. "Fine. Thanks, Doc."

"Let's go."

I follow him through the double doors and down two different corridors before stepping through the door he opens. A single bed occupies the room, and Evangeline is almost hidden under the blankets. Cables run from her hand and arm to the monitors beside her. My heart slows at hearing her rhythmic heartbeat, at seeing she's really okay.

Her skin is paler than usual, her body tiny in the large

bed, but she's here and breathing.

I step forward, wanting to get closer, but the doctor stops me with his hand. "Let her get some rest and take care of you in the meantime."

He walks me back through the double doors. "Let me know if you have any concerns or questions. I'll get someone for you." Then he heads straight for the nurses' desk.

Holden's in the same spot I left him. "Is she all right?"

I brush a hand over my face and nod. "Seems like it."

"Good." He regards the approaching nurse and juts his chin toward me. "I'll stay here until you're back in case anything happens. Get that nasty cut checked."

I don't tell him I have other places that also need attention. When the bomb exploded, I was able to spin us at the last second, which left me to take the brunt of the blast with my back. I wish there had been enough time to keep her head from hitting the ground when we landed, but I'll never regret using my body as a shield—just like she was trying to do when she launched herself at me a few seconds before the explosion went off.

Evangeline tried to save me.

Me.

The man she put in prison.

My head is spinning, trying once more to fit the puzzle pieces together that so blatantly don't want to fit.

From the looks of it, they keep getting more mismatched.

The nurse takes me to an exam room where she asks me a bunch of questions I mostly answer with a grunt. She eventually takes the hint and leaves me alone to change into the hospital gown she handed me.

For a moment, I consider ignoring her instructions, but

the unpleasant bite on my back changes my mind. I've only managed to remove my suit coat—or rather, what's left of it —when there's a knock at the door.

A man pokes his head in, gives me a once-over, and says, "Sorry, I thought you had already changed. I'll come back in a few minutes."

"Stay." I start unbuttoning my shirt.

"Are you sure?" The doctor sends me a pitiful look when I try to peel the shirt off and flinch.

I nod, and he steps inside. He seems young and might only be a few years out of medical school.

"Let me help." He puts his clipboard down, washes his hands, and puts on gloves.

We get the shirt off together, and the doctor curses under his breath at my exposed skin.

"I take it your back took the brunt of the explosion?"

I push a "Yeah" through clenched teeth and try not to cringe. But to no avail. He probes a skin patch, and searing pain slices across my shoulder blade where some shrapnel from the car must have cut me.

"That one will need stitches. Thankfully, most of the wounds aren't deep, and the burns appear to be first- and second-degree. You got really lucky." He scrutinizes the damage for several minutes, occasionally prodding at my skin, before he walks to the cabinets. "I need to clean your entire back first to see what needs sutures, but let's start with your face."

Several stitches and butterfly bandages later, I'm putting on the shirt Holden gave me. I think he said he had a change of clothes in the car he followed us with. Since it's Holden's, it's too big on me, but I don't even care. Nothing can keep me from going to Evangeline now that I'm all patched up and green-lighted to see her for more than just a glance.

Sometime during my exam, they brought her to another level. I catch up with Holden and what happened with the detective, then finally step past two of our security guards into Evangeline's room.

I step up to her bed and take her in, noticing all the things I couldn't see earlier from afar. The bandage wrapped around her head, the red gash at the corner of her lip, the streaks of dirt across her nose and temples. My fingers twitch, my hand halfway in the air, wanting to touch her, brush away the dirt, and make the wounds disappear.

But I stop and pull back, forcing myself to move away from the bed and to sit in the chair by the window instead.

Although I want to see those gorgeous brown eyes so badly, she needs her sleep more.

Later, I will get my answers.

Because Evangeline has secrets.

Possibly lots of them.

And she's going to tell me every single one.

My phone buzzes in my pocket, reminding me I still have a text message waiting from earlier.

CANARY

What a wasted opportunity to make her pay for what she did to you. It seems like the tables have turned.

I read the message several times, a sense of dread pooling heavily in my stomach.

We thought the bomb was supposed to be for me.

But was it actually for Evangeline?

CHAPTER 21

EVANGELINE

My mouth and throat are as dry as the desert, my lips cracked, and I wince at the sting in the corner of my mouth. The movement is minuscule at best, but it's enough to take the atrocious pounding in my head to another level. I squeeze my eyelids together even tighter.

The hammering is so intense, I can barely think past it.

And why am I so dang hot?

A bead of sweat runs down my nape, and I lift my hand to wipe it away while trying to pry my heavy eyelids open. They feel like they weigh fifty pounds each, and I settle on opening one eyelid halfway to start. It's probably better for my headache anyway.

My hand pauses halfway in the air. Not just because something is painfully tugging at it but also because of the sight in front of me.

It's Phoenix. *Phoenix.* He's sleeping only a few inches away from me.

My heart kicks into overdrive, forcing my brain to push the memories past the wall of pain.

Me on Phoenix's lap in his office. Getting ready for another gala event with my fiancé. The text message. The car bomb.

A sob breaks through my throat, scratching the walls along the way.

Phoenix's eyes fly open in alarm.

"You're okay." The words rush out of my mouth, followed by another sob.

"Shh, baby." Phoenix cradles my face, his thumb caressing my cheek in soothing strokes.

I sink into his touch and move toward him. I need more. He closes the distance between us when he sees I'm struggling and gently wraps his arm around me.

More sobs rack my body as I try to understand what happened and that we're both here. Both alive, both well. At least as well as anyone can be after an explosion went off mere feet away from them.

I bury my face in his chest and shut my eyes, letting all the emotions run their course while he holds me. And he lets me, rubbing soothing circles across my back, murmuring something I can't quite make out.

Despite everything that happened, I feel safe in this cocoon.

He saved you.

Memories of me running out of the house rush through my head, yelling at Phoenix, wanting him to run. Did I push him? Did I throw myself at him? I'm trying to remember, but my brain is fuzzy.

He grabbed me and ran until the explosion went off.

The explosion.

A real bomb.

Freddy.

He tried to kill Phoenix and almost killed both of us.

"Hold?" The name is a croak, but it must be enough.

Something soft presses against my forehead, like Phoenix just kissed it.

For some reason, that has more tears gathering in my eyes.

"He was still far enough behind you when the explosion went off. He's irritated he couldn't save anyone but unharmed."

"Thank God." I release a loud breath, my chest lighter at that knowledge.

I don't want to be responsible for anyone else getting hurt.

I can't be.

Too late for that, considering where you're at, isn't it?

I take in Phoenix again, this time more properly. There's a bandage on his forehead.

"You got hurt." It's not a question but a statement.

Unsurprisingly, he shrugs. "Just a few scratches."

I lift my hand toward his face, wanting to make sure he's okay, even though I know touching his face won't make a difference. But I don't get far, the stinging pain near my wrist returning, and I glare at the IV.

His eyebrows draw together at my wince. "Please don't. You're already hurt enough after what you did."

After what I did.

When I got the text message, I acted without thinking about the possible consequences. All I could think about was saving Phoenix. Nothing else mattered. But now, there's this enormous elephant in the room with us.

I close my eyes, shutting out the questions in his. I'm sure he has lots of them. And at the moment, I don't see a way out for myself. What plausible excuse could I have for knowing about the bomb without telling him the truth? Without telling him about the messages? About Freddy?

Sure, I could say nothing, but he wouldn't believe me. I think he's already suspicious about my nine-one-one call as it is. Now this? He won't leave it alone until I tell him.

Do you want to tell him?

This whole situation with Freddy has been eating at my soul for years, slowly disintegrating me from the inside out.

Message by message.

Terrible thing by terrible thing.

Phoenix's warm hand moves over my cheek and down my throat to rest on my pulse point there. His touch is a soothing balm to my soul and the only thing that keeps me tethered to this world.

His breathing is uneven, and I open my eyes at his next harsh exhale.

I almost wish I hadn't.

The expression in his eyes twists something in my stomach. It's raw and laced with emotions I'm not sure I've ever seen in him. Or anyone else, really. A vulnerability that feels like a knife to my sternum, ready to cut me wide open. For a moment, I imagine baring myself to him, letting him see all of the darkness and ugliness inside me. I can't help but wonder what would be worse: if he rejected me because it's so abhorrent or if he didn't.

And isn't that my answer right there? Because yes, deep down, I want to tell him. I want to tell him everything.

"Why did you do it?" He swallows. "Why did you save me?"

The question comes out quiet and shaky, a total contradiction to the unspoken words floating around us. They're *his* unspoken words, loud and stifling, trying to wrap a noose around my throat.

You could have let me die.

You could have escaped this life you so clearly don't want.

You could have gotten rid of your fiancé without lifting a finger.

You could have had the life you wanted.

Little does he know my life was already in shambles before he ever returned to it.

He isn't the detriment to my life he thinks he is, far from it.

And he didn't die.

Freddy didn't kill Phoenix like my sister.

Gripping his arm tightly, I tell him the truth. "I saved you because I don't want anything to happen to you."

"Angel." He says my nickname like a prayer, his voice shaky, pleading.

Then he leans in and presses his lips to mine. The barest touch. It's so tender it's almost too much.

My heart squeezes so tightly in my chest it steals my breath.

"I'm so sorry, Phoenix. I'm so sorry." The pain behind my rib cage is almost unbearable, the weight of this entire situation, of my life for the past few years, squeezing my soul mercilessly. "I want to tell you, I really do."

Phoenix pulls me back, and I relax in his warm embrace. With my head against his chest, I cry until I have no tears left.

SOFT MURMURS FILTER into my sleepy state, but the voice is still too far away to make out anything.

I swallow, immediately regretting it with my dry throat. The sound I make is something I'd imagine a dying frog makes.

"She's awake. I'll call you back."

The voice is louder now. Clear and urgent. Phoenix.

I squint at him through one eye, grateful when there's only a dull thrumming in my skull this time.

Phoenix leaves his spot by the window and makes his way toward me. "Sorry if I woke you up."

"Water," is all I manage to get out.

But he beats me to it, already holding a straw cup in his hand.

"Let me get you up first." He pushes a button on the side of the bed, and the upper half quietly whirrs up until I'm almost sitting.

When satisfied, he lets go of the button and lifts the cup to my mouth.

"Slowly. Just a few sips." His gaze is on my mouth as if he's ready to yank the cup away if I try to empty the whole thing in one go. "I already got a scolding from the nurse because I didn't get you any water earlier. Trust me, we don't want to get on her bad side any more than we already are."

One corner of his mouth ticks up, but it's more grimace than smile.

The water soothes the ache in my throat, and I keep drinking until Phoenix pulls it away with a chuckle. This time, it's genuine, and I automatically smile back as warmth spreads behind my rib cage.

There's a knock at the door before it opens, but my brain is still stuck on how Phoenix and I just smiled at each other.

Really smiled at each other.

Like we used to.

"I told you to let me know when she wakes up this time."

The firm voice drags my attention to the nurse walking toward me. She appears to be around my parents' age, but despite the sternness in her voice, she gives me a warm smile.

Her name tag says Cynthia.

"How are you feeling, sweetie?"

I take a moment to do a self-assessment. "Okay, I guess?"

She regards me. "Any pain?"

"I feel like half of my body is covered in bruises, but at least my head doesn't hurt as much as earlier."

She nods as if she suspected as much. "All in all, it sounds like you both got away fairly unscathed, considering the circumstances. Your head will likely hurt for a while, but your concussion is mild, so that's good. Rest and proper hydration are very important, especially in the next couple of days. It's pretty normal that physical activity, as well as any kind of screen time, reading, or listening to music can make symptoms worse, the same with loud sounds and bright lights. So let's avoid those for now. After two days, you can go back to light activities, but still keep it easy on the rest for the next week or two."

I process the information and nod. "So basically do nothing but sleep for the next two days?"

The machine next to the bed beeps, and she turns toward it with a chuckle to push a few buttons. "In a nutshell, yes. Rest, water, and healthy food. Then keep things easy and avoid anything that makes your symptoms worse."

She takes some notes and gives me a reassuring smile. "But your vitals are good, so hopefully your recovery will be on the short side. I'm going to let the doctor know you're awake."

"Thank you."

"Of course. I'll be back soon with more to drink and something to eat."

She leaves the room, and Phoenix comes to the bed.

"Hold is at the house. Is there anything you want him to bring?"

It's such a mundane question.

Do I need anything? Because I'm at the dang hospital.

When is someone stopping by to tell me all of this was just a dream? And in reality, I'm having a great time at college where I live a perfectly normal life with my friends and even have a boyfriend. Maybe Phoenix and I found our way to each other when we were younger, after all.

How utterly ridiculous and contradictory to how things actually played out.

"Eve?"

Phoenix's brows draw together. He looks me over, but instead of the anger or irritation I expect to see, it's worry.

He gives me a gentle smile. "It's okay if you don't need anything. Hopefully, you can go home tomorrow anyway."

"Sorry." I shake my head and wince at the pain. "My head is a little slow right now, but some comfy clothes would be nice. Something baggy?"

"Sure. I'll let him know."

"Thanks." I take a deep breath. "I . . . I'm still trying to process what happened. It feels so surreal."

He touches my fingertips with his at the edge of the bed. "Don't worry about any of this. I will find the bastard who did this and end him, and that's all you need to know right now while you rest."

I try to suppress a shiver, but it's pointless, and Phoenix pulls my blanket higher.

"Let me message Hold before I forget it."

He taps on his phone screen, and I stare at it, my heart beating wildly behind my rib cage.

Oh my God. I'm so stupid.

"Phoenix, where's my phone?" The first tendrils of panic slither through my body, and my breathing turns erratic. I stretch, glancing everywhere. "Shit, where is it? I . . . I need it."

Freddy.

What if he messaged again after the accident?

What if he did something to Ruby like he threatened so many times before?

And I'm here, completely clueless.

Phoenix's face appears right in front of mine, and his big hands cup my face. "Hey, shh. Eyes on me. Now take a deep breath. I've got you."

I nod, trying to match my breathing to his.

It takes the edge off my panic but doesn't entirely go away.

Phoenix sits on the edge of the mattress, taking both of my hands in his. "Your phone broke during the explosion, but Hold is working on transferring everything to a new one."

With my lips pressed together, I nod. "Okay, thank you."

He squeezes my hands. "Of course. Plus, you heard the nurse: no screen time for the next two days."

I chew on my lip, trying to come up with something to say that would make sense. "I know, I just need to check something quick and then I'll stay off it, promise."

He narrows his eyes at me but nods. "I already contacted your parents, and Hold said he'd let Ruby and Mason know what happened. I'll message them again to let them know you're okay but on a phone ban for the next two days, okay?"

I try to ignore the growing ball of worry in my chest and nod. "Thank you. I'm sure they're worried."

"Consider it done. I'll also get in touch with the school to figure out a plan for the next few weeks. I'm sure we can find a way to switch your classes online for the time being."

School wasn't even on my mind, but I'm glad he thought about it.

I whisper another, "Thank you," just as there's a knock at the door and it opens.

A tall man strolls in with a tablet in his hand. "Hey, I'm Dr. Chris. Good to see you awake, Miss Caldwell." He swings his gaze in Phoenix's direction. "How's your back? I told the nurses to give you some pain medicine if it's too much."

Phoenix sighs. "I'm fine."

The doctor lifts his hands in a calming gesture. "I just wanted you to know there are options."

Phoenix nods and turns toward me, and the doctor gets the cue.

I'm still stuck on how Phoenix's injuries seem bad enough for the doctor to think it warrants pain medicine, and the fact Phoenix didn't tell me about it.

"Now, to you, Miss Caldwell." He taps his tablet before peeking at the monitor next to me. "You suffered a mild concussion from the hit you took to the ground. The minor cuts should heal on their own, so no stitches for you. You will probably be sore for a while from the bruising. You both took the brunt with your backsides, one more than the other. Other than that, you're as good as new. And I'm happy you're still with us, both of you."

I try to smile at him, but my mouth doesn't want to work, no matter how much I try to tug it up in the corners.

I think it'll take some time to fully grasp I almost died.

The doctor goes over the dos and don'ts of treating a concussion again, but I only half listen. Eventually, he leaves, and the nurse returns with a small wagon in tow. I catch sight of a familiar black package next to the food tray. My body tenses immediately. It can't be.

Cynthia brings it over with a smile. "Someone had these flowers delivered for you."

CHAPTER 22

PHOENIX

Per hospital protocol, a nurse is accompanying us to the car, pushing Evangeline in a wheelchair next to me. Their snail's pace is testing every ounce of my self-control, and it takes all my willpower not to toss Evangeline over my shoulder and run to the waiting car with her.

My only goal is to get her safely into the car and away from the hospital as quickly as possible. To get her home and hide her away. Especially after someone sent her another bouquet of wilted roses. Eve's pretending it's not a big deal, but I can see right through it. Would she act the same if she knew I'm aware this wasn't the first one she got?

Better question yet, how would she act if she knew what Holden found on her mirrored phone?

We finally make it to the garage, where my best friend is already waiting for us next to a shiny new blacked-out SUV. I've never bought a vehicle as fast as I bought this one. When I was going to ask Holden to take care of it, he showed me three different models and told me to pick one.

There's no way in hell I would have any of us set foot in a vehicle that isn't the safest one out there, bombproof and all.

He sees us and steps forward.

Evangeline lets go of my hand, and I instantly miss the contact.

We're only a few feet away from the car, and the nurse stops. Evangeline takes that as a green light, gets up, and speed-walks to Holden.

The two of them embrace like long-lost friends, and even though I logically understand there's nothing between them, and we've all just gone through some trauma, I still don't like seeing her in another man's arms.

I huff an annoyed breath and shoot daggers in my best friend's direction.

Holden sees it and rolls his eyes, whispering something to Evangeline. He opens the car door for her, but she hesitates, staring at the car like she's never seen one before.

I step up behind her, shoving Holden out of the way. Not so subtly either.

Evangeline shoots me a glare over her shoulder but doesn't comment. Holden brought her one of my shirts and the smallest sweats he could find in my closet. I don't think that's what she had in mind when she asked for something comfortable and baggy, but she didn't complain either. Neither did I, because for some strange reason, I like seeing her in my clothes.

I put my hand on her arm. "You can get in. I promise it's safe."

"It's the best armored vehicle on the market right now. We would never risk your life," Holden chimes in.

She flinches and nods, staring at the ground.

Holden and I exchange a look.

Did we say something wrong?

Without another word, she steps up to the car, ducks her head, and slowly slides into the back seat, just like the doctor told her to.

Too bad, I have zero patience for it.

Something I have to deal with somehow.

I get in after her and shut the door while Holden slides into the front.

Our gazes meet in the rearview mirror.

"Is everything ready?" I ask.

He nods. "Yup. Just like we talked about."

A glance at Evangeline confirms she's buckled in. "Perfect. Let's go then."

Focusing on something other than Evangeline is nearly impossible. Her presence alone is a distraction, but now we also have the recent events hanging over us like a dark cloud. It's enormous and depressing, and hiding so many secrets it will inevitably hit us with a storm.

Evangeline and I are like that: two lives intermingled across so many paths, our lives could never be entirely disentangled.

Movement draws my attention to her fingers as she taps them rhythmically on her right leg. The motion is soft but fast until it stops.

What I wouldn't give to hear her play again.

"Hold," Evangeline sits up straighter in her seat, "did you bring my phone by any chance? Phoenix said you got a new one for me."

He clears his throat and gazes at me for a second, glancing her way when he's at a red light. "It's in your room."

"Oh." Her shoulders slump.

"Sorry, Princess. I wanted to bring it but then forgot."

The light turns green, and he focuses back on the road.

She waves him off. "No worries. Thanks for taking care of it for me, I appreciate it."

"Of course." He pauses. "Ruby wants you to call her when you can."

I've given up on stealth and switched to openly watching her conversation with Holden. It's so different from how our conversations go. They talk like two ordinary people, almost like . . . friends.

The way she and I used to talk.

Even though it was only several years ago, it feels like a lifetime.

But then, time goes by differently in prison.

I learned that one real quick.

But it gave Holden and me a lot of time to figure out my revenge plan. Maybe too much time. He was actually the one who suggested I should marry Evangeline. It was a joke at first, but then we realized how much she'd hate being my wife after the past we share.

We laughed about how ironic it would be for her to put me in prison, only to end up bound to me for the rest of her life. The situation would offer me unlimited access to her, allowing me to infiltrate her life and brain to figure out how to hurt her the most.

Now, I can confidently say that might have been the stupidest idea we've ever had.

Holden seems to be friends with her.

And me?

I have no clue what Evangeline and I are.

A mess, that's for sure.

I wouldn't consider us friends—though I'm not sure we were ever truly friends anyway—but I also haven't considered us enemies for a while either. This last week has changed everything I thought about her, about us. Now it's all upside down. To top it off, she just saved my life, and at this point, I'm pretty sure she didn't call the police that fateful night out of hate either.

There's still a mountain of lies and secrets between us, but somehow, we might have started to carve a small pathway toward each other. It's not an easy path to maneuver, and I'm sure we'll hit plenty of roadblocks along the way, but maybe, just maybe, there's a microscopic chance we could end up in a good spot together.

But first, I need answers. And I have to get Evangeline to give them to me. I need her to be the one who tells me what happened. I don't know why that's so important; I just know it is.

We wind up the driveway, and she exhales audibly. I don't blame her. Even though I know the entire house and property have been turned over with a fine-tooth comb and deemed as safe and secure as possible, I can't suppress the slight pressure that settles on my chest either when we drive past the house to park in the garage.

Holden pushes the button that closes the garage door behind us and gets out.

I look at Evangeline, making sure I have her attention. "I had the best security teams out here to ensure it's all safe, you hear me? You are mine to protect, and I will never let anything happen to you again."

She nods, but I can't disregard how she chews on the

corner of her bottom lip or how her hands have stopped drumming, both now clenched into tight fists.

I exit the car and open the door on her side. She blinks up at me with her big eyes but doesn't move.

Only when I offer her my hand does she slowly unclench her fingers to put them around my waiting palm. Her grip on me is tight, but I don't say anything about it, not even when she stands next to me and still holds on to me like her life depends on it.

She just went through something traumatic, we both did.

And I'm not here to judge her or tell her how to feel about it.

If it wasn't for her concussion and the headache she's been plagued by, I would have demanded answers at the hospital the second Holden told me what he'd discovered. And while it's killing me to wait even longer, I'll give her tonight to rest, but tomorrow all bets are off. At this point, figuring out this shit show—who's trying to kill us but also what the hell we are—is the only thing I can think about.

She tilts her head back to gaze at me. "Could you take me to my room, please? I think I need to lie down."

I dip my head. "Of course. Huxley made sure you have everything you need, and I'll have him get some food ready for you, okay?"

Her throat bobs with a swallow. "I'd like that, thank you."

"Anything in particular?"

She thinks about it, then we both blurt out, "Waffles!"

Her cheeks turn a soft pink, and I huff a surprised breath.

Holden comes up behind us. "Waffles? First pancakes, and now waffles? Do I even want to know?"

For a moment, Evangeline and I stare at each other with our gazes locked. The corners of her eyes crinkle slightly, and I can't look away.

She's so damn beautiful.

The second the thought races through my mind, she breaks eye contact and focuses on Holden.

"Waffles used to be my go-to food. I don't know why I was so obsessed with them, but I could eat them morning, noon, and night. Blueberry, plain, or chocolate chip. You name it, I loved them all."

"She went through phases where she ate them with whipped cream and chocolate sprinkles or bacon and melted cheese." My voice is quiet.

There's a rare peaceful expression on her beautiful face.

These memories are from an easier time, from a time in our lives when there was a real possibility of us ending up together, where I wanted more from her and told myself there might be a way to make it work. If anyone had told me she'd be the reason I ended up in prison one day, I'd have called them delusional and possibly punched them in the face for saying it in the first place.

But then, she'd probably feel the same if the roles were reversed and someone had predicted my engagement to her sister.

I didn't think I'd ever want to talk to Evangeline about Connie, but maybe I should. Unless I'm mistaken, she doesn't seem to know what happened between her sister and me.

Evangeline snorts, staring at Holden with her nose wrinkled. "Of course, the bacon and melted cheese was only on the plain waffle, you monster. I wasn't that gross with my concoctions."

Holden grins at her and hums under his breath.

Evangeline shakes her head at him and winces. "Ah, damn it, I forgot about my headache."

Like that, the bubble we escaped in for a few minutes pops, and we're back to reality. Back to where we're both injured. Since Evangeline got it worse than I did, I squeeze her hand and pull her after me into the house.

"You need to rest."

With her solemn expression firmly back in place, she whispers, "Okay."

Holden stays on the first level to check in with the security team while I walk up the stairs. At the top of them, I have the inexplicable urge to turn right to go to my bedroom, but I ignore it and swivel left to the other wing.

We enter her room, and she immediately stops, letting her gaze roam across everything.

I don't see anything amiss, so I ask, "What's wrong?"

"Everything's the same. It's weird."

Realization sinks in. "But nothing feels the same anymore."

She sighs. "Yeah."

While Holden took care of the mess out front, and our injuries will heal over the next few days and weeks, the place that suffered the most significant trauma is invisible to the naked eye. It's impossible to know how long those wounds will take to heal. The doubt, the fear, the confusion, the anger. No one can see that damage, but from the sound of it, Evangeline feels the change too. The essential makeup of myself, the person I thought I was, changed the second she threw herself at me and that bomb went off.

Many people deal with near-death experiences, but I'm not entirely sure what to make of mine or how to handle it.

Evangeline tugs her hand back, and I let go of it, instantly missing the connection when her fingers slip free from mine.

At the hospital, she told me she didn't want me to die and she was sorry.

My reaction was to kiss her.

If there was ever a fucked-up relationship, it's ours.

She goes to the nightstand and picks up the new cell phone. Glancing at me. Swiping across the screen. "Thanks again for this."

I take that as my cue to leave. "Of course. I'll make sure you'll get some food. Let us know if you need anything."

I want to say, "Let *me* know if you need anything," but I don't. I'm not sure where that ridiculous need to take care of her suddenly comes from, but it's loud and persistent. Just like it used to be when we were younger.

After knowing her for so long, I knew I could never get rid of my memories of her, but I thought my old feelings had successfully vanished with her betrayal. It turns out I was wrong, and they were only dormant this entire time, waiting for the first sunlight to kiss their skin so they could bloom once again.

"Thank you, Phoenix."

"No problem." I nod and step out of her room, forcing myself to walk away.

This is the first time I'm leaving her side since they allowed me into her hospital room, and it's almost painful to put distance between us. What if something happens to her while I'm gone? A few years ago, especially when the anger was fresh and taking over my brain, I would have said "good" and run the other way without looking back.

But I can't pretend that's who I am anymore. Despite my revenge plan, by the time I was released, my need for retribution was a mere baby flame compared to the inferno it was when I first learned about Evangeline's involvement in my arrest. Seeing her hasn't helped either, spending time with her even less. Holden and I suspected something wasn't right soon after she moved in here. What complicates things further is that, at her core, she still seems to be the same sweet girl I had a thing for when we were younger.

Holden waits at the landing for me, intercepting my frustrating attempt to organize my thoughts. "Office."

I follow him, going straight to the liquor cabinet to pour both of us a drink. The amber liquid burns down my throat, and I welcome the sting.

Holden drains the contents in one go as well, sighing loudly when he puts the glass back on the tray. "Much better."

He leans back against the large bookshelf and crosses his arms. "How's she doing?"

I shrug. "Honestly? No clue. The doctor doesn't expect any complications, so she'll be okay physically and should be back to normal in a week or two with plenty of rest. She was lucky."

I close my eyes, pushing away images of the explosion and how badly things could have ended.

"You both got lucky. Phoenix—"

I stare at my best friend. Waiting. "Show me."

He pulls two black phones out of the top drawer of the

desk. They're identical, except one of them has a note stuck between the phone and the clear case on the backside that says "old."

His fingers fly across the screen of the old mirrored phone, and after a few seconds, he hands it to me. "This is the text message she got right before the explosion. It's the reason you're still standing here."

My fingers squeeze the hard material as I read the words on the screen, then reread them.

FREDDY

What a shame to have that beautiful black car blown to pieces in a minute. Your fiancé could be gone alongside it, solving all your problems at once. Decisions, decisions. Tick tock, pet.

With my gaze still on the message, I say, "What. The. Fuck?"

Holden told me about the message when he found it but didn't mention the exact wording.

"I know." He goes back to crossing his massive arms over his chest. "I took apart the entire phone—the trash, the cloud, everything. This is the only message I could find from that sender. Of course, the number is untraceable, probably a burner phone, but it's saved in her contacts under that name, which makes me think this might not be the first time they contacted her."

"Why would someone plant a bomb on my car but then warn her with enough time to save me?" My head is spinning with this new information. "It makes no sense."

"It doesn't, no." He shakes his head, and a deep frown creases his forehead. "Also, the message only shows on the old phone, but it's gone on the new one. And it transferred everything else one to one, which makes me think these messages from him vanish, but this one somehow got captured. Maybe a glitch because of the explosion."

"That would explain why you couldn't find anything else from him anywhere."

"Yup." His frown deepens. "If we want to figure out what's going on, we need to get her to talk."

"Phoenix, nooooo." My voice is strained, the words scratching up my throat. I gulp in a deep breath, trying to eliminate this suffocating pressure in my chest that feels like it will crush my rib cage.

I yank the blanket off me and swing my legs over the side of the bed to stand. My steps are wobbly and uncoordinated. Baby deer steps.

But it doesn't matter. I need to get to him. I need to see him.

A sob interrupts my accelerated breathing at the very moment the door flies open. Holden rushes toward me, immediately wrapping me into his arms.

"Shh, Princess. You're okay."

"Phoenix. I need to . . . I need him." Loud and ugly sobs ricochet through my entire body. My brain is still halfway stuck in the nightmare that just ripped me out of my sleep.

While Holden's embrace is soothing, it's not the one I desperately need.

"I'm here, Angel. I'm right here."

I'm maneuvered between them until Phoenix's familiar scent envelops me, and he gently cups my face with his large hands.

"Nightmare?"

I nod and look at him through blurry eyes, reaching out to touch his cheek. To make sure he's really there and in one piece.

"You're safe. I swear to you, I'll kill anyone who tries to hurt you." He leans into my touch and closes his eyes.

I hiccup. "I was so scared he took you from me too. I wouldn't survive it."

His eyebrows almost touch as he stares down at me. "Who is he?"

The desperation in his eyes is a living thing, and the urge to tell him about Freddy, about everything, is even stronger than it was earlier.

I open my mouth, but no words come out. The fear coursing through my body is an invisible hand around my throat, cutting off all of my oxygen until I gasp.

Phoenix shares a look with Holden and says, "Let's get you back in bed."

My chest squeezes at the mere thought of this happening again.

The images flash behind my eyes. Me getting the text message but being too late. Phoenix glancing at me a nanosecond before the bomb explodes. Phoenix lying on the ground in a pool of blood. Dead.

Why does it have to feel so real?

My limbs shake, and I try to get closer to Phoenix, seeking his comfort and warmth. "Not here. I can't stay here after the nightmare."

After a moment of confusion, Phoenix nods. "Of course."

He says something to Holden before he picks me up gently and exits the room. I rest against his chest and listen to his heartbeat. It's erratic, but focusing on it slowly calms my breathing.

Phoenix moves slowly, with caution. Why does he have to make me feel like I'm precious cargo? We walk down the long hallways to get from one wing to another. In his room, he lays me down carefully on his bed and pulls the covers up to my neck.

Before he has a chance to get up, I grab his arm and hold on to it with the bit of strength I have. "Please don't go."

His gaze on me is intense and laced with something. Pain? No. That wouldn't make any sense.

"I wasn't planning on going anywhere." He glances behind him. "I'll just talk to Hold for a moment by the door."

Shifting forward, he presses his lips to my forehead. "I'll be right back."

My dying soul weeps in anguish at the gentle contact. To have the man I've wanted for most of my life so close to me, while also having done the most unspeakable and irreversible damage and loss to his life, is its own kind of twisted cruelty.

It's funny how the same person can be part of your life's happiest and worst memories. Almost like the universe can't decide if it wants to punish or reward you.

Maybe it's trying to teach me that life is as beautiful as it is ugly, and without the ugly, we couldn't experience the beauty.

Since I've been stuck on the ugly side of life for way too long now, I'm ready for the beautiful side.

I reluctantly release his arm, listening to his muffled footsteps as he crosses the carpeted room. My eyes close of their own accord, my body and mind dead tired. I try to listen to Phoenix and Holden, until I can't hear them anymore.

WHEN I WAKE UP, it's still dark outside, and Phoenix is right in front of me. He must have left a light on somewhere because the room is softly illuminated, allowing me to see him. His closed eyes, his steadily moving rib cage. I gaze over our bodies, with me under the blanket and him on top of it, close enough to touch, yet so far away. Except for one part. Phoenix's hand is resting on my hip as if he hoped his touch would keep my nightmares from returning.

Using this unexpected opportunity, I scan over his peaceful form, starting at the stubble on his chin. My hand aches to reach out and touch it, to find out if it's still prickly, or if it has reached that level of softness yet. I want to brush my finger down his straight nose until I reach his full lips. They're slightly parted, and I yearn to run my fingertips over them. Even more so, I want to kiss them. I want to kiss *him*.

My body hums at the memory of the two kisses we've shared. One passionate hate-kiss and a gentle we-just-escaped-death one. Both very different, both leading straight to this moment and the realization I'm attached to this man in ways that can never be undone.

There's still so much unsaid between us, so much pain and loss we can only hope to overcome one day, but right now, one thing is undeniable: I can breathe easier when he's nearby.

I also want to be stronger for him because he deserves it. He's already lost so much, and it's not his fault some psychopath decided to make me a target, inevitably dragging him down with me.

My eyes fixate on the bandage on Phoenix's forehead.

Will this ever end? How many more people will die or get injured?

In a twisted way, the explosion made me realize something crucial: people get hurt no matter what. Either Freddy has escalated for some reason and doesn't care anymore if anyone dies in his sick game, or this was his plan all along, and I was just stupid enough to believe he wouldn't hurt anyone ever again if I did what he asked me to do.

I stare at Phoenix for a while longer, calmed enough by his close proximity to fall back asleep.

When I wake up the next time, I'm alone in bed. Reaching out, I feel the warm sheets beside me. I blink, trying to adjust to the daylight streaming in through the windows. My gaze roams around the room until it settles on the bathroom door that's slightly ajar.

As if I'd willed it, the door moves and Phoenix steps out with only a towel wrapped around his narrow hips.

Heat grows in my chest and works its way toward my neck and face.

His surprised gaze meets mine. "You're awake."

I swallow and watch him walk toward me. "Just woke up."

He brushes a hand through his wet hair. "Sorry, I was hoping you wouldn't wake up while I was in the shower."

"It's okay." My voice is barely a whisper. I try to smile at him, but it feels more like a grimace, so I avert my gaze somewhere past him. Somewhere that isn't his beautiful face, or his toned chest, or his nipple piercing that glints in the light, or his intriguing tattoos, or the 'V' shape of his hips. Anywhere but there.

"Are you hungry?"

I tune in to my body and nod. "Maybe a little?"

"Did you eat your dinner last night?"

I lose my focus and look back up at him. "My dinner?"

"Yeah, after we returned from the hospital, Huxley brought you something, right?"

My brain isn't as fuzzy as before, but it still takes me a moment to remember what I did last night. "He did. I ate then texted Ruby, Mason, and Tyler, as well as my mom because surprise, she actually messaged to see if I was alive. I was planning on taking a bath, but I passed out before I could."

I peek down at my clothes. That would explain the oversized shirt and loose sweatpants I was still wearing, the same ones Holden dropped off for me at the hospital.

Phoenix ignores my snide remarks and asks, "Do you want to take a bath right now?"

"A bath?" More heat creeps up my neck at his question, and I want to hide under the blanket.

He nods. "You said you wanted to take one last night but fell asleep."

Stop being so weird. He didn't ask if you wanted to take a bath with him. He probably just wants to be nice because you saved his life.

Wait. Never mind, you put him in prison, so does that make you even?

You know, I put you in prison, but then three years later, I saved your life—that sort of thing.

Oh my God. Please, stop.

Great, now I'm yelling at myself inside my head.

"Eve?" Phoenix is giving me a concerned once-over.

I sigh and push up to a sitting position, wincing at how my entire body aches. "Uh, sorry. A bath actually sounds nice."

Maybe my muscles will relax in the hot water.

"I'll draw you one."

Phoenix's voice reminds me I'm not alone, regardless of how much time I spend in my head. His words finally process, and I open my mouth to tell him I can take one in my room, but the words die on my tongue.

My eyes go wide, and I cover my mouth with my hand. "Oh my God, Phoenix."

His name comes out all muffled, but I know he heard me because he stops and glances at me with a questioning expression.

I pull my hand off my mouth and point in his direction. "Your back."

Understanding crosses his features, and he lifts a shoulder. "It's nothing. I've had worse."

With that, he spins around and disappears into the bathroom.

He's had worse? His back looks like someone went at it

with a sharp rake, and the goal was to leave as little flesh unharmed as possible.

I'm still trying to sort through my muddled thoughts when he returns. This time, he's dressed in black sweats and a gray T-shirt that stretches across his broad chest.

He points his thumb toward the bathroom. "Do you need help?"

I blink and chuckle awkwardly. "Uh, no. I'm okay. Thank you."

His mouth draws into a line like he doesn't believe me.

To prove my point, I push my hands into the mattress and will my legs to hold me upright.

Thankfully, they do, or I would be screwed.

"Let me walk you into the bathroom, at least. I don't want you to fall." He sighs like I'm the most stubborn person he's ever met.

"Fine." I mutter the word, not admitting I'm secretly grateful for the help.

I'm pretty sure he knows it too when I cling to his arm like he's my life jacket and I'm about to drown if I let go.

He doesn't just deposit me at the door but takes me to the massive tub in the corner. It's one that doubles as a Jacuzzi and could probably fit several people.

"Thank you." I sit on the edge, letting out a relieved breath.

"No problem. I'll be in the bedroom if you need me."

"Okay." I watch him leave.

He stops in the doorway and turns around. "Eve?"

I swallow at my name on his lips. It has slipped out before, but now I can't remember when he last called me by my full name like he did at first. He's the only one who's ever called me Eve. Most other people call me Evie.

But not Phoenix. Never him.

My gaze is on my fingers as they tap on my leg.

I inhale deeply and say, "Can we talk when I'm done?"

Although it's just a simple question, the intent behind it turns my stomach sour. But I knew this wasn't going to be easy. I'm pretty sure this will suck pretty badly. But nothing has changed about my earlier epiphany or resolve. It's time. We both deserve some honesty, and I'll figure out the rest. I only hope I won't destroy his life even more.

His throat works on a swallow before he opens his mouth. "Of course. But will you answer one question for me before I leave?"

"Yes."

"Is the person who's responsible for the bomb also the reason why I was in prison?"

Our gazes lock, and I'm incapable of breaking eye contact. At this moment, I realize he doesn't need me to respond to his question because he already knows the answer. It's written all over his face: the disbelief and acceptance, the anger and sorrow.

The air in the room is stifling, threatening to pull me under, but I do what's been long overdue and what he deserves to happen: I give him a sliver of truth.

One word.

One word that will change everything.

"Yes."

CHAPTER 24

PHOENIX

I pace along the length of the room, back and forth. Back and forth.

What the fuck?

What. The. Fuck.

I had an inkling something happened back then, and it wasn't just Eve.

But I'm not sure I believed it.

It was so easy to let my anger consume me while I was in prison and couldn't see her. And then my mysterious person kept sending me pictures of her and how happy she was while I was in prison.

My mysterious person took pictures of her.

The person who told me I could call them Angel, which I refused to do for several reasons, one being I thought of Eve as Angel, and I didn't want the name reminder.

I saved them in my phone as Canary instead, like an informant.

Did Eve's person tell her their name is Freddy?

I'm two seconds away from storming into the bathroom to demand more answers.

I rake a hand through my hair.

Fuck.

There's a quiet knock on my door.

Holden. I texted him to come up.

I open the door, pressing my index finger to my lips and pointing at the bathroom door. I wanted to leave it open to hear her in case she needed help, but she looked so devastated after her admission that I wanted to give her some space.

I step out into the hallway but leave the door ajar.

Déjà vu hits me. How was it just a little over a week ago when we were in a similar situation after Eve's music room episode?

"What's going on? Is the princess okay?"

At first, it bothered me that Holden called her by a nickname like she was special. He did it as a joke at the beginning, but it didn't take long for him to start liking her, not that I blame him. The two of them have been spending a lot of time together. And this is Eve, the girl I still call Angel, not only because it's part of her name, but because she's always been a genuinely good person. So good I didn't want to taint her with my life, my family, and the cutthroat world I was always supposed to take over from my dad one day.

That's why it hit even harder when I heard her voice on the nine-one-one recording. She was the last person I ever expected to stab me in the back.

Turns out, that might still be true, after all.

"Phoenix."

"Sorry." I blink at Holden. "Eve admitted Freddy had something to do with my prison sentence."

His eyebrows shoot up his forehead. "What?"

"Yeah."

He scrubs a hand roughly over his beard. "Fuck. Is that the connection we've been missing?"

I shrug. "It's something."

"She didn't say who the guy was?"

After a glance through the gap in the door toward the bathroom, I lean against the hallway wall and close my eyes. "I don't think she knows who it is either."

Holden wraps one of his hands around the other, cracking his knuckles and filling the air with popping sounds. "Okay. Shit. I have to admit, I didn't see that coming. We knew something wasn't adding up, but this?"

I exhale loudly.

"But why would she put you in prison just because someone told her to? That doesn't make any sense."

"It doesn't."

He'd hit the nail right on the head. That's exactly where my brain is still stuck too.

"She didn't explain anything? Didn't say why she listened to some random person?"

I shake my head. "Trust me, I have a million questions and want answers to every single one, but she said she wanted to talk after her bath. I want to push her so badly, but the doctor said to keep things easy or the symptoms will get worse."

"Fair enough." Holden studies me for a long moment. "I bet she's been feeling like total shit since the explosion, and not just physically. I mean, this person pretty much texted her that you'd die unless she saved you. How fucked up is that?"

My chest expands, but it feels like my lungs aren't getting enough air.

He tilts his head to the side. "You know, there was no hesitation on her part either. She read the message and took off right away."

"She told me at the hospital that she didn't want me dead. She also apologized several times. I didn't understand what she was apologizing for, but maybe it makes more sense now."

"Man, I bet she feels guilty as fuck for everything." He shifts closer. "We need to figure out who's behind this before something else happens and they succeed with their murder attempts."

I nod, entirely on board with it.

"I'll hit up the other tech guys again that I know," he says. "Maybe one of them will be able to help now that we have some more info."

I push off the wall. "Thank you."

"No problem. I'll let you know as soon as I find out." He gets his phone out of his pocket.

"Hold."

His gaze snaps up.

I hope my hunch proves correct and we'll get one step closer to solving this puzzle. "Also, give them everything we have on our canary."

I see the moment it clicks for him, and his eyes widen. "Fuck me. Motherfucker. On it, boss."

His footsteps retreat, and I step back into the bedroom at the same time the bathroom door opens.

Eve pokes her head out. She clears her throat when she sees me across the room. "Uh, hey. Are those clothes on the counter for me?"

The gap in the door allows me to see a sliver of her body wrapped in one of my big towels with her bare legs on display.

I nod. "I can get you something else if you want. You seemed comfortable in them the—"

"No, they're perfect, thank you." The corners of her mouth lift into something that resembles a half-grimace, half-smile. "Mmm, okay, I'll be right out."

I'm still in the same spot when she steps out several minutes later, dressed in my clothes. The sweatshirt hangs loose on her frame, and the sweatpants are probably rolled up several times at the waist. But for some reason, I can't tear my eyes away from the sight.

She points at the table by the window where Huxley set up breakfast. "Is this for us?"

I nod, tracking her with my eyes as she strolls across the room and sits.

With her damp hair framing her face in waves and no makeup, she looks much like her younger self. Like the Eve I had a hard time staying away from.

Doesn't seem very different from now.

In a way yes, but so much has also changed.

My thoughts circle back to that one godforsaken night that still fills me with regret whenever I think about it.

Her sixteenth birthday.

I'd been so tired of resisting, of keeping her at arm's length. I was desperate for her attention, taking every morsel she threw my way. She was the forbidden fruit I wanted so badly, I couldn't handle it.

I had just given Eve her birthday present and was ready to find her again, to say fuck it all and take what I wanted. But then I got a text message from one of my father's enforcers. It was only an address, but I knew exactly what I'd be witnessing that night. What my dad considered part of my training for my future CEO position in the family company: blackmail, physical assault, threats of any kind. Whatever worked to get my father the companies he wanted for cheap so he could tear them apart and resell them for enormous profits. If there's one thing my father is good at, it's being a ruthless and calculated businessman.

That night, I watched my father's men beat a man unconscious to get the information my father was after.

Later that night, I heard from someone that Eve had disappeared with that douchebag, Tyler. While I wanted to find them—find him—and tear him limb from limb, I also told myself it was better this way. The reason why I had resisted her for so long was because I didn't want to drag her into this twisted and fucked-up family I was born into and put a target on her back for my dad to exploit and destroy. I wanted Eve to shine brightly and explore the world.

A noise drags me out of my thoughts, and Eve looks at me with an apology in her eyes.

"Sorry, I dropped my fork."

I inhale deeply, shaking those old thoughts off.

"No worries." I join her at the table, pleased when I see she's filled her plate with lots of fresh fruit, some fried eggs, and French toast.

I'm a routine person when it comes to my meals,

enjoying a vegetable-laden omelet every morning. But today, something urged me to follow in Eve's footsteps, and I fill my plate with a mix of everything.

We eat silently, glancing at the other when they aren't looking. Well, that's what Eve is doing. I'm not even hiding I'm staring, still hoping I'll suddenly be able to read her thoughts.

"How's your back? Does it hurt?" She moves the eggs around on her plate but raises her gaze at the end of her question.

I lift a shoulder and drop it. "It's okay. Nothing I can't handle."

She huffs a breath like she knew I'd say something like that.

Her hand tightens around her fork, and she guides it to her mouth. I watch the food disappear behind her full lips.

After a swallow, she goes back to pushing her eggs around. "I . . . mmm . . . I'm really sorry about your back and your other injuries. I don't think I've properly thanked you for what you did, so thank you."

A million unspoken things float between us.

"There's nothing to thank me for, Eve. If it weren't for you, I'd be dead."

She opens her mouth and closes it again.

It's easy to tell she doesn't like this topic by the way she averts her gaze and chews on the corner of her lip.

"Eve, who's Freddy?" I put down my fork.

She blows out a long breath and holds my gaze. "Listen, I want to tell you everything, but I need you to promise me something first."

"What?"

"I need you to not do anything rash, please. I haven't heard from Freddy since the explosion, so to be honest, I'm not completely sure what's going on, but this isn't just about you and me. There are other people involved who could get hurt."

I lean forward. "Other people? What are you talking about?"

She swallows. "Pretty much anyone who's close to me. My family, Ruby, Mason, Tyler. Thankfully, I haven't been close to anyone else since I started college, or they'd be targets as well."

"We need to find this guy. He tried to kill us. And he's the reason I was in prison. *Prison*, Eve. I was locked away for three years like a fucking animal. I had to spend most of my time crammed in a tiny cell, was beaten up for fun, had to eat food I'm pretty sure even stray dogs wouldn't eat, and was deprived of so many other things. I fucking deserve the truth."

Her eyes shimmer, and she nods.

With a firm grip on the imaginary knife, I twist it in deeper. Not because I want to hurt her, but because my desperation for her to lay it all out is pushing me from the inside. "Connie wouldn't have wanted this for us."

A lone tear escapes her eye and runs down her cheek. I'm not sure if that was the right or wrong thing to say, but as before, it's too late now.

Knowing someone's secrets is a weapon like no other.

I finally understand my dad's "words of wisdom," as he calls them. They're pretty much the company's unofficial mission statement at this point.

He failed to tell me, though, they can also turn on you at

any time, slicing you up from the inside until you slowly bleed to death.

And I'm so sick of it.

With no time to regret it, I open my mouth again, knowing my next words will completely change the trajectory of Evangeline and me.

"You knew that Connie was pregnant?"

She nods, suddenly looking a little paler.

Here we go.

"The baby wasn't mine."

CHAPTER 25

EVANGELINE

My heart pulses so violently I'm genuinely concerned it might explode.

I put my hand on my chest, as if that could keep it all together, and stare at Phoenix with my mouth hanging wide open.

"The baby wasn't mine."

My brain reboots, and I yell the first thing my mind can grasp, "She cheated on you?"

Phoenix shakes his head, still completely composed. "She didn't."

I rear back. "What? She didn't? But how is this possible then?"

Phoenix waves his index finger back and forth. "I can't be the only one handing out answers. A truth for a truth?"

He raises his brows, looking at me like he knows he's got me cornered, and I have nowhere else to go. He isn't wrong. He just doesn't know I was already planning on telling him everything today anyway.

So I push away the sense of dread that wants to overtake

my brain and nod. "Deal."

His mouth curves into a ghost of a smile because he knows exactly what he's doing.

Beautiful bastard.

I wait for him to tell me more, still in shock over his revelation. It also raises the question of what else he hasn't told me.

He raises an eyebrow. "I think it's your turn."

Of course. Dang it.

I open my mouth, still not completely sure where to even start, when he lifts his finger again.

"How did you know I was at the warehouse where they arrested me?"

Shit. Going straight for the throat.

My mouth is dry, and I reach for my juice, drinking the whole thing in one gulp.

Phoenix's gaze on me is intense.

Try to focus.

It wasn't his baby.

It. Wasn't. His. Baby.

I didn't kill his baby.

Oh my God, I didn't kill Phoenix's baby.

But you still killed your sister and her baby.

I cringe at the thought, then blurt out the words before I chicken out. "Text message."

Phoenix's expression doesn't change, like he expected this answer. "From Freddy?"

"Yes. He texted me to call nine-one-one, what to tell them, and the address."

He opens his mouth again, probably to ask more, and this time, I'm the one to lift my finger to interrupt him.

"My turn." I pause for a moment, my thoughts going a mile a minute. "If the baby wasn't yours, who was the father?"

"Chris Wellinger."

"What? Are you serious?" I'm yelling again, but I think we both know my composure left the room a long time ago. "You kidnapped and beat up the father of your fiancée's baby?"

Wow, that sounded bad in my head but even worse out loud.

"Yes." His gaze narrows on me for a split second as if to tell me I'm done with my turn. "Was that the first time Freddy contacted you when you called nine-one-one?"

Sweat forms at my nape, and I have to rub my hands on my pants several times to get rid of the clamminess.

Just tell him.

Soon, he'll know my worst secret. The one I'm most ashamed of and would gladly die for if I could have a redo.

I push back my shoulders and say, "No, it wasn't the first time."

His head moves up and down like he's nodding to himself, taking in the information and probably trying to connect the dots like I am.

Because apparently, Chris Wellinger, one of my dad's long-time business partners, was the father of my sister's unborn baby, and Phoenix kidnapped Chris and then went to prison for assault. My father hasn't mentioned Chris since, and I've never seen him at any events again either.

But if Phoenix wasn't the father, then . . . "Why were you marrying my sister when she was pregnant with someone else's baby?"

His answer is immediate. "She found herself in a shitty situation, and I wanted to help her, so I did and told her I'd marry her."

Time seems to slow down as I blink at him and try to process the news he just dropped on me.

Holy shit.

Can a heart and a brain explode at the same time?

"You." I point at him while simultaneously doing another poor imitation of a gaping fish. "You . . . you were going to marry my sister to help her because she was pregnant with someone else's baby?"

"Yes." He averts his gaze for the first time, picking at his pants. "Does it seem like such an outlandish thing that I'd want to help a friend?"

It takes my brain a moment to digest his words. Then I hold up my hand. "No, that's not what I meant. I'm just shocked. You guys looked so . . . so happy together. So in love. This is . . . wow."

He huffs. "That was the whole point, to make people believe the relationship was real. She was a good friend, so it was easy."

Easy. He said pretending to be in love with my sister was easy because she was his friend.

His *friend*.

My sister made me believe she was in love with Phoenix, the guy she knew I had a crush on. She knew she was going to destroy me with that. I kept telling myself I was happy for her, that if she and Phoenix were in love, he and I were clearly never meant to be. But they weren't. They fucking weren't in love. They were only friends.

Why didn't she tell me what was really going on? Why was she causing me so much pain on purpose?

Maybe things would have gone differently if she had told me the truth. Perhaps she would still be alive. The things I said to her that night. Oh my God.

I rub my forehead, a headache already brewing.

The past mixes with the present in such a twisted way that everything I thought I knew is turned upside down and tossed overboard.

"Eve."

My head snaps up. "Huh?"

"I asked when Freddy contacted you for the first time."

I avert my gaze because I can't watch him when he finds out what I did. My hands shake, and I wrap my arms around my stomach, sinking deeper into the chair. I want to disappear, be anywhere but here.

My voice sounds far away when I say, "A few days before the nine-one-one call."

"A few days before?"

I hear the confusion in his question, but I still don't lift my gaze.

My vision blurs. My legs bounce. I stare at my lap.

"Yes."

He shifts around. "What did he message you?"

"To call nine-one-one."

"About me?"

"Yes."

He doesn't wait for a second and fires off the next question. "But you didn't call them?"

I shake my head. "I didn't."

"Eve, look at me." He waits and waits, and then he's

suddenly on his knees in front of me, with his hands gently on the outside of my thighs. "What made you change your mind? Why did you call the cops a few days later?"

He stares at me like he can figure it all out as long as his gaze is on me.

The body tremors have reached uncontrollable levels, and I'm shaking violently from head to toe. The sensations attack me from all sides: the crawling feeling under my skin, my suddenly sluggish heartbeat, the unbearable pain in my chest, the dizziness and nausea.

I want to curl up into a tight ball and cease to exist.

My chin drops to my chest, and all of my emotions come out in a pained noise that sounds inhuman. "Because my sister died. I was supposed to make a phone call but didn't do it. I killed her, Phoenix. I'm the reason my sister is dead."

Phoenix's hands are on me. He pulls me into his arms. Gently. I bury my face into his chest, wanting nothing more than to disappear. I don't want to feel like this anymore. Pain, guilt, and shame are all ripping me apart from the inside.

Phoenix walks us to the bed and maneuvers us onto it, his embrace solid and unyielding, never letting go of me. He makes me feel safe in a way I've never felt before. Nothing bad can happen as long as I'm with him. It's a faulty notion, an illusion to screw with me because we both know we're not safe. No one is safe from the devil.

"Shh." Phoenix rubs his hand over my back.

My body seems to remember the soothing motion, immediately calming down. Silent tears run down my cheeks, but I do nothing to stop them. Weirdly enough, they offer me solace. Maybe I can cry all of this pain out once and for all.

"Eve, it wasn't your fault. You didn't know you were dealing with a psychopath. There was no way you could've known. You can't blame yourself."

It takes me several tries to get words out of my mouth. "If only I had told someone right away. Maybe things would have gone differently. But I thought it was just some idiot playing games."

He blows out a breath, the motion tickling my hair. "Most people wouldn't have taken it seriously, and I honestly don't think it would've made a difference had you told someone."

"I don't know. I just feel like I should have done something."

"Even if you'd gone to the police with one text message from what I assume is a burner phone, it wouldn't have mattered. If they had acted on it, which is doubtful, they probably wouldn't have found him in time."

In time to save my sister. That's what he's not saying.

And maybe he's right. That's the whole thing about retrospection and could haves and should haves. There's no way of knowing. Logically, it makes sense the police probably couldn't have prevented what happened. Involving them could have actually made things worse. But my heart doesn't want to hear anything about that. It's hurting, even after all this time, and I don't think it'll ever not hurt when I think about my sister. The grief is my living proof of how much I loved her. Just like there can't be happiness without unhappiness, maybe there can't be love without hate or loss either.

I sniff. "Connie didn't deserve this."

He shifts us around so we lie facing each other and cups my cheeks. "You're right, she didn't. But listen to me, you didn't deserve any of this either. And you certainly are not responsible for her death."

I stay quiet and focus on keeping my breathing as even as possible.

He wipes a thumb over my tears. "So you haven't told anyone about this in all these years?"

I close my eyes for a moment and shake my head.

"Eve."

His voice is laced with pain when he says my name.

I bite the inside of my cheek in response to hearing it. "I couldn't."

"You've been living with this secret, with this sorrow, all this time. I wish I would have known."

The torment in his eyes is almost too much, spearing me straight through the heart.

"I killed your fiancée and what I thought was your baby."

"Fuck." He exhales harshly, then closes the distance between us to wrap his arms around me. "Everything could have gone so differently. I was so confused, so hurt and angry, when I found out you were the one who called the police. I didn't understand why you hated me that much."

I'm pressed against his chest, and it's easier to talk when I don't have to see him. "I've never hated you, Phoenix. Not for a single day in my life, and trust me, I've tried."

I expect him to pull back, but he doesn't, allowing me to stay in this warm cocoon.

After a moment of silence, he says, "You know, there was a time when I was hoping you'd hate me."

I repeat his words in my head, but they don't make sense. "You *wanted* me to hate you?"

"Not really, but I didn't want to drag you into my messed-up world, so I kept telling myself if you hated me, at least you would take yourself out of this equation and move on."

"What equation?"

"The equation of you and me, Angel. The inevitability of us. I was trying so hard to stay away from you because I knew it would be better for you. It would allow you to follow your dreams and travel the world, enchanting millions of people with your music. I didn't want you to be stuck with me and the consequences of what it means to be the heir of Montgomery Enterprises. I never wanted that life for you."

My breath gets stuck in my chest.

I didn't imagine it.

He'd wanted me too.

I thought there would never be a future with Phoenix and tried to make peace with that, especially once he and Connie announced their engagement and she told me about the baby. I thought I'd dealt with it properly, healed as much as I could. I didn't expect this excruciating pain behind my rib cage at his admission, or that the loss of what could have been would threaten to tear me apart.

During this conversation, I've allowed myself to share a piece of my burden and secrets with another person for the first time. I never expected we'd end up here. With a heart I thought had healed enough to survive.

But I was wrong, so very wrong.

Now, I'm left with old wounds that have reopened to the point I'm not sure they'll ever fully close again.

We've been in some kind of limbo since our conversation last week, and I still can't get the image of Eve sobbing in my arms out of my head. She was clinging to my shirt like her life depended on it, and I was so relieved when her breathing finally evened out. She cried herself to sleep, utterly exhausted from the emotional hurricane our secrets had unleashed.

Maybe there were too many secrets.

Maybe they broke her.

Maybe *I* broke her.

Even though she tries to act normal, she's been quiet and withdrawn. Most of the time, she escapes into her schoolwork she's slowly been catching up with, or she zones out watching TV or reading a book. We've also been reviewing more real estate listings together, and she's been helping me smooth out a few more loose ends about the foundation. At first, I didn't want her to work too much, but I quickly realized it's one of the few times she has a spark in her eyes.

I'd gladly bleed myself dry if it spared her another second

of agony. But it doesn't matter how much I want to, I can't take away her pain. Instead, I stay by her side and watch her, making sure she eats enough and offering her comfort at night.

I want to be her compass, guiding her out of the darkness and back to me.

My phone vibrates on the table like a bad omen, and I glare at it. Phones have never been as ominous to me as they are now. I'm constantly waiting for a new message from whoever is behind this.

My father's name appears on the screen, and I sigh. He's been even more difficult to deal with since the explosion. Because how dare I almost get blown up and bring bad media to the company again?

Annoyance courses through me at having to leave Eve's side. I avoid it at all costs, more for my benefit than hers. Because just like she was having nightmares about me dying, I had the same about her.

I push out of my chair, and Eve looks up from her spot on the other side of the table.

I hold up my phone. "It's my dad, I have to take this."

The corner of her mouth twitches, but she doesn't smile —something she hasn't done much of all week.

Sometimes, I wish we never had that conversation. In a way, she seemed happier before. Happier in a situation that, in retrospect, might have been a little less fucked up than the aftermath our conversation has unearthed.

She makes a shooing motion with her hand. "Phoenix, I'm fine, just like the other five hundred and twenty-seven times I've told you. You can leave me alone for five minutes without supervision."

She's right.

Of course she's right.

But I can't help it.

We both know she isn't okay, even though she keeps telling me she is. Not that she should be after nearly getting killed and almost destroyed by my truths.

What made me tell her what really happened with her sister? I'd promised Connie not to tell anyone, but I couldn't keep it in any longer. Eve deserved to know. I *wanted* her to know. The truth must have been devastating for her, but I still hope it was the right thing to do. Even if this wound might never heal completely. I hope she'll see there's beauty in scars as they transform into reminders of our strength and resilience.

"I'll be right back." The phone stopped vibrating a while ago, and I'm still standing in the same spot.

She waves her hand toward the door again with a flicker of amusement in her eyes. "Go on, now."

I trudge toward the door, settled enough after seeing that tiny spark in her eyes. Does that mean I'm the reason for that flicker of life sometimes too? "Get Hold or Huxley if you need anything."

"Yes, sir."

I turn my back to her, so she can't see how those words affect me, and slip out of the library. I'm fully aware she didn't mean them in a sexual way, but my dick didn't get the memo. She seems to have a direct line to it, despite how worried I am about her, and waking up next to her all week has been absolute torture. Although, I'll gladly suffer if it means her nightmares stay away.

"Eve, if you think sleeping here with me will help with your nightmares, consider it done. You don't even have to ask."

What I really wanted to say was, "I don't give a damn what you want, I'm not leaving your side. Not now that I know the truth. Not when I know you didn't have a choice, suffered more of a loss, and lived in more anguish and sorrow in all those years than I could have ever imagined."

"I killed her, Phoenix. I'm the reason my sister is dead."

The pain and guilt have been eating away at her all those years. And even worse, she had to suffer in silence because she couldn't tell anyone.

And she's still suffering so much.

Every morning, I find her curled up with her arms wrapped tightly around herself, as if she'll fall apart otherwise.

I want to be the one to hold her every night, to offer her comfort and solace, to keep her safe. But I don't say any of those things, not wanting to make her uncomfortable when I'm glad she's at least next to me every night, even if she doesn't touch me.

I want that motherfucker who did this to suffer, to make him feel only a small portion of what he's caused. I want to wrap my hands around his throat and watch the life slowly, painfully drain out of his eyes. I want to know he will never feel an ounce of life in his body again because he deserves to rot in Hell for eternity.

The problem is, we're still not any closer to finding him. Holden says he's either using a burner phone, or one of those apps, making him untraceable. What makes this even harder is we don't know who would know so much about both Evangeline's life as well as mine. It could be one of the many enemies my father has made for all we know at this point, which is pretty much nothing.

I step into my office and shut the door behind me with more force than necessary.

Rain pounds on the window, the sky dark and glum like it's weeping for us—like it's seeking revenge for what happened, just like I am.

I dial my father's number without taking my eyes off the sky.

"What took you so long?" He doesn't care about niceties or manners.

When my father says jump, he expects you to do it as high as possible without further prompts.

There was a time when I appreciated his tenacity and drive and even admired the way he ruled his empire with an iron fist. I believed him when he told me it was necessary to keep people from stomping all over you. Once, I was impatiently awaiting that much power one day. Excited to have the respect of so many people simply for running a multi-billion-dollar company. That was before I went to prison.

"Phoenix." My father barks my name, his voice full of annoyance.

"Dad."

He exhales loudly, probably wondering why I'm such a disappointment.

"I wanted to make sure you'll be on your best behavior at the party this weekend. After—"

"What party are you talking about?"

"Where's your respect, Son? You know better than to interrupt me. And I'm talking about your engagement party. What else would I be talking about?"

My brain is spinning in circles, sifting through my memories but coming up empty. "This is the first I heard of the party."

"Can't trust anyone these days to do their fucking job. After the rather *inconvenient* event, Byron and I gave the okay to the wedding planner last week to put something together as soon as possible. The shareholders are getting anxious, and you know we can't have that happen again. So I expect an exceptional performance from you and the girl for some much-needed good press."

My ears are ringing, the words *rather inconvenient event* on repeat in my head.

"I'm sorry someone tried to kill me." No matter how hard I try, I can't keep the bite out of my voice. "And you're talking about my future wife, so how about you show her the proper respect and call her by her name?"

He laughs. He fucking laughs like the sociopath he is.

"Well, well. All it took was a small explosion for you to grow some balls, huh?"

I squeeze my free hand so hard my knuckles scream in pain. I'd refuse to believe this man was my father if I wasn't such a spitting image of him. When I was younger, I thought not being like him was bad and that I lacked what it took to be as successful as he was. Now, I see it for what it really is: a blessing.

I try to open my mouth to speak and give him a real piece of my mind, but my jaw is clenched so hard it's impossible to open.

My dad sighs, and it's easy to picture the exasperation on his face. "You're more dramatic by the day, just like your mother. Just smile for the camera and behave, something menial I assume you and your *fiancée* can manage for a few hours."

He says the word *fiancée* with so much disdain and sarcasm I'm surprised it's not dripping from my phone.

I need to end this call. "Of course, sir. Anything else?"

"I expect a report soon on how your little project is going. Once it's ready to launch, we'll ensure every news outlet covers it so you can be redeemed in public. It's taken long enough already as it is with all of these setbacks. The faster we can get this over with, the better. And stop requesting files from my employees. For all intents and purposes, you're not a part of my company at the moment and need to earn your way back into it first."

Over my dead body is the first thought that pops into my head, which might be too early to joke about, even though the sentiment hasn't changed. If I could get out of working for my dad without losing my entire inheritance, I'd be on that in a heartbeat. Plus, my grandfather wanted us to work together, and who am I to deny him his last wish?

I say, "Yes, sir," like the obedient son he expects me to be.

The line disconnects, because why would my father ever bother with pleasantries if it doesn't make him money?

The words my grandfather's friend uttered a while back about my dad pop into my mind.

"He's made a lot of enemies, and if you stand by his side, he'll drag you right to Hell with him."

Enemies who would get me locked up first and then try to kill me?

A war has broken out inside me, and I'm not sure which side will win: disgust for my father or the worry how Eve will react when she hears about our engagement party in less than a week, and the show we have to put on for everyone.

Eventually, the pounding rain and swaying trees calm me enough to see her. She doesn't deserve the leftovers of my anger and irritation that are solely my father's doing. Never hers. Not anymore.

I open my door and freeze when laughter travels down the hallway. Eve's laughter. A sound I've been longing to hear all week, despite knowing she might not be ready for it yet. Holden's laughter follows a moment later, mixing with hers. I was gone for less than half an hour, and he's accomplished what I've tried to do all week.

I love her beautiful smile, but nothing compares to her alluring laugh. It was one of my favorite things about her when we were younger. The days I heard her laugh were some of my happiest. Even my dad couldn't sour my mood then.

When was the last time I heard a real laugh from her? Jealousy wraps around my throat, squeezing with a sickening smile. I hate it, but I also welcome it. The pain is a reminder of my true feelings. How I ever managed to tell myself I hated this woman is beyond me. She still is the purest and most selfless person I know, and she deserves the world.

Footsteps echo through the halls, then stop somewhere close by. I poke my head out of my office like a creep to see what they're doing, only to draw back a split second later after seeing where they stopped: in front of the music room.

"Is today the day, Princess?" Holden sounds optimistic.

But he's met with silence, and I hate that I can't see her. I want to gauge her reaction and read every single millimeter of her face as I've done for so much of my life.

"Come on, then, Princess. Maybe tomorrow." Holden's voice is gentle yet still cheerful.

For a moment, I wonder if that's exactly what she needs right now and why they get along so well.

He's the light she needs.

I'm the darkness, only pulling her farther into the deep abyss.

Their footsteps pick back up, and I sink into the shadows of my office and close my eyes.

My head hurts.

They pause again, and Eve says, "Phoenix said he'd be right back."

Holden chuckles under his breath. "I'm sure something came up and he'll pop out of a dark corner any second. As your official knight in shining armor, he can't leave you alone for too long, right?"

Asshole.

There's Eve's laugh again. It's quiet but real.

Something in my chest settles into place upon hearing it.

Maybe I should give the bastard a raise.

They resume down the hallway and the stairs. I wait another minute to follow, both wanting to see Eve but also dreading to tell her the news.

CHAPTER 27

EVANGELINE

Every day I spend with Phoenix, I fall farther down the rabbit hole. By the end of the week, I crave his company. I'm so aware of him that I'm distracted by him lounging a few feet away from me on the couch. Currently, he's frowning at the tablet in his hands, possibly looking at something his father sent him since that always seems to frustrate him.

Unable to focus on my book, I gave up on reading a few minutes ago, playing with the PopSocket on the back of my e-reader instead. Pushing it down and pulling it back up. Push, pull. Push, pull. Pop, pop, pop.

"Angel."

His voice has a warning tone to it, and I stop immediately.

"Sorry."

"Ask what you want to ask."

I grimace. Of course, he sees right through me. "Are you sure?"

I internally cringe at the memory of how our conversation went last night when I asked him if he and Connie ever had sex. I didn't want to ask, but I *really* needed to know the answer. The relief that rushed through me when he told me their relationship was purely platonic almost knocked me off my feet.

Phoenix puts the tablet on the cushion next to him and turns my way. "That was our rule, right? AMA. Ask Me Anything, and you shall receive an answer." He bites the corner of his lip. "Maybe."

My gaze follows his movement, and I stare at his lips. Craving his company hasn't been the only urge that has grown. I'm also longing for his touch. Not just his lips or hands on me but also the comfort his embrace provides.

"Eve?"

Heat rises up my neck, but I pretend he didn't just catch me ogling him again. "Do you know how everything with Connie and Chris happened? Like were they dating, or was it a one-night stand situation? I still don't really know much about it."

Phoenix stares at me for a moment, like he's trying to decide how much to tell me. "She never told me when or how exactly it started, just that they were involved, and that he told her he was in the midst of separating from his wife, which wasn't easy because of the kids. They continued to meet in secret for months, and when she told him about the pregnancy, he laughed in her face and said she was delusional if she thought he'd want a baby with her."

"He said that?"

"That's what Connie told me."

"What an asshole." I mull over this new information. "I'm glad you beat him up."

The instant the words leave my lips, I slap a hand over my mouth, and Phoenix laughs. It's deep and rich, and my stomach does a weird flutter thing.

I chuckle. "I can't believe I just said that."

"I'm glad you did."

"Stop." I chuckle some more. "You know what I meant. I appreciate what you did for her. It means a lot."

With that, the happy moment is over before I'm ready, and something changes in Phoenix's expression.

"Since we're asking questions. Holden and I have been thinking about suspects. Did you ever have a hunch who Freddy could be? I'm sure you've thought about it plenty of times."

I sigh. "To the point of migraines. But no. For a while I suspected everyone, but no one made sense. No one I've ever met was outright hostile to me. So either Freddy is a good actor or I've never met him. Assuming it's a guy, of course."

"Yeah, I know exactly what you mean. I've been thinking too. Overanalyzing. Wondering who could be Freddy." He pauses. "Do you remember when I was in the city the week before the explosion?"

The week something changed between us. "Of course."

"I ran into two guys from school in the hotel lobby after one of my meetings. They came out of the hotel bar with a group of friends, all of them drunk off their asses. Anyway, they've always been total shitheads to me, but to a degree I didn't blame them because my dad slept with both of their moms, destroying at least one of the marriages as far as I know. Maybe both."

My eyes widen. "What on earth?"

His eyebrows lift. "I'm surprised you haven't heard about it since my dad never even tries to be discreet about his affairs. Not even for my sake. Once, in high school, I told him some of the women are my friends' moms and because he can't keep his dick in his pants, my friends turned on me. You know what he said? To stop being such a pussy and to use it as a learning experience to show them who's superior."

I'm so stunned, I just stare at him. "Your dad is just . . . wow, I don't know what to say. And then those guys stopped you at the hotel?"

He sighs. "Yeah. I saw Michael at another event last month, but he only sneered at me from across the room. This time, he got in my face. Both of their dads used to work for my dad, but I didn't know until later on they were fired. One, years ago, and the other just recently. Which might be the reason why they approached me now. Michael said I'm scum and don't belong in their circle after my prison time. That they should have kept me locked up forever because people like my dad and me always ruin everything. Then his best buddy, Owen, had to chime in too and—"

"Wait. Owen? My brother brought an Owen home once from college for some event. Preppy guy, sleazy smile, short blond curls. His dad used to work with my dad back then too. Dang it. What was his last name again? Something with R?"

Phoenix tilts his head to the side. "Rodgers?"

I wrinkle my nose. "Yes, that's him. Owen Rodgers. Total douchebag. Tried hitting on me and didn't take no for an answer. I'm pretty sure he was trying to get into my room that one night he stayed, but I made sure to lock my door when I went to bed."

Phoenix's eyes are small slits as he stares at me. "He what?"

"Nothing happened." I shrug and put my hand on his arm.

The veins in his neck pulse angrily. "Now it makes a lot more sense what he said."

"What did he say?"

His gaze softens a fraction when he looks at me. "That he hopes I'll rot in Hell with my prude bitch of a fiancée."

A laugh bursts out of me, and I wave my hand around in front of me. "I'm sorry. I know this isn't funny, but, man . . . it's just so stupid."

Now that I've started, I can't stop laughing. And it feels good, cathartic even, and so much better than crying too.

Phoenix stares at me with such an odd expression that I stop and brush over my face.

"Is there something on my face?"

He shakes his head and lifts his hand as if to touch me but drops it again. "No, everything's perfect."

His gaze is so intense my cheeks heat. "So, do you think one of them could be Freddy?"

He exhales loudly. "We checked them and their dads again, but without any luck. And like you said, it could be anyone, and it's not like we have any solid leads."

"Gosh. I wish it was over already." I grab my mug from the table and take a sip of my tea.

Phoenix clears his throat. "There's something I haven't told you yet."

I swallow the warm liquid so fast, it almost goes down the wrong pipe. "More secrets?"

"Yes and no." He pauses. "The only reason why I haven't told you yet is because he's been quiet for a while, and you've already had enough shit on your plate."

A chill goes down my spine. "He?"

"Someone's been sending me messages too, and I think it might be the same person as Freddy."

"What?" Tea splashes over my hands and clothes, but I ignore the mess. "Did he make you do things as well?"

He immediately shakes his head. "No. My messages weren't like yours, which is why I wasn't sure if they came from the same person. For me, it started a few weeks after I was arrested. My dad, being the controlling and shady person he is, had arranged a phone for me that I had access to when specific guards were on rotation. When I checked it a few weeks after my arrest, there was a message from my dad but also two messages from an unknown sender. One of them was the recording of your nine-one-one call."

I swallow, the guilt trying to eat me alive like every single time.

Phoenix blows out a breath. "He told me to call him Angel and was acting like he was my friend, helping me uncover your betrayal. From then on, I got messages from him several times a month, updating me about your life and sending pictures of you. Pictures of you smiling at school and having fun with your friends. Doing all the things I couldn't do because you took that from me. He stoked a fire in me until thoughts of revenge were all I could think of."

"He pitted us up against each other." The breath is stuck in my airway until I gasp. "And he told you to call him Angel?"

He nods.

I huff a laugh, but there's no humor in it. "He told me to call him Devil."

Phoenix shakes his head. "Very original. Angel and Devil."

I'm still reeling from all the new info. "I can't believe he was watching me the whole time and taking pictures of me."

Phoenix's Adam's apple bobs. "I'm not proud of myself, but nothing riled me up more than seeing you happy and free while I was locked away. At that point, I'd already met Holden, and since there was no hiding the phone from him, I told him everything. One time, I imagined how you'd react when you saw me again and realized that's probably the last thing you'd ever want to do. He joked about me marrying you, but over time, I became obsessed with the idea of making your life a living hell by forcing you to be with me every single day. The continued updates on you kept that obsession burning like a wildfire."

The words rush out of him, like his brain wants those nasty thoughts out of his head as quickly as possible.

I shake my head in a daze. "He knew exactly what he was doing."

"I hate myself for falling for the whole charade so easily."

Unable to stay away, I close the distance between us until I'm almost in his lap. "How could you not buy into it? You were in prison because of me. None of that was a lie, no matter how much I wish it was. I hated you for what you did to me and then my sister, but my heart still broke into a million pieces when I made that call."

With each new secret we reveal, a puzzle piece clicks into

place, exposing how endlessly screwed up this entire situation is. Way worse than I ever could have imagined.

The paranoia isn't helping either.

Just thinking about the engagement party tomorrow has me on edge. Will we be able to make it through the event without anything crazy happening?

Holden puts his phone away. "Showtime, Princess. Jo is here."

"Okay." I smile at him, hoping it comes off as real.

We're all on edge about having to attend our engagement party tonight. Not only did neither Phoenix nor I agree to it, but we were also almost killed two weeks ago.

Holden still doesn't like leaving me alone any more than Phoenix does. Although Phoenix is a lot more aggressive about it, which is completely unnecessary because I spend most of my time with him anyway.

There's a knock on the door, and Holden opens it.

We're back in my old room since it's easier to get ready here with Jo, while Phoenix gets dressed in his room in peace.

Jo maneuvers past Holden and toward me, sighing heavily when she takes in every detail of my face. "Oh, sweetie. You look like you haven't slept in a month."

I chuckle. "Please tell me how you really feel."

She winces. "Sorry. Bad habit."

Holden lifts a hand. "I'm out."

I wave back. "Later, alligator."

He rolls his eyes but can't hide how the corner of his mouth tilts up.

But I know Jo isn't wrong. I probably should have taken better care of myself in the past few weeks, but it just wasn't on my mind. During the day, I studied and helped Phoenix with some work for the foundation, and at night, we usually ended up on the couch together, him with his laptop or phone, and me with a good fantasy romance. As long as I kept busy and could dive into another world, my brain couldn't spiral too much.

Books have become my favorite way to escape, my personal sanctuary, offering me comfort in a way nothing else could.

Phoenix has only added to this. Talking to him has lifted a heavy weight off my shoulders, allowing something inside me to shift.

Is everything magically fine and dandy now? Absolutely one-hundred-percent not. We're still as deep in shit as before, but I also know I'm tired of crying, tired of feeling sad, frustrated, and depressed. I *want* a normal life, I've more than earned it.

Jo throws her arms around me, pulling me out of my thoughts. "I'm so relieved you're okay though. Looking shitty is better than being dead, and I'm so happy you're not dead."

I squeeze her back, basking in the embrace. "Thanks, Jo."

She shakes her head. "I was so surprised when Holden called me. If I were you, I'd probably never leave the house again, let alone go to a party."

I huff a breath. "Unfortunately, I don't have a choice."

"Of course you do. Say the word, and I'll get us some popcorn for a movie night instead."

I give her a half-smile. "I love the sound of that, but Phoenix needs me, and I want to do this for him."

She studies me for a while, and I see the urge in her eyes to say more, but she keeps it in for my sake. She'll never understand how much I appreciate her caring.

"Well then. Let's get you ready to wow the crowds."

Jo is a miracle worker. Because when I peek in the mirror a while later, there is no more trace of my disheveled self. My desolate, shattered side is hidden with a precision I wouldn't call possible if I wasn't staring at my reflection.

Before she leaves, Jo makes me promise to do a movie night with her sometime soon.

Once she's gone, I stay an extra minute.

When I finally open the door, Phoenix is casually leaning against the opposite wall. With his hands tucked in his pockets and his feet crossed at the ankles, his gaze bores into mine with such a magnitude, I feel it in my bones.

His gaze doesn't waver from mine as he pushes off the wall to close the distance between us. "There aren't enough words in this universe to describe how beautiful you are."

Something akin to wonder and serenity settles behind my breastbone, releasing a tender warmth into my bloodstream.

"Thank you." That warmth in my body turns into liquid heat the closer he gets. "You're very handsome yourself."

He stops a foot in front of me and holds out his hand, his eyes flaring the moment he catches sight of my engagement ring. My first one sadly didn't survive the explosion, so he had another one made. Only when I interlace my fingers with his does he let his gaze roam over my body, taking in every detail like it's been years since he's seen me and not hours.

I do the same with him, noticing how his wavy dark hair is artfully tousled, with a loose strand falling onto his forehead. His mesmerizing brown eyes lead to his straight nose and plush lips, and that angled jaw I want to nibble on. Lastly, there's the way he fills out his black suit that has my breath caught in my throat.

He's the depiction of male beauty, and no amount of staring will ever fill that need to feast my eyes on him.

And I've done plenty of that in the last two weeks. Actually, we've both been stealing peeks at each other. It's like neither one of us can look away for long.

"Shall we?" His voice is thick, his throat working on a swallow.

I nod and smile at him.

Tonight, I'm the happy fiancée of a man who can't get enough of me. A man who looks at his bride-to-be as if the world couldn't exist without her in it.

That's my role, and I will give it my all.

Tonight, I will pretend all of my younger self's dreams have come true.

And nothing can take that away from me, not even some psychopath out there.

～

PHOENIX HASN'T LET GO of me once tonight, just like he promised. If he isn't holding my hand, he touches my arm or lower back.

I can't say I mind.

Everything's gone smoothly so far. The ballroom at my parents' estate has been turned into something akin to a fairy tale with fresh flowers, twinkling strings of lights, and white and gold balloons everywhere. If guests were annoyed by the extra security measures when they arrived, no one has let on. Everyone has been kind, congratulating us, expressing their shock over what happened and relief that we got away unscathed.

But I'm sure I'm not the only one playing a role tonight. Everyone has to like us, be excited for us, and be happy we survived. At least to our faces.

My cheeks hurt from smiling so much, from pretending to be thrilled to be here, but I continue anyway.

Warm fingers move over my own.

Phoenix takes the glass out of my hand. "Excuse us. I think it's our turn to dance."

The words aren't for me, but for the man he was talking to.

I bite the inside of my cheek to keep from snorting as Phoenix leads me to the middle of the room, putting us at the center of attention for everyone to see.

He gives me a little spin, never letting go of my hand. My heartbeat quickens. He pulls me close to his body and rests his other hand on my lower back. My stomach flutters.

The orchestra starts a new song, "A Thousand Years," one of my favorites, and we sway across the polished floor in slow circles.

Phoenix closes his eyes for a moment, and when he

opens them back up, there's a solemn expression in them.

I brush a hand over his jaw. "Are you okay?"

He tilts his head as if my question takes him aback, and my thoughts pause briefly. Did I overstep somehow? Things have changed between us so quickly after we disentangled so many lies and revealed truths, I'm still not sure what that makes us. Friends?

Friends ask each other if they're okay, right?

Something inside me rebels at that thought, but I shove it away. Friends is good. Friends is preferable to enemies.

Phoenix nods. "Just tired of all the bullshit."

I smile at him and trail my fingers up his nape. "I'm sorry, baby."

We both freeze, and my eyes widen like saucers.

Heat rises into my cheeks, but I can't look away. There's something in his gaze that holds me captive. Storm clouds swirl in his dark irises, and I want to be brave enough to dance in the rain.

But I'm not. This time, I avert my gaze. "Sorry, that just popped out."

I try to draw back to allow some distance between us, but Phoenix only tightens his grip on me. "I don't give a fuck what you call me, so stop trying to get away from me. Now relax."

Obeying, I lean against his chest, happy to hide here for a while. With my eyes closed, I let the music wash over me and soothe my pounding heart.

"Will you play this for me at home?"

His words are a whisper against my hair, and my hand stills against his shoulder blade. I didn't even realize I'd been moving my fingers along to the music.

"Connie always talked about how much she loved watching you play. That nothing in this world could ever be as beautiful or as pure as when you sit down, put your hands on the keys, and allow yourself to be one with the music. She said the entire world deserves to hear your magic."

Tears prick my eyes, but I don't let them fall.

I want to smack his chest for choosing this moment to tell me something like this. But at the same time, I want to kiss him for sharing this with me. And he's right; Connie always was my biggest cheerleader. She pursued our dad's career, not only because she genuinely loved the business, but also because she knew it would allow me to live out my dreams.

And then it was all for nothing anyway.

No, none of that right now. I want to enjoy this moment with Phoenix and happy memories of my sister. I deserve that sliver of peace.

He rests his head on top of mine. "Just know that I'm ready whenever you're ready."

We stay on the dance floor for four more songs, and I never move out of his embrace. His heartbeat is steady under my ear, quickly turning into my favorite sound. Out of nowhere, a melody pops into my head, accompanying his heartbeat in the most beautiful way, and I can't contain the small gasp that bubbles up my throat. I haven't heard music in my head in so long, the pressure in the backs of my eyes comes back tenfold.

This entire time, I thought the silence was good, that it was exactly what I needed to heal, that it was better to forget the pain, but maybe I was wrong.

Maybe it was the silence that kept me from healing all

these years.

Maybe the silence was the price I paid for my wrongdo-ings, and now that Phoenix is back in my life and he knows the truth, we can heal together.

The melody flutters around in my mind like a loving caress, and I wonder if it could be my salvation.

Something urges me to look at Phoenix, to really *look* at him.

I know we're both playing a part tonight, but the man staring back at me right now is *my* Phoenix. The same one who told me none of the guys at school were good enough for me, and then tried to get me to promise I wouldn't date anyone until I was at least thirty. The guy who found me whenever there was a thunderstorm because he knew I loved them.

His eyes are kind and tender, even as he gazes down at me. So contrary to the steel that promised violence when he waltzed into the room at my birthday party what feels like an eternity ago.

"Thank you." I push onto my toes and press my lips gently against his. I don't move them; I don't open them.

This kiss isn't about lust.

This kiss isn't about pretense.

This kiss is about gratitude.

I was stuck in this cloud of darkness, and he just gave me back a piece I thought I'd lost forever.

This is a kiss about hope.

PHOENIX

"Shit, man." Holden cackles next to me like I just told him the funniest joke ever.

Sometimes, I'm worried about him.

"What's so funny?" Even though I'm talking to him, my gaze stays glued on Eve.

She's only a few feet away from us with her friends, which is too far for my taste. I promised Eve I wouldn't leave her side, but when her friends showed up, she gave me a pleading look, and I folded like a house of cards.

How bad of an idea would it be to strangle them for taking her away from me?

Not only did Ruby and Mason pop up right next to us on the dance floor, interrupting our precious time, but it was also right when I was about to ask Eve what she was thanking me for.

Now, I still don't know.

But something happened on the dance floor, that much I'm sure of.

Even the kiss felt different.

Holden steps in front of me, and I shift to the side to avoid losing sight of Eve.

He laughs again. "I've seen a lot in my life, but never a man so obsessed with a woman."

I merely shrug, because what's the point of denying it? We both know it's the truth.

"I always thought your fixation on her was a bit over the top, but she put you in prison, so I understood. But now I *really* understand."

I spare him a glance. But only for two seconds. "Understand what?"

"Oh no, I'm not telling you. Where would the fun be in that?"

This time, he gets a glare from me. "I don't even know what you're talking about anymore."

Holden grins. "I know, which is why this is so hilarious."

A low sound comes from my throat. "This guy doesn't know what's good for him, I swear."

Holden follows my gaze to Tyler, who has joined the trio, handing Eve a champagne glass from his tray with a smile. She takes it from him, and their fingers touch. I want to rip his clean off his hand.

I knew he would be here, we'd vetted everyone, but Holden told me we're not the assholes who keep scholarship kids from making some earnest money. That doesn't mean I have to like it though.

"Relax, dude. He reminds me of someone else who doesn't know what's good for him either." He wiggles his eyebrows at me. "Plus, haven't you heard that he and Ruby are an item now?"

That's news, but I still want to wipe the smirk off his face.

With my fist.

I glance back at the group. Tyler whispers something in Ruby's ear, and she giggles. Then he's off into the crowd. Eve peers at me over her shoulder, her lips curving into a genuine smile when our gazes meet.

I nod at Holden. "I think we've been here long enough. Let's say our goodbyes and go home."

"Couldn't agree more, *boss*."

He says "boss" like some people would say cockroach, and I mutter, "Asshole." His laughter follows me all the way to Eve.

I slide my arm around her waist, and my body instantly relaxes at the contact. I know it's stupid to think I can keep her safe as long as I'm by her side, but it's the only thing that calms me these days. I despise the moments I'm without her. Is that healthy? Probably not, but I don't give a fuck.

Like Holden pointed out, I'm a man obsessed.

I lean close to her ear and say, "Are you ready to leave?"

She shivers, and I bite my cheek to suppress my reaction.

The things I want to do to her.

But I don't think she's ready for that yet.

For now, the memory of her on my lap in my office has to be enough to hold me over.

Until she's ready for more.

Until I fully make her mine.

My dick twitches at the memory of her pussy pulsing around my fingers and the prospect of feeling her clench around my cock one day, and I have to pull away to put some space between us.

I head toward the exit, and Eve's parents step into our path. Alex is nowhere to be seen, which suits me just fine.

Audrey sweeps a glance over her daughter. "Evangeline, there you are. I thought we might miss you guys tonight. It's been so busy, and everyone always wants to chat."

Eve gives her mom a social smile, the one that doesn't reach her eyes. "Hi, yes, so busy. It's a lovely party, thank you for hosting."

Byron shakes my hand. "How's business going, Phoenix? I bet you're excited to be working with your father again soon?"

I barely manage to focus on him and the ridiculous words that are coming out of his mouth, giving him a simple, "Sure. Absolutely."

He seems satisfied with my answer and turns to his daughter. "I take it things are going *well*?"

It doesn't take a genius to know what he's referring to since the dollar signs are practically shimmering in his eyes. He and my dad are in the midst of closing the deal we promised him.

How pathetic. Sometimes I'm not sure which of our parents are worse. They're both greedy and cruel in their own ways.

I focus back on Eve to make sure she's okay just as she's squeezing my hand.

"Yup. Everything's going *super well*. Anyway, Mom, Dad, sorry to cut this short, but we were just about to head out. Phoenix has some important business waiting back at the house."

Her mom seems taken aback but quickly recovers. "Oh, sure."

Eve waves and says, "Oh, and by the way, thanks for sending me a message after the explosion to check in. I really appreciate the thought. Enjoy the rest of your evening."

I barely have time to take in the slightly confused expression on Audrey's face before Eve pulls me after her.

The conversation with my parents is thankfully even shorter. We swoop in, say thanks, and leave with a wave. All just for public appearances, of course.

Niko waits at the door for us. He's one of the security guys Holden assigned for me personally, among a few others. They've been at the house as added security for the past few weeks. As much as I prefer to have Holden by my side, we both felt better if he checked out the car himself before we left.

"Hey, Niko. How are you?" Eve smiles at him.

I grind my teeth but stay quiet. I have to get used to her knowing everyone's name and being friendly with the staff. Apparently, that's her thing.

"I'm well, miss, thank you for asking."

Thankfully, Niko knows what's good for him and nods curtly at Eve before averting his gaze.

"I told you to call me Evie like everyone else does."

The corner of his mouth twitches. "I remember, but I'd like to keep my job, miss."

Her mouth opens, and she whirls around.

I immediately hold up my hands. "No, not me."

Realization hits her features, and an irritated sound comes from her throat. "I think Hold and I need to have a little chat."

Niko swallows but stays quiet, leading us through the mansion and into the garage.

Everyone else has their drivers dropping them off and picking them up out front, but we didn't want to take any unnecessary risks.

Holden is waiting next to the car, and Eve immediately pokes his chest. "Did you tell your guys they have to call me miss?"

He grins. "Did you want them to call you Princess too?"

She groans. "Hold, be serious."

He sighs, like he's sad the fun is already over. "A lot of the guys prefer that small distance. It keeps their senses sharper when they're not overly friendly with their client."

She seems to mull over the information, the spot between her brows scrunched together. "That makes sense and no sense at the same time."

Holden nods. "We can talk about it later. Let's get out of here first."

"Fine."

She climbs into the SUV, and I follow her.

Holden navigates us back onto the main road, and with every mile we leave behind us, my body relaxes more.

Eve is quiet the whole drive home. For a moment, I wonder if she's asleep, but then I see her fingers tapping away on her legs. I want to slide across the middle seat to get to her, but then the moonlight illuminates her face through the window, showing me the gentle lift of her mouth.

I didn't intend to tell her about Connie and her music tonight. But when the orchestra played one of Eve's favorite songs, and she started moving her fingers on my back along with the melody, the words just spilled.

And I'm not sorry about it.

How could I be if they might have been precisely what she needed to hear?

Is that what the kiss was for?

Was that what she was thanking me for?

It was undoubtedly one of the most innocent kisses I've ever had. Yet, it felt like someone reached into my chest and took my heart in a chokehold.

We say goodnight to Holden, so he can check in with his team, and make our way up the stairs.

Up to my bedroom, that has slowly turned into *our* bedroom in the last few weeks.

Eve leaves for the bathroom to get ready while I take off my suit jacket by the couch, draping it over the back. My tie comes off next. I'm undoing the last button on my shirt when Eve calls my name.

I cross the room and push open the bathroom door, finding Eve in the middle of the ample space with her back to me.

She clears her throat and watches me over her shoulder. "Mmm, could you help me with the zipper, please? I got the top open but then got stuck halfway down."

"Sure." I stalk toward her, my gaze stuck on her long hair tumbling down her back. She must have taken it down the second she came in here.

I gather the soft strands in my hands and sweep them over her shoulder, grazing her skin in the process.

Eve shivers, just like earlier.

And just like earlier, my dick takes notice.

I stare at what's already exposed on her back and the small patches of her skin that are a little pinker than the rest. Newer. Freshly healed after the attack.

I brush my fingers over them. "Do they hurt?"

She shakes her head.

I touch every spot where she got hurt, some of them smooth skin and others scars. Goosebumps spread under my fingertips.

Then I kiss them—one by one.

"You're so beautiful."

Kiss.

"So brave."

Kiss.

"And strong."

I can't stop touching her, can't stop revering every wound and every scar.

This woman deserves to be worshiped.

I brush my hand down her back, finally making it to the zipper. Something like a whimper comes from her. I fix the zipper and pull it down her back tantalizingly slowly. Tracing every millimeter of freshly exposed skin. Until I feel the lace under my fingers. I continue, and then it's right in front of my eyes as the zipper reaches its final destination at the top of her ass. It's a black thong, and I wonder if it's the same one she wore when I made her come on my lap.

Unable to help myself, I press a finger behind the top seam and brush it left and right, left and right.

"Phoenix."

My name is a breathy whisper, snapping me out of my trance.

"Tell me to stop, Angel."

Eve doesn't answer. Instead, she lets go of the dress where she must have held it to her chest, and it falls to the floor in a heap, leaving her to stand there in nothing but that damn black thong.

Shit.

How many times have I envisioned a scenario like this before? How often did I imagine peeling off her clothes when we were younger? Fantasized about her perfect round hips? Wanting to grab handfuls of her ass and show her beautiful tits the appreciation they deserve?

I still haven't seen all of her, yet I already know she's just as spectacular as I knew she would be.

My cock is so hard, precum leaks onto my pants.

She's practically naked, within reach, and I'm still standing here like a prepubescent teenager who's never seen a girl before.

And she's allowing me to feast my eyes on her.

Angry thunder sounds outside, and I automatically step closer, bringing her backside flush to my front. There's no hiding my cock now.

Eve moans low in her throat at the contact and leans back against me.

I'm holding on to my sanity by a bare thread. "Last chance, Angel. If you want me to stop, tell me now. I don't think I can stop once I've touched you."

"Don't you dare stop." Eve tilts her chin in a way that allows me my first real look at the swell of her full breasts, her nipples hard and begging for my attention.

"Thank fuck."

I snap.

There's only one thought in my head before my body takes over.

This woman is my undoing.

Always has been and always will be.

Once I have her, this will be it for me. I will not let her go ever again. I don't think I could even if she asked me to.

My primal instincts quiet my mind.

I need to touch her. I need to feel her. I need to taste every inch of her. Mark her as mine.

Her thoughts seem to be aligned with mine because she spins around at the same time I grab for her, and together, we close every last gap between us. Maybe even more than the physical ones.

Her fingers dig into my nape while I reach around her to finally get my hands on her round ass. She jumps at the same time I lift her, and I blindly walk us into the bedroom.

My scalp screams in pain when she tugs at my hair, and I welcome the sting because I feel the same desperation.

Eve lets go of my hair, only to yank at my shirt, trying to force it off my arms.

She lets out a frustrated huff, realizing it won't come off while I carry her.

I chuckle.

And fuck, it feels good.

Every fiber of my being recognizes and wants her. Knowing she feels the same has something powerful coursing through my veins. It's not like anything I've never felt before.

I capture her mouth, unable to stare at those pouty lips for another moment without tasting them.

I finally reach the bed and lower us to the mattress.

Holding my weight as much as possible on my elbows, I press my cock against her pelvis, and we both moan.

With great difficulty, I pull away from her compelling lips

and kiss my way down her throat, across the elegant curves of her shoulder and collarbone until I reach her chest. Shifting my weight to one arm, I reach for her right breast and groan at the feel of it. Fuck. I massage it, then the other, sucking on one hard nipple.

Her floral scent infiltrates my senses, a smell I've associated with her for as long as I've known her, only adding to the insanity of this moment.

Eve arches her back, and my cock twitches at the evidence of her pleasure.

I shower both breasts with lavish attention, switching back and forth between licking, sucking, nibbling, and massaging, always listening to Eve's little gasps and moans whenever I do something she likes.

"Phoenix . . . need more . . . need to touch you."

I find my way back to her mouth. After another thorough kiss, I climb off her and walk to the end of the bed. I take a moment to treasure the sight of her lying on my bed. Spread out like the delicious feast she is—with her beautiful hair on my pillows, her flushed skin baring my marks, and eyes wild with arousal and desperation.

She's the most beautiful thing I've ever seen, and I'll never get my fill of her.

Her eyebrows bunch together in a cute frown, and she lets out a frustrated huff, much like earlier. "Why are you still dressed?"

Without taking my eyes off her, I slowly undo one of my cufflinks and let it fall to the floor. "Am I not fast enough for you?"

Her eyes widen for a fraction, a playful spark shining in them. "Maybe you need some help?"

I tilt my head to the side. "Come here and help me then."

She goes on all fours and crawls down the bed to me.

She's crawling to me with her heavy tits swaying left and right.

Fuck.

This is single-handedly the sexiest thing I've ever seen, and this moment will forever be burned into my memory.

The way she smirks at me, her gaze never leaving mine, tells me she knows exactly how much I like this.

When she reaches me, she doesn't go straight for my pants like I thought she would. Instead, she licks her way up from my navel to my chest.

CHAPTER 30

EVANGELINE

The nipple piercing glints in the dim light like it's waiting for me. I circle it with my tongue then bite his nipple gently. When Phoenix hisses, I do it again, this time also tugging a little at it.

Moving back, I stare straight at the tattoo over his heart. The compass tattoo. No matter how often I told myself it couldn't be true, here's the proof. Staring straight back at me. It bears a striking resemblance to my pendant, but it's so much more than that. Not just bigger but also more fleshed out. The details of the lines and arrows are amazing. Magnificent. Like him.

One day, I'll ask him about it.

But that day is not today.

Yet I can't help myself and press a kiss right in the center of it.

Phoenix groans, his erection hard against my stomach, distracting me enough that I trail my way back down his torso.

I kiss him over the fabric of his dress pants, gliding my nose up and down the length of his hard cock.

And there's a lot of it.

"Eve, I . . . fuck."

At first, I thought we'd go at each other like starved animals, and he'd just take me right there in the bathroom. On the counter, on the floor. I didn't even care as long as I could have him.

Something happened today when I heard that melody in my head.

It's like it unlocked a part of myself I wasn't privy to for the last three years.

It was hidden under a mountain of guilt and regret so big it wasn't strong enough to fight its way out.

Now, it's like a veil has been lifted in front of me.

I almost *died* two weeks ago. *We* almost died two weeks ago.

And I'm tired of holding back, of missing out. I'm not sure what this is between us, but I know he's the reason I feel more complete and alive than I have in so long. And I want more of it. So much more. I want all of it. All of him.

Unable to wait a second longer, I undo Phoenix's belt and zipper and push down his pants along with his boxers, gasping when his cock springs free. The urgency from earlier returns, and I lower my mouth on him without any preamble.

"Fucking hell." The noises that escape Phoenix are my new brand of aphrodisiac.

My corresponding arousal pulsates deep in my core.

His hands go into my hair, brushing it away from my face and holding it back in one fist.

I can't get enough of him. The sight of him in front of me. His large frame towering over me, his big cock in my mouth, so hot and smooth. His fist in my hair. It's such an intoxicating combination my clit buzzes.

"Eve . . . fuck . . . stop." He pulls at my hair.

My scalp sears in pain when I try to move forward on his cock.

"Sorry, but I need a minute. It's been a while." He lets go of me and steps back.

His cock springs free from my mouth, and he closes his eyes to take several deep inhales. I watch in amazement. He appears almost as affected by me as I am by him, like I'm his undoing just as much as he is mine.

My heart thumps wildly at the possibility.

Despite wanting to test his restraint once again, I lean back and sit on my feet. A whimper escapes my lips when I accidentally graze my clit, and his eyes immediately zone in on me.

He sweeps his thumb over my cheek, then my lips. "Look at you being such a good girl and waiting patiently."

"Phoenix." I seem unable to do anything but make noises and say his name.

His previous words finally filter through my haze. *It's been a while.* Did he mean what I think he meant?

"You haven't . . . all these years?"

It's hard to bring up that time in his life. Regardless of how things happened, the fact they did happen will never change.

He rakes a hand through his hair. "No."

"Me neither." The confession slips out of my mouth

before I think it through. I'm not sure I wanted him to know, but I can't take it back now.

To say he seems shocked is an understatement. "You didn't have sex the entire time I was gone?"

I shake my head, my lungs constricting. "I was too afraid something might happen to the person I got involved with."

"Angel." He pushes me back to the mattress and blankets me with his body. And then, he just holds me.

I wrap my arms around his neck and hold him as close as possible. Soaking in his warmth.

When I worry I might suffocate him, I lose my death grip.

He looks at me in a way no one besides him ever has. Like I'm something precious, something to be marveled at. For the first time, I feel cherished. I feel beautiful. I feel wanted.

My pulse quickens, and I whisper, "Kiss me."

He swallows loudly. And then he's right where I want him.

His lips are soft against mine as we both savor the contact. When his tongue enters my mouth, it's unhurried and gentle. This is, without a doubt, the most reverent kiss I've ever experienced, and against all odds, I hope it won't be my last.

Never being kissed again the way Phoenix kisses me right now would be an utter tragedy.

Despite my loud protests, he withdraws from my lips. I tilt my head to the side, exposing my neck like an offering. Unable to keep my eyes open, I close them and just feel. His lips slide down my throat and collarbone until he devours my breasts with the same detailed attention he did earlier. My entire body buzzes.

One hand rolls my nipple. A shot straight to my core. He

descends farther, circling my belly button. Nipping at my underwear.

"Lift your hips for me, Angel."

And I do, openly watching him. He grasps the corner of the lacy material and drags them off so slowly, I want to scream.

"Now open your legs and show me that perfect pussy."

I obey and he groans in response, not waiting for a single heartbeat. He lowers himself on the mattress and licks me once from my entrance to my clit.

I bow off the bed, moving against his mouth as he sucks on my tight bundle of nerves. Something akin to static electricity blasts through my entire body.

"Oh my God."

Fragments of an impending orgasm light up everywhere while he continues to test what I like, using his lips, tongue, and teeth in ways I didn't know were possible. He adds one finger, then two, pumping in and out of me. Rubbing that mysterious spot inside me I've only ever read about in books. And I'm done. I can't hold on any longer, my world exploding into a thousand sparks.

"Phoenix." I come with his name on my lips and a moan so loud, I'm not sure I can ever face anyone in this house again.

He pulls his attention away from my clit and kisses every inch of surrounding skin, lazily working his way back up my oversensitive body. I want to crush him to me, tell him to hurry, but I don't think I have enough energy left.

He's finally within reach, and I grab for him. Our lips touch in a searing kiss, and I taste myself on him.

"I want you inside me right now." I wrap my legs around his hips and push with the bit of strength that's left.

I gasp when his head slides in.

"Fuck, fuck, fuck." Phoenix stares at me with a painful expression. "I need . . . fuck . . . condom. I've never—"

I swallow. "I'm on the pill. So if you're okay with it, I'm—"

His lips crash on mine. I think he's trying to give me time to adjust to his considerable girth and length. But his control seems to slip halfway through, and he thrusts in all the way.

I gasp into his mouth, and he stills, mumbling, "Shit, baby, I'm so sorry."

He starts to pull back, but I cling to him.

"I'm okay, I'm okay. Just give me a moment."

"Fuuuuck, you're so tight."

I want to point out it's probably more because he's so big, but who cares? I'm deliciously full, and it's the best feeling ever.

"Okay, I think I'm good." I dig my heels into his ass.

I'm aching for him to move, and he finally rewards me with unrushed deep thrusts. A gasp escapes me every time he bottoms out and his pelvis hits mine.

My hands find their way back into his hair. Pressing into his scalp. I don't know if he can feel my next orgasm build, or if it's his own, but our kisses become more demanding.

He thrusts faster, harder. "Shit, you feel so good. I can't hold on much longer."

I say, "Then don't," and kiss him with everything I've got.

Either the words or actions spur him on because his movements become almost punishing, and I love every second of it.

He releases and groans loudly, triggering my orgasm.

"Jesus Christ, Angel, that was—"

He half collapses on top of me, and I don't mind one bit, muttering a weak, "Yeah" as we both try to catch our breaths.

Phoenix rolls us to the side and tucks me against him, pressing his lips to mine in a tender kiss.

"That was so much better than I ever imagined it would be."

His words sink in, and I swallow. "You've imagined us together?"

Phoenix chuckles. "Only a million times since I first saw you."

I should be flattered, euphoric even, that it was never one-sided like I thought, that I didn't imagine our attraction back then. But all my brain can think about is I'm responsible for him missing out on three years of his life. He'll never get the time back, and his past also still haunts him in his dreams. The knowledge chokes me.

"Hey, what's the sad face for?" He brushes my hair back and cradles my cheek.

"I don't know how you'll ever be able to forgive me for what I did." All the strength I felt earlier, all the bravado and positivity are suddenly gone. I feel more like my old shell again, those nasty thoughts infiltrating my piece of happiness and smashing it to smithereens.

Phoenix blows out a breath. "I was so angry with you when I found out you were the reason I was in prison. Absolutely livid. I channeled that into rage and plans for revenge. Although, I think deep down inside, I knew you'd never do something so callous to me. But it was easier to hate you than to deal with the pain."

Agony blooms in my chest.

"Listen," he pauses. "We both have a shit ton of baggage to work through and to disentangle, but I want to do that with you by my side. There's nothing to forgive. We both drew the short straw, and the only person who deserves forgiveness is you from yourself."

He touches his forehead to mine and clutches me to him while I fall apart.

"Plus, I would have never met Holden and his ugly ass otherwise."

Unable to help myself, I chuckle.

He wipes away any remaining tears and stares into my eyes. "I'm sorry you're hurting."

I sniffle. "I'm really sorry for what happened."

"I know you are, baby. But you didn't have a choice, and I'd never resent you for what happened now that I know the truth."

I sniffle.

He chews on his lip for a moment. "And you know what? I was able to think about this a bit more levelheaded lately, and I realized something. Whoever is behind those messages could have just made the call himself, so I probably would have ended up in prison regardless."

My lips part at the revelation, and Phoenix chuckles.

"Between the two of us, or three if you include Holden, we could probably keep a therapist occupied full time."

"I can't even tell you how badly I wanted to talk to someone about what happened. When I first told you, this huge weight dropped off my shoulders, and I wanted to weep in relief. It didn't take away my guilt or shame, but I guess there's a reason why people say talking is the best therapy."

He bumps his nose against mine. "And I'm always here to listen. But I'll look for someone who can be discreet if you want?"

I nod the second the words are out of his mouth. "I'd like that."

"Consider it done. Anything you want, and it's yours. Just say the words."

My head is spinning with everything that's happened today. So much, so fast. I feel it'll take a while to catch up, but I'm okay with that. Because, apparently, we're in this together.

Phoenix presses his lips to mine but doesn't linger. "Now you better get some sleep while you can because I'm not done with you yet. Not for a very long time."

To emphasize his words, his fingers leave my cheek to trail down the length of my body.

He squeezes my butt, and I yelp in surprise, trying to wiggle my way away to head to the bathroom. He follows close behind as I cross the room and lean into the shower to turn it on. Before I can step back, he grasps my hips and tugs me flush against his erection. I close my eyes and moan, moving against him without shame.

Being intimate with him, physically and emotionally, is my new safe space. The one place where I don't need to think and can get lost in our bodies and how he makes me feel.

His hand snakes around my middle and between my legs, rubbing my clit in lazy circles. The buildup isn't as fast this time but not any less potent. He pushes me forward with a hand on my back, and when I'm right on the edge of falling over, he thrusts inside me, taking me out of my head and to new places I haven't visited yet.

"Fuck, you look so good on my cock." He grabs my hair and yanks my head back so our gazes meet. "I'll never get enough of you, you hear me?"

Thrust.

"You're mine."

Thrust.

"And I will kill anyone who dares to take you away from me."

CHAPTER 31

PHOENIX

When I open my eyes and find the spot next to me empty, I immediately jump out of bed and grab my gun from the nightstand drawer.

No, no, no. Where is she?

I barely bother putting on my boxers before I yank open the door, ready to take on whoever I have to.

"Whoa. Easy there, tiger." Holden's walking down the hallway toward me, lifting his arms.

"Where is she?" I don't bother telling him who *she* is because he knows no one else would evoke this level of panic in me.

"She's fine . . . and safe." He nods in the direction of my open bedroom door. "Why don't you put on some clothes, and I'll show you."

I grumble something unintelligible under my breath but do as he says. Since I trust Holden, I stow away the gun and disappear into the bathroom.

Soon after, I join him again, this time fully dressed in sweatpants and a T-shirt. He ushers me past the closed music room. I stop and stare at the door, but my best friend steers me toward the staircase.

"Come on, I wanna show you."

Reluctantly, I follow him downstairs to his domain. Holden's pride and joy. I let him have full rein, and he transformed the room closest to the garage into a state-of-the-art security office, complete with an entire wall of monitors. When we enter, Niko and Darrell look up from their chairs, mumbling greetings.

Holden nods toward the door and says, "Time for a coffee break."

They hurry out of the room with a curt, "Yes, sir."

Holden points toward the middle screen in the top row, but I've already found her.

Eve is in the music room, sitting at the piano. And she's playing.

"She's been in there for the past hour." Holden sits in one of the unoccupied chairs, leaving me to stand alone.

"Can you turn it up?" I stare at the screen, unable to tear my gaze away from her.

"Sure. One sec." He clicks some buttons until music fills the room.

The melody is unfamiliar, but I'm immediately captivated by it. It's different from anything I've ever heard before. It starts sad and heavy but evolves into a happier, lighter tune. The music stops, and Eve takes her hands off the keys to write on a piece of paper. Then, she's back to playing the same melody as before but with a slight change toward the end.

My head snaps to Holden. "She's not just playing but composing?"

His grin is answer enough, but he nods anyway. "It seems like it."

My lips part, and I'm back to staring at the screen.

We're both quiet, content to watch her.

But Holden wouldn't be Holden if he could keep his mouth shut for long.

He clears his throat. "Something is different about her this morning. She came downstairs to get food before she practically skipped into the music room. Even when she was slamming the door in my face, she kept smiling and bouncing on her feet like an excited kid on Christmas morning."

I smile at his description, having witnessed Eve like that before.

He scoffs. "She must have had a *really* good night for her to be in such a good mood."

Last night wasn't just really good but incredible. Life-changing. For both of us, and for more reasons than just mind-blowing sex. I can't even describe it, nor will I try to explain it to Holden, but something big happened. I still feel it.

"We had a good night," I ignore his snort, "but her behavior isn't about that. This is about her music. She'd get like this whenever she had an idea for a new song. It lights her up from the inside, and she can't fully contain it. Some people are meant to shine like that."

This time, Holden doesn't give me a snarky reply, so I look at him. He's wearing an odd expression, like something I said upset him.

He lets out a sigh. "Yeah, I know what you mean."

The way he says it makes it sound like there's a story

behind it, but movement on the screen catches my eye before I can dig deeper.

Eve stands and stretches her arms overhead, leaning from one side to the other.

"What the fuck?" I see red and yank open the door to run upstairs. Why does she have so much skin on display?

I get to the music room just as Eve opens it. Her eyes go wide for a split second until she realizes it's me, and she gives me one of *my* broad smiles. It brightens her whole face, and it's pretty much impossible to be mad or irritated with her.

Before I can say anything, she jumps into my arms. "Hey."

Everything is forgotten the moment I catch her.

With her body flush with mine, my fingertips find the bare skin of her thighs. Eve is busy devouring my lips and digging her hands into the hair at my nape. It's wild and chaotic. Exhilarating. It's everything.

I walk us forward until I find purchase against the wall, needing to feel her even closer. I want to crawl under her skin to ensure my blood runs in her veins as strongly as hers runs in mine.

When I knead her soft *bare* ass cheeks, I remember why I raced here.

Shit. At least my frame should cover most of her in this position, in case anyone dares to watch us on the camera feed.

"Angel," her nickname comes out in a growl, "what are you wearing?"

She pulls back with puffy lips and glossy eyes.

Just the way I like it.

So damn beautiful and sexy.

She glances down at her body and shrugs. "I thought you like it when I wear your shirts."

I groan. "I do. But fuck, you need to wear more than just a pair of small panties underneath when you wander around the house, so you don't give my security team a show when you stretch."

Her mouth opens, then closes. "There are cameras in the music room?"

I shrug. "There are cameras pretty much everywhere in the house."

"In my room?"

Damn it. "Yes."

She narrows her eyes and sighs. "I shouldn't be surprised."

I stay silent.

"In *your* bedroom?" Her voice is about an octave higher than before.

I immediately shake my head. "No, of course not." Leaning close to her ear, I whisper, "What's underneath this shirt is for my eyes and my eyes only, understood? No one, and I mean, no one gets to see what's mine."

Her tongue darts out to lick my earlobe. "You know, I should be offended over your little caveman speech, but I'm not too ashamed to admit that it was a major turn-on."

A cough sounds behind me, and I close my eyes.

I know that cough.

Holden clears his throat. "For reasons beyond me, we can pretend I didn't hear what the princess just said."

Eve hides her face in my neck, and I shift a few inches to

the side to ensure I cover her entire body. All Holden can see are her legs wrapped around my waist.

"Anyway," he continues, undisturbed, "I realize this is a bad moment, but I just got a call from O'Neal. It's urgent."

That immediately gets my attention, and I stiffen. O'Neal is the detective we have deep in our pockets, and the reason why the police didn't bother us relentlessly after the car bomb.

I glance over my shoulder at my friend. "Did he say what it's about?"

"They got a tip and picked someone up. He hasn't confessed, but they found more of the same explosives that were used on your car at his house, and apparently other damning evidence." Holden huffs. "You will not believe who it is."

"Who?"

"Ben Rodgers."

I almost drop Eve at the news.

She looks back and forth between Holden and me with wide eyes, wriggling around in my arms to get down. "Owen's dad?"

I hear the same shock in her voice as I feel, and it takes all of my control to let her go slowly, still covering her in case her shirt rides up. "What the fuck? We checked him out."

Holden's features tighten. "I know."

Once Eve's feet hit the floor, she's a bundle of nerves. Pacing, wringing her fingers, glancing up and down, left and right, until she stares straight at Holden and inhales deeply like she needs to work herself up to the question. "Did they say what other evidence they found?"

He holds her gaze. "O'Neal said there were videos and photos of you from the last few years."

Her lip wobbles as she takes in that information.

"I will kill him." I pronounce each word slowly, trying to control the rising anger inside me before I do something I'll regret later. The need to pick up the nearest object and throw it is nearly impossible to subdue.

Holden turns toward me. "He said he can give you five minutes with him if you . . . you know, in case you had any *questions* for him."

Holden's doing a terrible job hiding the double meaning, but either Eve didn't hear it, or she's ignoring it.

The happiness and exuberance from just minutes ago are gone. She's clutching her arms to her chest, and her skin is visibly paler than before. She looks so broken, and I know she's lost in her memories.

I want to hold her and be there for her, but before I can step toward her, Holden speaks up again.

"Phoenix, if you want to do this, you have to leave right now. Niko and Darrell are waiting downstairs for you. Unless you want me to come with you?"

I shake my head. "No, you stay here with Eve."

Unable to leave without at least holding her in my arms one more time, I pull her close and tilt her face upward. She blinks at me with her lost gaze.

"I have to leave for a few hours, but Hold will stay with you, okay?"

I press my lips to hers before she can say anything, letting my senses wash over every detail of her. Then, I force myself to step back and head downstairs.

MY HAND CONNECTS with Ben's face again. This time, the asshole collapses, and a satisfying crunch of breaking bone occupies the air.

O'Neal steps between us, glaring down at the man as if he also wants to get a kick in while he's down. I certainly wouldn't hold him back.

"I'm afraid this is where the fun has to end. Any more, and no one will believe he fell down the stairs somewhere."

He cackles like this is just another ordinary day for him, and maybe it is, but I don't care. O'Neal is the reason I have this moment, so I can't complain about his police procedures or the lack thereof.

He grabs Ben by the back of his polo shirt and pulls him up. Blood gushes from his nose, dripping into his mouth and down his chin.

Although Holden and I considered him as a suspect, I never truly expected some run-of-the-mill middle-aged guy to be our psychopath. But then, it only proves you often have no idea what's a façade and what hides behind it. My father is a prime example of what evil can look like in a fit body and custom-tailored suit.

O'Neal drags Ben to his car. So far, he hasn't said a single word. His only reaction was surprise when I arrived that quickly morphed into disgust, right before my fist connected with his face.

Ben dips his head to get into the car.

I ask my question one last time. "Why did you do it?"

He spins around and sneers at me. "Because you and your precious fiancée were the easier targets."

"Easier than who?"

Spittle flies out of his mouth. "Your piece-of-shit father and hers. You're all a bunch of entitled assholes, and the world would be a better place without all of you. You deserve to rot in Hell."

O'Neal raises a brow at me before he pushes Ben inside the car. "Don't listen to him. He's a dickhead who'll be gone for a very, very long time."

I push my hands into my pockets, wincing when my knuckles brush the fabric. "Thanks for the call."

"Anytime. I'll let you know if we find anything else." He gives me a small salute and slips into his undercover police car.

I watch them leave, staring at the spot on the horizon where they disappeared long after they're gone.

A noise behind me snaps me out of my trance, and I turn to stare at Niko, who has one foot out of the SUV.

"You okay there, boss?"

I glance over at Darrell in the passenger seat, who's wearing a similar expression as Niko, furrowed brows and eyes full of concern. Maybe they're questioning my sanity, and I can't even blame them. These days, I'm right there with them. To be honest, I forgot they were even here, so perhaps they have a reason to worry.

"Let's go home." I walk toward the car.

Niko gets out to open the back door for me.

The drive is silent as I stare at the gray clouds, going over what just happened, trying to take every one of Ben's facial expressions and words apart. Over and over.

The world would be a better place without all of you.

The words still replay in my head during my walk from the garage into the kitchen.

Right now, I have two goals and two goals only.

First, getting a drink.

Second, getting lost in Eve until this day ends and I pass out from exhaustion.

Huxley's wiping a large bowl with a kitchen towel. He gives me a once-over, his eyes immediately widening. Damn it.

A glance at the time tells me it's dinner prep time. I should have paid more attention to the time and gone straight upstairs, reducing the risk of running into anyone.

"Sir. Are you all right?" He drops the towel and bowl and comes around the island. "Your shirt."

My hand goes toward where he's pointing on reflex, and he lets out a quiet gasp at the sight of my hand. A glance at my shirt confirms my suspicion that I must have gotten more than just my knuckles bloody.

"I'm fine." Ignoring my shirt and my hand, I focus on the long wall of cabinets and grab a glass from one.

Huxley intercepts me at the liquor tray. "Sir, please let me help."

The old man is fluttering around me like a nervous mother hen, and I don't care right now.

He almost pushes me aside, takes my favorite whiskey from the tray, and pours me a large heap.

"Thanks." I grunt out before drinking it in one go.

By the time I set down the glass, Huxley has produced a first aid kit, and is already rummaging around to get what he needs. I let him fret. He cleans my wounds, applies ointment, and bandages them. The sooner it's done, the sooner I can devour Eve.

That asshole psychopath will never touch her again, not even with a speck of his blood.

"It's been a while since I've had to patch someone up." Huxley gets rid of all evidence and smirks at me. "Your grandfather could be a bit of a hothead sometimes, especially when your grandmother was involved."

Despite the pain that hits me every time I think about my grandparents and that they were taken from us too early, I still have to chuckle at Huxley's comment.

"Your grandmother was incredibly protective too, but her ways were more . . . let's say more subtle than your grandfather's."

"They both loved fiercely and protected what was theirs." I've always wondered how my father became the person he is with such amazing parents. But then Grandpa would tell me he wasn't always like this, that somewhere he took a wrong path, listened to the wrong people, and became too greedy. I think they always hoped he'd change back into the man he used to be, the man I only know from stories.

Huxley nods. "That they did." He pauses for a moment. "They would have adored your Evangeline. Sometimes, I see the same spark in her eyes that I saw in your grandmother's."

Your Evangeline.

My Evangeline.

The only reason she's mine is because I forced her to marry me, a decision that was entirely led by my blind hatred for her.

Something tugs at the back of my brain. Something I

didn't even think about before. Because Huxley isn't wrong, Eve is a lot like my grandmother, and she wasn't a doormat.

I was so blinded by my hatred and my need for revenge that it didn't even occur to me that the Eve I used to know wouldn't just agree to marry me so quickly.

Yet, in less than a day, she went from proclaiming she'd never marry me to suddenly accepting the arrangement.

Fuck. Why didn't I see that before now?

With a quick "Thanks" to Huxley, I'm out of the room and on my way to find Eve.

I need answers, but first, I need her.

CHAPTER 32

EVANGELINE

Phoenix barrels into the music room, startling me so much I nearly fall off the bench.

My gaze snatches on his bandaged hand right away.

I shoot out of my seat. "What happened?"

I've been hiding here since he left, needing the escape only music—and now also Phoenix—can offer me after the news Holden dropped on us, impatiently waiting for his return.

We rush toward each other, diminishing every inch of space between us.

"It's nothing." He gathers me the second he's close enough.

One hand goes into my hair, the other presses against my lower back. He descends on my lips with a desperation that steals my breath.

Together, we move backward until I bump into the cool material of the piano. I get lost in his kiss, unable to ignore how my entire body comes to life under his touch.

326

Nothing, and no one, can render such an all-consuming fire inside me like this man can. He ignites me.

When we finally come up for air, I gasp and stare at the rapid rise and fall of his chest and what appears to be blood on his shirt.

My hand reaches for him. "Oh my God, are you okay?"

"I'm fine." He steps back.

I immediately mourn the loss of his proximity.

But then he holds out his uninjured hand toward me. "As much as I want to fuck you on this piano, I told you no one else gets to see what's mine. Say it."

I take his hand and stare at him. "Say what?"

"That you're mine."

I don't know what happened in the hours he was gone, but there's so much devastation in his gaze that my heart makes a sad extra thump.

I swallow and stare him straight in the eyes. "I'm yours."

The second the words are out of my mouth, he's back on me, that same wildness in every brush of his lips, every swipe of his tongue.

"Hold on." His hands go under my butt to lift me into his arms.

I circle my legs around his waist, and he carries me out of the music room.

Somehow, we end up in this position a lot.

Getting into the bedroom is a team effort, but neither one of us seems willing to let go, so we manage.

The second the door is closed behind us, all bets are off.

After Phoenix left earlier, I changed into a T-shirt and yoga pants, and Phoenix rids me of both, plus my bra and panties, in less than thirty seconds.

"I need you." His mouth is back on mine, his fingers trailing down my body until they disappear between my thighs. "Fuck, you're so wet."

He enters me, pumping in and out. Circling his slick fingers over my clit.

I throw my head back on a moan, slightly wobbling on my feet.

This man can make me forget my name, even though it seems like he's the one who's trying to forget something. But I'm okay with that, for now. I can, or rather, I *want* to be that escape for him, the person who takes him to a place where he can forget, where nothing but the two of us exists.

Without warning, he drops to his knees, and hooks one of my legs over his shoulder. His fingers sink into my butt cheeks to draw me toward his mouth. I only have a split second to sink my hands into his hair and to hold on for dear life.

Apparently, Phoenix is on a mission to kill me.

He doesn't just devour my pussy, he's going for utter destruction, holding me so close to him, I'm not even sure how he can breathe. When he sucks on my clit, then bites it and tongue-fucks me, I'm getting genuinely worried I might not survive this impending orgasm.

"Phoenix . . . Phoenix, I'm going to . . . oh my God, I can't."

Coherent thoughts leave my brain, my senses completely overwhelmed by the way his fingers dig into my butt, or how one of his fingers keeps circling my hole. The noises he makes are almost animalistic, and the scent of him, of us, permeates the air. My fingers tangle deeper into his soft hair, and I gaze down at him.

The sight of Phoenix on his knees in front of me is utterly mesmerizing, like I'm his queen, and he'd do anything for me.

Black dots send my vision hazy. He continues to lap at me like he can't get enough but always stops when I'm right at the edge.

"Don't you dare come until I'm inside you."

"Phoenix, please."

My moans turn into whimpers, and he finally takes pity on me. He slowly gets me back on my feet and sweeps me into his arms, not wasting a second—kissing me, laying me out on the bed, tearing off his clothes, grabbing my hips to flip me over onto my stomach, hauling me to the edge of the bed, and sinking into me with one big thrust.

"Fuuuuuuck." His groan is loud, etched with the same pain that shone in his eyes earlier.

As usual, he's my undoing, and my orgasm hits me with the power of a cracking lightning bolt.

His bandage grazes my hips, but I'm too far gone to worry about it right now. This, he, feels too good.

Every thrust hits home, his thighs slapping against mine, his balls creating extra friction. He moves one of his hands to my butt crack and circles my hole once more. It puckers, the anticipation, the forbidden aspect of whether he will do anything more, sending a zap straight to my clit.

"Come again for me."

Smack.

The slap to my butt is so unexpected, I freeze momentarily and then let out a long moan. The memory of what we shared in his office comes back to me, of how hard he made me come, how much I enjoyed that experience with him, even though I shouldn't have.

Things have changed so much between us since that moment, and now—just as then—he knows exactly what my body needs, maybe even better than I do.

A *smack* lands on my other cheek, and my eyes roll back.

"Look how well you take me, Angel. Your pussy was made for me." His breathing is labored, his movements frantic. "Fuck, come on my cock like the good girl you are. Now."

The last word comes out in a growl just as he brings his hands down on my ass cheeks again.

Smack.

Smack.

He makes some kind of spitting noise, and something wet hits my ass crack. Before I know what's happening, one of his fingers slides through it and pushes past my tight ring of muscle.

The foreign invasion is as surprising as it is intense, and I don't just come, I detonate.

My orgasm hits me so hard, I lose all feeling in my limbs and scream, my entire focus on that pulsing explosion in my core.

"Fuck, fuck, fuuuuuck." Phoenix comes with a roar.

His cock pulses inside me to the point where I'm not even sure where I end and he begins.

He collapses on top of me, his weight forcing me into the mattress without apology.

A huff of air escapes me.

"Sorry." He slowly detaches himself from me and withdraws.

The air smells of sex, and I inhale it like an addict.

There's only us. Nothing else matters.

Phoenix trails a finger up my inner thigh until he gets to where his cum has run down. He pauses, and I glance at him over my shoulder and how his gaze is zoned in on the spot he's touching.

My entire body shivers at the picture.

He moves his hand upward, tracing the wetness to where it came from. My eyes widen when the pressure on my skin increases, and he shoves his fingers inside me.

My brain short-circuits. Is he pushing his cum back in?

His expression is focused, and he keeps repeating the motion. Over and over until I squirm under his touch.

"Be still, Angel. I don't want you to waste a single drop."

His gaze meets mine, and time stops.

There's something in his eyes I've never seen before. I'm unsure what it is, but it tugs at an invisible string in my chest. It's the same feeling I used to get when I went on stage to perform. It's this electrifying and dizzying mix of excitement and anxiety.

Phoenix severs our connection to focus back on the spot between my legs. Not too long after, he stops, seemingly satisfied with his results. His arms gingerly move around my body, and he shifts me until we're both lying on the bed and I'm tightly in his arms.

I could stay here forever.

And for a moment, I allow myself to believe that's a possibility.

Ever since Holden came with the news earlier that they'd found the person, my Freddy, I couldn't shake the feeling that it would somehow mean the end of Phoenix and me.

"Is it really over?" My words are muffled against his warm chest, but I know he heard them because he stiffens.

The question is out of my mouth, and my breathing hitches.

What if he takes the question the wrong way?

His heart speeds up under my ear, so mine does too, always wanting to be in sync with his.

"I mean, Ben . . . Freddy. Was it really him?"

Phoenix lets out a sigh. "The police seem to think so, and he admitted it."

"Wow." I swallow. "That will take some getting used to. Does that . . . does that mean we can go back to our normal lives now?"

Phoenix is quiet for several long beats. "Is that what you want? To go back to your normal life?"

Panic squeezes my throat. Why does everything come out so wrong today?

"Yes, I guess? I mean, I'd really like to go back to school, meet my friends at the café, and return to the shelter. Those sorts of things. Back to how things were before."

His hand tightens on my waist. "Before when?"

The elephant in the room keeps growing, and I'm unsure who will be the first to break. I want to know his answer to the question circling our heads too, but I don't want to be the first one to answer it.

What if I put my heart out there and he doesn't want it? After everything that happened, I'm not sure I'd survive it if he told me he didn't want me anymore, that I should go back to the way things were before he barged back into my life.

There's one thing he doesn't understand: there's no before him. There's only with him and after him.

"Before when, Angel?"

I gnaw on my lip before giving him a morsel of truth. "The explosion."

I close my eyes.

I wait for him to tell me that's not what he wants.

"How fast can you get ready for a trip?" His breath whispers across my head. A moment later, his lips ghost over mine.

When my brain catches up with his question, I back away until I can see him. It's gotten dark outside, but the lamp on the nightstand illuminates the room with warm light. Phoenix watches me, his intense gaze unwavering.

"You want to go on a trip?"

He nods. "Just to lie low for a little while. I'd rather be safe than sorry. It'll also give the team and the police the chance to make sure Ben is really Freddy. Right now, it feels too good to be true."

I think about it for two seconds and say, "Depending on where you're planning to take me, I can be ready in less than an hour."

Because he isn't wrong. All of this happened so quickly, it still seems surreal. It will take some time to fully process the fact that the police caught Freddy. Right now, it still feels odd that Ben is my devil.

"I'll make the necessary calls so we can leave tomorrow."

Maybe we're both a bit crazy right now.

When we finally get to a point where we can go back to our normal lives without stalkers, psychopaths, and explosions, we escape.

The little voice in my head whispers, *"What if that's why he's doing this? Maybe he wants to stay in this bubble with you for a while longer too. Maybe he's just as afraid as you are of what's waiting on the other side, or that the police have the wrong guy despite the confession."*

Because what are we without all the secrets, lies, pain, and hurt?

Is there even an *us* without all of that?

CHAPTER 33

PHOENIX

Eve's delectable ass sways in front of my face, and I want to bite it.

"Welcome, Mr. Montgomery. It's so good to have you back on board with us." The slightly too-high voice coming from the top of the stairs is enough to deflate my throbbing cock.

"Michelle." I walk up the rest of the stairs and give the flight attendant a curt nod.

It didn't escape me that she ignored Eve ahead of me, and I curse the heavens that this was the flight crew on standby. But beggars can't be choosers, and while it'll cost me a lot of energy to ignore Michelle's specific brand of persistence, we'll somehow make it through the flight. It's not her fault my father has fucked her for years or that she thinks I'm the same.

I thought so too, at one point.

She leans in when I try to step past her but is forced to step back since the tank behind me gives me a push.

"Whoops, sorry." Holden chuckles.

I glare at him over my shoulder.

But then I see Michelle's gaze as she takes him in with that familiar spark in her eyes, and I smile at him. "No worries at all."

Let's see how he'll like that.

My smile becomes predatory. I turn back to my fiancée and find her on her toes, trying to get her bag into the overhead compartment. Her shirt has ridden up, and since I'm such a helpful person, I step up behind her and give the bag the shove it needs. My dick presses into her lower back, and the little minx pushes back against me.

This flight might be more interesting than I thought it would be. It's never too late for me to use the bedroom in the back for something other than sleeping.

Holden's groan sounds around us. "If you guys do this the entire time, I will drown myself in the ocean. At least have the decency to do it behind closed doors. I'm entirely okay with lying by the beach by myself, trust me."

Eve makes a choking noise. Her cheeks flush pink prior to peeking over my shoulder at our third wheel. "Sorry, Hold."

"It's okay, Princess. You didn't do anything wrong." He winks at her.

I already deeply regret bringing him.

But he deserves this break too. Plus, he wants to wait and see how this Ben mess plays out in the next week or so as well. And there was no way I was going to take someone else with us.

So here we are, a merry band of three.

We take our seats, Eve and me on one side of the aisle and Holden on the other. That guy needs both seats anyway with his frame.

Unfortunately, Michelle is back, giving us her flight safety and emergency speech. I try to tune her out, but ignoring her suggestive stares and winks is impossible. Even the massive ring on Eve's finger doesn't deter her, though I shouldn't be surprised matrimonial vows mean nothing to her.

They just so happen to mean something to me, though, at least where the woman next to me is concerned.

I ban all thoughts of our engagement going up in flames once I confront her. Yes, it's a possibility, but I'm not ready for that yet. I want to exist in this bubble while we're gone and have my fill of her.

Just in case.

Afterward, we'll have the conversation we need to have.

Evangeline leans in and says, "Did you have sex with her?"

I think she's trying to whisper, but if the snickers coming from the other side of the aisle are any indication, she wasn't as quiet as she'd hoped.

I sigh, purposefully not keeping my voice down. "Never have and never will."

Michelle stumbles over her next words but quickly catches herself, being the professional she is.

At least, there's that.

Eve's cheeks have turned a dark shade of pink while she listens to the instructions.

Ten minutes later, we finally take off. I go over some final paperwork for the foundation, which I'll hopefully be able to get off the ground soon. Eve has been my number one priority since the explosion, and everything else has taken a back seat.

Per typical bookworm fashion, Eve is cuddled up with a blanket and lost in a story on her e-reader. When we're high up in the air and the seat belt signs turn off, she's squirming.

I lean in. "You okay?"

"Yeah, all good." She glances at me before focusing back on her screen.

Such a liar.

She continues to squirm, and I put a hand on her thigh to make her stop.

Her gaze snaps to where I'm touching her before colliding with mine. Her pupils are larger than usual, and I tilt my head to study her. "What's going on in that pretty head of yours? You're not afraid of flying, are you?"

"Oh no." She shakes her head and glances at my lips for a moment, then mutters, "It's nothing."

Now I definitely know something is up.

My tongue darts out to glide over my bottom lip, and I lean in until we're face-to-face. "Tell me what's got you squirming like this."

She scrutinizes the cabin. Michelle is banging in the small kitchenette in the front, and Holden is softly snoring.

"I was just thinking about something."

"About what?"

"Have you ever . . . you know?" She nods toward the back of the plane.

I bite my cheek to keep from laughing. God, she's cute.

That's what's got her so worked up? "I haven't, no. Why? Are you offering?"

Her eyes widen, and she points at herself. "Me? Oh, I was just curious since I read this scene once in a book, so yeah. Forget I said anything."

"What scene?"

"Just this airplane sex scene."

Just this airplane sex scene? Is she for real right now?

"Actually, now that I think about it, I'm not sure they had sex. Maybe they weren't on an airplane either. No, wait, there was a flight attendant, so I guess they were. Anyway, it doesn't really matter. It would have been hot anywhere." She wrings her hands and looks anywhere but at me.

My cock grows behind my zipper, and I shift around to adjust it.

I touch her face, guiding her chin until her gaze collides with mine. There's an inferno in those irises. "Tell me what happens."

She licks her lips, and fuck, I want to drag her to the back so badly right now, but I also want to hear more about this. I want to know what she considers a hot scene, what turns her on and has her blush like this.

She raises her dark eyebrows. "You want to know what happened in the sex scene in the book?"

"Yes. Tell me."

I watch her throat bob several times. She swallows and nods, probably more to herself than me.

"Okay, mmm, so he tells her to go to her knees, and then he asks her if she wants him to feed her his cock. When she says yes, he tells her to beg for it. So she does, and then he tells her to open her mouth like a good girl, and then, you know, he puts it in, and . . . uh . . . does his thing. And then he asks her if she's wet. She nods, so he tells her to put her hand in her skirt and to make herself come."

The words tumble out of her like she's getting a prize for telling the scene as condensed and as quickly as possible.

And then she shrugs like she didn't just make me half come in my pants.

I squeeze her thigh. "How did the scene end?"

She bites her bottom lip and brings her roaming gaze back to mine. "The flight attendant knocked on the door just as they both came."

We stare at each other for a long time and then scramble up. I grab her wrist and pull her after me so fast she stumbles and bumps into my back.

The second I have her in the bedroom, I turn around and hold her against the door. "Fuck. I'm not sure I've ever been as turned on as when you talk about what gets you hot."

I slam my mouth on hers, plunging my tongue into her mouth and taking everything she offers.

When we come up for air, her eyes are glazed over and hooded.

My entire body is on fire, and I have to remind myself why it's a bad idea to fuck her against the door this very second. Not a bad idea, per se, but the desire to role-play with her is stronger. To see that burning lust in her gaze again. To feel the matching heat behind my rib cage.

"Get on your knees, Angel."

A little whimper escapes her, but she complies.

Shoving down my sweatpants and underwear, I squeeze my hand around my hard length and stroke it.

"Do you want me to feed you my cock?"

The spark in her eyes at my question is addicting, and I know I've found my new obsession with her: playing out every dirty scene she's ever read and was turned on by.

And I know she reads a lot.

Eve nods, waiting for further instructions.

"Then beg for my cock like the good girl you are."

A shudder runs through her, and my dick twitches inches from her face.

"Can I please suck your cock?" Her tongue darts out, and she licks off the beads of precum that have gathered at my tip. "Please, sir?"

"Fucking hell." Words flee my brain. I peer down at her and thrust my hips forward and my cock into her waiting mouth.

She takes me deep, switching between sucking and licking, with both of her hands wrapped around my shaft. When she gags, I'm already so close, I twitch on her tongue. As if that was her warning signal, she takes one of her hands off me and moves it between her legs instead, and I come without a warning.

Her eyes widen, but she swallows every last drop I give her. I'm on her the second she releases me. Yanking her up, removing her pants, picking her up, and pinning her against the wall. I'm already hard again, so I slam into her.

"Oh my God, Phoenix. I'm already so close."

Having her this turned on from playing out this scene and sucking me off has my vision go all hazy.

I take her mouth, swallow her moans, and pound into her like a madman possessed, not letting up on my punishing pace until she greedily clenches around me and I consume every last one of her cries.

This woman makes me lose all control, to the point where I'm not sure who I am anymore without her occupying my thoughts.

No matter where I'm at in life, this woman is my world.

My legs shake, and I walk us over to the bed. I lay her

down and draw out of her. After I remove the rest of her clothes in record time, I bury my face in her cunt and let her moans and gasps guide me. When she's close, I stop. She whimpers, squeezing her gorgeous tits in her hands, and I slap her clit and pussy.

"Oh my God." She bows off the bed. "Phoenix, please."

I do it again, unsure who's closer to losing their sanity.

Driving my cock back inside her slick heat, I revel in everything that's her.

Reality creeps in for a punishing moment, but I try to force it back out. I almost succeed. Almost. "Who do you belong to?"

I need her to say it so I can stay right here where I belong. With her.

Her walls clench around me, and she screams her release into the pillow she must have grabbed at some point.

She still hasn't answered me, but her orgasm triggers mine, and it's too late to hold it back. I come so hard I almost collapse on her, barely holding my weight on trembling arms.

Eve puts hers around my neck and pulls me down onto her. I roll us to our sides, trying to catch my breath before I look at her.

"It's you, Phoenix." She brushes my hair away from my forehead, a small, satisfied smile lifting her mouth. "I belong to you."

There's so much honesty in her gaze that my heart contracts.

It's almost too much.

I open my mouth to say something back, but there's a

knock on the door, officially ruining the moment. It's a loud and obnoxious knock, telling us exactly who it is.

Eve giggles before Holden's voice sounds through the door.

"Thanks for making me sit out here with a boner. I really appreciate it." He groans loudly. "Now get your asses out here because we're getting ready to land soon."

Eve and I gape at each other and laugh until my stomach hurts. She brushes her hand over my face, and I lean into it. It's perfect. Serene.

She presses a kiss to the corner of my mouth. "I've missed that laugh."

Memories of laughing with her when we were younger take over my mind: throwing her into the pool and her dunking me in retaliation. I return the kiss and stay there for several seconds. "I have too."

Another knock sounds at the door, this time more timid, and we both groan when Michelle tells us we have to return to our seats.

Reluctantly, we get dressed and walk back into the cabin, where Holden sits with a pillow on his lap, flipping us off.

"Hey, Princess."

She buckles in and regards Holden. "What?"

"Did Phoenix tell you the island is his? That he actually bought the whole damn thing?"

I groan and mumble, "Motherfucker."

Eve glances at me. "You did?"

I nod.

Holden chuckles, clearly enjoying this moment. "Ask him what it's called."

Curiosity shines in her eyes, and she leans into me. "What's the island called, baby?"

My eyes flare as her gaze collides with mine. "Careful, Angel."

She makes a pout. "Tell me."

"Angel Island."

What I don't tell her is I bought it the second I gained access to my trust fund at eighteen. That wasn't too long after I met her when she was only fifteen.

I didn't even tell Holden that part.

They don't need to know how truly obsessed I've been with her ever since I met her.

CHAPTER 34

EVANGELINE

I t's our last evening on this beautiful island—my island —and I never want to leave. Even though Phoenix and I have spent so much time together back in New York, this has felt different. It's like we both shed our expectations, the roles assigned to us. Underneath the façade we found the real us, the us that isn't defined by anyone or anything else.

I love that us so much.

And I think Phoenix does too.

Being here has given me hope, but I know we need to talk about how things will continue with us before we fly back home. At first, I didn't want to ruin this fantastic time. Now, it's a constant reminder creeping into our bubble, telling me I can't prolong this anymore.

Phoenix is in the shower after another day of relaxing at the beach, and I step out onto the sprawling patio, taking a few more pictures of the beautiful scenery to tease Ruby and Mason with. They are jealous whenever I send a new picture yet demand more every time.

I pass the hot tub we had a lot of fun in yesterday after

Holden retired for the night. Heat crawls up my neck, but I'm not mad. Phoenix keeps asking me about the books I've read, especially the spicy scenes, so who am I to say no to exploring some of my book fantasies in real life?

In an attempt to pause those memories for now, I keep walking. The wood of the patio seamlessly turns into warm sand under my toes. I love the feel of it. Up ahead, the man I was searching for is lounging on a chair with his phone in his hand. My steps are light as a feather, the sand swallowing all noise. It allows me to sneak up on him. To peek over his shoulder at a very familiar pop star on his screen. Just like last week when I caught him reading an article about her that he "stumbled upon by accident." Interesting.

Since I don't have a death wish, I slowly creep a few steps back before clearing my throat. "So you have a crush on Olivia Parker, huh?"

He bangs his head against the back of the chair and groans. "I'd be quiet about crushes if I were you, Miss 'harder, Phoenix, harder,' or I might come to some conclusions of my own."

His voice is several octaves higher as he imitates me, or tries to at least, because there's no way I sound anything like that. I hope.

There's no doubt I'm beet red, my face flaming with embarrassment, but it's Holden, so I still laugh and plop onto the lounge next to him. "You're mean."

"Don't dish it out if you can't take it, Princess. No pun intended."

"Oh my God, stop it." I smack his shoulder.

We both laugh.

Once I've calmed down, I point toward his phone. "She's

starting her world tour in a few months. Since I now know you're a fan too, does that mean you're coming with me next year when she's in New York?"

He shifts his focus back to the photo of Olivia still on the screen and huffs, which is pretty much like his version of no.

"Why not?" I pull up my legs and sit sideways to face him.

He scrubs a hand over his face, as if that would eliminate whatever he's tied up about. "I knew her when we were younger, and let's just say it didn't exactly end well, okay?"

The look he gives me could extinguish a fire, but not in a good way. I know it's not really directed at me personally, but I still cringe.

Then I gape at him for a solid minute until my brain reboots, mulling over what he just said. "Wait, wait. Back up for a second. You 'knew' Olivia Parker when you were younger, and it didn't exactly end well?" I make air quotes around *knew* because it sounds like the word needs extra attention.

"Yes."

"Aaaaaaand?" My brain still has a hard time catching up with the news. Holden, *my Holden*, knows my favorite singer.

"And nothing, Princess."

I throw my hands in the air. "That's all you're going to say about this?"

"Yes."

I grunt. "Why haven't you said anything? You know how obsessed I am with her. I've been playing her songs all week."

"I'm well aware of that. Thanks for that, by the way." He sighs like I'm the reason for his frustration.

"Are you telling me you started thinking about her again because of me?"

He shrugs.

"Do you want to see her?"

He doesn't say anything, and I feel like a dog with a bone.

Holden and Olivia Parker, who would have thought? But I can see it. They'd make a beautiful couple. Opposites attract and all.

I nod at him. "Let's go together. I bet she'd love to see you."

He gives me a pointed stare. "I wouldn't bet my money on that, Princess."

"Well, at least you'll know then, right? Isn't it better to fail at something than never try at all? What if she's your soulmate? Everyone deserves a chance with their soulmate."

Okay, maybe that's putting it on a bit thick, but I think everyone desires to be loved.

He raises an eyebrow and trains his razor-sharp gaze on me. "Are you talking from experience now that the stakes have changed?"

I tug at the hem of my shirt. "I don't know what you mean."

"You know exactly what I mean. Things aren't the same anymore as when you both entered this game."

I sigh, fully aware of his deflection. "I don't know if anything has changed. We haven't really talked about it."

He gets in my space. "Bullshit. Everything has changed, Princess, and you know it. Now the question is, do *you* want to take the risk? A wise person once told me everyone deserves a chance with their soulmate, so maybe it's time for you to make the first move. Happy endings only happen to those brave enough to conquer their fears."

I want to stick out my tongue at him for being cheeky, but his words hit home too much. It's everything I've been feeling, everything I've been worried about.

And damn him for being right. Of course I'm scared. Not wanting to bring this up with Phoenix is one-hundred-percent fear holding me back.

Noise comes from the house, and we both watch Phoenix approach. He eyes us with suspicion, his narrowed eyes moving back and forth between Holden and me like he could pluck out our thoughts by sheer will.

"Anything I should know about?" His words carry across the breeze.

I jump up and smile at him. "Yes. Holden and I will see Olivia Parker together when she's at Madison Square Garden next year. It's his early birthday present for me."

Phoenix shifts his gaze to Holden, tilting his head at his friend. "Is it now?"

Holden also stands, effectively towering over us, with that dang eyebrow raised again. "The princess thinks I need to conquer my fears."

"Conquer your fears? By going to a concert?" A noise escapes Phoenix like he's trying to hold back a laugh.

Holden rolls his shoulders. "Yup. Something about soul-mates and shit."

This time, Phoenix chuckles. As do I. When he says it like that, it does sound funny. But I've noticed that's his thing. No matter how sad or serious something is, Holden has a talent to make it sound silly. I once asked him why he went to prison, and he told me it was because sometimes you think you're a knight in shining armor but then it turns out you're just a villain in tinfoil after all.

The mountain of a man, who's somehow wormed his way into my heart too, grabs his things from the chair and gives us a little salute. "Anyway, you kids have fun with your own *conquests*."

He stomps up the path, turning left at the end to head to his bungalow.

Phoenix interlaces his fingers with mine and pulls me closer. "I'm not sure if poking the bear is the right thing to do here. Some things are better left in ruins."

Is he still talking about Holden or us?

Worry immediately takes over my brain, but I try to shake it off and say, "Maybe."

"I guess only time will tell." His lips meet mine in a gentle kiss. "Are you ready for dinner? I wanted to talk to you about something."

Dread hits my stomach like lead, but I smile at him. "Food sounds good."

I follow him to the house, knowing whatever comes next will change everything. But Holden was right; maybe it's time to conquer my fears. I can't give him the satisfaction of preaching to the choir when I don't follow my own advice.

Phoenix leads me through the house and up the flights of steps, his hand in mine the only thing that keeps me moving. I barely pay attention to our surroundings, halfway expecting to end up in the bedroom because we've been spending *a lot* of time there.

But we ascend one more flight of stairs until we push through a door that leads us onto the rooftop. We've been up here before, and it's a beautiful place with an infinity pool and the most stunning view of this tropical paradise. But something is different today. Not only is there a spectacular feast on a table for two, but the pool now also features gorgeous trays of chilled treats and drinks.

Pool floats.

"There you are." Phoenix walks into the kitchen of the pool house, his eyes taking me in from top to bottom in my bikini and thin cover-up. Lately, his gaze has lingered for longer, and I really hope it's because he's interested in me.

He swoops me into his big arms, crushing me against his chest. My heart pounds behind my rib cage, and I'm afraid he can feel it through the thin material separating us. He inhales, breathing me in, and goosebumps erupt on my body.

"Happy birthday, Angel." He stays there for one more deep inhale, then shifts his attention to the counter and the pool floats I put together.

Phantom pain pierces my heart, like every time thoughts of the night he broke my heart infiltrate my mind. First, he gave me my treasured compass necklace, and then he told me there was no place for someone like me in his life. How many times have I replayed that day? That night? And how things would have turned out if they had ended differently. Without him breaking my heart. Without me making a bunch of terrible decisions.

But I know I need to let go of that because things happened the way they did, and heedless of how many times I revisit the past and wish I could alter it, I can't.

Why is it sometimes so much easier to focus on the wrongdoings of the past than the possibilities of the future?

Ask him.

Ask him how things are going to continue between you.

Tell him how you want things to continue.

I'm catapulted back into the present, taking in the scene before me.

"Do you like it?" Phoenix studies me.

The setup is straight out of a fairy tale, with flowers and candles everywhere and soft music playing over hidden speakers. Now, all I need to figure out is whether this fairy tale will have a happily ever after or not.

"It's absolutely beautiful." I point at the pool and chuckle. "And these look so much better than mine did."

He lifts a shoulder. "Yours were perfect, just like you."

I gasp at his words just as my stomach growls, and he smirks at the sound.

"Let's feed your angry monster."

He pulls a chair out for me at the table and pushes it in when I'm ready. Then, he works on uncovering the dishes with a boyish grin. "What do you want first?"

All my favorite food from this week is laid out in front of me like a silent offering, and hope flares to life once more in my chest.

We both try some of everything, though I'd happily eat grilled pineapple for the rest of the evening.

Phoenix finishes first, watching me while I spoon the last bit of tiramisu out of my bowl.

He chuckles. "I don't think there's anything left in there."

I eye the leftovers in his bowl, but my stomach squeezes, and I reluctantly put my bowl and spoon down with a sigh. "That was delicious, thank you."

"Anything for you."

He sounds so genuine, his words surround me like a soft caress.

I know I shouldn't stare at him in an open invitation to ask me questions when I'm still not sure I want to know the answers to them. But I can't.

"Why did you agree to marry me?" His voice is even, but something in his gaze betrays his composure.

CHAPTER 35

PHOENIX

She swallows, letting out a reluctant sigh like she knew this would come up eventually. "Because *he* told me to."

"Why didn't you tell me?"

"Honestly? I just didn't want to think about him." She pulls at the hem of her skirt. "At the beginning, it didn't really matter anyway. Unless I wanted to risk someone getting hurt or worse, I was stuck in the engagement. And then so much happened, and things . . . things changed, and all I wanted to do was forget about my messed-up life and pretend everything's okay."

I nod, unsure of what to say.

Did she want to forget about us too?

I thought talking about this would help, but maybe it wasn't such a good idea, after all.

My gaze moves to the pool, the floating trays a stark reminder of one of the biggest regrets of my life.

"You know, I often think about that night, your birthday

party, and how different things could have been if I hadn't made you hate me."

"Why did you do it?"

Our gazes meet, and time stands still for a moment. "Because I knew I wasn't strong enough to stay away from you otherwise. I needed you to hate me. The older I got, the more fucked up my world got. I was drawn to you from the moment I first saw you, and I wanted you so badly. But I knew I'd eventually step into my father's footsteps. That's what he groomed me for, and somehow, he made me believe I wanted that power too."

My throat tightens, but I can't stop now. "He always said women made you weak, yet I wanted to be selfish and have you anyway. But you wanted to travel the world and play your music. Every time you talked about it, your entire face lit up, and you were wearing the most beautiful smile."

Eve sighs, remembering that time with me.

I lean forward, wanting her to understand my reasons. Or maybe I just want to make myself feel better about my past decisions. "You deserved that life, and I knew I couldn't give it to you. My future was dark and gloomy, whereas yours looked so bright. Taking that away from you would have meant watching the life drain out of your eyes, only leaving behind the same dull acceptance my mother has in hers. I saw how my dad treated my mother, how his business partners treated their women, and I didn't want you anywhere near that. You were so full of life, so eager to explore the world and lose yourself in your music, and I knew I could never drag you into my world where all of that would die eventually."

"There's no place for someone like you in my life." She

whispers the words I told her so many years ago and closes her eyes. "You were protecting me."

"I was trying to."

A single tear slips down her face, and I see the same grief in her eyes that surges in my chest. The grief over what we could have been. The version of us I destroyed because I made a choice for both of us—one I thought was the right one—only for it to have the worst possible outcome. Maybe Connie would still be alive if things had been different.

After what feels like an eternity, Eve says, "I know we can't change the past, and what's done is done. But if you could, what would you change?"

I bite my lip and try to stay calm. "Do you remember how I found you in the pool house on your birthday? You were making your pool floats."

She nods.

"I came up to you and gave you a hug and told you happy birthday."

"You did."

"If I could go back in time, I wouldn't have let you go. I would have held you and told you you were the most beautiful girl I'd ever seen, that none of the other guys were good enough for you because the only ring you were ever going to wear on your finger would be mine."

She presses her wobbling lips together and gazes at her lap. After several deep inhales, she looks back up, and the utter destruction in her eyes plunges a knife straight into my heart.

"And I wouldn't have believed you." Her voice is shaky.

I nod. "And I would have made it my daily mission to prove to you I meant every single word of it."

I thought it would feel good to have the truth out. I thought it would change things between us for the better. I didn't expect this level of torment and grief.

All I want to do is haul her into my arms and beg her for a real chance, but the fear of losing her again is paralyzing.

She gives me a teary smile. "Do you want to know what I wish I had done differently that day?"

I'm nodding before she ever finishes her sentence.

I might as well push the knife in to the hilt.

Eve pulls her lower lip into her mouth, gnawing on it.

One breath.

Two Breaths.

"I wish I would have told you none of the other guys could ever be good enough for me because they weren't you." Her hand goes to her necklace, toying with the charm. "You said the compass was supposed to be a reminder to keep moving forward in the direction of my goals, and I should have followed my heart and let it guide me toward you because I was utterly lost without you. And I should have told you all of this. I can't expect you to put your heart on the line without doing the same in return."

Her eyes search mine, her gaze unwavering, her voice steady.

My jaw clenches because I don't want to say what I have to say, but I know there's no way around this. "If the threat is really gone with Ben's arrest, the reason why you agreed to marry me and why I wanted to make this bargain in the first place are gone too."

And there it is—the biggest elephant of them all.

We stare at each other, and Eve is the first to end the silence.

"Would you break the engagement right now if I said that's what I wanted?"

I force myself to nod, knowing even if it came to this, I wouldn't let her go without a fight. But I keep that to myself for now, flexing my jaw so hard pain shoots through the lower half of my face.

Good.

The movement catches her eye before her gaze flicks up again. "Is that what you want, Phoenix? Do you want to break the engagement?"

"No." The word explodes through my clenched teeth, the sound low and menacing. "Do not mistake my agreement for compliance. I would chain you to my side if you let me."

Eve presses her hand on her chest but stays silent.

This has been a lot for both of us, but knowing she wanted me as badly as I wanted her when we were younger has taken my desperation, my obsession with her, to immeasurable heights.

I want her to be mine, but I also want her to choose me.

"The bigger question is, now that you can finally go after the life you've always dreamed of, do *you* want to end the engagement?"

CHAPTER 36

EVANGELINE

"Do you really have to go?" Phoenix brushes a lock of hair from my forehead, glaring at me from his spot beside me in the car.

I chuckle. "We've talked about this. Sometimes, we have to do things away from each other, and that's okay."

I play with his engagement ring, a sight that will never get old, especially now that I'm really engaged to Phoenix Montgomery. When he asked me if I wanted to end the engagement, I asked him in return how he felt about a long engagement. He said yes by devouring me on the edge of the pool. I know we'll probably need a lot of therapy to get to a healthy place, but at least we'll tackle this journey together.

I sigh. "Plus, Ruby said we've been back from our trip for a week, and sending daily selfies as proof of life isn't enough anymore. She'll show up at the house every day until you finally let me see them."

Phoenix huffs, clearly not amused. "That makes it sound like I'm holding you captive."

I move closer to whisper in his ear, "I like it when you

hold me captive. You know, there is this one scene with some restraints . . ."

Two groans sound in the car simultaneously, both for very different reasons.

Holden's is louder in the driver's seat. "Seriously, Princess. Have fucking mercy, will ya?"

Phoenix glares at him, and I touch his cheek to get his attention back.

"I haven't seen them in forever. And once they've grilled me about everything and see I'm well and alive, I'll be all yours again. Promise." I lean in and kiss him.

Getting lost in him has been my favorite pastime since our poolside conversation. We've been glued to each other's sides even more than before, whether we work, study, or relax. It's a craving we share and both happily indulge in.

Lucky for me, it was fall break at school this past week, giving me the time I needed to finally catch up with every-thing I've missed. Otherwise, I'm afraid, the lenience the teachers have given me with my recent schoolwork and assignments would have vanished into thin air.

In a few days, it's back to normal life, whatever that means anymore. I have a feeling it'll be a hard adjustment for both of us after spending almost every waking minute together for most of the last month.

"Fine." Phoenix glares past my shoulder at the café before pressing his lips against mine again. "Let me know when you're ready to leave."

"I told you, you don't have to wait. He's really gone."

His gaze is relentless. "Angel, we'll wait."

With Ben behind bars, I thought things would just be easy sailing from here on out, but I've quickly learned in the last two weeks you can't just undo years of fear and paranoia at the drop of a hat. It'll take some time for all of us to truly believe the threat is gone.

At least they're letting me go inside by myself. Baby steps.

"Fine, I'll keep you updated." I climb out of the car and blow him another kiss.

The moment I shut the door in his grumpy face, the door to the café flies open.

Ruby almost tackles me to the ground. "Evie, fucking finally."

I laugh and squeeze her tight. But something, or rather, someone, is missing, and I look around. "Where's Mase?"

She groans. "He's sick."

"What?"

"Yeah. He just texted. He left this morning to go shopping and to the gym and was supposed to meet us here after. Apparently, he puked, so he said he's heading home but to give you a hug."

"Well, that sucks."

Ruby keeps her limbs wrapped around me and pulls me toward the door. "It does, but I'm here, and I want to know everything."

Although my chest aches because Mason isn't here, I can't stop the happy smile over seeing Ruby.

Once we're inside and in our favorite corner booth, Ruby starts talking so fast, I laugh and wave my hands around to make her stop.

"Slow down. I didn't understand a single word you just said."

Tyler's arrival distracts me as he crosses the café and

puts two drinks on the table.

He leans down and gives me a side hug. "Hey, stranger. Good to see your face. Ruby was worried Phoenix and you might have killed each other after all."

"Nope. No killing anyone." I shake my head.

He grins at me. "I had to promise Ruby to help kidnap you if needed."

Ruby groans. "Oh, come on. I wasn't the only one who was a little worried when she suddenly canceled our coffee date, our first real chance of properly seeing her after the explosion. It was a tiny bit suspicious."

I lift my finger to interject, but she waves me off to continue.

"No, seeing you at your engagement party doesn't count because we only got to see you for like two minutes, with Phoenix and Holden sending us murderous glances the entire time. And then boom, he's dragging you on his private jet to take you to some faraway island. And all we got was a 'Don't worry about me. I'll call you when I'm back' message. Not cool. That sounded like something he would send us in your name if he decided to finish the job and throw your body out of the airplane somewhere."

She delivers the last line with a glare, and the intended guilt swirls in my stomach. I lift my hands in surrender, not even mentioning the daily pictures I've been sending. "You're right, you're right. I'm sorry. A lot happened, and I know I haven't been around much."

"Fine, you're forgiven." She leans forward with an eager smile. "But only if you tell us everything."

My smile slips a little, and I grab my drink to cover it up. I've talked to Phoenix about this exact scenario and have decided to keep my friends on a need-to-know basis regarding Freddy and my sister. I hate keeping them in the dark, but it's better this way.

Before I can say another word, the bell rings, and we all glance at the group of older people that walks through the door.

Tyler groans. "Figures."

Ruby waves him off. "Don't worry. I'll tell you all the gory details later."

They share a meaningful look, and he takes off with a sigh.

I tell her what we decided is safe information. Most of it is public knowledge now anyway after Ben's arrest, and the witnesses who have come forward to confirm his hatred for us and the scheming against our families. I keep things vague about what happened with Phoenix and me since so much would be tangled in lies and connected to Freddy. I don't want to lie to my friends, but it's too much baggage, and I don't need more people I love to have to shoulder it.

Ruby leans back and sips her drink. "So you basically just hung out at the house together? Both here and on the island?"

Her disappointment is written all over her face, and I chuckle.

"Pretty much, yeah. First out of necessity, but then also to spend more time together."

And then we move on, just like that. Ruby fills me on everything I've missed at school and parties. I'm sure she embellishes a story or two, but I don't even care. An hour later, my stomach hurts from all the laughter.

Tyler's been sitting with us during his downtime, adding

his own juicy details to the latest school gossip whenever he can. It feels good to spend some time with my friends, although I can't deny I already miss Phoenix like crazy.

Baby steps.

When Ruby finishes her drink, Tyler takes the empty cup and asks, "You want another one?"

She looks at her phone screen and back at him. "Are you still driving me to rehearsals?"

"Yeah. Shelly should be here any second to take over." He points toward the front door, just as his colleague walks in. "Ah, there she is. Perfect timing."

Ruby's gaze swings to me. "Since Tyler's playing chauffeur, I can stay another half an hour. Should we have one more?"

I nod and reach for my phone. "Sounds good. I'll text Phoenix to let him know I'll be ready in thirty minutes."

Tyler returns with our drinks a few minutes later and slides in next to Ruby. "I'm officially done for the day. What did I miss?"

My bladder uses that moment to yell at me, and I groan. "I'll be right back. Bathroom break."

Tyler whispers something in Ruby's ear, and I get up. Their hushed voices follow me all the way to the hallway in the corner, only cutting off when I step into the women's restroom.

I take care of business and wash my hands when heeled footsteps sound outside the door. It opens a split second later, just as I turn to grab some hand towels, and something sharp pierces my neck.

"I'm so sorry, Evie," are the last words I hear before someone catches me, and everything turns dark.

CHAPTER 37

PHOENIX

When I walk into the café, I don't see Eve anywhere. Ruby stands in the back, waving me over.

I glance past her into the hallway. The bathrooms are back here, as well as some storage rooms. "Where is she? Is she in the bathroom?"

My voice drips with frustration, although I know it's not Ruby's fault that I just got off the phone with my dad. He chewed me out for taking a vacation and said I'd never be successful with that lazy attitude. I never wanted to tell him to fuck off as much as I did just now. But as usual, he hung up before I could get a reply in. It's always the same with him, and I'm sick of it.

Ruby shakes her head, glancing around the almost empty café while she toys with the hem of her shirt.

Unease trickles down my neck, and when her gaze finally meets mine, I stiffen.

Something isn't right.

"What's going on, Ruby?"

She blinks up at me once, twice, and whispers, "Something's wrong with Evie, and I need you to come with me right now, okay? But you need to stay calm."

My stomach churns, and I lean into her space. "Where the fuck is she?"

I have to clench my hands at my sides. It's that or grabbing Ruby and shaking her until she tells me what's going on. But I know I couldn't be gentle, so I'd rather avoid that scenario, although I'm quickly getting to the point where I'm not sure I care.

Ruby jabs her thumb over her shoulder. "Out back. Come on."

She doesn't wait for my reaction, just spins on her heels, walks down the hallway toward the emergency exit, and pushes it open. Light filters in, momentarily blinding me until I follow her out, and my eyes adjust.

A quick look around makes one thing abundantly clear: no Eve.

Ready to rip Ruby a new one, I spin toward her. But this time, she's holding a gun aimed straight at me.

I freeze, my heart racing like it's trying to escape. "What the fuck is going on, Ruby?"

She swallows, her gaze flicking around the back alley. "We don't have much time, so I need you to listen to me very carefully, okay?"

I stare at her, not moving a muscle.

"We will get into the car behind me right now, and you'll follow the GPS directions. If you don't listen or try something stupid with me, something bad will happen to Evie." Her eyes are glassy, her voice monotone.

I don't hesitate for a second. I hold up my hands, walk toward the black Honda, and do exactly what she said. I could disarm her in seconds, but it's not worth the risk.

Eve's safety is my number one priority, and before anything else, I need to know where she is and make sure she's okay. One thing is for certain, though: whoever took Eve will pay—with their life.

Ruby joins me in the car with the gun trained on me the entire time. I turn the key, and the car comes to life with a roar. We leave the back alley in the opposite direction of where Holden is parked. There goes my small hope of driving past him and alerting him somehow.

When we enter the freeway, I watch her out of the corner of my eye. "Why are you doing this, Ruby?"

She's pushed against the door with her back, her right hand pointing at me with the gun. And I could be mistaken, but I'm pretty sure her entire arm is shaking. Is this her first time holding a gun?

"You know I will kill you if something happens to her, right?" I keep my gaze on the road, my hands crushing the steering wheel. "No one will touch her and get away with it."

She doesn't say anything.

We get off the freeway a few minutes later and enter a neighborhood with large properties, winding down road after road until the robotic voice says, "In two hundred feet, turn right."

The GPS leads us to a modern two-story family home, and the garage opens as we approach.

Fuck. I don't want to be so compliant, but what other choice do I have? I'd never forgive myself if something happened to Eve because of me.

The same thing Eve has done for years. Do things she'd never do otherwise to keep her loved ones safe.

Fuck. Fuck. Fuck.

It can't be.

Damn it. No.

That fucking bastard.

I drive inside the garage and park next to the family van.

"Empty your pockets and leave everything on the seat." Ruby opens her door. "Eve is in the basement. Let's go."

Eve is in the basement.

Ruby just said Eve is in the motherfucking basement. If a single hair on her head is out of place, I will take my time killing her.

But first, I need to get to Eve.

I unbuckle and exit the car, leaving my wallet, phone, and keys on the seat. My body is taut. On edge.

Sometimes, you have to be patient and let the other player make their move first so you can destroy them.

My father's words slice into my brain, and I clamp my jaw together.

Patience, my ass.

I'm barely holding on to my damn sanity but follow Ruby's vague instructions toward the staircases that lead upstairs and downstairs.

She waves her gun to motion for me to go first. I want to sprint downstairs to find Eve and rescue her, but I also don't want a bullet in the back of my head.

There's no door at the end of the staircase, so I walk through the doorframe and into the unfinished basement. Gray concrete floor and exposed framing and insulation gives the impression it's a construction site rather than the basement of an upper-middle-class house.

Unsure of where to go, I stop and scan my surroundings.

The left side of the basement is like an open area, whereas the right side has several unfinished rooms sectioned off, hiding them from my view.

Silence surrounds me, no matter how hard I strain my ears.

Where the fuck is Eve?

I'm about to ask Ruby when someone shouts, "All the way to the end and on the right."

Ruby makes a noise behind me, but I ignore her and do what the person said.

That voice.

Why does it sound familiar?

I try to stay calm and keep my footsteps at a normal pace when all I want to do is charge. But I need to get Eve out of here, and I can't do that if I'm dead before I ever get to her.

Trepidation fills every step I take toward the mentioned room. But I make it and get my first look inside the framed room. The fine hairs on the nape of my neck stand on end, followed by bile rising up my throat. I freeze, and Ruby bumps into me before peeking around me to see why I stopped.

I don't see her response, nor do I give a fuck.

All I can focus on is Eve curled up on a large metal bed in the middle of the room. And she isn't alone.

"Eve." Her name is laced with icy panic, the same one that's creeping up my hands and into my chest. "What the fuck did you do to her? I swear to God, if you hurt her . . ."

My body is tense. Trembling. I take in the scene in front of me, not wanting to miss anything. The bed is a king, if not bigger, the headboard made out of metal slats that are attached to poles on either side. The mattress is bare, but from here, it appears clean. At least something.

Eve doesn't seem to have any apparent injuries, but I can't be sure she's okay until I check.

She *has* to be okay.

If anyone deserves a fucking break from life, it's this woman. She's gone through so much already, and I will get her out of here, even if it's the last thing I do.

A bead of sweat rolls down my nape as I step forward, a low noise erupting from the back of my throat when the person sitting on the bed beside Eve puts a finger against his lips.

"Shh. We don't want to wake her up."

He's wearing a hoodie, and I can't see his face since he's watching Eve. He reaches for her cheek, caressing it in such a loving gesture that I see red.

I move before I realize what I'm doing, and he shoots up. I barrel forward until he aims a gun straight at my face and *tsks*.

"I wouldn't do that if I were you."

Warning bells go off, and I stop.

I don't dare move while I take him in. He's around my height, maybe an inch or two shorter, and not only is he wearing a hoodie but also a mask.

"Who are you?" My heart is beating like a drum. "And what the fuck is going on?"

He shrugs. "Just catching up with some old friends, that's all. We'll all have a great time together, won't we?"

That voice. Damn it. Where have I heard it before?

Eve lets out a little groan like she doesn't feel good, and my gaze flickers to her in a panic.

"What did you do to her?"

The guy puts his free hand on his chest. "*I* didn't do anything. But Ruby gave her some drugs to help her sleep."

Anger spirals up from the pit of my stomach, and I have to grind my molars to keep from reacting. If it wasn't for the gun, I'd strangle them both.

The psycho peeks around me and winks. I don't turn to see Ruby's reaction because there's no way I can take my eyes off Eve and this guy.

"Grab the handcuffs and put them on him."

My gaze snaps to him, and movement behind me tells me he was talking to Ruby.

He watches her before lifting his chin toward me. "Hands up in front of you."

Everything inside me fights his command, rage and fear struggling for dominance.

When I don't immediately react, he lowers the gun to point it at Eve.

Tilting his head side to side to crack his neck, he stares me straight in the eye. "I feel a little trigger-happy today, so don't tempt me."

Clenching my hands into fists, I lift them. Ruby steps in front of me without looking up, solely focused on her task: cuffing one hand, then the other. There's a long chain attached to the handcuffs, and the psycho grabs it. Without warning, he yanks me across the room to the other side of the bed, where he connects it to the side pole of the headboard. It's on the opposite side of Eve, and I hope like hell I can reach her.

He steps back and waves his gun around. "Since I'm such a nice person, I'm giving you a few feet to move around. If you don't behave, I'll take that privilege away. Are we clear?"

His intense stare is burning into the side of my head, so I give him what he wants and nod. He'll pay for all of this later.

"Good."

He walks toward the doorway, and this time, I drag my gaze long enough away from Eve to watch him nod toward the ceiling with the gun and say, "Don't do anything I wouldn't do. No, actually, please do. Either way, I'll enjoy the show."

His manic laughter follows him out of the barren room, and Ruby rushes after him when he calls her.

I scowl at the blinking camera in the top corner. That fucker is watching us.

For a moment, I just stand here, trying to get rid of some of this tension in my body. Every muscle is tight, every organ, my entire being on high alert.

Not understanding why we're in this situation only adds to the turmoil, because why the fuck does Ruby and a guy I might have possibly met before kidnap Eve and me?

Do they want money?

No. That doesn't make sense. Ruby comes from plenty of money too.

Eve groans again, interrupting my maddening thoughts. I stare at her limp form, wanting to climb on the bed and pull her into my arms. Badly. But I don't want to disturb her. She needs to sleep off as much of the drugs as she can. I'm sure the aftereffects of whatever they gave her won't be pretty when she wakes up.

As if she heard my thoughts, Eve rolls halfway on her back, and fuck. They handcuffed her too. The same way they restrained me, to the outside pole on the headboard. Damn it.

She mumbles something incoherent, and I throw all caution to the wind and get on the bed. I keep my movements as slow as possible in case she's nauseated. The small moan that escapes her lips doesn't make me hopeful.

"Angel, I'm right here." I face her, reaching forward to brush the hair away from her face, but the chain stops a few inches away.

Fucking bastard.

I squeeze my hands so hard some of the newly formed skin on my knuckles stretches too much and splits open.

Shit.

I take several deep breaths, trying to calm the ball of worry and foreboding that's currently twisting in my stomach. It's impossible, but at least I'm as quiet as possible. Eve will probably freak out enough as it is when she finally comes around.

Instead, I mimic her previous position and lie on my side to watch her chest rise and fall in rhythmic succession.

I will get us out of here.

There's no other option.

Nothing will happen to Eve, not on my watch.

She's gone through too much already.

I stretch my arms as far as they go, the movement allowing me to touch her elbow.

It's not much, but it's enough until I can gaze into those

beautiful eyes again. It's enough until I can hold her in my arms again. It's enough until I can spend the rest of my life with her by my side.

And so I watch over her, paying attention to every single movement she makes, while also staying alert in case someone comes back.

Eventually, her breathing quickens, and she smacks her lips. This time, she doesn't go back to sleep like before but groans. Her entire body shifts, and she slowly opens her eyes.

Since she's facing me, I'm the first thing she sees. One corner of her lip tugs upward for the barest hint of a half-smile before it falls again, her brain probably slowly catching on to something being wrong.

She blinks at me, the movement sluggish, her throat loudly working on a swallow. "Phoenix, I feel . . . funny."

The words come out slurred.

"It's okay, Angel. Everything will be okay." Since I don't know what or how much they gave her, I can't guess how long she'll feel like this. "I'm right here. Can you stretch your hands my way?"

It takes her a while, but she manages, and I eagerly touch her hands with mine. The contact calms me, at least a little.

Eve goes in and out of sleep a few more times until her gaze appears sharper and more alert, which is both good and bad.

Her eyes widen, and she takes in the scene before her. Me and my handcuffs, my attached chain that leads to the bed frame behind me, then back to her own, followed by a glance around the room.

"What's going on?" Her voice is shaky, her breaths coming fast now. Too fast. "Where are we?"

I squeeze her hands to get her attention. "Look at me. I need you to stay calm, okay? Can you breathe with me?"

She nods, and we take several slow inhales and exhales together until her breathing is mostly back to normal.

I hold on to her hands like they anchor me. "Do you remember how you got here?"

Her gaze moves away from mine, roaming all over the room like it helps her jog her memory. "Mmm, the last thing I remember is going to the bathroom at the café. I was washing my hands when someone came in and . . . and they grabbed me from behind and something pinched my neck."

She tries to detangle her right hand from mine, probably to touch the spot, but my grip on her is ironclad. I can't let her go right now. I just can't.

"The person." She pauses. "The person who did it said something to me." She draws in a sharp breath. "It sounded like . . . no, no, that's not possible."

I already know how that part of the story played out. I don't want to hurt her even more, but we're not in a position where tiptoeing around will do us any good. The faster we can figure out what's going on, the faster we can get out of here.

So I rip off the Band-Aid. "Ruby injected you with something. When I got to the café, she told me you were sick in the back, and I followed her outside. You were nowhere to be seen, of course, so she pointed a gun at me and made me drive to this neighborhood about fifteen minutes away."

She shakes her head and stares at me, her eyes glistening with tears. "No, that can't be. Why would she do that?"

A chuckle sounds around us. "Because Ruby's a good pet, just like you are, Evie."

My gaze snaps up at the same familiar voice as before, and I freeze when I see who's standing in the doorway.

No fucking way.

He's a dead man.

CHAPTER 38

EVANGELINE

Despite still feeling lousy, I go rigid the moment my brain registers not just the words spoken behind me but also the voice. On the outside, I'm utterly paralyzed. On the inside, fear threatens to squash my chest in a tight fist. My heart is rapping against my ribs so violently, it's ringing in my ears.

My breaths come in quick, rasping inhales, and I squeeze my eyes shut, hoping against all odds when I open them again, I'm at home tucked away safely in Phoenix's arms where he'll hold me the entire time I tell him about my nightmare.

But when I blink them open again, nothing has changed. Phoenix is now sitting behind me but still tied to the bed like an animal. Just like me. He's giving me the saddest look I've ever seen, as if he knows what I just did in my head, and he's devastated for me. With me. Because, surely, he doesn't want to be here anymore than I do.

A metallic sound vibrates at the bottom of the bed. I

flinch, snapping my gaze toward the noise. I immediately wish I hadn't.

Tyler, *my* Tyler, stands mere feet away from me, watching us with a broad smile and unmistakable glee in his eyes.

"Evie, I'm so happy you're awake. Sorry about the circumstances, but we're all finally together. At last." He paces the length of the bed, never taking his gaze off us once.

I track him with my eyes like he does, and his smile widens.

Am I hallucinating? This cannot be real. No. I . . . no.

My brain is trying to make sense of this, but I've got nothing. Absolutely nothing.

"Ty, what's going on? Let us go, please. Whatever it is you want, you'll get it. Anything. Please?" My voice isn't as strong as I'd like, but who am I kidding? I barely got the words through my trembling lips.

Phoenix stiffens at my words, and I'm unsure if it's because I said anything at all or because of what I said.

Tyler stops and regards me with pouty lips. "Aww, Evie, thank you for asking so nicely. But I'm afraid I can't do that."

The backs of my eyes burn at his reply.

Never in a million years would I have thought this guy, my friend, would do anything to me.

Not just your friend, but your friends. Plural.

I'm not even remotely stable enough to think about Ruby right now, and I'm glad she's not with him at this moment.

I try to focus on Phoenix's breathing to get my own under control. He's glaring daggers at Tyler, which I'm sure isn't helping our situation, but I can't blame him either. It's not every day you get kidnapped by people you considered your friends for years. Well, for me, at least. They're my friends, not Phoenix's.

I drag my attention away from my fiancé and focus on the real problem, trying to keep the panic at bay that wants to creep up my chest. "Why are you doing this, Ty? What do you want?"

"What do I want?" Tyler repeats my question in a mocking tone. He drags a chair across the floor and sits. "There are so many things I want. Most importantly, I want you to suffer. You both deserve everything that's been happening to you."

The sluggishness caused from the injection is still lingering, but my brain is fighting to catch up. A beat later, the word he says finally sets in. "You called . . . you called me—"

Tyler chuckles. "Ah, yes. I called you pet."

"No . . . no. That's impossible." The puzzle pieces rearrange in my brain until they form one really messy and horrifying picture. Even though I don't want to, I let go of Phoenix and push into a sitting position. I need at least a little bit of control. Even if it's nothing more than an illusion at best. "*You're* behind all the messages? All the . . . all the . . ."

"I will fucking kill you." Phoenix growls next to me and yanks at his chain.

My lungs struggle for air, but there's no oxygen. Soon after, it all sinks in, and I can't hold back the violent tremors that shake my entire body. "You . . . you killed my sister."

My breaths come too fast. Inhale, inhale, inhale.

Phoenix rattles the entire bed frame so hard, I shift on the mattress several times.

Tyler watches us with an amused smile.

I bite back the sobs that want to break free because Tyler doesn't deserve the satisfaction of watching me break down. He won't take more from me than he already has.

My sister.

Phoenix going to prison.

All those years I lived in fear for myself and my friends.

My engagement to Phoenix.

The explosion.

Thinking it was over when the police arrested Ben.

How stupid.

How utterly, utterly stupid.

All the while the real monster was right in front of me, watching the puppet show he created from the front row. My friend. My best friend's boyfriend.

Bile rises in my throat, and I barely turn my head in time to puke over the edge of the bed. I heave until my stomach is empty. Saliva drips out of my mouth while I try to catch my breath.

Footsteps come closer.

Someone pulls my hair hard enough for my head to snap back. Tyler's face appears only inches from mine. "Maybe things would have gone differently if you had listened back then."

"Take your fucking hands off of her." Phoenix's voice is menacing, and the bed shakes like we're in the middle of an earthquake.

Staring at Tyler, and into his familiar hazel eyes that are now filled with nothing but darkness, I let words slip free that I've never let myself say, let alone think. "It is not my fault she's dead. It is not my fault. You killed her. *You.*"

I don't just say them, I yell them. Right in his face.

I was holding on to that guilt, to that grief, for so long it became a living part of me. Always clinging to me, a shadow weighing me down. And now, that heavy weight slowly lifts off my shoulders.

Tyler lets go of my hair and shoves me back toward the mattress.

The air stalls in my lungs.

With his hands in his pockets, he stares at me with narrowed eyes.

My skin crawls.

The corners of his mouth lift into a poor imitation of a smile. "I don't care what you tell yourself, but it was your choice. You played with your sister's life, and you lost. I only did what I had to. You made me kill her. *You.*"

One beat.

Two beats.

Three beats.

"You're a fucking monster." A scream rips from my throat.

I yank on my restraints to grab him, but he jumps out of reach. The metal bites into my skin, trying to bury itself deep in my flesh. I welcome the pain and the anger that comes with it. It doesn't burden me like the fear and panic. Instead, it fuels me.

I want to kill him.

I *have* to kill him.

If Phoenix and I make it out of here alive, I know deep down in my soul that Tyler won't.

And that's a promise I intend to keep.

Tyler's headshake is accompanied by a crazy smile.

"Well, as much fun as this was, I've got things to do. But I'll be back later so we can talk more. Try to behave until then." He strolls toward the door and says, "Babe, clean up the mess she made."

And then he's gone, leaving behind a wreckage that is invisible to the naked eye.

My entire body shakes, convulsing. My mind isn't helping either, replaying what just happened in a loop.

Ruby walks in with a bucket and some wipes, jolting me out of my appalling thoughts.

I stare at my best friend in utter disbelief, lost for words until betrayal takes over and the pounding in my ears becomes almost unbearable. "Ruby, what the fuck is going on? Get us out of here. Now."

She glances at me, her eyes shining with tears, and shakes her head the tiniest bit.

A bead of sweat runs down my nape. I'm struggling, trying to keep my hysterical emotions under control. But it's no use. They bubble to the surface, and I yell, "Is he forcing you to do this? For fuck's sake, Ruby. Help us. Please."

When I think she might finally say something, she lowers her head and ignores me, cleaning my vomit in silence.

I want to shake her and scream in frustration.

Why the hell isn't she helping us?

Did I do something wrong for her to do something stupid like this? Is this the universe getting back at me for keeping so many secrets from her? Or is this about Phoenix and me? It would make sense since we're both here, both stuck in this fucked-up situation.

Phoenix told me Ruby drugged me and helped Tyler

kidnap both of us, but I still can't believe it. None of this can be real.

She drugged me.

My best friend.

She had tears in her eyes when she just looked at you.

Shit. She'd never do something like this willingly. I refuse to believe that.

I sense Phoenix's presence behind me, offering me silent support.

He probably wants to yell at Ruby too, but he also knows the chances of her talking to me are much higher than his.

Lowering my voice, I tell myself to stay collected and try one more time. "Ruby, please. Talk to me."

I watch her for a sign, anything.

But nothing.

Without another word or glance, she leaves. I fall back onto the bed in a mix of anger, fear, and hysteria, staring at the ceiling and trying my hardest to calm down my erratic heartbeat and shaking limbs.

"Angel."

My name is barely a whisper and laced with pain; the anger Phoenix showed Tyler gone now that it's just us.

Without uttering a word, I turn toward him and shuffle as close as my restraints allow. I'm forced to stop with several inches between our heads, but at least I can intertwine my fingers with his.

My wrists burn from yanking on my cuffs, and one quick look at Phoenix's wrists confirms we have matching red marks.

Being able to touch him is the only remnant of peace I have left in this fucked-up mess.

Phoenix holds on to me like he's afraid I'll disappear the moment he lets go.

I know the sentiment.

I don't ever want to let go of him either.

There's so much turmoil in his eyes, it's almost painful to see, but I don't avert my gaze. At least the pain means he's here with me, and while I should feel nothing but regret and devastation over his presence, I'm not strong enough to cling to anything but comfort and relief.

We might not make it out of here alive.

The terrifying thought hits my mind. A sledgehammer out to obliterate me.

No, no, no. No matter how much truth is in that one small sentence, I can't think like that. Tyler will let us go. He has to. He wouldn't really hurt us, would he?

He killed your sister.

Fuck.

My stomach churns, but I push the nausea down.

Phoenix rubs over the back of my hand, attempting to smile. "Tyler installed cameras, so he's probably watching us. Are you okay?"

Of course he's watching us. Considering everything he knows about me, about us, he probably has for years.

I swallow and nod. "Other than waiting to wake up from yet another nightmare? Yeah. Just a little headache and some nausea."

I take him in, cringing when I get another glimpse of the red marks on his wrists. They are a lot worse than mine. "You're hurt."

Another brush of his fingers. "Don't worry about me. I'll be fine. Even better once we're out of here."

A shiver courses through me, my clammy skin cooling off.

"You think he'll let us go?" My voice breaks, and I hate it. I want to be calm and collected, I want to be smart and savvy and figure out how to get us out of here. But fear clogs my brain, and it is hard to focus on anything else.

"I don't know if he will." Phoenix brushes his lips against my palm. "But he will pay for everything he did, I can promise you that."

I bite my lip to keep it from wobbling. "Yes."

My eyes sting, but I still refuse to let a single tear escape, holding on to them like they're my choice of rebellion.

Phoenix lets go of my hands and cups my face instead. "I can see your brain going a mile a minute, so I want you to listen to me very carefully right now."

I nod, placing my hands over his to savor as much of this connection as possible.

"I need you here with me, and there's no room for any of the guilt you're feeling. I don't blame you for anything that happened, and you can't change a damn thing either, regardless of how much you beat yourself up over it. It takes you away from me, and I won't allow it. I'm here, and I've got you. You can let go of all of it. You hear me? I. Got. You."

I blink at him, ignoring the taste of copper in my mouth that's slowly been collecting from biting my lip so hard.

His fingers move to my mouth, gently prying my lip from my grasp. "Once we're out of here, I want us to go after what we really want because I'm done denying myself. Life keeps leading me back to you because you're my end goal, my ultimate destination. I want you by my side forever, as my wife, and I cannot wait to show you how much I love you every single day until we're old and gray. It's you and me, Angel."

One tear slips out at his declaration. Phoenix lets it roll down my cheek and presses a gentle kiss to the back of my hand.

"I love you so much." Five whispered words are all I'm capable of getting out, but they are the most important words.

Phoenix's eyes brighten at my words. "I wanted to make you mine from the first time I saw you. I was delusional to think I could ever fight this pull between us. Even when I hated you, I still loved you."

Pain blossoms in my chest at his words because I know exactly what he's talking about. But just as quickly as the pain started, it's receding, extinguished by something much bigger, much more powerful. Trust. Trust in Phoenix. Trust in us. And trust in our love.

We've gone through so much, and we will not end here. We still have the rest of our story to write, and I will fight for every single word of it.

This little burst of hope is enough to calm the panic inside me. I'm sure it won't last for long, but I take any peace it offers me.

Phoenix raises my hands back to his mouth, peppering them with more kisses. The gesture is so comforting that a yawn escapes me.

He frowns at me. "You look exhausted. I wouldn't be surprised if you still had some leftover drugs in your system."

I yawn again. "I feel like I got run over by a bus."

"Try and get some sleep. I won't let anything happen to you."

I know he can't keep that promise, regardless of how much he wants to, but I nod anyway and close my eyes.

My thoughts are too loud, and just when I'm about to give up and open my eyes again, Phoenix brushes over my hands. I focus on the repetitive strokes, which slowly drown out my thoughts.

I wake up to yelling and pain.

CHAPTER 39

PHOENIX

"Don't touch her." I pull on the restraints and shoot a venomous glare in Tyler's direction, even though I know it's pointless.

Eve wakes up from the ruckus I create, and it kills me to watch Tyler unlock her chain without being able to interfere.

"Where are you taking her?" If I thought I felt rage toward Eve before, it's nothing compared to the plain fury I feel toward Tyler.

I've never hated another person in my life as much as I hate him. I want to pummel him into the ground with my bare hands until he's unrecognizable.

He drags her up by the chain, and she cries out.

I snarl at him, "You're as good as dead."

His gaze collides with mine. Like earlier, he smiles, right before he jerks on her chain so hard she falls out of bed.

Bastard.

I will kill him.

I will kill him.

I. Will. Kill. Him.

Tyler shifts his attention to her, caressing her hair before patting her head. "Such a pretty pet. Come on, let's go for a little walk."

Eve flinches and leans away from his touch.

Tyler laughs in response. "Naughty pet."

With an eyebrow wiggle at me, he spins and walks away, leaving Eve with no choice but to follow him or she'll be dragged. She looks at me over her shoulder with wild, terrified eyes and mouths the three words that are simultaneously like a balm and an arrow to my heart: *I love you.*

"Eeeeeeeve, Eeeeeeeve." I yank on my handcuffs, the metal noise loud in my ears.

I can't let her go with that disturbing piece of shit.

Clang.

I need to get to her.

Clang.

What if he hurts her?

Clang.

What if I never see her again? An icy chill curls up my spine.

Clang. Clang.

Blood runs down my wrists, a rush of debilitating fear mingling with it.

And she's gone.

"Fuck, fuck, fuck." The metal bites into my raw skin, and I drop my hands into my lap.

Think, Phoenix. Think.

But there's nothing.

I don't have my phone or any other way to contact someone, nor do I have any tools to get out of these handcuffs.

I have nothing.

Now that I'm alone, I turn away from the camera and let go of the brave face for a moment.

I breathe deeply, sitting limply with my hands still in my lap. I can't exhaust myself. I need to conserve every ounce of energy.

Think, Phoenix. Fuck. Think.

There's nothing I could use to try to free us, absolutely nothing. I stare blankly around the room. It's barren except for the bed and a chair in the far corner. It's a different kind of prison, this time made out of wood and insulation, but a prison all the same.

I still can't believe Tyler is the reason I was locked up. Or that I survived three years behind bars to have this be my end.

Sweat beads around my hairline, and I wipe it away, flinching when metal comes in contact with my raw skin.

I don't even know the guy.

What is he doing with her right now?

Where did he take her?

Is he touching her?

A feral growl comes from deep in my throat, and I wish I could punch something, or better yet, wrap my hands around Tyler's throat.

Why is he doing all of this?

I hate that none of this makes sense. It wouldn't change the situation to understand his reasons, but the confusion only adds to the mindfuck.

I sag against the metal headboard and push my handcuffs up my arms and as far away from my open skin as possible. It's not much, maybe an inch, but it gives my wrists at least a small break.

You should have thought about that sooner, dumbwit.

Well, it is what it is.

Closing my eyes, I tilt my head so it's angled toward the doorframe and listen. There's some chatter in the distance, but it's either too far away or too quiet to make out any details.

Tyler said he's taking her for a walk, so that means he'll bring her back, right? He *has* to.

There is no other option.

He'll die, no matter what. But if he hurts a single hair on her head, he'll be begging for a quick death. All the rage I built up behind bars toward Eve, the desire for vengeance, all of it finally has a real target. The real perpetrator.

An image of him lying in a puddle of his own blood and staring at me with vacant eyes flashes in my mind.

That's more like it.

He will find his end soon.

Footsteps sound downstairs, yanking me out of my daydream.

Tyler walks in first, Eve not far behind him.

I give her a once-over. She seems okay, nodding at me in reassurance. My heart finally slows down its erratic beat. Tyler fastens her chain back to the bed, and after another caress over her hair, he steps away and approaches my side. I flip around, not wanting to let that motherfucker out of my sight for even a second.

Tyler unlocks my chain and grabs it. At the same time, he pulls out his gun, pointing it directly at me. "Let's go."

Unease trickles like ice water through my veins, and I try not to dwell on how he didn't get his gun out for Eve but did for me.

One glance at Eve is all I manage before Tyler hauls me out of the room. There wasn't even enough time to tell her I love her. Anger and fear war side by side inside me. What if this was the last time I saw her?

Tyler pushes me toward the staircase. "Upstairs."

Fourteen. That's how many steps the sleek wooden staircase has. I counted them all in an effort to keep my cool. I'm no use to Eve if I'm dead. I need to play along with Tyler's game until I know how to get us out of here without putting Eve at risk. If he regularly takes us upstairs, maybe there's a way to overpower him here, especially if he takes off the handcuffs.

The light is bright as my feet hit the carpet, and it takes a second for my eyes to adjust.

Tyler jabs his gun into my back. "Kitchen."

I stiffen but shuffle toward the oversized kitchen island on the left where Ruby stands in front of a large window. The sun is setting behind her, and she briefly glances up when Tyler attaches my chain to one of the metal poles of the breakfast bar. No reaction. She simply focuses back on the food in front of her.

Tyler grabs a plate from her side of the kitchen island and dumps it unceremoniously on the floor before me with a huge smile. "Eat, pet."

Since he seems to take so much pleasure from the degradation, I don't blink an eye and sit. There's no point in pissing him off when I'm handcuffed to a metal pole, and he's the one with the gun.

There are two slices of bread, a banana, and string cheese on the plate.

I've had way worse in prison.

I pick up a slice of bread with shaky fingers, ripping off a piece to toss into my mouth.

Tyler's eyes are on me. I stare back and demolish my food. It's not much, but it's better than nothing. And I need every ounce of sustenance I can get right now. Who knows when he'll feed us next. He takes a bottle of water from the counter and throws it my way, narrowly missing my face.

Dickhead.

Although I remember Tyler from when we were younger, and I saw him at the café when I picked up Eve, I never really paid much attention to him. He's grown into his body since his scrawny teenage years, just like I did. His build is similar to mine, but I have ten or more pounds of muscle on me, thanks to Holden and his workout obsession.

Holden. What are the chances he'll miraculously find us? Since we had to hand over our phones, I doubt anyone can track our whereabouts, not even Holden with all of his skills and contacts. The psycho probably destroyed the devices. A flicker of hope flares inside me. Maybe there's a way Holden can figure out our last known location though?

Tyler's taking me in the same way I do him, his jaw clenching the entire time. We continue to stare at each other, and I take comfort in the fact that the hand holding the gun is facing the floor and not me.

I finish my water and screw the cap back on. "Why are you doing this, Tyler? If it's about money, it's easy to solve."

He scoffs. "You're just like your father. Immediately thinking it's all about the money."

"My dad?" I tilt my head to the side and frown.

What the fuck does he have to do with this?

"Yes, your dad." He strides a few steps into the living

room, then stops to glare at me, before walking some more. "You know, when I first met you, I thought maybe you were different from him, but then you looked down your nose at me the same way that arrogant ass did."

The more he talks, the more confused I get. Instead of answers, I'm left with a million questions. "I don't even know what you're talking about. What does my dad have to do with you kidnapping us? Is this all about him? Did he screw over your parents, and you're doing this for revenge?"

He glares at me and rushes over to where I'm still on the floor. My eyes widen, and I scoot back. Away from him. He takes my chain off the pole, his movements hasty and angry. He yanks me up without warning, and I groan when the metal bites into my burning skin.

Tyler jerks even harder, a sick, satisfied smile forming on his face. My stomach goes tight with knots.

He drags me across the room. "You have two minutes."

The air stalls in my lungs. Two minutes for what?

He shoves me through an open doorway and stalks off, leaving it wide open.

A bathroom. It's a fucking bathroom.

I blow out a breath and don't waste any time. I do my business, wash my hands, and splash water on my face. Movement up in the corner catches my eye. The red light of a camera blinks at me.

Fucker.

Was he watching Eve too?

I inhale deeply and repeat my new mantra. *Bide your time, and you'll get your revenge. Lose your cool and lose everything.*

More images of my hands squeezing around Tyler's throat soothe me.

As if summoned, he appears in the doorway, his gun trained on me. "Pick up your leash, pet, and hand it to me."

This pet thing is getting really old, but he clearly gets off on the shaming.

So I do as he says, and he yanks me out of the room. A hiss escapes my teeth, and I watch his pleased smile reappear.

"Let's head back downstairs to your betrothed. It will be a big day for all of us tomorrow, and you both need your rest." He rams his gun into my back hard enough for me to stumble.

A thousand ants seem to crawl over my skin.

Thankfully, I catch myself before I reach the staircase, carefully moving downstairs. The setting sun offers a new hurdle. It's dark in the space, with only a few high basement windows letting in light.

Every step toward the corner room is filled with new thoughts. I'm bigger than Tyler. I need to find a way to overpower him. The second he uncuffs me, I'll have to take my chances. If he never removes them, I need to find a moment when his guard is down. When he doesn't aim his damn gun at me.

Bide your time, and you'll get your revenge. Lose your cool and lose everything.

When the time is right, I'm going to take this bastard down.

I turn the corner into the room and sigh in relief when I see Eve sitting on the bed. She was probably waiting for me the same way I was waiting for her.

Tyler reattaches my chain and promptly walks toward the doorway. "Night, night, my pets. See you tomorrow."

Eve and I immediately turn toward one another, holding on to each other's hands like they're our lifelines.

I lean in as close as possible and open my mouth to say something, but Eve is faster.

"Ruby thinks he can't hear us if we whisper."

My eyes go wide. "Ruby talked to you?"

"No, but she had a message ready on her phone for me and slid it over with my food when Tyler was distracted."

I squeeze her hands, wanting her to say more. Wanting her to tell me something that will help us get out of here. "What did she say?"

Eve nods. "She wrote it like short bullet points, but basically she apologized and said Tyler is keeping Mason in one of the upstairs bedrooms, and he'll kill her and Mason if she disobeys."

"Anything else?"

Eve sighs. "Something about a signal jammer."

A low sound emerges from my throat. "Fuck. That complicates things."

"No cavalry, I'm guessing?"

"Not likely. I was pretty sure they took care of our phones so they can't be tracked, but Holden would try to get a hold of Ruby and Tyler after our disappearance since they were at the café as well. But they'll be untraceable with the jammer." I raise her hand to my lips, the contact comforting. It's nowhere the same as holding her in my arms, or kissing her, but it's better than nothing.

I tell her what transpired during my quick visit upstairs, and she seems just as confused as I feel.

"You know, although this seems a bit extreme, after what you told me about your dad, I wouldn't be surprised if someone came after him or even his family."

I nod. "Yeah. And that old investor even told me my dad has made a lot of enemies and tried to warn me. But when he said my dad would drag me right down to Hell with him, I never pictured anything like this."

We're both quiet, and I can tell by Eve's wandering gaze she's deep in thought.

Once she's done processing, she stares at me. I wish I could kiss away the frown lines on her forehead, but I can't, so smoothing them out with my fingers is the next best thing.

"Thanks." One side of her mouth quirks up and drops again. "You know what doesn't make any sense though? If this has something to do with your dad, how do I fit into all of this?"

I was thinking the same thing. "Maybe we underestimated how deep his feelings run for you. He's always looked at you a little more possessively than he should have."

Eve hums but doesn't say anything.

The silence hangs between us like a dark cloud until a panicked expression flitters across her beautiful face. "Do you really think we'll make it out of here alive?"

Her voice is so quiet, so broken, it rips my heart wide open.

I can't tell her that I don't know. That I'm scared shitless. That no matter how hard we'll try, it won't be enough, and we'll die here. An invisible weight presses on my chest for a moment, robbing me of breath.

"Yes." The word shoots out of my mouth, and I swallow the sudden lump in my throat. "We will."

She nods, but I'm not sure she believes me. I hate seeing her this worried, and a deep desire to ease that worry overcomes me.

Maybe we both need a distraction.

Eve—and her body—are my favorite escape, but for obvious reasons, that's not possible right now. One of her favorite escapes is romance novels, and if it helps keep her mind busy, we might have a chance.

"Angel."

"Yes?" Her mouth lifts a fraction at my nickname.

"Can I tell you a story?"

"Please." Even the dim light can't hide the spark in her eyes.

"All right." I clear my throat. "Once upon a time, there was a very handsome prince, and he fancied his new friend's younger sister. He'd never seen anyone as beautiful and sexy and magnificent as her, and when she smiled, his whole world tilted on its axis. She was the sunshine he never knew he was missing, and she quickly wormed her way into his heart. He—"

Eve huffs a breath. "That's one cheesy prince."

I tap my finger on her nose. "Quiet in the audience, please."

She presses her lips together but can't hide the twitch at the corners. "Sorry, I'll be good now. What happened next?"

My eyes fly open, and I start.

"What was that noise?" I stare straight at Phoenix, and his wide eyes mirror mine.

Unease darts through my body, and I hastily glance over my shoulder to see if someone's behind me.

My poor heart. I'm not sure how much more of this stress and anxiety it can take.

Tyler is responsible for this entire fucking mess. Everything that happened in the last few years, everything that led to this moment, it was all him. He changed my life in ways that can never be reversed or amended, and this entire time, he was my friend. At least, that's what he made me believe.

I blow out a breath and turn back to Phoenix to give him a small smile. "Hi."

He smiles back at me, reaching out to caress my cheek. "Hey."

This is what I need to focus on. My person. He's here with me, and I don't have to go through this hell alone. Not this time.

I have him to touch, to talk to, and to tell me stories like last night.

I don't remember falling asleep during his story, but I remember the warmth in my chest when I shut everything out and listened to his silly, over-the-top version of our fairy tale. Of course, we had a happily ever after. I wouldn't accept any other option.

Loud footsteps bounce down the stairs, and our moment of peace is gone. When the person gets closer, obnoxious whistling immediately identifies Tyler.

The weight on my chest grows heavier with each approaching footstep, and I inhale deeply in an attempt to lighten it. It doesn't work.

Phoenix is quiet next to me, both of us listening and anticipating what will happen next. Not knowing what nefarious thing Tyler might do. Not knowing if we'll survive to see another day. It's its own kind of torture.

With every footstep, my heart beats faster, harder, louder, and I hear my heartbeat everywhere. In my ears, my throat, even my mouth. It's loud. Suffocating.

Everything I thought about Tyler clearly went out the window, and now he's as predictable as any other psychopath. Ergo, not one single bit.

And to think I had . . . I did . . . with him. No, I can't.

"Rise and shine, my friends. It's your big day." Tyler strides into the room and claps, stopping at the foot of the bed with a big grin.

Every time I see him, it's like a brutal slap to the face. For years, Tyler played not just with my life but also with Phoenix's, and threatened my friends' lives, with my sister paying the ultimate price.

"What are you talking about?" Phoenix sends Tyler such a murderous glare, I'm disappointed he doesn't drop dead.

"Aww, come on. It's a surprise." Tyler raises his arms, the gun gleaming in the sunlight.

I swallow and move as far away from the edge of the bed as possible.

I don't like the gun or that nothing Tyler deems a surprise will be good.

"Evie, you're up first since you'll take longer." He walks to the head of the bed and uncuffs me.

"No, Tyler. Please. I . . . please let us go." My voice breaks as I shake my head and try to scoot back even farther.

Phoenix twists and gets on his knees, glaring at Tyler. "Come on, Tyler. We'll forget this ever happened."

He scoffs. "Yeah, I don't think so."

"Let's go, Evie."

Phoenix's nostrils flare. "Where are you taking her?"

"Down, boy." Tyler shoots Phoenix a pointed look, grabs my chain, and hauls me up. "Don't worry, I'll bring her back in one piece because Evie will be a good girl." He lifts the gun to my face and brushes the cool metal over my skin in a disturbing caress. "Won't you, Evie?"

My entire body shakes uncontrollably but I manage a nod, not daring to take my eyes off Tyler and his gun.

I don't ever want one this close to my face again.

He finally lowers it and moves backward toward the doorway, pulling me with him.

"Please, Ty." My eyes sting.

Tyler ignores me.

He winks at Phoenix before he walks out of the room. "I'll be back for you soon. Behave until then."

I cast one worried look at Phoenix, who's standing beside the bed now, his chain extended as far as it goes.

"Tyler, touch her and you'll die," he yells, his face contorted in a mixture of terror and fury.

I'm propelled through the doorway.

Tyler chuckles and leans close to me as if we're sharing a joke. "I think he hasn't quite grasped this concept of captor and prisoner, has he?"

My chest rises and falls with rapid breaths while Tyler leads me up the stairs. Instead of stopping in the kitchen, he yanks me up another flight to the second level.

Where is he taking me?

He's not going to do anything to me, is he?

My scalp prickles at the horrible thought, and my breaths quicken.

A loud noise comes from behind a closed door, and Tyler kicks it. "Stop the drama, Mason, or I'm going to do something worse than just gag you."

Nausea pools in my belly.

Mason. Mason is in there. And Tyler gagged him.

A harsh yank at my chain propels me forward, almost tripping me.

Tyler leads me into the room at the end of the hallway, a spacious, orange-and-red bedroom that appears to be the main bedroom. Ruby shoots up from the small chaise at the foot of the bed, wringing her hands in front of her.

What is she doing here?

Their gazes briefly meet before she averts hers, her hair covering half her face.

"She's all yours, babe. You know what to do, right?" Tyler

watches Ruby nod before he grasps my left hand. "You'll look spectacular."

With the gun still in one hand, he gets something out of his pocket with the other and gives it to Ruby.

I gasp when I see it's a small key. "Wh-what's going on?"

Ruby unlocks my handcuffs with trembling hands.

Tyler smiles at me widely. "Surprise, Evie. It's your wedding day. You're going to get married."

He puts the key back in his right pocket, and I watch him like a hawk. Right pocket. I need to remember that. Maybe there'll be a chance later to take it from him?

Tyler's words crash into my thoughts.

Surprise, Evie. It's your wedding day. You're going to get married.

Black dots dance across my vision, and I try to blink them away. A wave of dizziness follows, and I reach out to steady myself. Unfortunately, Tyler is closest to me, and I grab his arm. I want to flinch away from the contact, but my survival instinct has taken over to keep me from fainting. I don't ever want him to catch me unconscious. Who knows what he'll do to me.

Tyler frowns at me, holding on to me with both arms. "Don't worry. Everyone is nervous on their big day, and Ruby is here to help you get ready. I worked very hard to get my officiant license and a marriage license for you guys. It'll be great."

I shrink away from him and shield my body with my hands. "A marriage license?"

He gives me one of his twisted smiles. "Yeah, for you and Phoenix. Don't you want to get married?"

"Phoenix and I are getting married?" I mutter the words

more to myself, unable to wrap my head around this situation.

Why would Tyler want Phoenix and me to get married? To the extent that he gets an officiant license so he can do the ceremony? Is this another one of his twisted games? Marry us before he kills us?

It feels like the walls are shifting closer, and the desire to puke all over him is almost too strong to resist.

"Well, I'm going to leave you ladies to it." He trains his gaze on Ruby. "I'll be back to check on you guys. You know the rules. Don't disappoint me."

She nods, and he pats her head. Ruby closes her eyes and shudders in response. Her hair shifts to the side with the movement, revealing a split lip and the beginning of a bruise forming on her cheek. I press my lips together to keep from gasping out loud. He put his hands on her.

What I wouldn't give to push Tyler away from her, to slap him, or to force him to feel even a fraction of the pain and chaos he's caused in the last few years. To make him pay.

No, that wouldn't be enough. I want him dead. I've never wanted to kill anyone in my life, not even hit them. But Tyler? My Freddy? I *need* him dead. I have to know he'll never be able to hurt another soul ever again.

He leaves the room with a wave, and the door lock clicks from the outside.

I frown at Ruby, opening my mouth to say something, but she shakes her head and points around the room.

Cameras.

I spot three at first glance, but who knows how many more there are?

This fucking asshole.

I nod to tell her I understand and take several deep breaths, trying to calm down as much as possible now that Tyler isn't around. I need to use this time wisely, get as much info out of Ruby as possible. Maybe she has an idea. Maybe we can figure out together how to get out of here.

"Let's get you cleaned up. The bathroom is over here." She points at the door on the side of the room.

Ruby leads me to the bathroom where she disappears behind a stone partition in the back. My hands grow sweaty, and I wipe my damp palms on my leggings when the shower turns on.

A shower. Only a shower.

Ruby comes back and hands me a toothbrush.

I stare at it, and Ruby says, "It's new."

"I'm sorry." The apology flies from my lips, but Ruby shakes her head.

"*You* have nothing to apologize for."

I want to say, "Oh, but I do. If it weren't for me, you wouldn't be in this mess," but I'll save that conversation for another day.

Telling her I've been a shitty friend for the last few years, and that I've been keeping a million secrets from her, won't do me any good right now. Especially since I still don't even know what's going on.

I shove the toothbrush into my mouth and try to get a handle on my emotions.

After seeing the camera lineup in the bedroom, there may be more in the bathroom.

Ruby and I stare at each other as foam builds in my mouth.

Her throat moves on a swallow. "After your shower, I'll

help you with your makeup, hair, and dress. I also have some water and food for you in the bedroom. We have three hours."

I lean over the sink to spit out my toothpaste and rinse my mouth.

Ruby hands me a hand towel. "There's a small toilet room in the back, opposite the shower." She flinches. "Sorry, I probably should have told you that first."

"No worries." I put the towel down and take care of business before returning to Ruby.

A silent exchange occurs between us, and I take off my clothes, drop them on the floor, and step into the shower.

Yes, it's a bit weird, but being naked in front of Ruby right now is the least of my problems.

Once my hair is wet, I grab the shampoo bottle, but Ruby beats me to it. "Turn around. Let me do it."

I do as she says, stepping back to block most of the water from her.

She's close enough for me to feel her warm breath on my shoulder.

"I don't know what to do, Evie. He has his gun around me nonstop. Earlier, he . . . he tried to kiss me, and I cringed out of reflex. He backhanded me so hard I thought my cheekbone broke."

That explains the mark on her face and the split lip.

Sniffles break through her uneven breaths. All I want to do is turn around, wrap her in my arms, and tell her everything will be okay. But I don't do it. I can't. The last thing we need right now is to make things worse. The fact Tyler hit her when she refused to kiss him is bad enough, and we don't want to escalate his behavior.

I exhale loudly, the hold on my emotions slipping after her confession. "I cannot tell you how sorry I am that you got dragged into all of this, Ruby. Truly."

"It's not your fault he's crazy." Her hands leave my hair.

I step aside for her to wash off her hands.

"Rinse."

I step under the spray and wash off my hair, wishing the water could wash away my worries and problems alongside the shampoo. But when I reopen my eyes, I'm still in the same bathroom, still held prisoner.

Ruby puts conditioner in her hands, and I lean my head back to make it easier for her to apply. "Is Mase okay?"

"I think so." Ruby works the cream through my strands before massaging the leftovers into my scalp. "He made a bunch of noise, hoping that someone outside would hear him, so Tyler gagged him."

Oh, Mason.

"I think he also punched him, but I was in the kitchen when it happened."

"Ruby, why are you still here if he left you?"

She stops but doesn't take her hands out of my hair. "Evie, he said he'll kill all three of you if I try to run away. And I believe him."

Tyler's threats are simple yet effective. And the bastard knows it.

She sniffles again. "At the café, Tyler, he . . . he, after you left the booth for the bathroom, Tyler pulled me into the hallway. I thought he wanted to make out or something."

My body is feeling numb and utterly overwhelmed, but I welcome it at this point.

She laughs humorlessly. "When I got there, he covered

my mouth and told me what he wanted me to do. I thought he was crazy, so I shook my head. There was no way I was going to drug you and lead Phoenix to some house Tyler broke into. But then he held a gun to my head and showed me a picture of a gagged and bound Mason in his trunk. I was so terrified. I didn't want to do it, but I didn't want to die either. Or Mase. I couldn't risk it, Evie. I'm so sorry. Tyler said this was just a fun little game and it would all be over soon if I listened."

I don't point out that Tyler might have told her the truth and this will be over soon.

There's only one problem: he never told her we'd all make it out alive.

CHAPTER 41

PHOENIX

I straighten the deep-red bow tie around my neck and stare at my reflection in the mirror. Besides the dark circles under my eyes, the hardness in them, and the red, angry flesh circling my wrists, no one would be the wiser that I'm being forced to marry my fiancée at gunpoint.

I've wanted to call her my wife for so long that it's more than just a little unfortunate how things played into my deepest desire in such a fucked-up way.

Tyler steps into the small bathroom. He brought me here a while ago to get cleaned up and dressed for my wedding day.

My wedding day.

This guy is so screwed up, I don't even know where to start.

Fear is still a constant—both for Eve and me—but I'm also slowly getting frustrated. The anticipation of not knowing what his endgame is, or why he's doing this in the first place, has me on edge. I'm fidgety and jumpy.

"You clean up nicely." He smirks at me like we're best buddies. "Are you excited?"

I don't respond, but he doesn't seem bothered by it, laughing to himself.

"Fine. Have it your way and pout." He grabs my dangling handcuffs and clicks the second one in place. This time, without the chain though. Waving his gun toward the door, he hollers, "Let's roll. Your bride will be here soon. Back downstairs."

I pause when I walk through the doorway into the basement, and blink. Black balloons are tied to some of the wooden beams, and a congratulations banner is hanging from the ceiling. A chill coils up my spine. It looks terrifying.

"Do you like it?" Tyler gives me a shove from behind. "I wanted to make it special for you."

"You're sick." The words are out before I can keep them in. I know better than to make him angry, particularly when he presses a gun to my back.

Tyler chuckles. "Is that what you think? That I'm sick?"

I whirl around and lift an eyebrow, trying to appear unbothered. He doesn't need to know that worry and alarm are clawing at my throat.

Straightening my spine, I sweep my arms to gesture to the morbid wedding scene. "Why else would you do something like this?"

He shrugs like I'm overreacting. "Maybe I have my reasons."

I want to close the distance between us. Spit in his face. Make him cower in fear. Instead, I force my feet to remain in the same spot. "What reason could you possibly have for something fucked up like this? And I'm not just talking about kidnapping us. I'm talking about all the games you played with us for *years*. You killed Connie. You *killed* her, Tyler. You put me in prison. You tortured Eve for years, and then you planted a bomb on my car that almost killed us."

He rolls his eyes. He fucking rolls his eyes. "You're a little dramatic right now, don't you think?"

I've never wanted to murder someone with my bare hands like I do right now.

If I wasn't handcuffed, I would take my chances and jump him. And he knows that.

I still can't help but lean closer. "You think I'm a *little dramatic*?"

The words come out low and menacing, and Tyler sighs. "I'm marrying Evie and you. Isn't that what you wanted? To be honest, I thought you'd be happy about the wedding."

This son of a bitch.

He knows getting married under duress is straight out of a nightmare.

"Fine." His chest heaves on an inhale, and he checks his watch. "The girls will be here soon, so let's make this quick. You're clearly hung up on this, so I'll let you get in one hit. That'll make you feel better."

I rear back, unable to hide my surprise. "What are you talking about?"

He puts the hand with the gun behind his back and beckons me forward with the other. "Come on, I'll give you one freebie. Hit me."

Shaking my head in disbelief, I stare at him. He can't be serious.

He shrugs. "Fine, I'll go first."

Before I can register his words, he swings his fist at me.

He catches me so off guard that I don't have time to move out of the way entirely, and he connects with the side of my head. *Shit.*

Since I've participated in countless prison brawls, instinct takes over, and I push him back far enough to hit him with my cuffed fists. Once. Twice. Three times. He gets another hit in too, this time clipping my nose before cold metal touches my temple.

Fuck, fuck, fuck.

He *tsks* and taps my temple with the gun prior to hitting me hard enough with the butt of it to force me to my knees.

"Naughty, naughty. I said *one.*" His breathing is harsh as he paces back and forth.

When I stop feeling like I might pass out, I glance up at him. It takes a herculean effort to keep my mouth in a straight line at the sight of him. Blood is trickling from his nose onto his white shirt, and his left eye is slightly swollen.

Satisfaction courses through my veins strong enough to dull the pain of my injuries and that I probably don't look much better than him.

"Well," he raises his hands and drops them back to his sides, "do you feel better now?"

This guy is seriously unreal.

The only way I'd feel better is if he was dead at my feet.

Footsteps sound on the level right above our heads, and Tyler gasps.

He smiles at me, bloody teeth and all. "Here comes the bride."

The short-lived satisfaction of making him bleed disappears, as excitement to see Eve blends with worry.

We will survive today. We will fucking survive today.

Pushing back on my feet isn't easy, but I manage. The handkerchief from my breast pocket is the only tissue alternative I have, so I use it to wipe as much blood from my face as possible. It's quite the task without a mirror.

The footsteps are on the steps leading to us now, so I give up on my face and jam the fabric back into my pocket.

My gaze is zeroed in on the doorway because, despite the sickening circumstances, I don't want to miss a single glance of my bride.

Eve turns the corner, and my breath catches in my throat.

Her deep-crimson gown matches my bow tie, and her dark hair frames her face in silky waves. She's absolutely breathtaking.

Our gazes collide, and the shy smile vanishes the second she gets a good look at me.

"Oh my God, what happened?" Without pause, she grabs two handfuls of her thick skirt, lifts it, and hurries over. "Phoenix, are you okay?"

Her focus is entirely on me, and since Tyler's clearing his throat, I'm guessing he doesn't like that fact.

We both eye him, but his gaze is on Eve only.

"Get out of line again like this, and you'll regret it. Are we clear?"

Eve swallows and nods, her focus dropping to the floor.

Tyler motions behind him. "Come on, babe, we don't have all day. Let's get this party started."

Ruby steps closer, and I narrow my eyes at the state of her face. That bastard put his hands on her? One moment is all I need. One moment without handcuffs where I won't risk anyone's life, and this guy is dead.

Tyler pulls a stack of note cards from his back pocket and clears his throat. "Everyone in position."

Ruby makes her way to a spot near the end of the room and motions for Eve and me to follow. We join her, and Ruby glances at us.

"Just pretend you're walking down an aisle toward him from here. First groom, then the bride."

Something unspoken passes between Ruby and Eve, and I wonder if they had a chance to talk. Were they able to come up with a plan to escape? Ruby squeezes Eve's arm and hurries toward Tyler.

Eve studies me and whispers, "You okay?"

I nod. Instead of answering her question, I say, "You look beautiful."

What if this is the last time I see her? We both know Tyler isn't marrying us out of the goodness of his heart. He must have something else planned, but what? This could be his grand finale. I just don't know what happens after, which is incredibly nerve-racking.

Eve does a crap job hiding her worry and fear too.

She barely manages a smile because of her trembling chin. "Thank you."

"Phoenix, over here." Tyler's voice grates on my ears.

I hate that I wasn't able to finish the job and beat his face in.

Grabbing Eve's hands, I squeeze them and mouth, "I love you."

This is not the end. We will get out of here. We will survive.

I walk toward Tyler, with my hands curled into fists in front of me.

Showtime.

Once I've taken my spot, we all turn our heads toward Eve. I feast my eyes on my beautiful bride, committing every detail to memory.

Tyler ruins the moment when he curses under his breath.

"Stop." He barks something at Ruby, who runs into one of the sectioned-off rooms and rushes to Eve with something in her hand.

Eve gasps.

Ruby holds out the item to her. Eve's hands shake, but she accepts the dark bundle. I have a good guess what it might be.

That sicko.

"Perfect." Tyler's voice is giddy. "Music, please."

I detest him more with every passing second

Ruby uses her phone, and after a few seconds, the "Bridal Chorus" fills the air.

Eve's chest heaves as she ambles toward me. Despite the situation, there's a flutter in my stomach, and I watch her every step. She's a vision in her nontraditional dress, which is quite fitting, considering the majority of our relationship has been pretty nontraditional too.

The fairy tale version of us I told Eve about yesterday is so far from reality it's laughable. But that doesn't mean we shouldn't get the ending we want.

Many roads lead to a happily ever after, and if ours is tainted by violence and murder, so be it. I'm happy to bathe in the blood of our enemies if it means I'll have her forever.

It will be well worth it to kill Tyler to get Eve out of here alive.

Eve reaches us, and now that I get a better glimpse, my

guess is confirmed. A bouquet of dark-red wilted roses. The same ones Tyler sent Eve before.

I cannot wait until this asshole is as dead as these flowers.

Ruby takes the bouquet from Eve, and Tyler clears his voice.

"We've gathered here today to celebrate the union of these two lovebirds." He smiles as if he's genuinely happy.

Eve intertwines her hands with mine, a luxury I'm glad the handcuffs allow.

"Did you hear that, old man?"

I frown at Tyler's words. Did he just call me old man?

He grins at us and rubs his hands. "My bad, I totally forgot about the other surprise." He rushes to the chair next to his little podium and turns around a laptop.

My mouth falls open when I get a look at the screen. "Dad?"

Tyler waves me off. "He isn't allowed to talk right now, as you can see, so don't bother."

Duct tape covers my dad's mouth, and his murderous gaze glares straight at the camera.

"What the fuck is going on?" I slowly feel like I'm losing my mind with all of Tyler's damn "surprises."

Tyler narrows his eyes at me. "I'll tell you what's going on later. Right now, we have a wedding ceremony to complete first." He gestures with his gun toward Evie.

I swallow and face Eve. Slowly, I unclench my teeth. I just need to focus on her and zone Tyler out. I can do that.

"So, where were we?" Tyler scowls at his cards. "Oh yes, we're gathered here today. Yada, yada, yada. Until death do us part." He wiggles his eyebrows and smiles at his last words.

Is that supposed to be a hint at what's to come? Bile bubbles up from my stomach at the prospect. He throws card after card on the floor until he gets to the last one.

"Evangeline Caldwell, do you take Phoenix Montgomery to be your lawfully wedded husband, and so on?"

Eve looks at me with so much turmoil in her eyes, my heart stutters, followed by this falling, spinning-down feeling.

When she doesn't answer immediately, Tyler approaches her and puts his gun to her temple. She flinches and closes her eyes.

I'm immobilized. One wrong move. One wrong word, and he might shoot her right in front of me.

A realization clicks into place. I would follow her.

Tyler's jaw tics. "I said, Evangeline Caldwell, will you —"

"Yes, yes, yes, I do." The words rush out of her mouth, her eyes shining with a layer of moisture that wasn't there a moment ago. She takes the unfamiliar ring Tyler holds out and slips it on my finger, a single tear running down her cheek.

Another thing this bastard will pay for. How many tears has she shed because of him? He'll pay for every single one of them.

Tyler grins. "Good pet." His attention shifts to me. "Your turn. Phoenix Montgomery, will you—?"

"I do." There isn't a single ounce of doubt in my voice as I glide the engagement ring I got for her back on her finger. Where it belongs.

Tyler chuckles. "So eager. I love it. Tenacity undoubtedly

runs in the family, doesn't it? By the power vested in me by the state of New York, I now pronounce you husband and wife. You may kiss the bride."

While I can't take my eyes off Eve, my brain is still hung up on what Tyler said.

"I said, kiss the fucking bride." Tyler aims the gun at me again. "Or do you need me to show you how it's done? I know exactly how she likes it, don't I, Evie?"

Red-hot anger courses through my veins at his words.

It's one thing to have a suspicion and another to have it confirmed, especially in a moment like this.

Eve hisses, trying to tug her hands out of my too-firm grasp.

"Sorry." I immediately let her go.

Tyler chuckles like the psycho he is. "I'm sorry. Is that a sore spot for you, Phoenix?" He waves his gun around. "Why don't you show me how it's done? Theoretically, you're supposed to teach me stuff, right?"

Tyler distracts me on purpose, feeding me these little hints and riddles that drive me insane. I'm about to turn to him to tell him to just spit it out already when Eve gets in my space. She cups my cheeks and presses her lips to mine. We stay like this for several moments before we pull apart.

Tyler moves so close, his breath drifts over my neck. "No, that was not it. You can do better. Now."

CHAPTER 42

EVANGELINE

There's nothing but pain and regret in Phoenix's eyes, but he closes the distance and takes my mouth like he would if we were alone.

I can almost hear his words in my head.

I got you. You can let go.

So I close my eyes and shut out the world, not allowing anything in except Phoenix: his mouth on mine, his tongue teasing me in the best possible way, and our hands intertwined.

Noise filters in, Tyler's clapping ruining this peaceful moment.

Phoenix and I separate with heavy breaths, and all eyes are on us.

A lump catches in my throat, promising to choke off my air, and I take a step closer to Phoenix.

Tyler whistles. "Now that's what I'm talking about. Well done, bro. Well done." He moves his attention to the computer screen to stare at Phoenix's dad. "Do you want to tell him, or should I?" He waits for a moment while the older man continues to stare daggers at him, the tape still over his mouth. Tyler nods at the screen. "Okay, fine, have it your way. I'll tell him."

He faces Phoenix and opens his arms. "I'm your long-lost brother."

There's nothing but silence before Tyler cracks up, smacking his thigh repeatedly with his hand. "Just kidding. The long-lost part, I mean, not the brother."

Oh my God.

No, that can't be right. Tyler and Phoenix are brothers?

Holy shit.

I blink and gape at the two men. Phoenix is stiff as a board as he stares at Tyler, who only scoffs.

"I know, we look nothing alike. Well, mostly. But the DNA tests confirmed it. Thank goodness I take after my mother, or I couldn't have pulled off half of this entertaining shit."

A cold mask settles on Phoenix's face, and he shrugs. "So all of this is some twisted revenge because my dad didn't acknowledge you?"

Tyler's nostrils flare, and he glowers at Phoenix. "*This* was for two purposes. To show *our* father he made the wrong choice when he turned me away, and because *you're* just as big of a prick as he is and deserved to be taken down a notch."

He paces. "You know, when my mom got sick and we were forced to move here, I didn't know who my dad was. But then my aunt let something slip about when my mom was younger, and I started digging, all of my nerdy computer skills finally paying off. After I realized dear old Dad was a total schmuck, I wanted to give you a chance. I thought, hey, maybe he was treating you like shit too, and we could bond over it. Especially after I found out he forged your grandfather's will to cheat you out of your inheritance. But then *you* weren't any better than him, acting like I was some dog shit beneath your shoe."

Phoenix is frowning but stays quiet, and Tyler continues.

"You were so aloof, acting like you were better than me, like you were the king of the castle and everyone else was just a peasant. Everyone . . . except *her*."

His finger points at me, and ice shoots through my veins.

He continues, "You had such a hard time keeping your eyes off her, so I began talking to her. When I saw how you glared at me, I took it as a challenge and became friends with her. And then I fucked her just because I could."

Nausea rolls through my body at the scene Tyler paints. I knew he wasn't right in the head, but this is really fucked up.

A humorless laugh escapes him. "And you know what this bitch did when I took her virginity? She said *your* fucking name before she passed out."

He swings his ruthless stare in my direction. There isn't an ounce left of the friendly, upbeat guy I thought I knew.

The corners of his mouth curl in a snarl. "So *she* had to pay too."

To imagine that one small moment like that, a drunken mistake, set off such an avalanche of devastation and pain.

I press my lips together so hard they feel like they might burst.

And that's when all hell breaks loose.

Phoenix launches himself at Tyler so fast, they smack to the floor with a loud thud. The chair goes flying, the laptop smashing into dozens of pieces on impact.

"Nooooo." I move toward the two men, panic overtaking my body. "Phoenix, please, no."

What the hell was he thinking? Tyler has a fucking gun.

They wrestle, fists flying, insults shouted, and then, the gun sails out of the heap. Tyler and Phoenix break apart, trying to get it. I run toward it too, but Ruby is faster. She grabs it, points toward where Tyler is still sprawled on the floor several feet away, and pulls the trigger.

The gunshot fills the air, and for a moment, I can't hear anything but the loud ringing in my ears.

Blinking, I stare at the scene in front of me.

Tyler charges toward Ruby with his mouth open in a war cry. "You fucking bitch."

My stomach free-falls when I catch sight of the gun on the floor right next to where Ruby is standing, immobilized. Did she drop it? Tyler picks it up and smacks her straight in the temple with it. Ruby goes down like a sack of potatoes, an eerie crack filling the room when her head hits the floor.

"Oh my gosh." I cover my mouth and rush toward her. "Ruby, no."

My voice is shrill and loud, amplifying the ringing in my ears even more.

There's blood on the floor next to where she collapsed. Already so much blood. How is that possible? And she isn't moving.

I need to get to her. I need to make sure she's okay.

Tyler hobbles into my path, blocking her from view. "Don't even think about it."

I peer down at the blood running from his pant leg. She got him. Ruby really shot him, though clearly nowhere fatal.

And she paid for it. My God. "Please, Tyler, let me see if she's okay."

Phoenix groans, and I glance at him. Despite being a bloody mess, I think he's okay. But Ruby . . .

I stare at her lifeless body again, and silent tears run down my face.

Tyler waves his gun at Phoenix, motioning for him to get up. "I will enjoy the next part of our program even more now. Everything is so much more intense when emotions run high."

The words come out in a low, feral tone, eliciting goose-bumps all over my body.

He kidnapped us, chained us to a bed, forced us to get married, and potentially just killed Ruby. What could he possibly be excited about after all of this?

But there is undeniable glee in his eyes that not even his injuries can seem to rob him of. And while Ruby was the one to shoot him, Phoenix did some damage too. Joining the bloody nose and the swollen eye from earlier, Tyler now also has a split lip that mirrors Ruby's and a nasty cut on his eyebrow. He could star in a horror movie.

Phoenix strides toward us, and I immediately grab his hand. Although the contact won't be able to sever the tendrils of panic seizing my chest, I feel stronger when we're together.

Thankfully, he looks better than Tyler, still only a small gash on his temple.

"Back to the room. Now." Tyler gives us both a shove toward the corner of the basement.

Each footstep, every click of my heels on the unfinished concrete floor, feels like a bad omen.

Please, just let him chain us back to the bed and leave.

I can't believe I just thought that, but it's the truth. In a twisted way, after everything that happened, that would be the best-case scenario right now. Other than being released or rescued, of course, but I'm not even entertaining either of those options right now, not with the gun aimed at me.

Now that shots have been fired, and Tyler got injured, I'm afraid his breaking point is just around the corner.

Tears quickly blur my vision, and I have the urge to cover my mouth to hold the fear inside.

I don't want to die. I really don't.

So many times over the years, I've wondered if it wouldn't be better if I just ceased to exist. If that would ease my suffering and pain and keep others from hurting too. All this time, I thought I was the catalyst for all the awful things that had happened. That somehow, I did something to attract a psychopath, and now he's trying to ruin my life and everyone I care about.

But it's not my fault; it never was.

And now, more than ever, I want to live. I want this nightmare to be over for good. I want the life Phoenix promised me. I want *my* life back with him by my side.

We have to get out of this.

I know not everyone gets their happy ending, but damn it, we deserve it.

I deserve it.

In the bedroom, Tyler attaches Phoenix to the chain on the bed before he pulls me toward the chair in the corner. My heart is pounding. My limbs shaking. He hooks me to a chain that's secured to the wall and out of Phoenix's reach, which I'm guessing is exactly why Tyler chose this spot.

Although this guy is clearly not right in the head, unfortunately, he's also not stupid.

My palms are damp, my mouth dry. A single bead of sweat skitters down my spine until it disappears beneath my dress.

Phoenix stands next to the bed with the chain stretched as far as it goes. My lips tremble as I watch him struggle. I want to tell him to stop hurting himself further, but I know it would do no good.

Instead, I turn my attention to Tyler. "Ty, let Phoenix go, please. I'll stay here with you."

Tyler lifts his hand toward my face.

Don't flinch, don't flinch, don't flinch.

"Evie, you're so sweet to offer, but I'm afraid I have to decline."

Phoenix growls. He's a wild animal, drawing his lips back to bare his teeth at Tyler. "Touch her, and you'll die."

He sounds utterly feral, fighting for me, trying to protect me. Although he must be just as exhausted and as scared as I am. Terrified, angry, and sad. Something unlocks inside me, a permission to fully feel everything I've hidden for so many years, and to finally act on it to get my revenge.

Knowing that Tyler is Freddy means there's nothing hanging over my head. The people he threatened me with are all in this house, one of them locked away, another one possibly dead, and my soulmate fighting for me like my life means more than his. Like he couldn't live in a world I didn't exist.

He deserves the same commitment from me. Because I'd die for him too.

Tyler takes a step toward me, and Phoenix lunges forward, despite his already extended arms and chain. He yanks at it anyway, over and over and over.

Almost there, baby.

A chuckle escapes Tyler. "Relax, bro. I just want to help Evie out of her dress. Ruby was supposed to do that, but well." He shrugs like Ruby's life means nothing to him. She never mattered. Nothing does. "Since she's a bit indisposed at the moment, I'll do it. Plus, it all stays in the family, right?"

Bile rises in my throat at Tyler's comment, but I push it away.

Phoenix shakes his head. "No."

The one word holds so much menace that my disgust for Tyler is quickly exchanged with worry for Phoenix.

But like the loon Tyler is, he only grins at Phoenix.

I want to wipe his ugly grin off his face and shove it down his throat.

And I will. Soon.

I focus on the man in front of me, not on Tyler when he steps behind me to get started at my pearls.

It's easy to see that Phoenix doesn't want to take his eyes off Tyler, but since I continue to stare at him, he finally glances at me.

My husband.

I'm married to Phoenix.

Our wedding took place under duress and the worst circumstances I could think of.

And I'm not sure if it makes me a little unstable, but I'm happy about officially being his wife.

My heart has expanded exponentially for him, and I've never felt so genuinely happy as I am with him. Together.

And whatever happens next, nothing can take that away from me.

CHAPTER 43

PHOENIX

Tyler touches Eve, and I'm forced to watch. I'm two seconds away from ripping my hands off to get to her, no matter how much my wrists scream at me.

This is my wife. It should be me doing this. Not this excuse of a human.

"How many of these damn pearls are there?" Tyler heaves a sigh, as if the poor bastard is actually inconvenienced.

If it was me, I'd savor each pearl, unwrapping my wife inch by inch like the present she is.

The fact it's another thing he's taken away from me only adds to the mental shit list I already have for him.

Tyler's frustration is getting the best of him, and he yanks on the back of the dress so hard that Eve is tightening the grip on the back of the chair for balance.

Several pearls pop off the dress and scatter around the room, and I want to pick them all up and shove them down his throat.

"Fucking finally." Tyler takes a step back. "Show your husband the underwear I got you."

This guy knows how to play his sick mindfuck games, I'll give him that much. He knows exactly what buttons to push to get the biggest reaction out of us.

Boiling with fury, I grind my teeth so hard it hurts. But I welcome the pain and hold on to it. It's so much better than this constant fear and unease Tyler's instilled in me.

I tighten my hands into fists when Eve gasps. Her hands try to grasp the front of the dress, but it's too late. It's already sliding down her waist and legs, pooling in a puffy heap on the floor. And fuck. This woman. My wife. I hate it, but she's an absolute stunner in the black panties and bra set.

"What do you think, brother? I did good, didn't I?" He reaches out with his hand.

I hold my breath and snap at him, "No."

I'm not sure how much more I can take. It's absolute torture.

If he'd only come a little closer.

I avert my gaze from him to Eve. She's already watching me. There's something in her gaze I can't identify. I can't even tell if it's good or bad. At first, it seems like she's calm, but then her chest expands on an extra-long inhale, and she mouths my new favorite three words.

I. Love. You.

A *swoosh* sound fills the air around me, and I blink. Then I blink again. Eve is in the middle of doing a one-eighty with the chair clasped in her hands, swinging it straight toward Tyler's head. She catches him so off guard that the wooden legs connect full-on with his head. His eyes go wide, and he stumbles back a step. Then two. She swings it again. He crumples to the floor. Fuck. He's on the floor, not moving.

"Oh my God, oh my God, oh my God. Is he dead?" Eve's breaths come in harsh bursts. She's trying to get to Tyler, only to stop short.

Fucking chain.

"You did so good, Angel." And she did. So good. But shit, he fell in the wrong direction, away from both of us toward the foot of the bed. "Give me a second."

I move closer to the headboard, which gives my wrists the relief they've been begging for, and try to force the bed back with my legs. Turning around, I push with all my strength. I don't know where the hell this bed is from, but it's heavy as hell.

"Keep your eye on him." Once the bed is far enough back, I grab the headboard and pull it sideways toward where Tyler is lying. It's a process, and by the time I'm halfway across the room, my shirt is soaked in sweat.

"Almost there."

Eve's voice is lighter than I've heard it in the last two days.

It gives me hope. The bed bumps into the corner behind me, and I can't go any farther. Tyler is almost within reach, so I sink to the floor and wrap my feet around his legs to drag him toward me, which isn't as easy as I thought it would be.

"Come on, come on, come on." I clench my teeth, wishing I could get a better grip on him.

Eve is leaning on the chair, watching the scene with knitted brows. "Just a little more, baby."

I don't look at her, not wanting to waste a precious

second, but I feel that tether inside me that connects us. It gives me strength.

We're going to make it out of here alive. Together.

I'm finally able to reach Tyler with my hands after what feels like forever. I haul him far enough toward me to get the keys out of his pocket.

Thank fuck.

I fumble with the keys. It's not as easy to unlock your own handcuffs as I expected it to be. When I finally get them open, they fall to the floor with a satisfying *clunk*.

I scramble up, my entire focus now on Eve. Getting to her. Freeing her. Going home with her.

Her expression suddenly changes, her eyes bulging. She screams, "Phoenix, watch out! Down."

I dive toward her at the same instant a shot rings in the air.

But I'm not fast enough, and the bullet grazes my arm. My skin is on fire, the pain stealing my breath momentarily.

"No, no, no." Eve strains to get to me.

But I'm too far away.

I toss her the key and another shot goes off. "Eve, get down. Now."

This time, I jump out of the way, scrambling around the corner of the bed to put as much distance as possible between us.

Shit, shit, shit. What now?

"I thought maybe we could get through this, you know." Tyler's staggers toward me, his words slow and a little slurry.

Since there's no real cover for me to take, I wait until he's close enough and lunge straight for him. I collide with him, ramming my head straight into his middle, and we crash into the wall. The wooden beams vibrate under the attack, but that deters neither of us. Tyler's fist connects with the side of my head, taking the dull headache to an excruciating level.

The sudden dizziness and blurry vision are disorienting, and I twist away from him, allowing him to get in another punch. This time to my stomach. I wince at the assault, but the new pain distracts me to the point the fog clears in my brain. It's enough for adrenaline to do its job, and my angry bull resurfaces.

After a punch from me and a tackle from him, we roll around on the floor, a tangle of limbs. Fighting for dominance. I hit Tyler in the same spot on his temple as before, and he squeezes his eyes shut and sways. I use that moment to get the gun but never make it there. Tyler pulls my legs out from under me, knocking the breath out of my lungs.

I accidentally kick the gun, and it slides across the floor to the other side of the room.

Tyler pushes himself up on all fours. I grab the chain and wrap it around his neck from behind. His hands tighten around the metal links, trying to tug them off, but I hold it as tightly as possible.

By the time he sputters and lets go, my reserves are depleted. Tyler's hands fall limp before him. Without any strength left, the weight of his body propels me forward.

Then things get a little blurry. Tyler either faked his loss of consciousness or he got a superhuman adrenaline hit. Because one moment he's limp, and the next, he's reached the gun and points it at me.

This time, the bullet hits me in the shoulder, near my throat. There's a snap, and then nothing but a white-hot burn like someone is jabbing me with a fire iron.

My vision darkens at the corners.

Tyler sways and drops the gun, and it slides under the bed. I clench my teeth hard to fight off the excruciating pain and dig deep to find every last remaining ounce of my energy to get to him.

He's closer to Eve now than he is to me, and I can't let that happen.

Tyler is not going to leave this room alive.

This is for Eve. This is for Connie. This is for me.

The pain is almost unbearable, but I push into a sitting position. Tyler groans.

When I see why, the ache in my chest almost explodes.

Eve has jumped on his back, with her legs wrapped around his waist and her chain around his neck.

Fuck me.

That's my wife.

Her eyes are dark, her face tight with determination. And she yanks on the chain with a grunt.

Her arm muscles strain, but she twists and pulls, not letting go. Not when Tyler tries to yank at the chain, not when he claws and punches at her legs and arms. Nothing. He's too weak right now, and she hangs on for dear life, until, eventually, he collapses like a dropped rag doll. Eve tumbles with him, her fall cushioned by his body underneath her, her hands still holding on to that chain.

Waiting, waiting, waiting.

Tyler doesn't move, and his vacant eyes are the last thing I see when I crash to the floor too.

CHAPTER 44

EVANGELINE

The scream that leaves my throat sounds inhuman.

"Phoenix, no. No."

My airways are painfully tight, contracting with each sob that overtakes my body.

Thank goodness Tyler had been so focused on Phoenix that he didn't realize how close he'd come to me and my chain. Nothing has ever felt as satisfying as Tyler collapsing to the floor.

I gaze at his blank stare, and with a swallow, I touch his throat to check for a pulse. Nausea rolls through my stomach at feeling his skin under mine. I wait. One second. Two. I take deep breaths through my nose. But there's nothing. No pulse. No heartbeat.

He's dead. He's really dead.

Freddy is dead.

Oh my God.

No matter how satisfying it might be to get the gun and empty the remainder of the magazine into him, I need to get to Phoenix.

I rush to him, panic prickling my soul when I see him. So much blood has collected around his body.

So much blood.

He's utterly still and unmoving.

"No, please, dear God. No."

My breaths are short, quick pants as I fall to my knees beside him. Blood coats half of his face, and he's pale. Too pale.

I glide my shaky fingers up his neck, trying to search for his pulse. The second I find it, I half collapse on his body in relief but quickly pull myself up again. "Hang in there, baby, please. I'm going to get you help, I promise."

I don't want to leave him, but he needs an ambulance. Quickly.

For a moment, my muscles freeze.

You can do this, Eve. It's over. Tyler can't hurt you anymore. You did it. And now you need to get your husband the help he needs.

A shudder shakes me out of my stupor, and I go back to Tyler and pat my hands over his pants. I hate every second of being so close to him, of having my hands on him, but I need to find . . . Yes. I feel the hard rectangular shape in his left pocket and reach into it to tug it out.

My hands shake so badly it takes me several swipes to bring the screen to life. The locked screen. "Fuck, fuck, fuck."

I swipe again and feel disgust and gratitude rush my system at the fingerprint access.

Of course.

On a deep inhale, I grab his limp hand and situate his thumb over the screen. It takes me numerous tries, but the phone finally unlocks.

"Come on, come on." I push the green phone button, type in nine-one-one, and wait. But nothing happens. "No, please."

I hold the phone away from my ear and stare at the corner of the screen. No service.

The jammer.

Shit.

I have no idea where it is. Shit, I don't even know what it looks like.

No, no, no.

We didn't get this far to fail now. It's not over yet.

A sob racks my body. I move back to Phoenix and press my lips to his, but then I'm up. I hold the phone in a death grip and sprint out of the room, gasping at Ruby's unmoving form.

Fuck.

I already forgot about my best friend again.

Tears fall to the floor as I crouch beside her, dropping the phone to search for her pulse. Hers is easier to find than Phoenix's, stronger under my fingertips. Thank goodness.

A soft groan escapes her mouth, and I shush her. "Don't move, Ruby. You'll be okay. I'm getting help."

Jumping up, I grab the phone once more and touch the screen to keep it unlocked. I race through the house until I reach the front door. It's heavy in my hand, but I haul it open and run down the front steps. I race down the long driveway toward the street that lies beyond, my gaze constantly flicking to the phone to see if the service has returned.

I don't know how far the reach of the signal jammer goes, so I keep pushing my tired legs. Ignoring the bite on the bottom of my bare feet slapping on the concrete and pebbles.

The crisp fall air bites at my skin, goosebumps immediately spreading over my entire body.

Despite feeling like I'm about to collapse, I make it to the road and take a left turn on instinct. A strangled sound leaves my lips when two network bars appear on the screen. Oh my God. Finally, I crumble to the ground and repeat my earlier call.

"Nine-one-one, what's your emergency?"

"Can you track the location of my phone?" My breathing is so loud I hope the woman on the other end of the line can make out the words.

"Give me one second." She's quiet for two beats. "Yes, I got you."

"I was kidnapped. One person is dead, two injured."

My eyes flare. My thoughts rearrange.

Mason. Fuck.

"Maybe three."

"Ma'am, are you injured? Can you tell me more—"

I hang up and dial the next number, this one longer than the first.

The call connects, but I'm greeted by silence. "Hold?"

"Princess? Fuck."

My sobs are loud and ugly the moment I hear his voice.

He's talking to me, but I can't make out the words.

"Hold, he shot Phoenix. His pulse . . . it was so weak." I hiccup and bite my lip, trying to calm down, but it's useless.

Holden repeats something.

This time, I catch the end. "Stay. One minute."

I nod, even though he can't see me. I couldn't move if I wanted to.

And then he's there.

As are others.

There's a lot of noise. And flashing lights. And people.

"Princess."

And then I'm in Holden's arms, wrapped tightly against his warm chest. Someone takes the phone from me, and something soft wraps around me, covering me, and it vaguely registers I'm still only in my underwear.

I sag against him, tears rolling down my cheeks and onto his shirt. "Phoenix. Shot. Basement."

"Fuck." He cradles me tighter, his fingers tightening around my body before he relaxes them. "Tyler?"

"Dead."

He blows out a breath. "Ruby and Mason?"

"Ruby injured in the basement. Mason upstairs. Save Phoenix. Please, Hold." The words slip out of my mouth between sobs while Holden barks orders at people and sirens sound in the distance.

I nestle closer against Holden's warmth.

"They got him, Princess. They're taking him to the hospital, and we'll be right behind him, okay? Get some rest."

As if his words turned off the power switch in my body, a sudden wave of exhaustion washes over me. My eyes are too heavy to keep open, and I close them for a moment. Just one moment.

WHEN I OPEN my eyes again, it takes me several attempts to blink away the blurriness. Eventually, Holden's face becomes sharper.

The events rush back into my head with the magnitude of a bulldozer, and I gasp, "Phoenix?"

One corner of his mouth lifts in an attempt of a smile, but that's all it is, an attempt. "He lost a lot of blood, and they rushed him into emergency surgery. There hasn't been any update yet."

"What? No." I try to sit up, but for some reason, the blanket is tucked in on my sides, and panic rises in my throat at being restrained. My heart immediately gallops, the machine next to me speeding up in tandem until an alarm sounds.

A moment later, the door flies open, and a nurse walks in. Holden steps aside. "She just woke up."

"Shh, Evangeline. It's okay, you're safe now." She pushes a few buttons on the machine until the beeping stops. A syringe appears out of nowhere, and she injects it into my IV.

I avert my gaze away from her and over to Holden.

The nurse holds my arms down. "You'll feel better in just a moment. Everything's all right."

A sudden calmness spreads through my limbs, and I relax.

Holden's sad look still pierces me straight through the heart though, and I hold out my hand to him. The nurse stops him, and they exchange a few hushed words. Eventually, she leaves, and he comes to my side.

"I can't make it without him. If he doesn't survive, I don't want to either." The words all blur together in my head, and I close my eyes after seeing Holden's glistening eyes.

There's only so much I can take.

～

THE MEDICINE the nurse gave me did a number on me. I'm not sure if it was supposed to knock me out as much as it did, but for the next few hours, I go in and out of sleep. It reminds me too much of waking up after Ruby drugged me. I hate it.

The room is dark when I peel my eyelids back and feel a little more alert. It's an effort, but eventually, I manage to keep them open.

"Hold?" The name is barely audible, my throat too dry to talk.

Footsteps hurry toward me.

"Hey, Princess." A chair scrapes across the floor. "How are you feeling?"

How do I feel?

Holden hands me a cup of water with a straw, and I take slow sips.

I'm utterly drained, that's for sure.

"Phoenix?" His name is full of anguish and worry as my brain fully wakes up, quickly overriding my nervous system with a wave of anxiety and dread.

Hold nods. "He's out of surgery. They're keeping a close eye on him for the next twenty-four hours, but they're hopeful."

My eyes burn, but I nod at him. "O . . . Okay."

"Shh." Holden covers my hand with his. He gives it a gentle squeeze. "You guys are both going to be okay, and that motherfucker is dead."

Having it officially confirmed eases a small part of my chest. We stay like this for a moment, and I close my eyes.

Inhale.

Exhale.

Inhale.

Exhale.

"It's really over?" I stare into Holden's eyes, needing to hear it again.

His lips press into a tight-lipped smile. "It is, Princess. And as soon as Phoenix is cleared, I'll take you to him."

My vision blurs again, but I blink to bring Holden back into focus.

"I'm so sorry I failed you." Holden's hand is still on mine, but he averts his gaze to the floor. "If you hadn't done what you did, the ambulance might not have made it there in time."

"Hold, no . . . don't."

A muscle tics when he finally glances at me again. "You're the reason he's still alive, Eve."

"I . . . I . . ." I don't know what to say.

And it doesn't matter anyway. The only thing that matters is that he's going to be okay. "What about Ruby and Mase?"

Hold clears his throat. "Ruby suffered a fractured skull, but the doctor said she should be okay again in a few months. Mason only had some minor injuries."

"Thank goodness." I blow out a long breath, the relief of the entire situation almost overwhelming.

The door opens, and the same nurse from my last hospital visit walks in, her shoes coming to a squeaking halt when she sees us.

"Well, hello there, Sleeping Beauty. Glad to see you awake. We have to stop meeting like this." She gives me a smile and a wink before shifting her attention to Hold to glare at him. "And you, young man, were supposed to tell us when she woke up. What is it with you guys never listening?"

He has the decency to look flustered. "Sorry, Nurse Cynthia."

"Uh-huh, that's right." She comes to the other side of my bed, checks the monitors, and gets the stethoscope from around her neck to check my vitals. Her watchful gaze inspects my face. "How are you feeling, sweetie?"

Holden's unanswered question from earlier comes back. "Mmm, okay, I think."

"Does anything hurt?" She moves the round metal piece over my chest, listening intently while I inhale and exhale.

I shake my head, taking a moment to inventory my body. "I don't think so. Mainly just my wrists."

Her expression falls at the mention of my wrists, but she forces her lips to move upward again. "I'm glad you got away better than your husband."

Her words repeat in my head.

Your husband.

My husband.

A vague memory of yelling at Holden that I need to see Phoenix, and that he's my husband, dashes into my mind.

"Can I . . . can I see him?" I clear my throat, sending her a pleading gaze. "Please?"

She tilts her head to the side, a frown growing between her brows, and I get ready for her rejection.

After a sigh, she blinks at me. "I know they brought him to a room, but let me see how he's doing first, okay?"

I nod, sad but hopeful I'll be able to see Phoenix soon. I need to see him alive and doing well with my own eyes.

A big yawn takes over my mouth, and my eyes droop.

This stupid medicine. I never want anything like this ever again. Feeling loopy is officially on my bad list.

Cynthia huffs a laugh and pats my hand. "Why don't you rest for a while, and I'll be back before you know it?"

I want to tell her no, that I don't want to sleep any more. I want to stay awake and see Phoenix. But whatever medicine is left in my body has other plans.

STRONG ARMS PUSH under my body, lifting me effortlessly off the mattress.

A high-pitched sound leaves my throat as I'm pulled against a warm chest.

"Just me, Princess. You're safe."

I hum low in my throat, the gentle rocking motion of Holden carrying me reminding me of our little vacation. Of being in the ocean with the soft waves lapping up my body and surrounding me in a tender caress.

My eyes stay shut until he places me down again, and I gingerly pry them open.

The large white-and-gray room is almost identical to the one we just left, except for one significant difference. There's a second bed a few feet away from mine, and Phoenix's large frame takes up almost the entire mattress. He's on his back with cables coming out from under the covers attached to several machines.

I take him in, my eyes feasting on as much of him as they can manage from this angle.

Straining my neck, I roam over the bandages from one wound, with the other hiding under the fabric. Since I'm facing his right side, I can't see the temple injury or anything else on his face. My gaze stops at his wrapped wrists for several beats before I stare at the healthy rise and fall of his chest, nearly breaking down at the sight of it.

Holden's still next to my bed, his gaze fixed on his best friend. I grab his hand and squeeze it. When he looks down at me with shiny eyes, I whisper, "Thank you."

He squeezes my fingers back and gives me a tight nod. We stay like this until he points toward the oversized chair in the corner, where he settles in for the night.

I plan on not moving a single muscle the entire night, watching over Phoenix until he opens his eyes.

CHAPTER 45

PHOENIX

"I'm not sure who's worse, you or Nurse Holden over there." I growl, my displeasure vibrating low in my throat.

Eve chuckles. "Stop being such a grump. Maybe you're just a terrible patient."

Holden walks over to us, raised brows in tow. "A very ungrateful patient too."

I shake my head. "Nope. You guys are definitely the problem. I'm fine. I can get up and do things myself."

"Dude." Holden lifts his hand like he plans to push me back on the mattress and hold me there. "You got shot and had emergency surgery. You almost died. One inch to the left, and—"

"Trust me, I'm well aware I got lucky. But we've been home for almost three weeks now, and you guys still act like I got shot yesterday."

Eve sidles up next to him, giving me her best glare. "The doctor said you have to take it easy for at least four to six weeks."

I nod. "Easy, yes. But he didn't say I needed to be chained to the bed."

She flinches at the choice of words, and I immediately say, "Sorry, I didn't . . . ah, shit."

Her features soften. "I know you didn't, don't worry about it."

Eve climbs onto the bed and snuggles up to me with her head on my good side. "We just want you to heal as quickly as possible and not be in more pain than necessary."

I press my lips to her forehead, swallowing the hiss that wants to escape at the shift. "I know."

And I do know. I wouldn't feel any different if the roles were reversed, but I also hate being so confined. I want to get up and do things. Move around. Feel productive.

I want to live.

Be with my wife.

I breathe her in, her floral scent filling my nostrils. "You know, the doctor also said during my last checkup that I'm cleared for minor physical activities. I just can't overdo it."

I wiggle my brows, and Eve laughs.

"Aaaaand that's my cue to leave." Holden snatches something from the side table and heads toward the bedroom door. "Holler if you need anything."

"Sorry," Eve yells after him, unable to hide the giggle in her voice. "And thank you."

"Yes, thank you, Holden," I repeat her words.

"No problem."

The door clicks shut behind him, and then it's just Eve and me. My wife and me.

I smile at her. "Hi."

The corners of her eyes crinkle as she chuckles. "Hey, handsome."

I lift my right hand and wince. But I want to touch her badly enough to ignore it for at least a little while. Long enough to brush my fingers over her cheek. Along her jaw. Her lips. "So, how about that minor physical activity?"

She buries her face into my good shoulder. "I am not going to have sex with you."

I grunt. "Party pooper. How about you sit on my face and suffocate me with that sweet pussy of yours?"

Her laughter is muffled. "Oh my God, you're terrible."

I inhale deeply. "I just finally want to fuck my wife."

That sobers her up, and she looks at me somberly. "I know. I can't wait to be with you again too. But it's not worth it if it prolongs your recovery time. Your health is my number one priority. *You* are my number one priority."

"Of course, you have to be perfectly reasonable, kind, and lovable about denying me. Figures."

She shakes her head, giving me the soft smile that's reserved just for me.

"But . . ." She pushes herself up enough to press her lips against mine, not pulling away.

I coax her mouth open and gently stroke my tongue against hers.

When she leans back, her gaze is a little hazy, and I wonder if she's as high on this connection between us as I am.

She licks her lips and sits back on her heels. "But you're right, the doctor did say light physical activity is okay. In moderation."

Crawling down the mattress, she settles between my

spread legs. Her fingers gentle and careful as she tugs them into the low-hung waistband of my sweats and pulls them down. I groan at the same time my cock springs free, already hard as a rock.

"Looks like someone is happy to see me." Eve encircles my length with one hand and swipes her thumb over the tip.

"So very happy."

She bends down and slowly wraps her lips around my crown, causing buzzing electricity to flood my veins.

My hips spasm, and it takes all my willpower to keep them from bucking up like I want to. "Fuck, Angel. Yes. Suck me deep. I want to see you choke on my cock."

I grab as many pillows as possible with my good hand and deposit them under my head.

The view is absolute perfection.

I hiss when Eve takes me in all the way, and my tip touches the back of her throat. Her eyes water, and I brush my hand over her hair, forehead, and cheek. Any part I can reach in my position.

Our gazes collide, and I hiss at the picture she's presenting.

"You're so beautiful with your lips wrapped tightly around my cock." I groan and lift my hips.

She shakes her head slightly at my movement, and I curse my injuries for the millionth time.

Focus on the fact you survived and left that hellhole with your wife.

Eve touches my balls, gently massaging them in her hand while sucking in earnest. The telltale sign of my balls tingling begins, and I drive deeper into her mouth, keeping my movement shallow.

"Fuck. I'm going to come." Two more thrusts, and I still in Eve's warm mouth, gazing at my wife, who swallows every last drop of cum I give her.

She draws back, and my slick cock falls out of her mouth. My gaze immediately zeroes in on her swollen lips.

She licks them, the corners pulling into a proud smirk. "Not a drop spilled."

"Come here." I reach for her, drawing her up as much as she lets me. Once she's close enough, I plunge my tongue into her mouth and show her exactly what I think about her performance. When we part, I gently bite her lip. "Your bedside manners are fantastic."

Eve laughs, and I soak up every second of the musical sound.

I brush a strand of hair off her forehead. "Maybe I should get you a sexy nurse outfit?"

She's still laughing. "So I can scare the staff?"

I haul her against me. "No one's going to see you in it but me."

"Oh yeah?"

Her breath fans against my neck, and her scent immediately intoxicates me.

Which reminds me of another one.

"Touch yourself and give me a taste with your fingers."

Her eyes widen. Her pupils grow. She just stares at me for a moment, biting her lip. Her hand descends her torso, and heat shoots to my groin. Soon after, her fingers disappear beneath the waistband of her leggings.

Shit. That's so fucking hot.

She closes her eyes and rocks against her hand, letting out a little gasp.

"How wet are you, baby?" I stare at her parted lips.

"Soaked."

One word, and my control slips further.

"Did you get all wet sucking off your husband's cock?"

A sharp breath. A curt nod. A shy glance. And then that damn lip bite again.

"Let me suck those fingers off. Let me taste my wife."

With a whimper, she draws her hand from her leggings and brings it to my mouth. I groan and take one finger between my lips. It's just as good as I remember. I lap at each finger, swirling my tongue around every digit until they're all clean.

"Angel." My voice is husky, the desperation in it as clear as day. "Take off your clothes and go to the edge of the bed. On your hands and knees."

"Phoenix." She says my name like it has ten syllables.

I touch my lips against hers for a lazy moment. "It's my time to make you feel good. I promise I'll be careful, okay?"

Her nod is quick, eager. Just the way I like it.

My gaze is glued to her, watching her undress and get into position. I move off the bed and take a sip of my water. Standing at the end of the bed, I'm offered one of the most perfect views. Eve's pussy glistens with arousal, and my dick stirs in my pants with renewed interest. But this isn't about me. I put the cup away and lower myself to my knees behind Eve.

A deep inhale later, I lean forward and do one languid lick from her clit to her ass.

Eve moans and jerks against me. "Oh my God, Phoenix."

I give her ass an appreciative slap and put the ice cube I took from my water cup into my mouth.

After swirling it around for several seconds, I tuck it between my lips and attack her pussy in earnest. Dragging the ice cube over her folds, circling her clit, teasing her entrance. Faster than planned, the ice cube turns to cold water in my mouth, and I crush the rest of it. Once it's gone, I thrust my cold tongue deep into her cunt, showing her everything I wish I could do to her with my cock. Soon.

Her moans are all I hear, her pussy all I see and taste.

"More, baby. Please, more," Eve begs, "I'm so close. Just a—"

"Come for me, Angel. Be a good wife and coat your husband's fingers."

I thrust two fingers deep inside her, curling them against her sensitive softness, and she pulses around them. I take that as my cue and attack her clit, sucking on it, pressing my flat tongue over it while continuing to pump my fingers into her.

"Fuck, yes. Oh my God. Yeeees." Eve moans loudly, her release running down my fingers just like I wanted.

I retrieve them and lap at her pussy, staying away from her oversensitive clit until her spasms subside, and Eve collapses forward onto the mattress. My hand has a mind of its own. I grab a handful of her ass, massaging one round cheek then giving the other side the same treatment.

Eventually, I step away with a groan. "I'll be back. I need a cold shower."

Eve chuckles but follows me into the shower a minute later, replacing the cold water with her mouth and gorgeous tits that I wash off very thoroughly after giving her the most satisfying pearl necklace.

LATER THAT EVENING, we're cuddled up on the couch with Eve safely tucked under my arm. The same way we've been doing since I was released from the hospital, and she was sure I wasn't lying about it not hurting, at least not in that instance. Sometimes, there are moments when a little pain is worth having her closer or satisfied.

Eve turns to look at me. "How did your meeting go with the lawyers?"

I blow out a breath. "Good, I think. There's a lot to unravel, a lot of paperwork to go through, and even more cleanup to do. My father screwed over a lot of people, but I'm optimistic, especially now that we have some of my grandpa's closest employees back. They'll be a huge help in returning the company to what my grandpa intended it to be. It'll be a lot of work but worth it in the end."

Her lips curve up. "So worth it. I can't wait to see all the things you'll accomplish."

"Thank you." I lean down to kiss her forehead. "Having you by my side will make all the backlash and resistance we face more tolerable. There are a lot of people who aren't happy my dad left the country before anyone could ask him any questions, and now, they just want someone to blame."

Although I'd love to give my dad a piece of my mind, I'm glad he disappeared. I don't know if he'll ever return, but I've never felt this at peace than without his presence in my life. The fact that my mom left with him annoys me, but when Holden asked me if I wanted him to search for them, I told him not to bother. They made their choices, and I'm making mine.

Sometimes, life is better without certain people in it, even if they're your own flesh and blood. And I know Eve feels the same way, having cut ties with her parents once she was ready to face them. Even my presence didn't deter her father from throwing threats her way, and that was before I told him that any deals between Caldwell & Company and Montgomery Enterprises are terminated.

It was bittersweet when Holden and our team looked into Tyler's allegations and discovered he had actually told the truth. The company was supposed to go to me once I had my college degree, something my father had purposefully hidden from me since he wanted the company all to himself for as long as possible. Once power hungry, always power hungry.

We also uncovered that my father fired anyone who didn't agree with his often aggressive or illegal ways of conducting business.

Thankfully, many of them have agreed to return to help dig up the poison my father spread within the company and beyond, so we can rebuild it the right way as soon as possible.

Eve presses her lips to mine in a soft kiss. "You'll do amazing. I don't have a single doubt about that."

I sigh. "I'm just glad I don't have to do it alone."

Enter Holden. He's been the most significant resource I've ever encountered, especially in all things security. While I was at the hospital, he assembled a team to tear apart Tyler's apartment and everything he owned. Holden said Tyler—my half brother—had footage of my dad, me, Eve, and dozens of other people, dating back to when he moved to New York. Including blackmail material for Ben Rodgers that was way worse than what he took the fall for. On top of that, he had a ton of audio recordings that were definitely illegally obtained and what Holden called a very obsessive trail of miscellaneous documents and items. It seems like Tyler was on his A game when it came to blackmailing people. Holden almost sounded impressed.

"Do not attempt to understand why a dysfunctional person does what they do. There's no logic behind it."

Who would have thought therapy could be so insightful?

What started as a joke has quickly turned into reality where the three of us—Holden, Eve, and I—keep a therapist busy full time. Sort of. While we didn't hire anyone full time, we see someone several times a week. Sometimes alone, other times together, depending on the topics and issues. I have felt oddly relieved and energized as a result. It's nice to finally talk to someone about everything I, and we, have gone through.

Eve drags her fingernails over my arm, and I sigh.

"That feels so good."

She presses a kiss to my chest. "You have a great team, which will only grow over time."

My mind returns to our conversation about work, and I clear my throat. "Speaking of great team, there was something else I was thinking about."

"Oh yeah, what's that?"

I swallow. "I want to talk to the board and see how they feel about someone else taking over, or at the very least, share my responsibilities."

A slight crease forms between Eve's brows. "But . . . you've always wanted to be CEO."

"I used to . . . before. But my priorities have changed." I

grasp her hand, playing with the wedding ring on her finger. "Not only do I want to focus more on the foundation and expand our work, but I also want to travel the world with you and be there when you play your concerts. I can't do that if I'm stuck behind a desk for twelve-plus hours most days. And to be honest, I've realized I'm not really that interested in the company anymore anyway. I'd much rather make a difference in the world in a way that's meaningful to me. And I want to do it with you by my side. You're my priority now."

Her lower lip quivers as she nods at me. "I just want you to be happy."

"I'm happy when I'm with you, Angel. Everything else is just a bonus."

She clears her throat. "You know, I've done some thinking too. Working with you on the foundation has been more fun than I ever could have imagined it would be, and now that this nightmare is finally over, I'd like to be more involved. I was actually wondering if maybe there's a way to get Doreen on board, and together, we can find a way to combine the women's shelter and the teen safe house. You were talking about getting a large property anyway, so there'd be enough room for everyone, and maybe they could help each other."

"I like the sound of that." I pause for a moment, still mulling over what she just said. "But what about your dreams of traveling the tworld and playing your music?"

"I've talked to Dr. Johnson about this, and I realized a part of me had those dreams because I wanted to escape my life here. We both know I was never truly a part of my family, at least not where my parents and brother were concerned.

Now that we've mostly cut ties, all of that pressure and impulse to flee has gone away with it."

I study her closely, glad when her features stay relaxed. In a twisted way of fate, a lot of good has come from our messed-up situation.

She continues, "I'd still like to travel, and maybe do a performance every once in a while, but I'd also like to try my hand at other things. Explore studio work some more, maybe film music, collaborations with other artists, compose a bunch of different songs and upload them online, that sort of thing. Work that will fulfill me but will also allow me a lot of flexibility. For the first time, I'm content and excited to see what the future will bring. With you by my side, because you make everything better."

There's a lightness in her face I've never seen before. True happiness. I want to wake up to this spark in her eyes for the rest of my life. "You amaze me."

She gives me a watery smile. "I love you."

I tilt her chin back and cover her lips with mine. "I love you more."

We both have to sort through a lot of baggage that has accumulated over the last few years, probably most of our lives, but now that no one is trying to murder or ruin us, we can focus on writing the rest of our story the way it was always supposed to be written.

Together.

Forever.

EPILOGUE
EVANGELINE

"Best early birthday present ever." I throw myself at Holden, who catches me with a grunt.

He pulls back and shakes his head. "I think you already said that about ten times on the drive here."

Here is Madison Square Garden, where Olivia Parker performs tonight to a sold-out audience, just like every other concert on her tour. While the backstage passes are technically my present, Mason, Ruby, and I also use tonight to celebrate our bachelor degrees. It took a lot of studying and catching up, but somehow, we all managed with weekly study dates at Phoenix's—no, *our*—house.

"And you'll probably hear it another ten times before the day is over," I squeal.

Holden sighs and shifts us around. "Dude, get your wife off me, please."

I sense Phoenix's presence behind me in the long backstage tunnel before the breath of his chuckle hits my neck, and he presses a soft kiss to my nape.

Then he steps back. "Nope. Your idea. Your problem."

I can't see what's happening behind my back, but since Phoenix chuckles again, I'm pretty sure Holden flipped him off or something equally theatric.

"Angel."

Phoenix's low rasp has the desired effect, and I let go of Holden, who exhales heavily like the drama queen he is.

The door to the men's restroom behind Holden opens, and Mason exits.

Before I can signal anything to Mason, he takes one look at Holden and says, "Nice photo," while patting his back.

Not two seconds later, Holden growls, "Princess," when it clicks why I really attacked him like I did.

It's entirely his fault though.

Phoenix is leaning against the brick wall, delicious in dark jeans and a fitted light-gray T-shirt. I've tried everything, but he refused to wear one of the Olivia Parker shirts I got us. Okay, maybe he bent me over his desk and fucked me so thoroughly that I agreed he didn't need to wear one.

Anyway, his loss.

Ruby is standing a few feet away from us, sporting the same fan shirt as Mason and I do, and I've decided Holden isn't getting out of it either. Hence, the large photo I just taped to his back.

I lean against Phoenix with my back to his front, releasing a happy sigh when he wraps his arms around my middle.

With my gaze on Holden, I raise both hands to the sides

like a scale. "Picture on your back, or Olivia T-shirt. You promised we'd be concert buddies. This is part of it." I push my lower lip out, knowing I'm not playing fair, but the time for caring is over.

He growls at me. "Fine. Give me the damn shirt."

I hurry to grab it from my bag just as a door opens a few feet away, and a tall, skinny guy rushes out, bringing a ton of noise from the backstage rooms with him. He freezes the second he sees all of us and turns bright red. He stares at us like a deer caught in the headlights, his knuckles white on the still-open door.

Loud voices filter out from behind him.

A woman says, "I can't believe you think this is okay. Someone took photos of me in my underwear and posted them online. Without my permission."

The response is immediate, exasperation clear in the man's voice. "Come on, Olivia, be real. This is how things work, and you know it. It's not even full-on nudes. No biggie."

There's a moment of silence before the woman replies, "I can't deal with this right now. I . . . I have to go."

We're all standing there as the skinny guy finally lets go of the door, and it shuts with a loud *thud*. He shuffles on his feet, and we continue to stare at each other awkwardly.

"Mmh, Miss Parker will be right out."

He spins on his heels and speed-walks away.

No one speaks, everyone unsure of what we just overheard.

The silence is broken when Phoenix takes the T-shirt from my hand and tosses it straight at Holden's face.

He glares at both of us in return, and I'm quick to hold up my hands to proclaim my innocence but can't help myself and whisper, "Hurry up."

He rolls his eyes at me, not for the first time today either, and I can't wait for him to get over this mood and return to his usual perky self.

Much to everyone's surprise—I think Mason's gasp was the loudest—Holden doesn't put on the shirt over the one he's already wearing, but instead, we watch him pull his black shirt off and toss it at a chuckling Phoenix.

Holden tugs the new shirt over his head at the exact moment the door opens again, and Olivia Parker steps out. Her gaze darts around, immediately landing on Holden, who's frozen with one arm in the T-shirt and the other still out, exposing most of his chiseled torso. And boy, he is ripped with a capital R.

Secretly, I've been waiting to see how Olivia reacts to seeing Holden again, especially since he still hasn't told me what went down between them. And she doesn't disappoint. She goes rigid and blinks as if she's trying to discern whether she's seeing a mirage.

Her sharp inhale is a bonus. She lets her gaze roam over Holden's chest and abs, down his black jeans and scuffed brown boots, before returning to his face. "Holden?"

He finally manages to push his other arm into the sleeve and pulls the shirt down. "Hey, Hurricane."

Olivia closes the distance between them and flings herself at Holden, much like I did earlier, but to a much better reception. He wraps his arms tightly around her and burrows his face into her neck, and I hear her muffled, "I can't believe you're really here" against his shoulder before she draws back and knees him in the balls.

Holden sinks to the floor, and we all gasp.

For a moment, he's silent.

Then he hisses through his teeth, "Looks like someone's still mad."

"Screw you." She spins on her heel and steps toward me, stopping a few feet before me, this time with a beautiful smile. "You must be Evangeline."

My manners kick in, and I shake her outstretched hand on autopilot. "Evie, please."

She winks. "Evie, it is. I'm so sorry about this." She points her thumb over her shoulder at Holden. "Please don't hold it against me. He knows he deserved much worse. But anyway, it's so nice to meet you, and I'm thrilled to have you here tonight. I'm obsessed with your music."

It takes me a few seconds to reboot my brain, and all I manage to stutter is, "Uh . . . thank you."

Did she seriously just compliment *my* music?

Thank you, universe, for blowing up my music online.

Never in a million years did I think my covers and originals would reach someone like Olivia though. This must be a dream. Someone pinch me.

Mentally, I add a *Sorry, Hold. I'll be outraged on your behalf once I'm down from cloud nine.*

She waves her hand around our little group. "Thank you all for being here. It means a lot."

Everyone talks over each other, and Olivia chuckles. The ominous door opens again, and Gavin Bryce walks out— Olivia's manager and rumored boyfriend.

Holden pushes himself off the floor, and Gavin frowns at us.

Without a hello, he dismisses us, his gaze zeroing in on Olivia. "Backstage, now."

Her chest heaves. She says goodbye to us, not sparing a glance in Holden's direction. "I hope you'll enjoy the show. And happy birthday, Evangeline. I'd like to get in touch with you sometime soon if that's okay."

I nod like a robot and wave after my girl crush, who just kneed my best friend in the balls.

WHEN WE'RE BACK at the house hours later, my throat is sore, my voice pretty much gone, and I've never been happier. Phoenix stands by the open car door in the garage, waiting for me to get out. When I finally move my tired butt, he turns around and crouches.

"Hop on."

I smile. "Best day ever."

He chuckles. "So you've said."

I climb on, and he stands, walking us through the garage and into the house. I press my nose into his neck, enjoying the smell of cologne, leftover heat from tonight, and something male that's uniquely Phoenix. I have no clue how he manages to get up the stairs with my extra weight on his back, but somehow, he makes it to our bedroom, where he deposits me on the bed.

He turns to leave, but I grab his shirt and haul him toward me, capturing his lips with mine. "Thank you for today. It seriously was amazing. A million times better than I thought it would be."

Shifting his weight onto his elbows, he stares into my eyes and brushes my hair back with both hands. The motion is soothing and comforting, and I hum in pleasure.

"Most of it was Holden's doing, but I think you've already thanked him about seventy-five times." He presses his lips together to keep from laughing.

"What was up with him today anyway? I mean, besides the whole kick to the balls. He was already cranky before that, but then he clearly enjoyed the show."

Phoenix shrugs. "He hasn't told me much either, but they definitely have a complicated history. I think that much is clear."

I nod, lost in thought, replaying everything that happened today for the millionth time. "I thought he was going to go after Olivia's manager when he came out and took her away so rudely. Not that I blame him, that guy is an asshole. I wonder what she sees in him since she seems like such a nice woman."

He taps his index finger on my nose. "You, of all people, should know you can't always trust what you see in public. Some people hide their demons better than others."

His comment throws me back into my mind, flitting around too fast for me to make out anything until it stops at an image of my best friend. "At least Ruby seemed to have a good time."

Phoenix nods. "She did."

Ruby has had the most challenging time adjusting after Tyler's kidnapping last year. She's retreated into herself, now merely a shell of her old self. We've all been trying to help, but there's only so much we can do from the outside.

"She'll get better, Angel."

"I hope so. I miss my friend."

"I know you do."

We're quiet until Phoenix's lips find mine in a soft kiss. "I'm sorry you're hurting."

"I just want to help her. It's been almost a year."

"She needs to figure it out by herself. Remember what Dr. Johnson said. Everyone handles trauma differently, and that's normal. You're there for her, and she knows it. She'll talk to you when she's ready."

"Yeah." I exhale loudly, always frustrated when we talk about Ruby. I hate feeling so helpless.

Once Ruby, Mason, and I recovered after the Tyler incident, we sat together, and I told them everything. We cried for hours, our eyes and faces swollen and blotchy by the time the night ended. We all know that life will never be the same after what happened, but we're trying our best. And while I've talked to Phoenix, Holden, and Dr. Johnson about everything that transpired in great detail, Ruby and Mason seem to just want to forget. And that's fair too.

Phoenix gives me a gentle smile. "Do you want to take a bath?"

I frown. "A bath? Now? It's past midnight."

He only shrugs. "So what? It'll relax you."

Warm water lapping around me does sound good. "Okay. But only if you'll join me."

"Anything for you." He rolls off me, pulling me with him.

Hand in hand, we walk to the bathroom, where Phoenix turns on the water and pours a generous amount of the lavender bath soap I like into the large tub. It only takes a few seconds for the air to change and the floral scent to surround us.

I grab the hem of my shirt to take it off, but Phoenix stops me with a hand on mine.

"Let me."

I blink at him but nod. "Okay."

Phoenix takes his time undressing me. Trailing kisses over every inch of newly exposed flesh. I moan when his mouth meets my hip bone, following an invisible path down to my clit.

He drags my panties down my legs. "Hold on to the counter, and put one leg around my shoulder."

I follow his command, and he continues his slow assault between my legs. Dragging slow, languid licks down my center. Circling his tongue around my clit.

Without thinking, I tilt my hips, lazily rocking them against his face. His hands move around my hips toward my butt, squeezing and massaging. Dragging a finger through my wetness, spreading it over my butthole, and slowly pushing in.

My orgasm hits me out of nowhere, but Phoenix doesn't let go, staying on his knees to pepper my stomach with gentle kisses.

With the last of my strength, I pull him up and devour his mouth. "Take off your clothes and get in the tub, babe. I want you to fuck me."

He huffs a laugh. "Yes, ma'am."

Once we're in the water, I straddle his lap, and he enters me. Stretches me. Fills me. Owns me.

I lean down and steal a kiss. "I love you."

"I love *you*, Angel. Marry me again?"

After a gasp, I smile wide against his mouth and nod. "I'll always say yes to you."

He shows his approval by fucking me so hard, I forget my name.

AUTHOR NOTE

Thank you so much for picking up *Tangled In Lies*. It means the absolute world to me.

If you enjoyed Phoenix and Eve's story, I'd be honored if you told a friend.

For more books (including Holden and Olivia's) and bonus scenes (including several for Phoenix and Eve), please visit my website at
www.jasminmiller.com

xoxo, Jasmin

Acknowledgments

This is MY book. Not my story, but *my* book. You are probably wondering what on earth I'm babbling about, and I don't blame you. I'm not even sure I can put it into words to make sense, but I've never enjoyed writing a book as much as this one. It didn't pour out of me, but I loved every moment of writing it, which, for some reason, just never happened before. So, for the first time, it truly feels like MY book. Let's stop the confusion right there. lol

Although Phoenix and Eve's story has nothing to do with me, or anything that's ever happened to me in the bigger sense, I love it more than I could ever tell you, and I hope that's visible on every page. Or at least most of them. Ha.

So, to make this even more awkward, I'd like to apologize to myself. Sorry for saying no to ideas and for ignoring gut feelings. I should have listened sooner. But we're here now, and I couldn't be happier about that. Thanks for hanging around so long and not giving up on me.

Now, to my husband. That poor man. The crazy things he had to listen to for this book, the excitement he had to witness over things no sane person should probably ever get excited about. The patience he tries to extend to me even when he's a walking zombie from working a ton. I love you! 

To Jo. I still want to equally apologize and thank you for

what you did for me. Seriously. It's something I'll never take for granted. Thank you, thank you, thank you!! I'm so incredibly grateful for your help and for knowing you!! ♥

To Lynn. Boy, oh boy, where to start with you? The story wouldn't be what it is now without you. No doubt about that. Not as a whole but especially not that one specific part. You know which one. Lol. Thank you for being there for me and for not holding back. You're incredible, and I'm so grateful to have you in my corner. ♥

To Alicia. Thank you for always believing in me. It means more than I could ever tell you. Borahae.

To Becca. Thank you for keeping me sane, or at least trying to. I'd be in a much worse space without you. ♥

To Kim Namjoon, Kim Seokjin, Min Yoongi, Jung Hoseok, Park Jimin, Kim Taehyung, and Jeon Jungkook. You guys left a hole in my heart, and I miss you. Be safe and hurry back! *finger hearts*

As always, a massive shout-out to my incredible editors and proofreader, Rebecca, Emmy, and Karen. And my cover designer queen, Najla. You guys are fantastic. Thank you for all the hard work.

Thank you to Courtney for the extra eyes and the love. I appreciate it so much! ☺

A big thank you to Emma, Allison, and Christina for reading it early and for all the help. Your love and excitement mean the absolute world to me. You know how to make me feel special. ♥

To all my ARC readers, I can't tell you how much I appreciate that you signed up to receive an early copy. That you were interested in the first place. Forever, thank you! ♥

And now to my readers. Please know that I don't take it

lightly that you picked my book from the millions of books available. It warms my heart, and there aren't enough words to thank you! I hope you enjoyed the time with my story and my characters, and I hope I'll see you again. Until then, sending much love. ♥ ♥ ♥

ABOUT THE AUTHOR

Jasmin Miller is a professional lover of books and cake (preferably together) as well as a fangirl extraordinaire. She loves to read and write about anything romantic and never misses a chance to swoon over characters. Originally from Germany, she now lives in the western US with her husband and three little humans that keep her busy day and night.

If you liked *Tangled In Lies* and would like to know more about Jasmin and her books, please sign up for her newsletter on her website. She'd love to connect with you.

www.jasminmiller.com
jasminmillerbooks@gmail.com
Facebook.com/jasminmillerwrites
Instagram.com/jasminmiller
Twitter.com/JasminMiller_
Facebook.com/groups/jasminmillerpeeps
tiktok.com/@jasminmillerbooks

* 9 7 8 1 9 6 3 7 8 8 0 0 6 *